Additional praise for *Havoc's Sword*

"Solid seafaring historical. Lambdin's customary good humor, well-wrought naval battles, and use of every ruse de guerre in the book provide enough moment-to-moment pleasure to keep this long-running adventure series afloat."

—*Publishers Weekly*

Praise for Dewey Lambdin's Alan Lewrie adventures

"Brilliantly styled. This outing matches the darkness of Lambdin's second installment in the series. Sizzlingly tropical and stuffed to the beams with salty parlance."

—*Kirkus* (on *Sea of Grey*)

"The lively pace and white-knuckle battle scenes should make this another winner with Lambdin's fans."

—*Publishers Weekly* (on *Sea of Grey*)

"Lambdin is back in full stride. This is one of those books you finish with a chuckle, sorry that you've reached the last page."

—*Charleston Post & Courier* (on *Sea of Grey*)

"An entertaining book . . . rich in dialogue from the era."

—*Chattanooga Times Free Press* (on *Sea of Grey*)

"A hugely likable hero, a huge cast of sharply drawn supporting characters: there's nothing missing. Wonderful stuff."

—*Kirkus*

Also by Dewey Lambdin

The King's Coat

The French Admiral

The King's Commission

The King's Privateer

The Gun Ketch

H.M.S. Cockerel

A King's Commander

Jester's Fortune

King's Captain

Sea of Grey

Havoc's Sword

Dewey Lambdin

THOMAS DUNNE BOOKS
ST. MARTIN'S GRIFFIN
NEW YORK

This one is for . . .

Sam and Salvador, at my favourite "watering hole," Darfon's. And for all their lovely "beer-slingers," Stephanie, Rachel, Charlsi, Dezerae, Boo, Courtney, and "Skank"—none of whom are waiting on a record deal on Music Row, if that's possible in Nashville!

Thanks for all the bottles of "Loudmouth Lite," and may none of you ever experience a personal life as tumultuous as that of that rogue Alan Lewrie.

THOMAS DUNNE BOOKS.
An imprint of St. Martin's Press.

HAVOC'S SWORD. Copyright © 2003 by Dewey Lambdin. All rights reserved. Printed in the United States of America. For information, address St. Martin's Press, 175 Fifth Avenue, New York, N.Y. 10010.

www.stmartins.com

Library of Congress Cataloging-in-Publication Data

Lambdin, Dewey.
    Havoc's sword : an Alan Lewrie naval adventure / Dewey Lambdin.
        p. cm.
    ISBN 0-312-28688-0 (hc)
    ISBN 0-312-31548-1 (pbk)
    EAN 978-0312-31548-1
    1. Lewrie, Alan (Fictitious character)—Fiction. 2. Great Britain—History, Naval—18th century—Fiction. 3. British—Caribbean Area—Fiction. 4. Caribbean Area—Fiction. 5. Privateering—Fiction. I. Title.

PS3562.A435H388 2003
813'.54—dc21   003046835

D 10 9 8

"All pity chok'd with custom of fell deeds;
And Caesar's spirit, ranging for revenge,
With Ate by his side come hot from Hell,
Shall in these confines with a monarch's voice
Cry 'Havoc!' and let slip the dogs of war . . ."

Julius Caesar, Act III, Sc. 1 269–273
William Shakespeare

PROLOGUE

Gaudent perfusi sanguine fratrum;
exsilioque domos et dulcia limina mutant
atque alio patrium quaerunt sub sole iacentem.

Gleefully they steep themselves in their brothers' blood;
for exile they change their sweet homes and hearths
and seek a country that lies beneath an alien sun.
                                        –GEORGICS, BOOK II, 510-512
                                        PUBLIUS VERGILIUS MARO

*C*lerk Etienne de Gougne heaved a fretful sigh after surveying the large salon, just off the equally seedy entrance hall of the commandeered mansion. With grips still in hand, and rolled up charts still crammed under his arm-pits, he squinted his eyes in dread of the tirade to come once *Le Capitaine* saw the place. He wished that just once he had had the tiniest dash of courage; else, his master's transfer to Guadeloupe, and this foetid clime, could have been his excuse to enter the service of some other official, perhaps even in his own beloved and exhilarating Paris, instead of letting himself be meekly dragged, ever demeaned and terrified, from one arse-end of the world to another.

Etienne de Gougne could smirk, though, in his mousy little way, that the bulk of *Le Capitaine*'s wrath would fall upon the person who'd *chosen* this abandoned mansion so blithely and carelessly, the despised *Lieutenant de Vaisseau* Jules Hainaut, for once, the swaggering *poseur*, that jumped-up *lout*, that . . . !

"God's Noodle, what a pig-sty!" Lt. Hainaut said from the doorway, making the little clerk "Eep" in sudden dread, drop his precious charts in a hollow, "bonking" jumble, his grips thudding to the floor, and making him spin about.

"Oh! Lieutenant, don't do that, I beg you," de Gougne said as he bent to gather his things; though secretly pleased to see the look of consternation on the handsome young sprig's face as he realised his error.

"Good Christ," Lt. Jules Hainaut breathed, taking in just how shabby the interior was; when it had looked *so* promising and grand in his too-brief visit the day before, when he'd stood on the veranda and had merely peeked in through the smutted window panes, *assuming* . . . !

"This won't do," Hainaut stated, shaking his head, "no, not at all. You'd better get our gang of *noirs* to muck all this out before *Le Capitaine* arrives, little mouse."

Ordering the timid clerk about always made Hainaut feel better. He stalked into the salon, elegant and expensive new boots drumming on the loose wood-parquet floor, savouring the creak-squeak of excellently made leather. His left hand grasped the hilt of his ornately chased smallsword, his right hand fisted to his hip, the arm akimbo, his mind scheming quickly on how to recover from this disaster.

This spacious salon on the east side of the house had lost its window panes, and the winds and rains had gotten in, along with a scattering of leaves, palm fronds, and red-brown, wooly furze off the tropical trees. The window shutters hung nearly paintless, scabbed, broken-slatted and crooked. A skift of bright glass shards littered the floor, along with a few dead birds and a skeletal rat, now collapsed upon itself, and swarming with ants. Even as Hainaut fanned himself in the closeness of the airless salon with his gilt-laced fore-and-aft bicorne hat, he saw a lizard of some kind scuttle from the shutters to seize a cockroach nigh as big as his thumb, and he could hear the 'crunch' all the way across the room. To make things even worse, an entire flotilla, a whole shoal of cockroaches, fled at that seizure from beneath a torn and tilt-legged sofa to flood along the baseboard, before swirling beneath it like a spill of dark ale!

Jules Hainaut *knew* that he was in trouble; *Le Capitaine* would have him strangled for such carelessness, for heaping one more demeaning slight upon him, after the several he had suffered from the local officials since they had come ashore on Guadeloupe.

Working for *Le Capitaine* was rewarding at times, profitable in monetary matters and the best of confiscated or "commandeered" goods . . . such as his ornate sword, which formerly had been the property of an elderly junior admiral without the proper zeal and ruthlessness of a true revolutionary. *"You wish it? Take it,"* *Le Capitaine* had told Hainaut after the court-martial for failure and Royalist sentiments, as it lay on the judge's table after the guilty party had been hauled out— blade exposed and point toward the doomed, signifying a verdict of guilty.

Rewarding and pleasing for Jules Hainaut, too, was the aura of fear he could create by merely stating whom he worked for, trading on *Le Capitaine*'s dread reputation. His new boots the cobbler had made *gratis*, pouring heart and soul into the workmanship and materials as if his life had depended on it. His uniforms, if not free, were gotten at a large, shuddery, discount.

But, his superior didn't suffer fools or slackers gladly, and more than one promising and well-connected young officer had had his head lopped off for less. Now, *what to do, what to do?* Hainaut dithered, all the while in an outward pose of a man with few cares, but for this mere *trifle.*

Jumped-up, foreign farm-hand! Clerk de Gougne silently sneered as he gathered up his traps; *can't even speak good French,* he circumspectly scoffed with a Parisian's disdain for anything provincial, or anyone born outside *La Belle France.*

Jules Hainaut no longer looked it, but he *had* been born a farmboy, in the Austrian Netherlands, his parents the sketchiest sort of "out-lander" French. He'd fled potato-grubbing early, had gone to sea at fourteen, still nigh-illiterate, and had drifted into the old Royal French Navy just before the start of the Revolution.

Just a lowly *matelot* with grandiose dreams of being *somebody* or something, some day, he'd seen quickly how the prevailing winds stood, and had gladly (if not wholeheartedly) embraced Republicanism and the Jacobism of the *sans culottes* as a way to advance himself. He bought a tricolour revolutionary's cockade and red-wool tassel cap, and had worn them with outward pride, had shouted "Down with the Aristos" the loudest, and had ridden the coat-tails of the Terror, help-ing to purge the navy of Royalists and aristocrats, earning a share of the loot taken from them, moving up in rank, in "dead men's shoes." For once, his lack of education, his humble beginnings, and his out-landness had worked for him, for he was held up as a shining example of how the ideals of the Revolution would spread all round the world and conquer the old order.

Most of the rhetoric was Greek to Hainaut, just loud twaddle to be tolerated—but it paid well to listen and cheer. And the raids and arrests, as a "virtuous" commoner armed to the teeth and given the awesome power of weaponry over the rich, the titled, and their minions and lick-spittle servants, was a heady thing, indeed. And the cheers!

Escorting accused prisoners through the seaport streets, eyes open for the prettiest women and girls who threw corsages, and now and then *themselves*, at such a well-knit and stalwart young patriot. Then, when he had been urged to turn informer and spy upon suspect shipmates, surviving officers, and town citizens, and he'd come to court to testify, tricked out in his scrubbed-up, borrowed best, Hainaut had gotten even more favourable attention . . . from the young female citizens most of all!

After all, it wasn't as if the people he'd testified against were all *that* innocent, and if *he* hadn't done it, there were two dozen more eager to make names for themselves standing in line behind him, so what did it matter when "traitors" were trundled to the guillotines in the big tumbrils, to fill the baskets with their heads. They were not family, they weren't friends of his, and most had been unattractive or outright ugly, or simply not clever enough to keep their mouths shut and dissemble the latest revolutionary cant, which could change from month to month as the various factions in the Assembly rose or fell.

Hainaut had advanced to the rank of *Timmonier*, the trusty Coxswain to a rising young star of a Lieutenant who had come up from the lower deck, just as he had. He ate better than most, drank very well, and had first pick of the loot, could make a pig of himself every night of the week, and had thought he had risen high . . . when he had met the man who would change his life.

He knew he'd met *real* power when his Lieutenant had nearly shat his *culottes* in fear of him after one interview. He knew he'd met the consummate unscrupulous cynic, out to use the Revolution to claw back his former honours and position; and, perhaps, *Le Capitaine* had seen a fellow spirit in Hainaut, despite his outward protestations of adoration for the Revolution.

That quickly, he'd become an *Aspirant* entitled to wear steel on his hip, not a crude seaman's cutlass, but a midshipman's dirk of honour, even if his uniform had been a rag-picker's off-day *ensemble*. Hainaut had thrown himself into pleasing *Le Capitaine* during the purging of the Bordeaux fleet, and later in the Mediterranean, when they ran the infiltrating spy-boats, the coastal raiding ships, and small convoys to support the army facing the Piedmontese, the Genoese, Neapolitan, and much-vaunted Austrian armies.

And it *hadn't* been Hainaut's fault when his small warship under an idiot captain had been taken by the British, when *Le Capitaine* had trusted him to supervise the mission, and "wet his feet" as a fighting sailor. A few weeks on parole on Corsica (rather pleasant, that!) and he'd been exchanged for a British midshipman, and warmly welcomed back into *Le Capitaine*'s service—though the idiot had gotten "chopped" for failure!

Now Jules Hainaut was a seasoned *Lieutenant de Vaisseau*, polished and groomed, tutored and "pampered," and, did he continue pleasing his superior, the aspirations of commanding a small warship, later becoming a *Capitaine de Vaisseau* in charge of a tall, swift frigate of his own, were not beyond his reach.

If he survived this little disaster!

And it certainly looked hopeless.

Lt. Hainaut damned the Governor-General, Citizen Victor Hugues, for this insult. There were much nicer mansions to be had in the neat little community of Bas Fort, and much closer to the local seat of power, too. He suspected that Governor-General Hugues (a *light*-skinned Mulatto *gens du couleur*, but still a *noir*, Lt. Hainaut accused!) wanted to show how unimpressed he was by the arrival of *Le Capitaine*, a possible rival for his position, or a spy for the Directory, despite all their fulsome introductory letters from Paris.

Fanning himself some more, Lt. Hainaut paced about in the foyer, admiring the gloss of his boot-toes, testing the formerly shiny Cuban mahoghany inlaid parquet. With a preparatory sigh of disappointment, Hainaut went to the double doors of the west-side salon, which were barely ajar; pocket doors, which hissed into their recesses barely at a touch, of the finest craftsmanship.

"Ah! Better!" he cheered. Drapes still hung, the windows were still glazed, chandeliers were still whole, and the furniture was worn but useable; in point of fact, this second salon was jam-packed with a jumble of furniture, as if two or three other mansions had been looted and the contents stored in this one! And behind the salon was a room of equal spaciousness, filled with several sets of dining room furnishings. Hainaut doubted there would be plates, cutlery, or serving pieces in there, but they'd brought their own, enough to serve for a few weeks 'til another "warehouse" of confiscated goods could be "shopped."

"*Garçon chef!*" Hainaut barked over his shoulder, to summon the "head boy" of the work-gang they had been loaned. "*Ici, vite!*"

"*Oui, bas?*" he answered when he came.

"This salon will be my master's private office," Hainaut said, briskly rubbing his hands in relief. "That dining room, there. Clean it out. It will become *Le Maître*'s bed-chamber, *comprendre?* Office, here . . . bed-chamber, there, *hein?*"

"*Oui, bas. Je comprend,*" the solidly built man responded.

"Send *garçons* above-stairs. Surely, there's bed furniture. Find best, and fetch it down, to . . . there," Hainaut instructed, pointing up, then to the dining room. "Bedding and such . . . *comprendre literies, hein?*" he said in *pidgin* French, since he hadn't heard passable French from the island Blacks since stepping ashore; they uttered a soft, and liquid, Creole *patois*.

"*Oui, bas, comprend la literie,*" the headman assured him, talking as slowly as Hainaut, as if to covertly twit him back. "Pillows, sheets, and mattresses. Send boys for the best. Make house *nouveau* clean . . . *tout d'abord,*" he vowed. "Be *très élégant.*"

"It had *better* be," Hainaut said with a miffed sniff, unfamiliar with *noirs*, but suspecting that he was slyly being japed. "Some men to sickle the grass, prune the bushes, too. Re-hang the shutters, there," he said, pointing again. "Paint walls, if paper is hopeless. Nail the parquet down. Floor? Loose floor pieces, *hein?* Make smooth?"

"Ah, *oui,*" the gang leader replied, with a resigned shrug.

"All done by sundown, *comprendre?*" Hainaut gleefully insisted.

The *noir* winced and sucked his teeth, but nodded assent.

"That room, there . . . be office for the little mouse clerk," Lt. Hainaut slyly instructed. "*Small* bed-cot, unbroken desk, and chest of drawers. Nothing *good*, mind. Well, get cracking. *Vite, vite!*"

Hainaut turned and trotted up the staircase, without a thought for the herculean task he'd just assigned, and did they *not* get it all presentable, well . . . too bad for the *garçon chef!* That was what whips were good for, Hainaut casually supposed, *pour encourager les autres*, so they *saw* the price of failure. Even Hugues, part-Black himself, had kept a *form* of slavery on Guadeloupe after the *noirs* had been "freed." Poorly paid, closely supervised labour gangs might *not* emulate the bloody massacres of former masters that had torn Saint Domingue to shreds. Idle hands were the Devil's workshop!

"*Magnifique!*" Hainaut whispered on entering the former master's and mistress's chambers on the east side front. It was bigger than the salon below it, fronted by a deep, cool balcony and two sets of double doors, with separate shutter doors on the outside. The imported furnishings were suitable for a rich *aristo*'s Paris *maison*; settees, chairs and draperies in expensive *moiré* silks, elegantly carved night-tables, card tables, and chairs, lamp stands ... with no windows facing the Nor'east Trades, the room had stayed pristine, despite being rifled.

"*Garçon chef*, up here, *vite!*" Hainaut barked.

A younger, scrawnier *noir* trotted into the chamber, the leader's assistant, the *sous-chef d'équipage*. "*Oui, bas?*" he asked.

"Run tell your chef that all *this* goes downstairs to my master's bed-chamber. Second-best from the other front room, move in here, for me. I'll take this room, *comprendre?*"

"Uhh," this one answered, scratching his pate. "Too fast ..."

"Dammit!" Hainaut snapped impatiently, seizing the man by his arm to lead him to the other bed-chamber, shoving him inside. "Furnishings of *here*, move to grand chamber. Furnishings in *chambre grande* you move below, *comprendre, hein? Du verdammte dreckig monstrosität?*" he swore, unconsciously falling back on the bastard German of his youth.

"Exchange, *oui, bas?*" the Black supposed, in a sullen voice.

"*Oui*, damn you ... exchange."

"Ah, *mais oui ... rapidement!*" the slave beamed.

"Go *do* it, then ... *rapidement*," Hainaut disgustedly sneered.

He strode back to the grand bed-chamber to savour his new digs, fanning with his hat some more, walking out on the wide balcony, where tall trees shaded him from the morning sun, where woven cane chaises and side-tables awaited, and a spectacular view presented itself. And he could have sworn that the temperature dropped a quick ten degrees or more, in obedience to the Trade winds.

He tipped trash from a cane chair and sat down, thinking it was a mortal pity that his grand new bed-chamber could never be used for sport, but his master was ... touchy, when it came to seeing his aide taking pleasures under his very nose, while his own tastes were so ... *outré*. Darker recollections made Hainaut shiver. His master taking pleasure was not something he would ever wish to see; things best left in the dark, in prison cellars, with the younger, weaker, and frailer girls, the better. *Mon Dieu, merde alors!* Hainaut silently quailed, as some of the work gang came up to begin moving things around at his bidding.

Well, with his naval salary and *Le Maître*'s now-and-then admiring largesse, he could hire a tiny but elegant *pied-à-terre* room in one of the better harbour lodgings for sport. And his off-duty, moment-of-arising view would be splendid, at any rate.

Guadeloupe was nearly two islands, pinched in to a narrow cause-way just north and west of Pointe-à-Pitre's environs that linked Grande-Terre, on which he stood, and Basse-Terre. Grande-Terre ran East-West, low and lushly verdant despite its exposure to the Nor'east Trades, all the way to Pointe des Chateaux and the farther islet of Désirade where dark Atlantic rollers met the turquoise Caribbean.

Basse-Terre ran North-South, also incredibly green but mountain-ous, dominated by the peak of the dormant volcano La Soufrière, tilled as orderly as terrace farms round Marseilles, its shore fringed with a series of neat little villages and white-sand beach hamlets along its eastern, windward shore across the great harbour in which he stood.

Petit-Bourg, Ste.-Marie, where Christopher Columbus was reputed to have first landed, Capesterre Belle-Eau south of there, before the coastline curved about Sou'west, hiding Trois Rivières, the Vieux Fort, and the other, lee-side harbour of Basse-Terre.

So beautiful, Hainaut marvelled, so *pleasingly* alien, for once. After the bleakness of the rocky, wave-punched coasts of Europe; Biscay waters, Baltic, the German Sea, or *Le Maître*'s beloved Channel ports in Brittany, even the softer Mediterranean or Italian shores, this was wondrous.

A grand view, he thought; it would have to suffice. And did *Le Maître*'s plans spin out in even somewhat proper order, or yield success in half the measure he'd schemed, he would be worked so hard that a *view* might be all the satisfaction a harried aide might have.

Though it had taken a fair number of kicks and slaps, the house was ready for its new master's arrival. The jingle and rumble of the coach-and-four on the roundabout sand-shell drive brought out Hainaut, de Gougne, and the most docile, willing, and least threatening Blacks whom Hainaut had decided to employ. They had been sluiced down at the well in the back yard and hurriedly garbed in clean slop-clothing, to stand muster by the drive. Enticing aromas from the sep-arate cooking shed wafted coach-ward, tall beeswax candles fluttered in the windows, and both closed lanthorns and open torches beamed welcoming cheer from the drive and the wide, deep veranda.

The coach rocked to a stop and an armed guard in the uniform of Naval Infantry leaped down from the boot to fold down the metal step and open the near-side door before springing to rigid attention, his musket unslung and held at Present Arms, his face a patient blank no matter that the senior passenger took half an hour to alight; and God help the man who innocently sprang to assist him!

The fingers of a left hand curled about the door frame, a brass tip on a stout ebony walking-stick, then a man's right boot emerged, blindly groping for the step, as someone grunted to shift his weight.

"*Zut! Beurk! Ouf, ailé! Merde alors! Horreur . . . une bête!*" Weak cries of alarm sussurated from the aligned Blacks, who to a man crossed themselves or made warding signs against the Evil Eye, wail-ing "*Le Diable!*" and making Hainaut turn to cuff or curse them to worshipful silence.

Le Maître—*Le Capitaine*—in Paris and Toulon *Le Hideux* but *never* in his or his minion's hearing—alit at last, standing on his own feet, surveying the house front with a suspicious scowl.

Clump, shuffle, *tick* . . . clump, shuffle, *tick* on the firmly laid pavers of the sand-and-brick walk between the freshly pruned flowering *bou-gainvillea*, as *Capitaine de Vaisseau* Guillaume Choundas made a tor-turous way forward. His right foot in a regular high-topped boot almost *demanded* firm ground before the ham-strung left leg in an iron-braced-and-bound boot swished limply ahead, with the bright brass ferrule of the stout walking-stick swung out ahead for balance, to ring against the stones.

Guillaume Choundas's right sleeve was pinned up high under his heavily gilt epaulette, folded so it displayed gold buttons and wide oak-leaf embroidery, near where a sergeant would show chevrons. It was a full-dress coat more suited to a junior admiral, but very few in the Caribbean (or Europe, either) would *dare* to question his right to wear it. More gilt oak-leaf showed on the high red collar, and on the thighs of his dark blue breeches, too.

A large and elaborate bicorne hat slashed fore-and-aft atop his head, raked aggressively low over his eyes; eight centimeters of gold edge lace, loop and button and tassels gilt as well, with a *tricolore* cockade on one side, and blue-white-red egret plumes nodding above the crease. Below the hat, though. . . .

Capitaine Choundas's face was half-covered with a stiffened silk mask that disguised a cruel, deep-scarred ruin, the result of a ghastly wound suffered long ago, a sword cut that had slashed upwards to slice one eye and his brow in half almost vertically, shattered the eye socket, chopped off one nostril and X-ed both lips to a horror worthy of an Hieronymous Bosch painting of a demon. The mask had been expanded lately to cover the nose completely, but there was no concealing the split lips that had healed in a rictus of rage.

"Welcome, *mon Capitaine!*" Hainaut exclaimed, stepping off the veranda to greet him and sweep an arm to encompass the house. "All is ready for you, in your grand new lodgings! Supper will be served just as soon as you wish, *m'sieur!*"

"As I expected, *cher* Jules," Choundas replied, almost registering pleasure for a glimmering moment, that just as quickly disappeared, "given your zeal. Though I have not yet seen inside . . . *hein?*" he came close to almost making a *jest*. "These dumb beasts are to be our house servants?" he concluded with a normal frown.

"Such as they are, *m'sieur*. Best of a poor lot," Hainaut told him, with a disparaging Gallic shrug. "I returned those that did not please to Governor Hugues, to make what use of them he will. Do a few more officials arrive in need of servants, he'll be reduced to the *very* dregs of the government supply, *n'est-ce pas, mon Capitaine?*" he concluded with a devious simper.

"Think I am *Le Diable*, do you?" Choundas asked the Blacks lined up for inspection, almost jovially, soft-voiced, as he clump-ticked to within a few feet of them, making them shrink back a pace. He removed his hat, baring florid ginger-red hair. "Ah, *mais oui*," he said with a shrug. Hat tucked under his good arm, he lifted the mask. "I *am!*" he thundered, making the Blacks whine, cringe, visibly shake, and almost piss their slop-trousers.

"I will be served with alacrity, with diligence, and with *quiet!* The one who raises his voice inside, who annoys me, he'll be flayed to his bones and fed to the sharks . . . alive! Do *not* make me take notice of you, *comprende?* You've *had* your one curious look, and last winces! The next one of you who looks at me askance and even *thinks* that I am disgusting I will have boiled in hot tar and crucified, head-down!"

He let the mask drop back into place, shuffled its seating, and thrust his hat back onto his head.

"You had *better* fear me, *mon garçons*," he threatened. "and do my bidding as quietly and un-noticed as mice. Now, go! *Allez, vite!*"

They scampered in a twinkling.

Pleased with himself, Choundas turned once more to Lt. Hainaut. "Let us see what you have accomplished, Jules. By the way, we will be having dinner guests. You know the gallant *Capitaine* Desplan?"

"But of course, *maître. Capitaine* Desplan? Welcome," Hainaut piped up to the captain of the *Le Bouclier* frigate, as if they hadn't spent nearly six weeks aboard her, in cheek-to-jowl company.

Choundas stomped up to the wood veranda while Hainaut made his welcomes to the other captains of their acquaintance off the 20-gunned corvettes that had escorted their older 28-gun frigate and a storeship; *Capitaine de Frégate* Griot of *Le Gascon*, a stout little fellow of dark features, and the much taller and paler *Capitaine de Frégate* Mac-Pherson off *La Résolue*, an *émigré* Jacobite Scot whose family had fled to France after the failure of Bonnie Prince Charlie Stuart in 1745.

Another officer, a mere *Lieutenant de Vaisseau*, had alit from the carriage, too, one who hung back shyly. "*Et vous, m'sieur?*"

"That is Lieutenant Récamier, Jules," Choundas informed him as he stood, impatiently rapping his stick on the veranda to hurry them inside. "Formerly of the schooner *L'Incendiare*. He is most familiar with Caribbean waters, and has a most intriguing tale to tell. After dessert and brandy, we must avail ourselves of his experience. Come, *messieurs* . . . let us share a glass of wine, and discover what an island cook can do with victuals."

Ah, him! Hainaut thought with malicious glee, having read after-action reports of *L'Incendiare*'s loss. It was no wonder that the poor fellow was diffident! Hainaut wasn't sure whether Lt. Récamier was to be the main course, the dessert, or the postprandial entertainment.

"*Bienvenu, M'sieur* Récamier," he said, though, putting his best face of ignorant affability on, and extending a proper Republican hand to shake. "I trust you'll enjoy our offerings for supper."

They had sailed with an extensive wine cellar, and the casks and crates had been ashore long enough for ship-stirred lees to settle, or be carefully filtered when decanted, so Choundas set a good table. Lt. Hainaut saw to that. The soup was a bland, cool celery broth, the fish a fresh-caught pompano served with a local delicacy, *crabes farcis*. A locally grown salad course with onions, cucumbers, and carrots, zested with *vinaigrette* and lime juice. The main course chickens were on the tough, small, and stringy side, on a rice *pilaf*; still on the bone, but for Choundas's plate, which had been picked off and diced for easier one-handed eating. A *touch* dry and over-cooked, pan-fried, but enlivened with enough exotic hot sauces and Caribbean spices to make an equivalent to a Hindee curry, normally used to mask a tainted dish.

Hainaut, Griot, Desplan, and MacPherson dug in with a will, delighted with fresh shore viands after weeks of salt-meat junk, sending servants back for more crisp and piping-hot baguettes time after time, after the dreary monotony of stale or weeviled ship's biscuit.

Choundas occupied the head of the table, with *Capitaine* Desplan in the place of honour to his right, and Griot to his left. Récamier was to Griot's left, opposite Hainaut, and—two empty chairs down—at the foot of the table sat poor clerk Etienne de Gougne.

The little clerk abstemiously took wee bites, then chewed seemingly forever before swallowing, before the tiniest sips of wine.

Hainaut had seen to it that his dishes had been over-seasoned, knowing the timid little clerk's penchant for the blander and creamier Parisian cooking. Each bite seemed a torture of Hell-fire, though he would be loath to do or say a thing about it. And if he pushed his plate away, he wouldn't get anything else!

Lt. Récamier was another spare diner and imbiber, as if trying to keep his wits about him and hope to be forgotten, perhaps. Sooner or later, though, *Le Maître* would get around to him, Hainaut was sure.

"Stupid waste of the fleet," Choundas groused, on his favourite peeve for the umpteenth time, "when it would have been better to work them up with weeks of training at sea, before gadding off on their adventures. We will never meet the *biftecks* on an equal footing until our seamanship and our cooperation between ships and senior officers markedly improves. Been that way for years," Choundas groused, shoving his food about his plate with his specially made all-in-one utensil, a pewter fork and spoon on one end, and a thin scoop on the other. "In the *aristo* navy," he sneered, "we swung at anchor most of the time, convenient to *shore* comforts, and got sent out on overseas adventures by foppish, ignorant *fools*, trusting that time on-passage would smooth out the rough spots. What idiocy!"

"If only our superiors would have heeded your suggestions, *mon Capitaine*," Desplan of *Le Bouclier* sympathised, toadying up agreeably, as was his wont since they had first set foot on his decks.

"One devoutly wishes that you could be appointed to the Ministry, *Capitaine* Choundas," the dark-visaged, hawk-nosed Griot suggested. "Scourge out the useless place-keepers, and put *real* sailors in charge."

They were *so* obsequious that Hainaut had to stifle a groan of derision. Toadying was pointless for Griot. He was a Breton, one of *Le Maître's* fabled Celts, descended from the bold seafarers of Brittany, of the same blood as Choundas, scions of the ancient Veneti. To hear Choundas tell it (and endlessly *re*-tell it!) the Veneti had been *deep*-water sailors in their stout oak ships, as daring as the Phoenicians, and *might* have crossed the trackless oceans to discover the New World long before Columbus; who had *almost* out-fought Julius Caesar's fleet of eggshell-thin, coast-hugging, *oared* triremes during the Gallic Wars.

No, Griot had no need to lick *Le Maître's* arse; his heritage was his pass to promotion and favour.

Desplan, too. Before the Revolution, Desplan had been a mere midshipman, a commoner who could not expect to rise much higher than *Lieutenant de Vaisseau* in royal service without money, connections, or the rare chance to shine with a spectacular feat of derring-do gaining him notice at the royal court. Desplan, however, was from Quimper, a fluent speaker of the ancient Breton tongue that King Louis's officials had fought to suppress. He and Capt. Choundas had slanged whole afternoons away on-passage, Desplan even daring to compose heroic poems set in the glorious old days—then *read* them . . . *aloud*! first in Breton, then in French for the unenlightened.

Capitaine MacPherson, though . . . hmmm, Hainaut considered, giving him a perusal under his lashes as he took a long sip of *vin ordinaire*. The man was tall, lean, and raw-boned, as gingery-blond as Choundas, but more weathered, his skin more amenable to harsh sunlight. Scottish; *ergo*, some sort of Celt. But most unfortunately and overtly Catholic, of the most egregiously self-effacing and *devout* kind.

Not the best thing to be, or practice so openly, these days in a nation, under a regime, that had closed great cathedrals and tiny chapels, confiscated the great wealth and lands of Holy Mother Church, and turned them all into Temples of Reason, where the *genius* of Man was celebrated.

His *corvette, La Résolue,* was a smartly-run ship, though, kept in perfect trim, her crew intensely drilled and disciplined with a gruff fairness. Their stormy passage had proved MacPherson to be a tarry, hoary-handed "tarpaulin man" as the British, the "Bloodies," said. It was possible that MacPherson would prosper under Choundas's command . . . but never shine.

". . . what Admiral de Brueys will accomplish with the Mediterranean fleet, well," Choundas was raspingly continuing. He stopped in mid-carp, pressed his napkin to his lips to stifle a belch, and bent at the waist as if in pain. *"Mon Dieu,* take this *merde* away!"

He shoved his plate halfway to the fruit *compote* on the glossy wood surface, and flung his all-in-one utensil after it in a sudden fit of rage. "Damned *nègres!* All fire and peppers!" he gravelled, glaring at Hainaut as if it were his fault; making Hainaut cringe to think that his plate and the "loaded" one meant for de Gougne had been confused!

"She'll not do it again, *m'sieur!*" Hainaut hotly vowed, rising. "I'll fetch you a *blanc-manger,* at once, to ease you."

Le Maître had been suffering stomach troubles ever since he had gotten his orders to sail for the Caribbean. Was his mentor ailing . . . was it something serious enough to threaten Hainaut's comfortable and lucrative billet? He dashed off towards the cooking shed.

"Oui, go!" Choundas snapped, stifling another painful burning and eructation. "And give that *salope* a whack or two as warning! Pardons, *messieurs.* Foreign service has ruined my tripes as sure as grape-shot. I could *almost* savour Chinese cooking. Mandarin was best, subtle and elegant both in taste and presentation. Hoisin, from the far north, or Cantonese, though . . . all devil's piss, garlic and fire, bah! Does that *nègre* cow's-hide mean to *poison* me?"

"It has been known to happen, *m'sieur le Capitaine,*" Lt. Récamier spoke up for the first time in half an hour, still diffident. "Though it means the slaughter of the entire house-slave staff . . . if they are *caught* at it. Many an overly cruel master or mistress has died, under mysterious circumstances, in the islands. Sometimes, the 'witch' worked by *Voudoun* poisons are so subtle, even the ablest physicians can't say the cause was not natural. *Les noirs* have a thousand ways to get back

at Europeans. Scorches on new clothing, pets gone missing, lost spoons
. . . anything. Drip at a time, never anything worthy of a beating. I
think your *chinois* would call it 'the death of a thousand cuts', *n'est-ce
pas?* A drip-at-a-time water torture?"

"Indeed," Guillaume Choundas archly drawled back, though with
a glint of sudden wariness in his good eye.

"Here you are, *m'sieur*," Hainaut said, returning with a dish of
whipped and sweetened wheat flour. He retrieved the utensil, wiped
it on his waist-coat, and handed it to Choundas.

After a few moments, and a few spoonfuls, *Le Maître* seemed much
eased, and the wary, uncomfortable silence ended. Hainaut returned
to his own supper, enjoying its taste, even if it had cooled while he
was away on his urgent errand.

"De Brueys," Choundas dyspeptically snapped, picking up where
he had left off. "A cautious old fellow. Perhaps more suited to a shore
or port command than a fighting fleet, *hein?* Too set in his ways, the
old idle *aristo* ways. Needs everything just so, a set-piece that advances
in understandable steps. We must thank our lucky stars, *messieurs*, that
we are not part of his folly. That little tuft-hunter whose army he
carries, General Bonaparte, is sure to overreach, and lead a great part
of our navy into trouble. Better we take Malta as planned, land and
conquer the Kingdom of Naples second, *then* cross and conquer Sicily,
cutting the Mediterranean in two, before any *farther* efforts. Give the
bifteck Admiral Jervis a real headache and run him back to Lisbon,
again. Then, properly shaken down and trained in seamanship, the
Adriatic, the Aegean Sea, and the Ottoman Turk lands could be ours
by simply opening our hands to pluck them. *Oui*. Dearly as we would
wish to partake in honour and glory for *La Belle France*, and the
Revolution's expansion to all of Europe, we must be thankful that we
are out here, where adventures just as grand await us."

Like proper little sychophants appreciative of their superior's acuity
and bold strategic thinking, the diners almost stood to clap.

Hainaut didn't *quite* remember it that way. When orders had come
from the five demi-gods who comprised the Directory in Paris, in
point of fact, his master had raged and cursed, throwing things to the
four winds, howling about Betrayal, Exile, and scourging the "New
Men," the slimy-slick attorney-poseurs who'd supplanted the bold fire-
brands of the Revolution, shuffling those who'd worked the hardest
off stage to be forgotten and dismissed without reward! A brace of

prisoners in for minor offences had been half-dead before *Le Maître* had spent his rage!

It was, though, the story of his master's embittered life, to be used as a cat's-paw to the rich and titled wastrels, even in the days when he was slim, stalwart, and handsome in his own fashion. Now it was exile to the Sugar Islands, where ugly, crippled embarassments could succumb to a myriad of plagues and fevers, un-looked-for and un-loved!

Hainaut grimaced a tad, recalling Choundas's slim successes in the Mediterranean, his next thankless assignment to outfit General Humbert's expedition to Ireland in a squadron of frigates. It hadn't been *his* fault that Lord Cornwallis's army had cornered the small army of Humbert's, forcing its semi-honourable surrender, and a slaughter of its ill-armed, ill-trained Irish rebel auxiliaries . . .

Last year in the Batavian Republic, formerly Holland, training and encouraging jury-armed merchant ships into frigates and corvettes and scouting vessels . . . only to see the *bifteck* Admiral Duncan sweep them from the seas at the Battle of Camperdown, for the scouts failed their main body. That hadn't been his fault, either, but . . .

Hainaut wondered, again, whether he had hitched his waggon to an ill-favoured star, or remained in Choundas's harness perhaps too long. Did *Le Maître* fail out here, this would be his last chance, and Hainaut could sink back into the pool of mediocre junior officers, living only on his meagre pay, with all hopes of future advancement blocked . . .

Choundas rang a tiny porcelain bell to summon dessert. Slaves rushed to dole out soft, doughy, and sugar-crusted pastry shells filled with fresh local berries sopping in heavy whipped cream. Dessert wine and brandy were fetched out as well.

The Directory, and the Assembly, gave short shrift to failures, Jules Hainaut glumly speculated as he tried a bite of the dessert and found it better than succulent, almost *too* sweet; though they did not execute as many as they had in the earlier days, Hainaut speculated. Even powerful Robespierre had lost his head as an embarassment! Choundas . . . perhaps. But never a handsome, cunning fellow such as he! *He* knew when to jump, and profit by it!

Promised me a command, he did, Hainaut thought; *not a privateer, but a National Ship.* It was the donkey's carrot that Choundas had

hung before his eyes, what he had groomed him for—not to be his
footman, his catch-fart, his dog's-body, forever! That's what the de
Gougnes of this world were for, after all!

"Excellent," Choundas grunted in rare praise of his berry tart.
"Though, *cher* Hainaut, you must also remind that *peau de vache* that
portions must be cut smaller for me in future."

"I'll see to it, *m'sieur*," Hainaut swore, beaming at his mentor, already laying an agreeable aura in which he could sooner or later pose
his request for a chance to shine on his own.

"The brandy, now, I think, *messieurs?*" Choundas announced. "And
we shall now partake of Lieutenant Récamier's vast experience and his
wisdom!" Making Récamier stiffen in dread; which reaction pleased
Le Maître no end.

After all, Machiavelli had said it was better to be feared than loved.

Though Lieutenant Récamier knew that "Le Hideux" loved to make
examples of failures in the performance of their duty to the Republic
and the navy, the fellow had kept a cool head throughout supper,
believing that a bold front of honour impugned, his truth insulted,
would serve him better than coming over all meek or fearful, of being
willing to admit error but vowing to do better next time . . . if allowed.

Hainaut had been mildly amazed that Récamier had so kept his wits
about him that he'd not even fidgeted, or plucked with his fingers at
the tablecloth or his napkin, either—his hands had stayed innocently
inert, rising only to gesture, or draw his actions against the British
frigate that had destroyed his command, and captured the American
smuggling brig in his charge, using the tip of his knife on his placemat.

They had both anchored for the night off St. John's island in the
masterless Danish Virgins; yes, he'd seen the frigate, lit up like a
whaler hard at work boiling down a catch for its oil, he admitted to
them; a clever ruse.

Yes, there she'd been at dawn, as his schooner and the brig had set
sail, revealed as a British warship, and he had turned at once to in-
terpose his small ship between them and had been the first to fire.
Fifteen minutes altogether, he had traded fire with the *Biftecks*, his
puny 6-pounders against 12-pounders, until forced to bear away after
a roundshot had shattered his schooner's helm. Before relieving tackle

could be rigged to the rudder post, his little ship had struck a badly charted shoal, ripping her bows open, stranding her forward third high and dry, and dis-masting her in an instant.

"Unlike *some, m'sieur Capitaine*, I did *not* fire a few shots to salvage honour before striking!" Lt. Récamier had sulkily declared to one and all, eyes level, broodingly aflame, as if ready to dare anyone to a duel for his good name. "I had thought to lure the 'Bloody' ship onto the shoal in close pursuit, but my charts were old, so . . ."

Hainaut had scoffed to himself, sure that Récamier was lying as boldly as a street vendor with a tray of "confiscated *aristo*" pocket watches, but, strangely, Capt. Choundas had not challenged him over it. And who was to say, since *L'Incendiare* had not rated a sailing master, leaving her navigation to her low-ranking captain—and all of those charts were now lost with her; quite conveniently, he thought!

Yes, the British frigate had broken off pursuit of the brig to fetch-to and lower two boats filled with "redcoat" Marines and sailors, then had headed West-Nor'west into the vast sound east of St. Thomas to catch the brig—which she did, Récamier had witnessed from a high vantage point ashore through his telescope, and saw them sailing back down a very narrow channel into the sound where she fetched-to, again, to recover her boats and men.

Yes, Récamier had gotten all his crew, including his seriously wounded and maimed men, into his own boats and had rowed ashore on St. John, but only after making sure that his command was well alight, his colours still flying in fiery defiance, and all her damning correspondence rescued, jettisoned in weighted bags or boxes, or left to burn. His precious commission papers and *rôle d'equipage* as proof of being a proper warship he had salvaged, which had proved of great value when he had sailed over to St. Thomas a day later and presented himself to the Danish authorities, who had shrugged off the more-punctilious formalities of internment and had treated his wounded well, before providing a cartel ship to return him and his men to Guade-loupe—the Danish fee for such "compassionate" offices a steep one.

"And how close-aboard were the British boats when you left your command, Lieutenant?" Choundas had probed.

"More than four long musket shots, *m'sieur*, perhaps less," Lt. Ré-camier had replied, his eyes a tad *too* unblinking over that point, as if trying too hard to be believed.

"Describe them," Choundas had demanded.

"Hmmm . . . tarred hulls, *m'sieur*, perhaps dull black paint? The gunwales and waterline boot-stripes were cream or pale yellow. White oars . . . ?" He had vaguely shrugged, taking a sip of wine, at last.

"Any name displayed, *mon cher* Lieutenant?" Choundas had almost purred, as if beguiling him into an inescapable trap, making Hainaut lick his lips in expectation, sure that Récamier had gone over-side in haste, not sticking around to take note of such things.

"*Proteus, m'sieur,*" Récamier had calmly and certainly answered, though. "Block letters in gilt, either side of the lead boat's bows. And the officer in charge, he shouted the ship's name, as well. *Very* bad French, of course. 'Here am I, His *Frégate Les Rois* . . . His Twelfth Night Cake's ship! *Proteus!*" Récamier had tittered, making the others laugh. *Les Rois*, not *Le Roi—quel drôle!* And that error had carried such versimilitude that Captain Choundas had chuckled along (briefly, mind) with the rest, dismissing his suspicions. Only an English ignoramus, so arrogantly unschooled in any language but his own, could mistake the possessive "Majesty's" with the plural "*Les Rois,*" which any French toddler knew meant a Christmastide treat!

In point of fact, Lt. Récamier had picked out the lettering from a *very* safe half-mile distant with a strong glass, abandoning ship as soon as the "Bloodies" had fetched-to, sure of what was coming, and averse to languishing for years in a prison hulk or scraping by on a pittance in an enemy harbour town on parole, with barely two *sou* to rub together, unable to afford his usual wine, women, and song, and women! And it was the *biftecks* who had fired his ship, after sorting through his papers, which he had left scattered 'cross his great-cabins, leaving his false Letter of Marque and Reprisal, taking only his true naval commission! Leaving orders signed by the newly arrived *Capitaine de Vaisseau* Guillaume Choundas, and did he ever discover *that*, well . . . ! Even being kin by marriage to the estimable Admiral de Brueys would not save him from the guillotine's blade.

"A most unfortunate turn of fate, then," Choundas had decided, motioning for *Capitaine* Griot to top up Récamier's wineglass at last. "But they did not get your ship, or her papers. She did not go into English Harbour with that damnable British flag above her own colours."

"Not into English Harbour, *m'sieur, non,*" Récamier had objected. "Once her boats were recovered, she sailed West, not South. I watched her 'til her t'gallants dropped below the horizon. I suspect that she was not part of the Antigua squadron, but was from Jamaica, instead."

"How odd," Choundas had pondered, leaning back in his chair and staring at the ceiling, as if easing a cramp from sitting so long.

"Poaching, perhaps?" *Capitaine de Frégate* MacPherson had japed. "With the British troops gone from Saint Domingue, their frigates are under-employed that far West. Do they loan frigates to the squadrons out of Antigua, our tasks will be more difficult, with more patrollers at sea opposing us."

"*Proteus,*" Hainaut had mused. "Did not the London papers last year mention her? Was she not at Camperduin, against our pitiful allies, the Batavians?" he posed, using the Dutch-Flemish pronunciation of the battle's name. "I seem to recall . . . took a prize, another frigate . . . something?" he had trailed off, vague, and "foxed" by then on his master's wine.

"*Oui,* look into that, Etienne," Choundas had ordered.

"*Certainement, m'sieur,*" the harried little clerk had said with a quick bob of his balding head, scribbling notes to himself on scrap paper with an ever-present pencil from his waist-coat pockets.

"Well, *mon cher* Récamier," Choundas had concluded their supper with an air approaching *bonhomie,* "it is too bad that your *L'Incendiare* was lost, along with the 'Ami' brig and all her supplies, but no blame can be laid against you, you did your best, after all, *hein?*"

"*Merci, m'sieur,*" Récamier had replied, nodding curtly, as if it were true, and no more than his right, with no sign of relief to his demeanour.

"I cannot promise you another command, though, not for some time," Choundas had informed him. "You understand that a new ship may be seen as a reward, *n'est-ce pas?* The British *knight* their captains when they lose after a well-fought action. We . . . do *not.* But I am sure that a shore posting, for a year or two . . . at your current salary rate, of course . . . might prove instructive . . . and rewarding."

Choundas had looked down his ravaged, shiny-masked nose, as if to say that he *knew* about Récamier's three current *amours,* besides his reasonably well-connected young and attractive wife back in Bordeaux.

"I serve at your command, of course, *m'sieur.*" Récamier shrugged back, with just the right "eager" note of toadying, but nothing *too* thick or oily.

"It has been a long day, *messieurs,* and I am weary. Instructive and pleasant as our supper has been, I bid you a good night," Choundas had determined, painfully, stiffly scraping his chair back on the bare parquet floor, and using his stick to rise, most creaky, by then.

Quick handshakes, quick, insincere thanks and compliments were exchanged, Récamier out the door first, then MacPherson and Griot, in order of seniority dates on their commissions; lastly, Capt. Desplan doffed his undonned hat and backed off the wide front veranda to enter the waiting coach that the Black *garçon chef* had whistled up for them. All of them, but Lt. Récamier most of all, were glad to be gone, free of their superior's mercurial, and scathing, temper.

Choundas stood by the door, half slumped in weariness and lingering pain of his ancient wounds, leaning heavily on his walking-stick before turning to clump-swish back into the foyer.

"He lies like a dog, *oui*, Jules," Choundas said with a snarl of anger, and a touch of resignation. "Oh, his surviving crewmen said he fought well, but as for the rest, hmmm . . ."

"Then why did you not . . . ?"

"Because he did not *cringe, cher* Jules!" Choundas barked with a tinge of wonderment in his voice. "Young Récamier has hair on his arse, to face me so coolly. A man of many parts, he is, and most of them calm, calculating, and brave. He is not a timid, cringing *shop*-keeper! *And* his wife is a distant cousin to Admiral de Brueys, and the Directory would look even *more* unfavourably upon me did I harvest the lad's head," Choundas concluded with a world-weary sigh and shrug. "He will not make that set of errors again; he is one who can learn from his mistakes. Of *course*, he panicked when he ran aground, most likely his first time, *hein?* I doubt he left his little ship so late as he claims. His Boatswain swears that smoke was visible when he got into his boat, though the real fire did not come 'til later, when the *biftecks* got aboard her . . . but he *did* see to his men, his wounded, so to punish him severely would degrade the morale of our *matelots*, did a popular and caring officer get guillotined for placing their safety as paramount."

"But he should have fired her at once, even leaving his wounded to burn with her, *m'sieur?*" Hainaut queried, aghast at the obvious conclusion, and posing his question most carefully.

"*Certainement*," Choundas callously snapped. "Such sentiment is *bourgeois* twaddle left over from the old regime, Hainaut. Hardly suitable to a commited son of the Revolution and the Republic. One cannot make the omelette without breaking the eggs, *n'est-ce pas?* Or, as the great American revolutionary Jefferson said, 'The tree of revolution must now and then be watered with the blood of patriots and tyrants.' "

"Well, Lieutenant Récamier will have plenty of time to think on his error, and repent of it, *m'sieur*," Hainaut snidely tittered.

"A year at least, before we employ him again," Choundas mused, yawning loudly and widely, unable to cover his mouth. "Unless the need for officers at sea forces my hand. Say, six months?"

"If you wish to *really* rub his lesson in, *m'sieur*," Hainaut posed, carefully daring to advance his own career, "you could even send *me* to sea before him. In the next suitable prize. A fast American schooner, perhaps . . ."

"Perhaps so, Hainaut. Perhaps so," Choundas *seemed* to promise, before another gargantuan yawn overtook him. "It *is* late. The guards are posted? The doors and windows locked for the night? *Bon. Garçon!* Light me to my chamber!" he barked at the older chief servant.

"Good night, *m'sieur*," Hainaut bade him. "Sleep well in your new bed . . . your first night in your grand new house."

"Thank you, Jules, I believe I will," Choundas said over his shoulder as he shrugged the right side of his ornate coat off, letting it fall down to his left wrist, with the servant fretting about him.

Hainaut turned to ascend the stairs to his own lofty chambers, but had only taken a step or two when he heard de Gougne scuttle across the foyer from his miserable quarters to *Le Maître's*, in evident haste and concern, so Hainaut halted and leaned far out, hoping to overhear what seemed so urgent to the little mouse, what made him so fearful.

" . . . *Proteus* . . . Camperduin . . . the *Orangespruit* frigate. . . . in the *Gazette* and *Marine Chronicle* . . . mumble-mumble hum-um . . ."

"*Putain!*" he heard Choundas bellow. "*Mon cul! Ce salaud de . . .* Lewrie? That bastard, that son of a whore is out *here?*" his superior screamed, instantly so enraged that anyone who crossed him would die, as sure as Fate! The stout walking-stick swished the air, something expensive and frangible shattered . . . several breakable somethings!

Oh-oh! Hainaut cravenly thought. His *bête noire*, that bane of his very life, the author of his wounds and disfigurements was nearby?

"*Merde alors, putain!* That shit, that . . . cunt! This time, I'll kill him, this time . . . !"

Lewrie! Hainaut thought, not daring to breathe or draw attention to himself that might make him a target. *Now, Récamier's bane . . . and mine, too. He captured me, once . . .*

More things went smash, the *garçon chef* yelped in sudden pain, then stumbled out of the bed-chamber into the office as if physically hurled . . . immediately followed by the little mouse, de Gougne, who was guarding his head with the sheaf of papers, his face terror-pale.

Suddenly, the idea of getting a small ship of his own to command seemed a trifle *less* attractive, Hainaut thought, *quietly* tip-toeing up the stairs for safety. Better would be to go as a lieutenant aboard a much larger man o' war, *Capitaine* Desplan's frigate, say, with so many large guns and such stout sides . . . under an experienced older captain who'd know how to deal with such a clever scourge.

BOOK ONE

Di, talem terris avertite pestem!
Nec visu facilis nec dictu adfabilis ulli.

Ye god, take such a pest away from Earth!
In aspect foreboding, in speech to be accosted by none.
—*Aeneid*, Book III, 620-621
Publius Vergilius Maro

CHAPTER ONE

S ah?" a voice intruded on his dreams, interrupting a matter of great import, the fate of the ship, of England . . . something that, at that instant, was but seconds from its penultimate deciding, for good or ill. "Sah, time t'wake, sah."

"Grr . . . ack!" the dreamer exclaimed, which could have stood for "Ease your helm" or "All Hands to the braces"—to him, anyway, as the "deck" rocked and shuddered alarmingly. "Whazzuh?" he queried.

"Be almos' four o' de mornin', sah," Coxswain Andrews insisted, using his weight upon a knee to jounce the soft, civilian mattress. A hand was pent in indecision above the hero, as he pondered laying hands on a gentleman . . . or dashing a ladle of cool water from the laving bowl on his head, then run and blame it on a house-servant!

"But . . . !" Captain Alan Lewrie, RN, commanding officer of HMS *Proteus*, Fifth Rate frigate, managed in reply, heavily smacking his lips and creaking one eye open to peruse the ceiling, one which he did not in *any* wise recognise. Too many damn' cherubs, and such!

"G'mornin', sah," Andrews said.

"Aarrr . . ." Lewrie commented. It had been such a *vivid* dream, one which might have been mere *seconds* from revealing or concluding or fulfilling . . . something. Whatever it had been, it had left him with a cock-stand worthy of a marlingspike. "Time, is it?"

"Aye, sah," Andrews replied, stepping away from the bed. "Dey be coffee belowstairs, black an' hot, Cap'm. Mistah Cashman, he's up already, an' 'is coachman's gettin' de 'quipage hitched."

"Right, then," Lewrie said with a sigh and a yawn, chiding himself for sharing that third bottle of wine with his host, "Kit," after supper. He should have known better, should have kept a soberer head, and . . .

Damn *that ceiling!* Lewrie thought, scowling as he sat up in bed: *Eros and arrows, bare-titted shepherd girls, and clouds . . . thought I was gone over to Heaven for a second or two!*

He flung back the single sheet that covered him, swung his legs out to plant his bare feet on the naked wood floor . . . swayed a bit as the last of the wine fumes rose with him, and belched.

"Bloody hell," he gravelled, massaging his eyes with the heels of his palms. "Why can't people shoot each other at reasonable hours? Is it light yet, Andrews?"

"Just a tad o' false dawn, sah," Andrews said from the bureau, where he was brushing Lewrie's dress coat. Sure enough, the scene in the tall French doors leading to the upper balcony was night-dark with only a hint of darker trees swaying against skies just barely brushed with grey. "Touch o' fog'r mist, too, sah," Andrews said, frowning.

"Ummph," Lewrie commented, bracing his hands on the bed to get himself upright. With one eye still shut and the other squinted, he shambled to the wash-hand stand and laving bowl, to the ewer full of cool well-water, 'coz *God*, was he thirsty!

"Mind d'ose . . ." Andrews cautioned, too late.

"Oww! Shit-*fire*! Mmmm! Dammit t' hell!"

He'd stubbed his toes on a dark leather chest, just one of many in the room, as Kit Cashman packed up his household for his removal from Jamaica in the next few weeks.

Two tumblers of water, a quick slosh and scrub on his face and neck, a cursory sponge-down against the humid cool of a tropic morning, and he was primed to part the flaps of his thin cotton underdrawers for a *long* "tinkle" into the night-jar. Feeling *some* more human, at last, he sat on a spindly side-chair to don his white silk hose and bind them behind his knees, pull on a fresh pair of light sailcloth breeches, and slip into his new-blacked Hessian boots. Andrews stood by patiently, offering him a clean silk shirt with a moderately ruffled breast inset and cuffs, helped him bind on his neck-stock, then held out a cotton waist-coat so he could slip into it. His slim sword baldric looped atop that, from right shoulder to left hip, with a gleaming oval brass breastplate at the centre of his chest. Then came the kerseymere wool coat, the full-dress version with the gilt-lace buttonholes, buttons and pocket detailings, and the single fringed gold epaulet of a captain of less than three years' seniority that rode on his right shoulder.

Lewrie turned to the mirror above the wash-hand stand, to drag both hands through his hair to "Welsh" comb it with his fingers; back above his ears on the sides, where thick and slightly wiry hair of mid-brown, almost light-brown, and further gilt by harsh sunlight off seas innumerable by then, curled over ears and temples almost like the bust of a long-gone Roman, gathered in a fashionable swirl low on his forehead. Andrew plucked at his collar to tug his short, spriggish queue of hair to lie outside the tall-collared coat and fiddled with the narrow band and bow of black silk which bound it.

Lewrie had shaved the morning before, so that wouldn't delay him. He rubbed his stubble, adjudging his "phyz." Firm skin, a lean face, a long-passage sailor's permanent tan ... the upright puckered line of a sword-cut on his left cheek, from a foolish duel of his own long ago. Permanent squint-lines round his eyes, now, though *merry-lookin'* ... ? Frown lines, or *grin* lines at the corners of his mouth ... and eyes of startling colour, light grey or blue, by temper. They looked a trifle grey, this bloody pre-morning ... and a touch of "bleary" and red-shot, too, he speculated. But, altogether, not a *bad* phyz.

"Yah hat, sah," Andrews said, handing him the best one from a thin wooden box, Gilt cords and tassels just so, cockade and the dog-vane, loop, and button gleaming, the gold lacing round the edges bright and buttery-yellow, instead of verdigrised by sea-air like his oldest one.

"Well, then ... coffee, didje say?"

Blam! From the lower porch, the front veranda, a pistol firing as loud and terrier-bark-sharp as a four-pounder, making them both jump!

"Bloody man!" Lewrie snapped, reclaiming his calm. "What need of *more* practice? Went through a *pound* o' powder, yesterday and last night! Tell cook I'll want some toast and jam with my coffee, too."

"Aye, sah," Andrews replied as Lewrie strode to the door, with at least the outward appearance of firm-minded purpose, and *sober* control of himself. At least he avoided the various boxes and chests.

Blam!

"That'd be de lef' hand, I reckon," Andrews muttered.

"Morning, Nimrod," Lewrie bade his host, standing bare-headed by a whitewashed column on the veranda, balancing cup and saucer, and savouring his second refill of coffee, heavily laced with local-made brown sugar, and thick cream fresh-stripped from the teat. The smell of burned gunpowder lay heavy on the air, and a small cumulus cloud of nitres and exploded sulfurs mingled with the predawn fog.

"Ah, good morning, Alan me old," Lieutenant-Colonel Christopher Cashman answered right gaily for such an ungodly hour, turning to face him as his man-servant quickly reloaded the pair of duelling pistols. A scarecrow figure of straw stuffed into white nankeen slop-trousers and loose shirt, already holed with long practice, stood beyond the shell-and-sand drive, the requisite fifteen paces from Cashman's line in the sand, and the rickety folding field-table that bore his arsenal.

"Sleep well?" Lewrie enquired as he lifted a thick slice of hot, toasted bread, slathered with fresh butter and mango jam, to his lips.

"As peaceful, and as undisturbed, as a babe," Cashman boasted, with a chuckle and a wide grin, and Lewrie had to admit that he *seemed* in fine fettle, clear-eyed and "tail's-up" with gleeful anticipation, not dread, of facing another man's levelled pistol not an hour hence. "Not Nimrod, though . . . that's huntin'. Nay, rather I fancy meself an Achilles this mornin'. Ready to slay my Hector and be done."

He was dressed for it, of a certainty, with the care and forethought required of a man who'd shortly "blaze." Silk shirts were *de rigueur*, more easily drawn, in whole patches, from bullet wounds. Kit wore white cotton breeches, freshly boiled in lye soap, thoroughly rinsed in clean well-water and air-dried on a line strung on the upper balcony, above the miasmas and smuts of the daily traffic to the house, and the risk of tropical "infusions" that came from damp soils. Tall black-and-brown-topped riding boots completed his ensemble; thick'uns, *almost* proof against a stray ball, or a snakebite, too.

"And I'm . . . ?" Lewrie asked with a small, approving laugh, never the greatest of Greek scholars.

"My Ulysses, Alan . . . ever the crafty bastard, haha!"

"Didn't he make off with most of the loot in the end?" Lewrie wondered aloud.

"Lost it all by shipwreck, then went home to his wife, at the last," Cashman said, picking up a newly loaded pistol and taking his stance, side-on to the target, to present the slimmest right profile to a return ball, pistol cocked and his forearm vertical, the long barrel in perfect alignment with his forearm, mortally intent . . .

Bloody bastard! Lewrie cringed; *just had t'remind me o' bein' on the outs with the wife back home!* He rather doubted that Caroline was pining away and spinning wool as faithfully as . . . Penelope, was it? Not that Caroline, a paragon of virtue to his "crow-cock" Corinthian nature, would *ever* cuckold *him* . . . would she?

Down went the right arm, hinging like a heavy gate beam, and the pistol and forearm were as straight and steady as a sword blade, and, *Bang!* Another .63 calibre lead ball plumbed the red wool Valentine's heart pinned to the straw man, now almost punched or clipped into the form of a many-layered cockade, or a rose blossom.

"Steady, is it? There's a wonder . . . after last night," Alan said, thinking that even one as cocksure as Cashman could use a little encouraging toadying, that hour of the morning.

"Three shared bottles, and a brandy night-cap? Mere piffle," Cashman scoffed. "Nought t'fuddle a *soldier's* constitution. Though *you* look a tad 'foxed,' still. Thought sailors could hold their wine, b'God! Game enough for't, I trust?"

"Oh, I'll toe up proper, Kit, no worries," Lewrie answered, an angry second from a harsher retort. Cashman was not the same man he'd been over supper. Today, he had his "battle-face" on, and friendship, or another's feelings, could be go-to-hell. He had a foe to kill, and consideration had little to do with it. Now, did he survive, and succeed, he'd be puffed full of relief and joy, and breakfast would be a nigh-hysterically blissful explosion of high-cockalorum. But that was for later.

Lewrie polished off his toast and took a sip of his coffee, as Cashman snatched up the second pistol of a sudden, back to the target, pistol and forearm vertical again but close to his chest, to quickly spin on the balls of his feet, take stance, and fire. Another cloud of gunsmoke wreathed him, but he was smiling. His snap-shot had hit.

"Awake enough now, are ye?" Cashman snapped. "Let's be about it, then. Here comes the coach. And God help Ledyard Beauman!"

CHAPTER TWO

Cashman's feud, his almost Corsican *vendetta* versus ex-Colonel Ledyard Beauman had been going on for months, Lewrie sourly thought as the coach-and-four jounced and rumbled over the irregularities in the sand-and-shell road, with both pairs of pistols in boxes in his lap. He sat facing aft, while Cashman took the rear seat facing forward, arms folded across his chest, chin down, and his face made of ruddy granite, centred on the rear bench with no need of support from the coach's padded sides or window sills. Lewrie was crammed into the fore-left corner, more than willing to wilt against leather and an open window sill. Not a word had passed between them in the quarter-hour since they'd entered the coach.

End o' my *relations with the Beaumans, root an' branch*, Lewrie told himself in the uncomfortable silence; *and by* God *but they're rich and influential!* Should've *begged off, but.... a friend's a friend, a promise is a promise.*

Odds were, Kit would blast Ledyard Beauman's heart clean out of his chest, drop him like a pole-axed heifer for veal, and the Beaumans would blame *him*, damn' em! for agreeing to be Cashman's second, whichever way it went. The father was retired back in England, the sort of huntin', shootin', tenant-whippin', crop-tramplin' fool of the squirearchy . . . but with so much money to sling around, he appeared *so* much more civilised when he sat on his coin-purse, and surely was more than welcome round Whitehall, the Admiralty, Board of Trade, the Court, and Parliament, with half a dozen "bought" Members from his *own* Rotten Boroughs to do his bidding in Commons, mayhap even a "skint" peer dependent upon his largesse to look out for his interests in Lords, too!

One letter from his son Hugh, now in charge of their plantings and enterprises here in Jamaica, and they could ruin him! Not that he stood in particularly "good odour," already, for all his successes at sea. The longer the war against Revolutionary France and her unlikely ally Spain continued, the more "priggish" people were getting, he had noticed. Smallish peccadilloes and indiscretions so easily dismissed back in the '70s and '80s were now nearly the stuff of scandal.

Lewrie blamed the Wesley brothers, the Hannah Moores, and the William Wilberforces, and all their goose-eyed, slack-jawed tribe, for meddling, sermonising . . . Reformers . . . for mucking things up with all their "shalt-nots" and "viewing with alarm," their evangelising, their . . . revival-ising! Why, did they keep their mass-crowd preaching up, not only would fox-hunting and steeple-chasing go by the board, there'd be an end to bear-baiting, dog or cock-fighting, boys beating the bounds every spring, morris dancing, and cricket, too!

And fucking and adultery would be right-out, of course.

It *was* a mortal pity. Here he was, a True Blue Heart of Oak, a bold Sea Officer of the Crown, and *just* because he'd kept a courtesan for a year or so, had an affair with a young widow who'd produced him a child on the wrong side of the blanket . . . Even the two medals tinkling together on his chest for Saint Vincent and Camperdown meant nothing.

Without a career, without a commission or ship, he'd be back in England, permanently on half-pay, and facing a hostile wife, a clutch of estranged children, a too-fond *amour* with a bastard, so blissful she'd cry their "love" from the rooftops . . . and *another* Beauman, his old love Lucy, more than ready to spite him and spread every sort of malicious rumour in the better reaches of English Society, from Land's End to John O' Groats!

If only Ledyard'd had a bit *o' brains in his head!* Lewrie sadly contemplated.

But, no, he hadn't. His older brother, Hugh, had funded a local regiment of volunteers, had urged their swaggerin'-handsome and capable neighbour, Christopher Cashman, the distinguished ex-soldier, to take charge and mould it into a creditable unit, with that jingle-brained, ne'er-do-well, indolent fop Ledyard taking the honourific office, with no real responsibility, as Colonel of the Regiment. All he had to do was show up once a month on Mess Night, be fawned over by the locally raised officers much like him—idle second or third planters' sons. And what harm could've come from that? So *utterly* useless, surely he could *soldier* for a spell . . . or, pretend to!

But Ledyard had gotten it in his head that *any* damn fool with *book-learnin'* could be a military genius. Washington, Gage, and Green for examples in the recent past inspired him, accounts of Caesar's Gallic Wars, of Hannibal and Lake Trasimeno, Scipio Africanus who'd crushed Hannibal and Carthage; Marlborough, even that Puritan bastard Cromwell had quite turned his noggin. So, when the regiment had sailed to Saint Domingue to fight those ex-slave armies of Toussaint L'Ouverture (*another* self-educated general) Ledyard had taken command. In the smoke and confusion of their first battle near Port-au-Prince, he'd gotten a third of his men murdered or wounded or captured by those blood-thirsty rebel slaves, whose battle song was "Kill All the Whites" or something near-like it, had caused a general panic and rout of half the *army*, then had dashed off atop his blooded stallion with his cronies and toadies croaking in his wake, and had left poor Cashman to clean up the mess, and *naturally* it was not a bit of *his* fault, but Cashman's panic, or misunderstanding of orders!

Cashman had been ready to sell up, anyway, and leave Jamaica for someplace new in the United States of America, change from being landed to a new career, one which didn't require slaves, for he was heart-sick of the institution. A successful last campaign season, and he could've resigned his commission, perhaps even *sold* it to an aspiring major . . . though colonelcies weren't bought or sold in the Regular Army, Jamaica was another kettle of fish, and a "rancid" one at that, where sharp practice was more easily tolerated, or ignored.

Now, though, smeared in the local newspapers, by rumour and the sneers of the richer, his repute, and his property, weren't worth half a crown to the pound, and no matter how the duel ended, he'd be forced to slink off with but a pittance of his massive investment, the fruits of his adult life as a soldier and looter and speculator barely enough for a fresh start, and then only did he think small, not over-reach!

Oh yes, Ledyard, and all the Beaumans, had a lot to answer for!
A little heart's blood would pay for all.

The coach turned off the coast road and skreaked steeply downhill for
a space, the wood brake-shoes ready to begin smoking as they made
for the agreed-upon stretch of low-tide beach, where the footing would
be firm. With a last thudding toss and clatter that came nigh to hurling
them into each other, the coach gained the flatter ground of the strand,
and the wheels hissed like hungry dragons over sandier grit and thin
soil, the clopping of hooves subdued to the rushing and faint water-
drumming of a ship underway.

"Hmmm," Lewrie commented, taking off his large cocked hat to
stick out his head for a look-see. He'd have said something inane and
redundant such as "we're here," had it not been for the razory glints
in Cashman's eyes for disturbing his deep, silent contemplations. For
a ha'penny, Lewrie realised, Kit would have bitten his head off!

"Hope Ledyard's been shriven," Lewrie said, instead, twisting on a
wry, lop-sided grin. "Whatever it is the vicars do for the half-dead."

Cashman, enveloped by a silk-lined cape, merely nodded, though
there was a hint of amusement to the set of his mouth.

The coach body rocked on its thick leather suspension straps, and
the horses blew and shook their heads as Andrews and the old Black
man-servant that Cashman had brought along sprang down to open
the door for them. Lewrie went out first, the two boxes of pistols
awkward under his left arm, the expensive wood cases chafing on the
hilt of his hanger. He donned his hat, took a deep breath, and looked
about their killing ground.

There was very little wind, just the mildest little zephyrs off the
sea, the last afterthought of the steady night-winds; not enough to stir
the thin mists in the forest above the beach and the coast road, the
tendrils of fog that slunk stealthily through the lower scrub of the
beach, the manchineel trees and sea-grapes, the withering saplings and
wire grasses, the low runners that snaked across the sands. Down the
beach, a little to the East'rd, stood a pair of coach-and-fours, a table
set up closer to the proper sea-washed beach sands, and a party of
caped men who stood waiting for him. Some smoked clay pipes or
the Spanish-style *cigarillos* that were coming into vogue, and he could

see the faint gleam of coin-silver flasks as they were tipped up for a sip, the sheen of larger silver or crystal wineglasses as men drank to kill boredom, dread, impatience, or terror. As Lewrie began to plod towards them through the deep, dry-sucking coarser sand of the beach above the high-tide line and the over-wash barrow behind it, the men in the other party left their coaches and strode out toward that table, so he short-tacked to intercept them, the heels of his Hessian boots sinking in, his ankles quickly beginning to ache from the unnatural, enforced gait where toes stayed elevated and rarely had any purchase, where even rough-seasoned soles clumsily skidded and slipped.

There were two coaches, and at least three saddle horses, back of the beach, making Lewrie frown a little as he turned his head for a cursory look; one ornate and its doors emblazoned with a fanciful escutcheon the Beaumans didn't exactly merit. The second coach was plainer, well worn and a touch seedy, its team of four mis-matched and the typical runtish, slab-shanked beasts found in the Colonies. Lewrie deemed that one the surgeon's. The saddle horses, though . . . there was an agreed-upon limit to how many gentlemen were allowed as witnesses, participants, and seconds. Were they cheating? He would not put it past them, and looked more closely at the trees, where some sharpshooter might be lurking.

"Ah, Captain Lewrie!" the older gentleman, a Mr. Hendricks, and a well-respected squire, planter, and magistrate, called out of a sudden, as if to draw his attention to the immediate field, which made Lewrie even more suspicious. As his second, Lewrie literally held Cashman's honour and safety in his hands, not merely the pettifogging details of well-established custom, usage, and *punctilio*.

"Mister Hendricks, good morning, sir," Lewrie replied, halting short of the inviting table—*tables*, he took note. There were four, in all, three in one row, well separated from one another, with the one in the centre draped in white cloth and agleam with a surgeon's field kit of instruments, the vials, powders, and such with which to save the life of the loser. The farthest table bore two cases of pistols, two pairs of long-barreled death. Their table —so far—was bare.

"You know Mister Trollope, the surgeon."

"Sir," Lewrie intoned, doffing his hat.

"Captain Sellers, of course, Colonel Beauman's second."

"Captain Sellers."

"Captain Lewrie," that weedy worthy answered with the merest tilt of his head and a hand that just approached his own cocked hat in a returning salute, his tone icy and top-lofty, looking down his nose.

Kin o' the dead man, o' course, Lewrie told himself; *'spose he has cause t'look gloomy, knowin' his cousin's about t'get knackered.*

"Geratt, the surgeon's assistant." Hendricks went on, waving an arm in the general direction of a mousy little fuss-budget with his hands held rodent-like in the middle of his chest. "And Mister Hugh Beauman."

"Sir," Lewrie solemnly said in greeting, with a faint bow and another doff of his hat. He was surprised that the elder brother gave him a doff and bow of equal courtesy . . . since he looked as if he had breakfasted on glass splinters and was trying to pass them *without* a roar of agony. His grimace was worthy of a hanged spaniel.

"Your principal, Colonel Cashman, is come, sir?" Mr. Hendricks softly enquired, sounding the opening bars of the "dance of honour."

"He has, sir," Lewrie formally intoned, casting his eyes to the slim fop, Captain Sellers. "And yours, Captain Sellers?" Lewrie asked (rather politely, he thought!), but Sellers, still clad in his full regimentals, despite the fact that the 15th West Indies had been mustered out a month before, took umbrage and looked even farther down his nose.

"Damn you, he has, sir!" Sellers shot back. "The Colonel is more than ready!"

"Tut, now, Captain Sellers," Hendricks mournfully chid him with a grimace of distaste. "Decorum, hmm?"

"Aye," Lewrie could not help tacking on to nettle the little bantam cock, his eyes gone wintry steel-grey despite the feral grin on his face. "*Someone*'s about t'die, the next few minutes. 'Twas 'blaze 'til death or severe wounding,' d'ye recall, sir? And . . . do you prefer the *pretence* of still holding active commission, mind that I out-rank you . . . and tread wary . . . *sir.*"

"Now see here . . . !" Sellers spluttered, one hand upon the hilt of his smallsword—his *left,* Lewrie took note with a smirk of derision, not the right, with which to draw it and *do* anything.

"Gentlemen, please—!" Mr. Hendricks objected, meekly scandalised by their behaviour.

"Damn yer eyes, Lewrie!" Hugh Beauman barked in a husky *basso.* "Impertinent . . . swaggerin', damme-boy . . . *tcha!*"

It must have been born in the blood, that all the Beauman men chopped their thoughts into the pithiest shards of sentences that stood in the stead of another man's entire full minute of prosing!

"Mister Beauman, please," Hendricks insisted, recalling his own dignities in Jamaican Society. "The both of you, sirs . . . for shame!"

"My pardons, sir, but Captain Sellers rowed me beyond all temperance," Lewrie was first to apologise, doffing his hat again. "I do not *yet* feel need to demand his apology . . . or satisfaction for such a slight upon the field on honour. You have *my* abject apology, sir."

Think that'un over, toady! Lewrie smugly thought, bestowing his best beatific smile on Hendricks, his Number One "shit-eatin' grin" on Sellers. *You wish it, we'll make this like a double weddin'! Two for the price of one!*

Hendricks rounded slowly on Capt. Sellers, who could do nothing but flummox, redden, fidget, and bob his head as he mumbled like sentiments over his error.

"The occasion for two gentlemen to meet upon the field of honour is a sad, regrettable, yet solemn, uhm, occasion," Mr. Hendricks gloomily intoned. "And there is no place for . . ."

Christ on a crutch, he makes it sound *like a wedding preamble!* Lewrie thought, lowering his head and biting the lining of his cheeks to keep from snickering, despite all solemnity. *'Does anyone object t'these two lunaticks blowin' their guts out, speak now, or forever hold yer peace?'* *Gawd!*

"I charge you now, sirs, is there not another course of action by which the parties may obtain satisfaction without the useless effusion of blood?" Hendricks almost chanted, sounding more like a judge or priest than a referee. "Even at this last moment, can we not walk away after shaking hands, and forgive all enmities? Captain Lewrie?"

"I regret that there is not, Mister Hendricks," Lewrie replied. "My principal is adamant that both public, and private, slurs against his character and military prowess, his pride and his honour, have no other recourse. The hurt inflicted is too grievous."

"Captain Sellers? Mister Beauman, as his brother—"

"The Colonel stands by his account of his actions on Saint Domingue, sir, and is in no wise responsible for the characterisations in the papers, nor the rumours in Society, but holds steadfast to his opinion of his former subordinate's behaviour as the truth of the matter. Therefore, he cannot, and will not, retreat from his position without a grievous loss of his own honour and credence," Capt. Sellers recited, his speech all but written on his coat cuff, Lewrie suspected, and rehearsed all the previous day and in the coach on the way here.

Well, somebody's doomed, then, Lewrie glumly thought. Neither man *could* demur without suffering the ultimate penalties. The label of Coward or Poltroon would be the worst, with Liar and Weasel coming in strong seconds. Did Ledyard Beauman withdraw, he'd not only become a *pariah* in Jamaica and the entire Caribbean, but in England as well, did he scurry there to hide his shame. His supposedly "accurate" account of the 15th's role outside Port-au-Prince would be exposed as the total fabrication it was, and the entire Beauman clan would become a laughingstock.

"Mister Beauman?" Hendricks pressed in a near-whisper.

"Stands by it," Hugh Beauman nigh-growled, stone-faced. " 'Tis too late now. Duel it is. Be about it, hey?"

Damn my eyes, but the bastard's good as slain his brother, for his own damn' pride! Lewrie gawped to himself; *'twas* Hugh *who made him soldier,* knowin' *he'd be hopeless.*

"Having failed to reconcile the gentlemen, we must proceed," Mr. Hendricks ceremoniously announced; like a Romish priest who, the weekly notices over, reverts to Latin for the daily offices of the Mass. "The agreement is for the exchange of fire from pistols at fifteen paces . . . the principals to continue firing until such time as one, or both, are mortally struck or incapable of continuing. Those are still the conditions, sirs?" he asked Sellers and Lewrie, peering at each in turn.

"It is, sir," both seconds intoned, almost as one, putting Alan in mind of Divine Services, again—"The Lord be with you" from the vicar, the congregants responding "And also with you."

"Each party supplies two brace of weapons. I have seen Captain Sellers's. Captain Lewrie, d'ye have Colonel Cashman's? Then, please be so good as to place them on yon table and open the boxes so that I and my assistant, and Captain Sellers, may inspect them. After which, you will be free to inspect those brought by Colonel Ledyard Beauman."

"Very good, sir," Lewrie replied, walking back to the bare and rickety table indicated, at the south end of the beach. They had chosen this cove and beach for its privacy, as well as the fact that it lay nearly Sou-Sou'west to Nor-Nor'east, so the rising sun would not be in either party's eyes. He opened the boxes to display the pistols, and their accoutrements; the lidded pocket full of spare flints, the wire vent-pricks in their own depression, the brass rammers slotted in velvet, the bright powder flasks in their snugly sculpted holes, and five new-cast lead balls for each weapon in troughs, gleaming prettily, like spare rings in a lady's jewelry case.

Mr. Hendricks was a good judge of weapons, perhaps from a long experience with the *code duello* and the arguments of his neighbours. He pricked the vents with the wires to determine that a double-charge was not already loaded, let the rammers drop down the barrels to coax a clean, and empty, "ring" from each pistol, checking closely for any hidden rifling—smoothbores, only, thankee, no cheating!—then watched warily as Lewrie charged all four with powder, added ball and wadding, flipped open the raspy frizzens to prime the pans, then shut them and left them un-cocked, the hammers touched only to adjudge how snugly their flints and leathers were screwed down in the dog's-jaws.

"Discriminatin' taste in arms, the both of them," Mr. Hendricks commented as they repeated the process at Beauman's table. "The best Mantons or Twiggs, and these Philadelphia-made beauties!" he exulted over a pair of ten-inch barreled, silver-chased, and gold-leafed .54-calibre pistols with glossy burled-walnut furniture. "Though I note that Colonel Cashman favours the heavier Mantons, of sixty-three calibre. Ahem, I think we're done. Let us now repair to my neutral table . . . that'un yonder before the others, and complete our preparations, gentlemen. I have the coin."

He produced a large Spanish silver piece-of-eight, showed them the reverse and obverse, the "head" and the "tail," and poised it upon the nail of his right thumb.

"First, for the south position. Choose, Captain Sellers."

"Uhmm . . . heads," Sellers blurted after a brief hesitation.

"And tails it is. Captain Lewrie, your principal will be posted on the south end of the beach, and yours, Captain Sellers, will hold the north end of the touch line."

"Mmmph," Sellers grunted, not greatly disappointed; at that hour there was no superiority to either position. The sun would not interfere, nor would the land breeze when it sprang up be strong enough to deviate a bullet's trajectory.

"The first brace of pistols to be used," Hendricks continued in a solemn drone. "Heads for Colonel Cashman's, tails will be for Colonel Beauman's. Captain Lewrie?"

"Heads," Lewrie decided quickly.

"And heads it is. Please be so good as to fetch the initial pair to this table, Captain Lewrie. Captain Sellers, oblige as well by bringing forth your choice of pistols, should a second exchange be necessary?"

Lewrie was partial to Mantons, as was Christopher Cashman, so he brought over the box containing the 9-inch barreled Mantons, first, as Sellers returned with a box containing the silver-chased Philadelphia duellers.

"All that remains then, gentlemen, is to announce to your principals that, barring a last-minute reconciliation, the field is ready for their appearances," Hendricks concluded.

Lewrie bowed himself away and strode back through the deep sand to the waiting coach, all his senses as tautly alert and alive as if it were he who would "blaze," savouring the dawn as if it were *his* last.

False dawn had become a grey but promising predawn, the colours of beach, forests, and the sea turning more vibrant. The inshore waters were turning topaz, the deeps beyond shading off to a blue-grey, barely stirring at slack water of the tide, at the death of the night breezes and the Nor'east Trades.

Tan upper beach, littered with desperate growth, the crown and over-wash barrow bearded with tall reeds that faintly swayed to what little breeze sprang up in fitful puffs; the greyed shell-litter near the crowns, sloughing downward to the hard-pan as if smoothed by some titanic sculptor's hands, to the last, wide taupe and greyed-wet sands where a grown man's boots could barely leave an impression.

Sand, the wet, the cool but muggy tidal marsh aroma, the crisp tang of crystalled salt, the kelp and iodine and blood-copper odours off the wider, open sea assailed his nose, wakening the memories of a half of his life near, or on, the sea.

Lovely damn' mornin'! he thought; *what a damn-fool time t'die!*

He leaned into the open coach door; no Cashman! Had he deloped?

"Kit?" he softly called, walking round the team of horses.

"Ready, are we?" Cashman gravelled, his voice a tad hoarse.

"All's in order. You've the south end, and your own barkers. For the first shots, at least," Lewrie told him as Cashman cast aside his cloak at last, tossing it to his coachee.

Odd damn' reek! Lewrie thought, looking at a scuffed-up pile of sand on the far side of the coach: *'Tis puke!* he realised. *Puke and piss.*

"Pen quill down me throat," Cashman explained. "No trouble in emptying the ol' bladder, though. Does the hapless bastard get lucky, I'll not have coffee kill me slowly. Never do battle on a full stomach, don't ye know. The death o' many a good man, victuals."

"I'll keep that in mind," Lewrie somberly told him.

Lewrie looked off to the forests above the beach, chilling, as he realised that he'd been horribly remiss, that all the *minutiae* had made his suspicions quite fly his head! Two coaches and three horses— Who'd ridden, who'd coached? And *was* there someone lurking over yonder with a rifled weapon?

"Er, Andrews, a word, please. The man-servant, too, if you will fetch him along," Lewrie said, turning from his principal. "Do you keep a keen weather eye peeled on those trees, lad. You see some devilment lurkin', you sing out, hear me? I don't trust the Beaumans not to mark their cards . . . that Sellers bastard, most of all."

"I'll do it, sah," Andrews vowed, scowling intensely, and the black man-servant to Cashman nodded just as assuredly.

Only a tad reassured, Lewrie caught up with Kit, who had gone on by himself, single-mindedly plodding along through the loose sands, head up, clad only in shirt and breeches, his stock gone and collars undone, and his sleaves rolled halfway to his elbows.

"What was *that* about?" Kit snippishly demanded.

"Keepin' 'em occupied and neutral, so no one could accuse us of under-handed doings," Lewrie lied, thinking that the best thing he could do for Kit at that moment was to keep his mind on his foe, without another dread that would keep him looking over his shoulder.

"Ummph!" Cashman said with a snort of understanding.

"Well, there he is," Lewrie pointed out, cringing to say such an inane thing, after all.

Ledyard Beauman was coming toward them across the deep sands, a tad unsteady to their eyes, even at that distance. He was tricked out in the full regimentals of the old, disbanded, 15th, as was his cousin Captain Sellers; black-and-tan riding boots, buff breeches and waist-coat, a gaudy cocked hat awash in white egret feathers and gilt lace, and the heavily gilded, almost burgundy-red coat with buff, gilt, and crimson facings and buttonholes.

"Dear God, is that a uniform . . . wearin' a man?" Lewrie said in a soft, amused whisper.

"No, Alan, 'tis a corpse in fancy dress," Cashman growled.

CHAPTER THREE

$\mathcal{G}$od help him, Ledyard Beauman had never made an imposing figure in his life. Lewrie could recall the whippet-skinny little shit from '81 or '82 in his midshipman days, sporting exaggerated Macaroni fashions *years* after they'd gone out of style back in England, right down to the bright silk or satin shoes with tall red-painted heels, and gilt buckles paved with diamond chips. Now, even in full martial "fig"—minus his hundred-guinea smallsword—he more resembled a pathetic footman masquerading in his master's clothes as part of the mummers' crews on Christmas Eve, when times turn topsy-turvy 'twixt servants and masters; but without the innate authority or wit to play the Lord of Misrule.

Mr. Hendricks summoned principals and seconds to him, just by the last edge of the upper beach.

"Gentlemen, I feel bound by Christian duty to appeal to you one last time. Are you so determined, so prejudiced against conciliation, that no plea, no logic, might move you from your intent?" the dignified older fellow implored.

"I am determined, sir," Christopher Cashman quickly answered, in a cold, brusque manner.

"I, too, am . . . ready, sir," Ledyard Beauman said, though in a voice more fluttery, and fainter. His eyes were red and puffy, as if he had suffered a tormented, sleepless night, and they shimmered and darted, like a mouse seeking a bolt-hole. He did not *quite* shudder, he did not chatter his teeth in terror; his jaws were clamped much too tight for that, and his hands were hidden behind his back.

Near miss'd stop his heart, Lewrie speculated; almost feeling a spurt of pity for Ledyard, who was *trying* to play up game: *One 'Boh' to a goose'd make him fill his breeches! Surely, he must know how good Kit is! Has he ever bla₂ed?*

"Then it is my sad duty to allow you gentlemen to proceed," Mr. Hendricks declaimed. "Colonel Beauman, your post is to the north, and Colonel Cashman, yours is to the south. A toe-line has been drawn in the sands. The coin toss has awarded the first pair of pistols to Colonel Cashman. In a moment or so, when both are ready, each will take up a pistol from this case, *strictly* keeping it un-cocked until commanded. You will take up positions, either side of the toe-line, back-to-back. When I ascertain that you are, in all respects, prepared, I will charge you to cock your locks, and you will hold your pistols vertical. I will say 'begin your pace' and start a count, thusly . . . 'and one, and two, and three,' until I reach the number seven. That will represent fourteen paces, together, with a pace more between you to be determined at the toe-line, equalling the agreed fifteen paces.

"At the count of *seven*, mind, and not a *jot* before," Hendricks intoned, "you may turn and fire at your pleasure. I advert to you now, sirs, the man who turns to fire *before* the count of seven, it will be my, and the innocent party's second's, duty to shoot down. Do you understand me plainly in that regard, sirs?"

"Absolutely, sir," Cashman replied, breezily, this time, as if impatient to get it over with.

"I do, sir," Ledyard agreed, with a bob of his head, gulping as if just now realising how fatal this was going to be. Lewrie caught a faint whiff of brandy on the scant wind, and it wasn't from the surgeon's table. On close perusal, Lewrie could espy a wet stain on Ledyard Beauman's waist-coat. He had obviously partaken of a liberal measure of Dutch Courage back at his coach, poor Devil.

"Now, does the first to fire miss his aim, sirs, and the second delay his response, the first party must stand and receive," Hendricks further grimly cautioned, "as is expected of a proper gentleman."

"No worries," Cashman almost chuckled. Rather evilly, in fact.

Ledyard could but goggle and bob, gulping dry-mouthed.

"Do both parties miss on the first exchange, you will, upon my command, immediately turn your backs, keeping your fifteen paces separation and wait 'til your seconds fetch you a fresh pistol, which shall be uncocked, from those supplied by Colonel Beauman. Do you understand, Captain Lewrie? Captain Sellers? As soon as both parties are re-armed, I will call 'Ready' again, and a new count of three. At *three* you will be free to cock, turn, and fire once more. After that *second* exchange, assuming neither gentlemen is struck, a brief pause in the proceedings will be allowed while fresh pistols will be provided, and we shall begin, again, back-to-back at the touch-line, using the initial procedure. Is all that clearly understood by all participants?"

"Understood," Christopher coolly said.

"Ah, yes," Ledyard managed.

"It has been stipulated that this is, unfortunately, a duel to the death or incapacitation by a severe wound," Mr. Hendricks added. "Should one, or both, of you fall wounded, I, and Surgeon Trollope, will determine whether the injured party is able to rise and continue. This stipulation, demanded by Colonel Cashman, shall not admit of any superficial wounding to fulfill his desire for satisfaction."

"Barbaric," Hugh Beauman sourly sniffed, half to himself.

"Then why did your principal agree to it, sir?" Mr. Hendricks countered. "Proceedings shall be halted so the injured party may be examined, and queries made to determine whether both principals feel that honour has been satisfied. Should we continue after a wounding, I shall repeat my exposition of the original rules. The seconds . . ."

Lewrie perked up, and watched Capt. Sellers stiffen with importance, before turning his full attention to Hendricks's mournful face.

"You will each take up *one* pistol," Hendricks instructed sternly. "You will each take post to my right and left, apart from your principals, but slightly ahead of me. Your pistols will remain un-cocked until such time as either party commits a shameful act by turning early or attempting to violate the accepted rules of the *code duello*. Only *then* will it be your duty to protect your principal, and I assure you that *I* will fire, should such a heinous deed occur to mar the honour of the field. A second, should *he* commit such a violation, will also be shot down. Understood?"

"Perfectly, sir," Lewrie said, before turning to face Sellers and lift a quizzical, deriding brow at him. Sellers reddened, again, and tossed his head in anger.

"Are you both determined, then, let us be about it, sirs. Do you take positions, and we shall begin," Hendricks ended with a sigh.

Hendricks at the apex of a fatal triangle, slightly above the duellists at the top of the slope of hard sand; Lewrie and Sellers two paces lower than the referees, their places juggled until Hendricks was fussily satisfied. Beauman and Kit either side of that heel-dragged furrow in the sand, back-to-back but not touching, about a pace apart—also fussily placed by the demanding Hendricks.

Lewrie hoisted his borrowed Manton pistol to the vertical, his right arm pressed against his chest, the fire-lock safely un-cocked, and his body turned so that Hendricks could see his actions, turned to keep an eye on Ledyard Beauman when he paced up the beach; turned, to keep one wary eye on Sellers, too, who would be doing the same upon Cashman, and Lewrie, as well!

'Bye, Ledyard, Lewrie snarkily thought, seeing the man's ashen look toward his elder brother, a silly, lop-sided grin of dread, and farewell; *write and tell us what Hell's like.*

Lewrie swivelled to see what Hugh Beauman made of his brother's hapless expression, but that worthy was implacable. Hugh Beauman stood far back, hands clasped behind his back, heaving a great, re-signed sigh of parting. A brief farewell grin creased his granite features.

He turned back to the principals, making a quick prayer for his old friend's success and safety, that he'd shoot straight and true and put a quick end to this, and a mercifully quick end of Ledyard, too. A man so foppish, petulant, and weak *couldn't* win! The world would be a boresome place, did Kit fall and leave this Mortal Coil.

Kit had been gazing out to sea, savouring perhaps his last precious taste of Life, but he did turn briefly, saw Lewrie's concern, and re-warded him with a quick lift of his chin, a faint grin, and even a wink!

"Ready, Colonel Beauman?" the doughty Hendricks called over the mewing of the gulls. "Ready, Colonel Cashman?" Some seabirds glided down near the duellists, some flapping in place against the faint wind, as if begging for tossed morsels.

"Ready," Cashman cried.

"Er . . . yes," Ledyard Beauman managed. "Ready."

"Cock your locks! Begin your pace. And one, and two . . ."

Kit marched in short parade steps; Ledyard took childish giant strides, as if to turn fifteen paces into a furlong. "And four, and five, and six . . . !"

" 'Ware!" Lewrie cried as Ledyard lost his nerve and turned too early, boots skidding on the hard sand, and levelling his pistol. The shout made Kit jerk to a stop, flinch, and start to turn about, and . . . *Blam!*

Ledyard had fired at Kit Cashman's back!

"Damn you!" Lewrie shouted, cocking his pistol and bringing it up to aim, with a quick plea for permission from Mr. Hendricks.

"Shit!" Cashman grunted. A pistol ball had struck him 'twixt his neck and the end of his left shoulder, bursting a bloom of scarlet on his white shirt!

"Well, damme!" Mr. Hendricks barked, his pistol now cocked and ready, but unsure of how to proceed. "Shame, sir! Now, stand and . . ."

"Stand and receive, ya bastard!" Cashman roared as he completed his hunching turn and straightened his back.

"He's wounded, wait, wait!" Ledyard demanded, dancing from one foot to the other. "Examine him, he has t'stop, mean t'say. Wait!"

"You must stand and receive, first, sir," the disgusted umpire Mr. Hendricks ordained, his voice gone disdainfully formal.

"God *above*, you said, *no!*" Ledyard wheedled as Cashman raised his pistol, his body turned sideways-on as if Beauman still held shot in his locker, a practiced, instinctive pose. He grimly took aim . . .

Lewrie was dumb-struck, and enrapted. One *couldn't* look away from such a shameful cock-up! Ledyard's terror-dance, the mounting horror in his whitened face, benumbed him. Would Ledyard drop to beg, or simply break and run?

And Kit was taking slow, careful aim, *savouring* Ledyard's fear, his teeth bared in the smile of a snarling wolf, *making* him suffer, as Ledyard was forced to look down that wide, fateful bore!

Sellers broke position! His left hand clawed under his uniform coat for a hidden pistol, sprinting toward Ledyard Beauman and tossing him the ready-cocked, silver-chased "barker," who gawped at it like a drowning man would stare desperately at an offered rope-end.

Blam!

The pistol flew toward Ledyard, who stopped shuffling, stretched out to catch it, but his shirt billowed at the waist as a ball punched him backwards, blood sheeting in an instant eruption, driving him down to fall on his rump with his arms still out-stretched for the gun like a stiff porcelain doll, legs and feet splayed heel-down in a vee!

Captain Sellers switched hands, flung up his right with his illegal pistol cocked, and aimed at Kit Cashman.

Blam-blam! as Lewrie shot quickly, he and Hendricks firing at nigh the same time, and Ledyard's cousin jerked and grunted as life was hammered from him, to drop lifeless across the lap of his kin he'd hoped to save!

"Disgusting," Mr. Hendricks hissed, outraged. "Despicable!"

A gruff cry of pain from behind, from Hugh Beauman, to see both slain, then a brief silence, even from the gulls.

"Oh, Charlie," they could clearly hear Ledyard Beauman weakly say to his cousin, giving him a shake or two. "Ye fell down."

Ledyard noticed his own wound, at last, the gout of blood that stained his breeches and shirt, that trickled from his fingertips as he probed the hole in his belly, just below his waistband, and began to moan, fret, and pluck at the cloth, still numbed.

"Damn my eyes, sir, but *never* have I witnessed such a craven, ungentlemanly. . . . !" doughty Hendricks was declaiming as Surgeon Mister Trollope and his assistant rushed to Beauman's side to drag away Capt. Sellers's body. Ledyard at last toppled on his right side, his knees drawn up in fetal position, whimpering with realisation.

Kit! Lewrie dropped his pistol where he stood and sprinted to Cashman's side as he strode up-beach, himself. He held his pistol in his right hand, that hand pressed to the top of his left shoulder, his left arm dangling rigid at his side.

"Alan, ol' son. The bloody idiot *winged* me, can ye feature it? Look-see how bad it is, will you, there's a good fellow." Cashman was grinning; now a stoic *rictus* of manful self-control . . . and a bemused puzzlement.

"Uhm . . . ragged, but clean through yer meat," Lewrie announced after a long look under the torn shirt where two plum-coloured holes, front and back, almost made a single bear-bite. "Don't *think* he struck bone, but you'd best let that Trollope fella ascertain that. They're a tad busy at the moment, don't ye know, but if needs must, I could do a fotherin' patch over it 'til they're free." Lewrie made it a jape, equally manful and dismissive of suffering, to perk him up and "play up game." He offered his pocket flask of brandy. "I could get your man-servant, or Andrews, do a little *obeah* witchy-work. Make a poultice . . . herbs and fish-guts?"

The very idea made Cashman dry-retch and wobble on his pins, a cold sweat popping out on his face as he staggered.

"Here, son, yer lookin' peaky. Sit ye down for a spell and be easy," Lewrie said, helping him down, taking his pistol. "Here, one of you! Mister . . . Geratt, is it?" he cried for a saw-bones.

The assistant surgeon came running, and Mr. Hendricks trundled down to see to him as well. "Your wound is grievous, Colonel Cashman?"

"Not a bit of it, sir," Cashman shrugged off, seconded at once by Mr. Geratt's pooh-poohing noises, and the assurance that no bones were broken as he swabbed, probed for cloth and such in the trough of the wound, and snipped away the odd ragged edge or two before binding and bandaging him and rigging a sling to immobilise Cashman's arm.

"Must apologise, Mister Hendricks," Cashman said, making a *moue* of regret. "Had we known such would occur, I'd have *never* . . . !"

"Not *your* fault, sirs," Hendricks quickly disabused him of all blame. "Mister Ledyard Beauman, in the end, was no gentleman, nor was his cousin. This will redound to no good credit, or credence to their cause. Rest assured that a *factual* account of this morning's scandalous doin's will be known far and wide. Uhm . . . I've always been partial t'dark rum, m'self, when revival is needed. You will allow me, Colonel Cashman?" he said, fetching out his own red leather bottle of heady-smelling dark rum, from which Cashman gratefully sucked. Geratt insisted on a tincture of laudanum be mixed with the rum, in a small silver two-dram cup.

"God, their poor family, though," Hendricks sadly intoned.

The rum (rather a lot of it) and the laudanum availed Kit most wondrous. Within minutes he was on his feet again, his pain muted and his colour back. Lewrie, Andrews, and the man-servant packed their paraphernalia and began to assist him towards his waiting carriage, a last gracious *adieu* said and *congé* made to the referees and surgeons for their good offices.

"Well, damme," Kit sighed, gritting his teeth as they shoved him to a seat on the coach's rear leather bench. " 'Twas such a *good* shirt, too . . . the most cunning lace-work, and all. That shit was so cross-eyed 'foxed,' I didn't think he could even hit the *ground* in one shot, much less . . ."

"Your shot was a good'un, though, and he's done for, so put it down to blind beginner's luck," Lewrie said, tucking the rolled cape and other stuff to either side of him to bolster him from sliding back and forth. "Three, four days o' Hell, he has t'look forward to. You did good work, Kit."

Lewrie's last sight of Ledyard Beauman (a wolfishly satisfied one, thankee!) he was curled up and gasping like a landed fish, agony beginning to course outward from his wound with each pulsing beat of his heart, the raw fire in his belly stoking hotter and hotter as the numbness that follows wounding wore off. Belly wounds were fatal and inflicted the sufferings of the Damned before the victims departed the Mortal Coil. Cashman should have been cackling with glee over his long-awaited victory.

"Won't be much joy at our breakfast, Alan, sorry," Cashman said. "Might cry off, just go home and. . . ."

"You can't, and you know it," Lewrie countered, still fussing, with the man-servant's assistance. "Laudanum, rum, and brandy on your empty stomach? A hearty breakfast's the best thing for you. And in public, where you put on the proper airs, else folk'll think that he's *succeeded* at something for once in his miserable life."

They'd made reservations at a very public tavern in Kingston to show off and crow.

"You know the drill . . . *modest* joy, stern duty done. Sad wonder at his baseness, add that'un," Lewrie babbled. "The fewer details, the better . . . 'no questions, please, it was just *too* egregious.' Make 'em ask of Hendricks and the surgeons. Hell, make 'em call upon the Beaumans if they wish to swoon o'er the sordid details!"

"Will you all quit fussing over me?" Cashman carped, squinting at Lewrie, half-amused and half-rankled to be so cosseted. "I am nowhere *near* a piteous . . . dodderer!"

"Just wanted yer great arse wedged in," Lewrie complained as he suddenly left off and took his own seat, "so yer coachee don't rattle ye half t'death 'fore we get to the tavern, you fool."

"Alan," Cashman said softly, reaching out to touch him on his knee, "had I come close t'losin' such a fine friend as you, I'd most like fret a little, too." He chuckled, laughing off such a frank admission between two English gentlemen.

"Well, there it is, then," Lewrie grumped back, immensely glad that he, and the world, still had Kit Cashman to make it a vivid place. "All in?" he called, leaning out the coach window. "Right, then, let's whip up and go. I must own I'm famished, and. . . ."

"Wait!" Cashman suddenly demanded, leaning forward, wincing at the effort. "Just for a bit! There . . . ye hear it?"

Suspension straps creaking as Andrews and the man-servant took seats by the coachee or at the postillion bench at the rear, the stamp and whuffle of the team, the jingle of bitts and reins.

"What? Oh . . ." Lewrie asked, but heard the answer.

Ledyard Beauman's pain, as they moved him in a litter from the beach to his family coach, sounded inordinate. Surely, he was still curled up like a singed worm on his side, legs drawn up, arms crossed low on his stomach as if cramping from too many green apples.

Ledyard Beauman was thinly, femininely, keening and screaming.

"Ah!" Cashman said, beaming, most happily sleepy-eyed from laudanum and liquor, but suddenly hugely content. "Damn my eyes, but did ya ever hear such a pleasin' sound, yer whole bleedin' life?"

CHAPTER FOUR

*O*f course, Kit Cashman couldn't resist the celebration. Breakfast had been laid on at Baltazar's, the discrete and elegant Kingston eatery, at tables on the raised section overlooking brick-enclosed fountains, trellises, and herb gardens. Kit's friends, former officers of the 15th who inclined to his cause, and well-wishers made it a jolly affair, with many toasts made and drunk, and champagne cups had sloshed about like so many watering cans might *flood* those herb gardens and small lawn. There *was* food; Lewrie was pretty-well sure of that . . . but no matter how comestible, and welcome by that hour of the morning, the victuals were definite also-rans. Fried eggs, tatty hash, fletches of bacon and small chops, heaps of thick-sliced toast, and the requisite butter and jams, had first been heartily swallowed, but had later become more akin to party favours, or missiles to be flung or trampled.

The nigh-White waitress, a local who always seemed to serve Cashman whenever he and Lewrie had dined there, was in attendance, more as a guest than a servitor, half of her time spent lolling in Kit's lap, shrieking and guzzling, bussing and petting the hero of the hour, with her ornate hair unwinding rather fetchingly.

More girls of the town, most "no better than they should be," began to turn up as the morning drew on towards 9:00 A.M., and it looked fair to becoming one of those all-day celebrations, with Baltazar's reserved and shut to public custom 'til next noon. Fine for Kit, but he had duties.

After two last fortifying cups of black coffee, drunk standing by the common room bar, he reclaimed his sword and hat and departed, sure that he wouldn't be missed 'til tea-time . . . if then.

On the short (but a *bit* unsteady, thankee!) stroll to the dock, Lewrie and Andrews felt the eyes of the town bore into them, heard the faint hum-um of whispered conversation. Some sounded scandalised, but more than half seemed secretly pleased, yet too daunted by Beauman wealth and influence to cheer them openly. However the news had come, by fast rider or forest drums, the outcome of the duel seemed known as soon as they'd clattered into Kingston!

All this public notice made Lewrie check to see if his breeches flap was buttoned more than once as they threaded the last gawping clot of fellow officers, merchant captains and crewmen, stevedores and servants on the stone quay just in front of The Grapes; some glaring at him so severely he expected to be called out as he waited for his gig to arrive.

"Done for two of 'em, 'e did!" Lewrie heard one of his oarsmen off his own boat whisper, beamingly jubilant. And how the devil news of the cock-up had reached the ship before he did, he had *no* way of knowing!

"Welcome back aboard, sir," Lieutenant Adair crisply said, his small-sword drawn and held before his face in salute as Lewrie climbed aboard HMS *Proteus* and took the on-deck crew's salute amid a trill of bosun's calls.

"Mister Adair," Lewrie said, with a brief nod to his Third Officer, now confirmed and possessed of his commission, no longer an acting lieutenant; putting his mute "Captain's Face" back on. "Thankee, sir. Dismiss the side party, and return the hands to their duties."

"Message from the flag's come aboard for you, sir," Adair said, coughing into his fist.

"Oh, damn," Lewrie said, wincing at that news. He was nowhere *near* sober enough for official doings. Did Admiral Parker abhor duelling? Or did he loathe affairs of honour turning into Cheapside shootouts? Either way, the summons boded ill.

" 'Twas a lieutenant fetched it, sir," Adair informed him.

Worse and worse, Lewrie thought; *not a Middy's errand, but. . . .*

"Drew straws, did you?" Lewrie snorted, hands in the small of his back. "Diced t'see who'd have to tell me?"

"Uhm, seniority, sir," Lt. Adair mumbled, blushing as Lewrie twigged to the fact that Langlie, Catterall, and Adair had all felt the summons was Trouble, capital T, and had all turned queasy. For all of their proven courage as Commission Sea Officers, it now appeared there were *some* things that'd make 'em blanch!

"And you couldn't find little Larkin or Burns," Lewrie assumed aloud, almost chuckling. His newest, junior-most midshipmen, one a Bog-Irish squire's by-blow, uniformed so poorly it looked as if he'd robbed a scarecrow, and t'other a blinkless, drooling lack-wit.

"Couldn't *find* 'em, sir," Adair admitted. "Most-like, they're still hiding in the cable-tiers or furled themselves aloft in the main course."

"Goes t'prove, then, that one, or both, just *may* be smarter than we give 'em credit for," Lewrie replied. "Well, give it me, then."

Andrews slunk below with his shore-going bag while Lewrie broke the wax seal and unfolded the single-page note. He glanced over toward the Palisades, the long, natural seawall, where stood Giddy House, and the shore residence where Admiral Parker entertained.

"Pass word for my Cox'n, Mister Adair. 'Vast there, you men. Back into the boat," Lewrie snapped. "We're bound away." He stuck the letter into a side pocket of his coat, and wishing that he *had* shaved before the duel, that he *didn't* subtly reek of the wine-table at such a pagan hour . . . or that there seemed to be some sticky, reddish jam patches, some greasy flung-chop smuts, and some scrambled egg stains on breeches, waist-coat, and shirt cuffs at the moment.

The letter stressed his reporting "Instanter," underlined twice with some force, so there went a change of clothing, or a sponge-down.

Should've stuck with just throwin' bread rolls, Lewrie sighed to himself as the gig's crew reassembled, as Andrews reappeared to muster them. *And damme, but don't he look natty! Took time t'scrub . . . the bastard!*

"Uhm," Andrews muttered, showing his captain the damp towel and tall pewter mug of sudsy water that he'd fetched along. "Mebbe on de way ovah, sah, we could, aahh, touch ya up a tad?"

"I take back everything I just thought about you," Lewrie said with a grateful smile as the bosun's calls *phweeped* again to salute his departure, leaving Andrews in befuddlement as he doffed his hat and scampered back down the man-ropes and battens to the waiting gig.

CHAPTER FIVE

'Twas Giddy House, the old pile that served as administrative head-quarters, not the stately, welcoming, and airy Admiralty House where Admiral Sir Hyde Parker resided, that was Lewrie's destination. He was escorted to the offices of Staff Captain Sir Edward Charles. Was there a piss-proud, drunken, officious prig who despised him more (in the Caribbean, at least) Lewrie had yet to encounter him. He steeled himself for a long, rambling, and abusive tirade before the double doors swung back to admit him.

A rap upon those doors, and the announcement that he had come at long last drew a "Hah! Come!" roar—Sir Edward's high-handed snip of "Got ye now, ye bastard!" with an admixture of the enticing coo a starving bridge troll might employ to lure a tasty stray child.

Hat under his arm, with the broken dog's vane and egg-stained front averted, Lewrie entered the "devil's den."

"Captain Lewrie!" Captain Charles growled, his blood-shot eyes given youth and clarity by this chance for "comeuppance." "Hah, sir! Damme, a waiter tip his tray o'er ye, did he? The publican's drinks tray, more like. Dis-reput-able, sir, most!" he sneered, savouring the word. " 'Tis a wonder yer shirt-tail's still in. How dare . . . !"

"Disreputable, aye," another voice chimed in, snatching Lewrie's attention to a civilian who stood near the bookcases at the darker end of the spacious offices, in a sombre suit of black "ditto" enlivened by a green satin waist-coat, and grinning like a sardonic devil.

Christ, just shoot me now! Lewrie goggled, half of a mind to do a bolt. *Not him, not another hare-brained . . . !*

"Mister. . . . ?" Lewrie managed to say, unsure whether Peel would be under some new alias, or was the Foreign Office spy still sailing under his own colours. Peel, ex-Captain of Household Cavalry, John . . . no it had been *James* . . . James Peel; right-hand man to that devious old cut-throat, Zachariah Twigg, in the Mediterranean, several years before.

"You recall me, surely, Captain Lewrie," Peel (or whomever) said with a taunting smirk over his obvious discomfiture.

"Oh, indeed, sir . . . with fondly remembered shudders of dread," Lewrie countered with equal banter to his tone. "Though how you *wish* to be named, this time, is . . . ?" he concluded with a mystified shrug.

"It's still Peel, Captain Lewrie," Peel chuckled, coming up to take hands with him. "It serves as good as any. Been years, has it not, sir? Good to see you again."

"Wish I could say the same, Mister Peel," Lewrie lightly replied. "But where you and your old master turn up, there's no one safe. And how is. . . . ?"

"Allow me to name to you my new superior, Captain Lewrie," Peel said, deflecting the question, and turning them to face the other man, who had been lingering near a tall bookcase now burdened with reports and returns rather than books. Lewrie wondered how he could have missed the peacock. "The Honourable Grenville Pelham . . . here is our Captain Alan Lewrie, in the flesh at last. Captain Lewrie, Mister Grenville Pelham."

"Ah-de-do," Pelham intoned in a high-bred Oxonian voice as he allowed his hand to be shaken, preferring to be grasped by the fingers, not a hearty palm-to-palm greeting. "Heard much about you, Captain . . . much, indeed."

"Mister Pelham, sir, an honour to make your acquaintance."

No, it ain't, but what else can y'say, Lewrie snidely thought.

The Honourable Grenville Pelham, obviously someone's "promising git," was a brisk, wee sprout for all his high-nosed manner, a thoroughbred colt. Compared to Peel's sombre suiting, though, Pelham was rigged out in a cream-white linen coat and breeches, cuffs, collar, and lapels trimmed in dark green satin, with a light green waist-coat of nubby silk, all sprigged with looping gilt embroidery. Black shoes and white silk stockings, *large* brass buttons on coat and waistcoat, shoe and knee buckles that Lewrie suspected were gold, not brass.

And, dammit, but Pelham seemed awfully young to be Peel's, or anyone's, superior; why, he couldn't be beyond his mid-twenties! This dandy-prat put Lewrie in mind of Rear Admiral Nelson, greyhound lean, full of nervous energy, forever wavering 'twixt the languid airs of a proper Crown official and the titters of an impish University boy.

Pelham wore his own hair, fashionably long and wavy, but clipped in the back where a gentleman's queue should ride atop his stiff stand-and-fall collar. His face was pale and peeling with sunburn, his eyes bright and snapping blue—though squinted at the moment, as if just a touch leery, and darting as if impatient with the social amenities.

"Didn't do half of what I'm reputed, sir," Lewrie said, determined to make a decent impression on *somebody*, given the state of his own attire, and employing his gruffest "gentleman sea-dog" air. "It's all a slander."

"Uhm, quite," Pelham said, disengaging his fingers as if discomfited. "Though you must admit, you are. . . . renowned, Captain."

"Good God, off on the wrong foot already, are we?" Lewrie felt emboldened (or enough disgruntled by that tone) to remark. "I assume you spoke with Mister Twigg before sailing out here? Then you heard only the naughty bits."

"Ahem, well. . . ." Pelham commented, unsure what to make of that. "Let us begin, then. Thankee, Captain Charles. . . . Sir Edward. That is all that we require. We'll not take long, I assure you."

Pelham turned to beam false cheer at the man commonly known on the West Indies Station as "The Wine Cask," a hair away from shooing him from his very own office! Which prompted Lewrie to turn about and bestow his own "shit-eatin' " grin on that worthy, as well.

"Ah, hmm. Well, o' course, Mister Pelham," Capt. Charles said, flummoxed, with much throat-clearing and frowning. "Anything for the Crown, though?" Capt. Charles grumbled, slyly making his complaint known as he snatched up a thick stack of loose papers, files, and ledger books as if salvaging an inheritance—and gave his wine service a longing, famished, look; perhaps to gauge how much was left in the decanter, did they *dare* partake while he was away! With a few more stammers, he departed with a bow, and an ominous "We must discuss things later, Captain Lewrie!" before the twin doors to his office suite clicked shut behind him.

Pelham did, indeed, amble over to the desk and pour himself a goodly measure of the white wine, after scrounging about for an unused glass in the set of four, all of which seemed to have been employed at some time or other since sunrise. "Dear Lord, he's the taste of a Philistine! *Not* what I'd call even a *poor* vintage. Has a taste, and the finish, more like . . . horse liniment!" the young man snickered.

"May I, sir?" Lewrie bade, and Pelham offered the glass for his tasting. Lewrie merely sniffed it, though, and returned it. "That's Navy-issue white wine, Mister Pelham. We call it 'Miss Taylor', and a bad vinegar it is, too. It's damn' cheap, and he can indent for it from the stores house, just down the quay. By the ten-gallon cask . . . then lose the chits, which all come through *him*, d'ye see. A dirty business." Lewrie jadedly "tsk-tsked" to Mr. Pelham in hopes that he might report the bitter man's peccadilloes. "And aye, Navy surgeons *can*, and *have*, used it as a liniment."

"You *wish* a glass, then, sir?" Pelham seemed to tease.

"No, thankee kindly. Bit early for me," Lewrie beamed back.

"Really," Pelham drawled, rightly skeptical of that claim, in light of Lewrie's dishevelment, and his breath. "Gentlemen, be seated, please," he bade instead, making free with Capt. Charles's furniture, and seeming to dither as to whether he himself should sit in authority behind the desk or appear more "convivial" in one of the club chairs. He chose the chair, sweeping the long, but narrow-cut tail of his coat back with an elegant swish as he plopped down and crossed his legs at the knee, with his hands in his lap.

"All the 'go,' is it?" Lewrie asked, tongue-in-cheek, to bring the younker down a peg. "We're years behind London fashions, out here. I haven't seen a coat such as yours . . . cut so high to the waist, with the tails beginning so far back. Damme, you make me wish the name of your tailor, Mister Pelham. Or yours, Captain Peel!"

Now that they were in private, Pelham no longer had to pretend to be amused. He raised one eyebrow, his face stony, resting his elbows on the chair arms and steepling his fingers in front of his mouth, whilst Mr. Peel coughed into a fist in warning.

"In answer to your earlier question, Captain Lewrie, Zachariah Twigg is now most honourably retired, though frequently consulted for his vast knowledge. Mister Twigg was one of my mentors, d'ye see, and as soon as I was given this assignment, I, and Captain Peel, were quick to call on him for background material. You will be relieved to know . . . or, not, given your past relations with that worthy . . . that he keeps well, in the main, though his constitution will no longer admit to the travail of overseas adventures," Pelham prosed, high-nosed from being twitted by a mere . . . sailor. "We spent the better part of a day and a night in his company. And when your presence in the Caribbean was revealed to us, naturally we discussed your, ah . . . attributes. And your sense of wit," Pelham concluded with a sniff.

"Well, what *is* the old saying . . . 'Forewarned is forearmed'?" Lewrie breezed off, unabashed. "And what was the old fart's advice to you? 'Don't take any guff off him? Keep a weather-eye peeled for his foolishness,' was it?"

"Something very much like that," Pelham rejoined, harumphing.

"Mister Twigg sends you his warmest regards, Captain Lewrie," Peel said, interjecting to keep their initial interview running smooth, and perhaps to allay any rancour. "Believe it or not," Peel went on, with a knowing smirk.

"Pardon me, sir, but that's 'fiddler's pay,' " Lewrie commented. "Mere thanks and wine . . . less the wine. And easy for him to say after all the shitten messes he got me into. Told you all our doings together, did he?" he said, returning his attention to Pelham. "The Far East and then the Mediterranean? Well, here's another platitude for you . . . 'Once bitten, twice shy,' Mister Pelham. So you will understand why I have my qualms at being dragooned into *another* neck-or-nothing affair, one involving that ogre Choundas, most especially."

Pelham and Peel exchanged glances, at that.

"That *is* why you're here, I take it," Lewrie stated. "He's in the Caribbean, I'm in the Caribbean, and suddenly here comes a brace o' spies from the Foreign Office just slaverin' t'put me back in harness to deal with the bastard, just *one more time*," he sneered. "*Thought* I was summoned t'be broken for seconding my friend at his duel, which turned to shit, by the way . . . what with Charles an' Admiral Parker so tight with the planter family we just winnowed, but no . . . to my lights, it's even worse. Beggin' yer pardon, o' course." Lewrie said, facetiously bowing from the waist in his chair.

"You are *demurring* from such duty, sir?" Pelham charily asked.

"Damme, you know I can't, Mister Pelham," Lewrie snapped back.

"You surely hold sealed orders up your sleeve, directing me to aid you, no matter what I think of it. Don't you." It was not a question.

"Yes, I do, Captain Lewrie," Pelham quirkily informed him, with a faint, superior grin. "Believe me, I *do* understand, should you hold any misgivings." And he seemed so sincere that Lewrie could almost believe him . . . for a moment. "And, yes, Mister Twigg also discovered to me all your past doings. And, again, yes . . . my mentor told me how you react when pushed. That since it is beyond your power to demur, or be *too* truculent and insubordinate when handed extraordinary duty beyond your customary brief . . . that your last refuge is an acid and sarcastic wit. Which wit will *seem* to border upon insubordination, and truculence. I was strongly advised to make allowances for when you suffer the odd 'snit,' Captain Lewrie."

That old bastard Twigg knows me too *well!* Lewrie thought with a wince.

"Mister Twigg, despite his vast wisdom, and his unbroken string of successes," Pelham drawled, fingers steepled once more to feign the sagacity that a man in his position should possess, "was, believe it or not, always more sanguine, more . . . easy-going than I. More accepting of those who would frustrate his efforts, or gainsay his directives. I believe you will find me to be a *fairly* tolerant and forgiving fellow, Captain Lewrie . . . but only up to a point, and no further."

Threaten me, *would you?* Lewrie heatedly thought, utterly nettled by then; *you damn' puppy!* It was like being chided by one of his sons.

"Perhaps because he had more experience dealing with *people*, not *things*, Mister Pelham," Lewrie pointedly drawled back, crossing his own legs at the knee and pretending to flick lint from his breeches. "Nor did he, no matter his necessity or impatience, ever confuse the two."

Good God! Lewrie thought, wincing again; *did I actually compliment the old cut-throat? Mine arse on a band-box!*

"Now that we know where we stand . . ." Mr. Peel tried to mollify.

"Quite, Mister Peel," Lewrie quickly said, accepting his offer to move along before he reached over and slapped the wee fool silly. "You're here, I'm your cat's-paw, you've press-ganged me, and there it is, then. You might as well tell it me."

"Ahem," Peel said, seizing the initiative so his superior could sit silent and gather his aplomb before speaking too rashly. "As you may assume, Mister Pelham and I are not to be revealed as Crown agents,

Captain Lewrie. The Governor-General, his excellency the Earl of Balcarres . . . Admiral Sir Hyde Parker and some few of his senior officers, are aware of our true identities. To the general population, we're to be known as speculators, out from London to make our fortunes. Mister Pelham will pose as the younger son of a wealthy, landed family, seeking acreage, and I will make myself known as the family's advisor from Coutts' Bank . . . a junior partner sent to determine the practicality of the enterprise."

"Junior to old Mister Simon Silberberg, hmm?" Lewrie chuckled in knowing understanding, recalling one of Mr. Twigg's old aliases.

"Just so, sir," Peel replied, nodding and tipping him a wink.

"And since I also bank with Coutts, my being seen with you is perfectly innocent, I take it, Mister Peel?" Lewrie said, grinning.

"Exactly, sir," Peel agreed. "My presence is also, uhm . . . to be a voice of reason and temperance upon the impetuous Mister Pelham. Serving a second role as a *factotum* to his family's legitimate worry."

"His governess, aye," Lewrie could not help suggesting with a leer. "Such a frenetic, *easily* aroused young fellow."

"Ahem," Pelham objected to be so characterised, despite a role of a light-headed young wastrel as his agreed alias.

"My, how believable," Lewrie went on, cooing. "It has such a . . . versimilitude."

"Quite," Peel agreed, hiding a smile; which made Lewrie wonder what an experienced agent such as Peel, himself once a protégé under Twigg's tutelage, thought of being supplanted as the senior man on the mission by a less-experienced "comer" with better connexions, interest, and patronage.

"So, what's the plan, then?" Lewrie asked, deciding they might as well get down to it. "What part of Choundas d'ye want me to lop off this time?"

Dammit, though—there was another of those guarded looks back and forth 'twixt Pelham and Peel.

"This does concern Choundas, doesn't it?" Lewrie pressed.

"Well, it is, and it does," Pelham answered with an inscrutable smile. "Though not completely," he maddeningly hinted.

"There's bigger fish to fry than him?" Lewrie asked, puzzled.

"Indeed, Captain Lewrie," Pelham told him with a condescending little chuckle. "There still remains the larger matter of winning the French colony of Saint Domingue for the Crown."

"We just *lost* it," Lewrie all but yelped in surprise. "Or had you not heard? Our army beaten . . . evacuated, root and branch?"

"Nothing is ever *completely* lost, Captain Lewrie," Pelham said, looking down his long, aristocratic nose, and still wearing a superior grin. "So long as we remain at war with France, the game's not ended. Oh, I'll allow that the French, with this Toussaint L'Ouverture and his tag-rag-and-bobtail slave rabble as their instrument, have outscored us, the last few innings. But barring a sudden declaration of peace, the game is still afoot . . . and it is now our turn before the stumps."

"With what?" Lewrie petulantly demanded, trying to picture the Saint Domingue soldiery and Pelham on a cricket pitch. "We sending in another army?"

"What may not be gained by force of arms, sir," the elegant wee Pelham chuckled, in a conspiratorial whisper, "may yet be won with the application of guile, bribery, and diplomacy."

Lewrie had a sudden sinking feeling that this would not be in any way a straightforward proposition—and why he had hoped that it would, he couldn't imagine. He knew in his bones that this time, he would really be in for a spell of "war on the cheap."

CHAPTER SIX

*L*ooks hellish-lost t'me!" Lewrie grumbled, wishing that Capt. Charles's wine was but a *tad* drinkable. He felt badly in need of some.

"To all intents and purposes, it does appear so," Pelham said, "but appearances can deceive, sir. We have our sources in France who tell us that the Directory in Paris, and the Assembly, have their suspicions as to whether Saint Domingue *has* been won for France, or does L'Ouverture have designs of his own which may result in a loss after all. There are mercantile forces of great influence who demand Saint Domingue return to immediate profitability, both for their own gain, and for the Republic's. They want their lands, and their money back, even does the trade in cocoa, sugar, cotton, coffee, and tobacco go in American hulls. Once exports are sold in American ports, profit is easily exchanged from United States banks to French banks."

"The United States is at war with France," Lewrie pointed out.

"Not officially," Pelham countered, "and American merchantmen, along with Portuguese, Danish, and Swedish traders, enter the colony's ports daily. As captain of a blockading frigate you surely know how impossible it is to stop supposedly neutral trade, so long as their cargoes are innocent, and no military supplies are discovered."

"Granted," Lewrie moodily agreed.

"A return to profitability, though, a quick one," Pelham continued, "would require a return to the *status quo ante* on the island. That is to say, the presence of a French garrison army, the dismissal of the ex-slave armies, and this L'Ouverture creature being supplanted by a new, *French*—White—Governor-General. But," Pelham posed, "What if L'Ouverture doesn't *want* supplanting? Hmm? What if he owns to dreams of grandeur? He's a simple African, a former slave, at best one generation from the customs of some barbaric kingdom, and a crude kingship recalled from his bed-time stories. And what worries France is that, perhaps, *Liberté, Egalité et Fraternité* cannot extend to all, not if the plantations must be productive, again. That would mean the return to human bondage. You know of Leger Sonthonax, Lewrie?"

"A horse, showed well at New Market?" Lewrie quipped.

"The former governor of Saint Domingue," Pelham exclaimed, not sure if Lewrie was being witty, or sublimely un-informed. "Soon as he kicked our forces off, L'Ouverture finagled to send Sonthonax back to France to represent the colony. Sonthonax is a staunch revolutionary, the bloody sort, who *more* than decimated the colony's Whites with his guillotines, worse than the Terror of '93 in France. He's a bit of a loose cannon, as you sailors might say . . . *loves* the Blacks! Said in public he wished he *was* Black, more than once. All that 'noble savage' rot of Rousseau's, don't ye know."

"Then who better to send to Paris," Lewrie assumed aloud.

"Laveaux, t'other ranking Frenchman in the colony," Pelham said. "He, at least, is a cultured, aristocratic holdover from the old days of the *ancien régime*, and a whole lot cleverer and subtler than Leger Sonthonax, more skilled in faction intrigues. Just as 'beloved' with L'Ouverture, we're told, and leagues more able. The question is, why did L'Ouverture send Sonthonax, instead of Laveaux? Sonthonax is not in good loaf in Paris. Too fractious a man, but deuced lucky in being out of the country when his worst enemies got the chop. As he did in the latest instance, landing in France just as Robespierre went under the guillotine and lost his head," Pelham snickered.

"Robespierre, d'ye say!" Lewrie cried, perking up. "The ogre finally got his, hey? Why, that's marvellous news."

Wish we could drink to that! Lewrie dryly thought.

"But did L'Ouverture *hope* that Sonthonax would be eliminated?" Pelham asked the aether, and leaned back in his chair, staring at the old, water-spotted plaster ceiling. "Is Laveaux more bendable to his

will, should he declare total independence? Or is Laveaux less powerful to control events . . ."

"And, with Sonthonax chopped first, would L'Ouverture despatch
Laveaux to face the wrath of the Directory next," Peel chimed in with
a sage expression, "leaving him in sole control?"

"No matter," Pelham said with a disappointed sniff. "Sonthonax
survived the latest power shift, and is recently returned, with fresh
orders from the Directory. But with his power diminished in favour
of another . . . so we are *informed*," Pelham simply had to leer, "who's
to decide whether L'Ouverture has outlived his brief usefulness after
he expelled our armies. Whether his rival, General Rigaud, might be
more amenable to France's long-term interests. Rigaud has created
what he calls a Mulatto Republic in South Province, round Jacmel and
Jéremie, with most of the educated Free Blacks and educated Mulattoes
rallied to him. He's betrayed L'Ouverture more than once, changed
sides right in the middle of a battle. In the brief period both served
under the Spanish, when the Dons had designs on the whole island of
Hispaniola, their relations were quite bitter."

"But, sir," Lewrie happily pointed out, if only to scotch the superior,
insider's, smirk on Pelham's phyz, "once our troops landed, they became tight as ticks. Our General Maitland offered Rigaud just about
everything but his virgin daughter to change sides, but Rigaud spurned
our every blandishment."

"Only so long as *we* were there," Mr. Peel calmly dismissed with
a study of his fingernails. "We evil White Devils who'd have put 'em
back in chains . . . and slew 'em by battalions, atrocity for atrocity."

"I absolutely refuse to countenance any tales of British atrocities,"
Pelham retorted. "They're all a pack of lies dreamt up by the Directory, and stuck in their papers to poison the other powers against us!
Rigaud, though . . . now we're gone, he has no *reason* to stay true to
L'Ouverture. Both are so ambitious, they're *sure* to fall out, then make
another bloody 'War of the Skin' to determine who rules over what
still stands when it's ended. Does L'Ouverture win, t'will be the illiterate and barbaric ex-slaves oppressing the educated, the half-caste,
and the remaining Whites, and reduce Saint Domingue to the back-
wardness of the Dahomey jungles. No, no, 'twould be better, all round,
if Rigaud came out on top, and his more-civilised followers. We could
deal with Rigaud, who at least is somewhat sophisticated, an educated

man schooled in France, seen the wider world, raised as good as a
European by his own White father. . . ."

"Eats with a knife and fork," Mr. Peel interjected, feigning an air
of wonder, which subtle jape went right past Pelham, but put Lewrie
to coughing into *his* fist.

"As you say, sir," Pelham snapped, stiffening. "Rigaud can see the
commercial realities of re-establishing trade relations with other powers. A man who realises whose Navy rules the seas. A man who sees
that any hope of American trade is futile, given the vulnerability of
Yankee merchant ships, and the utter weakness of the new United
States Navy. And, God knows, does either L'Ouverture or Rigaud
hope that the French restore their trade or naval presence, they've
another thing coming!"

"So . . . you want my help to get to Rigaud," Lewrie surmised in
dread of just up and sailing into Jacmel like a fart in a trance. "We
offer him whatever it takes to buy him over, before the French or the
Yankees make him a better offer? God above . . ."

"We would prefer Rigaud to L'Ouverture, yayss," Pelham drawled
so coolly and casually that it made Lewrie's nape hairs stand on end.

"You won't mind, do I *not* go ashore with you, when you dine
with either or both," Lewrie scoffed. "Good God, man! L'Ouverture,
Rigaud . . . Christophe or that brute Dessalines, none of the Black generals'd give a tinker's damn for your offers. They'd torture you for
six days runnin', and put your head on a pole the seventh! Heard their
favourite song, have you? Goes, ummm . . .

" '*Eh eh, bomba, heu heu! Canga, bafio té! Canga, moune de lé!
Canga, do ki la! Canga, li'!*' " Lewrie grunt-chanted, pounding the time
on the arm of his chair and bob-thrusting from the waist.

"Mmmm," Mr. Peel chuckled. "Catchy."

"It means, 'We swear to kill all the Whites and take all their possessions,' Mister Pelham," Lewrie harshly translated. " 'Let us die if
we fail to keep this vow.' Well, they've done for their White owners,
and a whole British army, and they'll do for you if you go there."

"Oh, rot!" Pelham countered, as if jadedly amused. "Just like the
Terror in France, the bulk of the killing is done with. Laveaux, and
Sonthonax, saw to that. Why, L'Ouverture's offered amnesty to *émi-
grés* who came back with our army, amnesty and return of their estates
to any White planters who'll return to the back-country and get 'em
running, again. *Pay* the workers, this time, of course. Those who

won't lose all claim to their former fortunes. Sonthonax and Laveaux
have enough influence and control over the ugly little monkey to place
experienced White officers over his Black regiments, make him see the
sense of appointing clever local-born Whites in civil government positions. Guaranteed the safety of any White, even *children*, who'll teach
reading, writing, and sums, e'en on the remotest plantations."

"All of whom, you hope, will turn on him, once Rigaud announces
that he's the boss-cock," Lewrie charily speculated; all that was new
to *him*, but it didn't signify. " 'Cause former masters'd never abide a
savage ex-slave regime, but they could almost tolerate a moderate, and
educated pack o' half-breeds who can at least speak *some* sort o' Frog,
dress like them . . . *live* like them . . ."

"Who can eat with a knife and fork, yes," Peel reiterated.

"That is the hope," Pelham admitted, blithely unworried by any
mere quibble. "That, once Rigaud and L'Ouverture fall out, as men
do, sooner or later, Rigaud will have the troops, artillery, and support
of the prominent, leading elements in the colony, and civil government
appointees swinging his way. From what we know of his forces, he
has excellent prospects of success. And," Pelham related, bestowing
another of those clever little simpers, "even he cannot, both sides're
locked in a draining war that sooner or later ends in weary stalemate.
At which time our trade, protection, and good offices will appear more
than welcome . . . gaining us what we seek whether Rigaud wins, or
not."

"Slamming the door on American aspirations to extend trade into
the colony, thence to dominate the entire Caribbean," Peel took up
the tale, since Pelham's cleverness had seemed to exhaust him for the
moment; "retaining and protecting our own stakes in the Sugar Isles;
and getting *us* access to a colony that was wealthier than all ours put
together, before the war began. We must keep a wary eye on the
Americans, Captain Lewrie. Else, they'll swamp us with their skinflint
Yankee traders and their wiles, and we'll gradually lose all we own
out here."

God, but it was a vaunting scheme, and all back-alley ambushes
and under-handed devilment. Lewrie studied Pelham, who was fussing
at his neck-stock, now wilted with perspiration, and wondered whether
it was his own scheme, one that would make his name and career in
government, or was the preening little pop-in-jay some clever fellow's
avid apostle. *Must've looked just* inspired *back in London*, Lewrie

sneered in silence; *gentlemens' club, drawing room, over port? And scads of clean, unwrinkled maps! Gawd . . . was this old Twigg's last, glorious riposte? A guarantee of knighthood, even in retirement? It'd be just like him, it has that same fresh-blood smell.*

"Well, it all sounds promising," Lewrie said, lying damn' well. "And Choundas is . . . what? Going to beat you to it?"

"Ah, Choundas!" Pelham exclaimed, now revived, and rubbing his hands wolfishly. "We have our sources, don't ye know, Lewrie, even in Paris, the Directory, and the Ministry of Marine."

Oh God, here we go, again! Lewrie quietly groaned to himself.

"He was despatched to Guadeloupe with two missions," Mr. Pelham enthusiastically told him. "The overt one is to organise, arm, and run privateers and smaller National ships as raiders, working for *another* Mulatto, Victor Hugues, now promoted to greater responsibility. Amazin', ain't it. So many coloureds in French service . . ." he simpered. "His second mission is to smuggle arms and supplies into Saint Domingue, land agents, and perhaps even speed the export of the money crops," Pelham said, then turned sly, again. "To give his support and aid to . . . ?" He paused, as if awaiting applause.

I'll kill him, he keeps that up! Lewrie promised himself.

"To one or t'other," Lewrie finished for him, "L'Ouverture, or Rigaud, whichever looks t'be the winner, so France keeps it, no matter who gets betrayed."

"Erm . . . exactly," Pelham admitted with a petulant snap of his jaws. "Got it in one, Captain Lewrie! Now, we also know that France has sent out yet *another* man to keep an eye on L'Ouverture, Laveaux, and Sonthonax, see which way the wind is blowing, and determine which of *them* gets the chop, and try on Rigaud as a replacement, if he gets displeased with L'Ouverture."

"So if Rigaud looks as if he'll go the distance, Choundas and this new man do the dirty work for us?" Lewrie asked, his head cocked over in disbelief. "Mean t'say, they back Rigaud, we *let* 'em? Just get out of their way? *Help* Choundas along?"

"Well, at the least, turn a *half*-blind eye," Mr. Pelham chuckled, after a long ponder. "So long as things go our way, that is."

"Mine arse on a band-box!" Lewrie all but yelped.

"I know that Guillaume Choundas is your particular *bête noire*, Captain Lewrie," Pelham dismissively said to soothe him, patronisingly, "and you'd like nothing better than to carve him into cutlets, but . . .

the old monster's played the cat's-paw for France, so who's to say he can't be *our* cat's-paw for a bit, and all unwitting? Wouldn't that be delicious? Oh, decimate his privateers should you meet them, it goes without saying. Gather information from the prizes you might take, in particular any written directives from Choundas himself, so we can do a bit of forgery to sow distrust and confusion, should the need arise . . . and, do you meet up with one of his men o' war, of course you will be free to engage her, and fetch me prisoners to interrogate. Can't let Choundas think he's a *completely* free hand, ha!"

"One would hope not, sir," Lewrie gruffly said, most unamused.

"You're here, he's here, *you* know he's here, and we will make sure that *he* knows of your presence, does he not already," Mr. Pelham cackled with glee from his schemes. You're *his* nemesis, too, ye know. The temptation to do for you, on his part, *must* distract him from the proper discharge of his mission. That, and your preying upon his too-few ships, will blunt whatever aid he can deliver either L'Ouverture or Rigaud, making Britain, in the end, appear the best choice to who-ever wins over yonder. Either one, really," Pelham confessed, almost whispering to impart his inside knowledge once again, "so long as he is dependent upon the Crown for his continued peace and prosperity. I do believe we might even tolerate an independent, abolitionist, Black Republic to gain that end, Captain Lewrie."

"But preferably under Rigaud," Lewrie said, sniffing sourly in world-weary amazement at *that* revelation.

"Of course," Pelham answered, shutting his eyes and nodding as if saying "Ever and Amen" in his family's pew-box.

"Slave or free, no matter?" Lewrie pressed, a dubious brow up.

"Mmm," Pelham uttered, nodding again over steepled hands, as if the re-enslavement of nearly 300,000 people was simply a cost of doing business. "As to that, this new man out from Paris is just the fellow to stir *that* pot. General Hédouville. Have you heard of him, Captain Lewrie?" Pelham asked expectantly, as if preparing to be clever again.

"Not in this life, no," Lewrie slowly intoned, preparing himself.

"Hédouville's a bloodthirsty butcher," Pelham was happy to say. "Conquered the Royalist enclaves in the Vendée region in the early days of their Revolution . . . rather brutally. A 'Monsieur Guillotine' and a real terror. He'll sort things out in quick order, most-like. Get the colony aboil, likely purge Citizen Sonthonax, perhaps even La-veaux as well. We still have got agents and influence on the island to prompt Hédouville to do just that. And, launch Rigaud at L'Ouverture if God is just, and our slanders take root," Pelham sniggered. "*He's* the new power over yonder, is Hédouville."

Lewrie looked away towards Peel, rolling his eyes, just about fed up with Pelham's "how shall we torment the headmaster?" titterings. He found an equally unimpressed ally in Peel, whose blank attentiveness relaxed enough to curl up his lips in the faintest of weary smiles.

"Hédouville is reputed to be blunt, direct, and quick off the mark," Peel said. "Once he's made up his mind, he's very hard to divert. Much like a Spanish fighting bull, beguiled by the cape. None too clever, really, but a force of nature once set in motion. The ideal instrument for the Directory." Peel had a clever simper of his own. "We pour our subtle poisons in his ears, and mayhem and disorder will surely follow, in short order."

"Well, you seem to have it all arranged," Lewrie said, surrendering to Fate; especially when it seemed he had so little choice, else. "My congratulations on a most knacky plan, sirs."

"Well, thankee, Captain Lewrie," Pelham smirked, overcome by the required, befitting modesty of an Englishman accused of being *too* clever by half, no matter how well it secretly pleased him. "Not *all* my doing, but . . ."

"Hopefully," Peel said, rising at last as if the tedious task was outlined well enough for even Lewrie to follow it, "this may make up for the fact that, since this war began in '93, we've lost untold millions of pounds, and over one hundred thousand men trying to take all the French 'Sugar Isles' . . . half of 'em dead and wasted, t'other half so fever-raddled they're unfit for future service. Damn 'em, *all* these tropic pest holes. Look so beguiling, but . . ."

And Pitt and Dundas didn't see that goin' in? Lewrie cynically asked himself as he got to his feet as well. *It ain't like the French could hold 'em if their fleet can't get t'sea. Better we'd blockaded 'em, let 'em rot on the vine, so the Frogs didn't get ha'pence o' good from 'em.*

But it didn't appear likely that the Prime Minister, nor the Secretary of State for War, would have asked him his opinion then, or would much care for his chary opinion of them now. No, they were too damned "brilliant," too full of themselves, just like their wee minion Pelham. He felt it would be an excruciatingly frustrating adventure.

"Orders for me and my ship, then, sirs?" Lewrie asked.

"As I earlier stated, Captain Lewrie," Pelham energetically said, shooting upright and resetting the cut of his cuffs and waist-coat, playing with the lapels of his coat to tug them fashionably snug across his shoulders and the back of his neck. "Raid, cruise, make a right nuisance of yourself versus Choundas's ships. I have arranged a roving, open brief for you with Admiral Parker, so . . . wherever, and whenever you and Mister Peel wish, or are led by the evidence you may discover. I am *not* squeamish as to the means you employ. So long as the end is attained," Pelham coldly stated.

That sounded promising, even was he saddled with Peel as supercargo, a slab of "live lumber" who would surely, sooner or later, try to boss him about as if he were in actual command.

"Oh . . . joy," Lewrie growled in a monotone, looking at Peel.

"I *promise* I'll be *gentle*, captain, sir!" Peel chuckled, voice pitched high and virginally sing-song, drawing Lewrie's wry amusement.

"And Choundas," Lewrie insisted, wary of oral instructions from such a man as Pelham. "What of him, for now? Do I just watch, stand aloof 'til we get what we want from his efforts, or . . . ?"

"As Mister Zachariah Twigg once instructed you, in the Mediterranean I believe it was, sir," Pelham intoned, high-nosed and for once in deadly earnest, "you are, sir, given opportunity, no matter how early or late in our plans, 'to kill him dead,' and put paid to his noxious existence."

"Well, good God, why didn't ye just *say* so!" Lewrie exclaimed in great relief, forced to laugh out loud at such long-delayed end to such a tortuous preamble. "Could've saved us all the palaver."

"Guillaume Choundas, sir," Pelham piously declared, "is still possessed of such demonic cleverness that, despite his monstrous soul, and his ogreish appearance, he was *not* sent out here by his masters as an exile. Mister Twigg, and Captain Peel, both have stressed just how dangerous he remains. Most-like, does he *fail* out here, that's an end to his usefulness to them, *but* . . . we cannot take the risk of him popping up somewhere else, in future. His head on a platter might mean a knighthood to the one who fetches it. As Salome was rewarded when she brought King Herod the head of John the Baptist."

"B'lieve she's the one *demanded* Saint John's head, after Herod saw her dance, sir," Mr. Peel corrected, coughing into his fist.

"Quibble, quibble, quibble," Pelham groused, waving off petty, inconsequential facts, and laughing at his mistake. "It don't signify, Mister Peel. Lewrie gets my meaning."

"Indeed I do, sir," Lewrie vowed, though irked by Pelham's iffy lure and mixed messages, as if he needed any further incentives to pursue Choundas, or was so venal as to fall for such a faithless promise.

"Working together, again, after all this time, sir," Peel said, feigning fond reverie, making Lewrie stifle a lewd comment and a snort of sarcasm. They'd gotten on much like mating hedgehogs, really; testy and spiky. "What jolly times they were!"

"Well, there you are, then!" Pelham concluded, pleased that their pairing, and their plot, was off on a good footing. Or so he blithely assumed. "Let us not waste a single hour."

"Uhm . . . best let me avail myself of that 'Miss Taylor,' after all, Mister Pelham," Lewrie said, changing the subject before he broke out in peels of laughter at just how dense Pelham really was.

"*That* horrid stuff, Captain Lewrie?" Pelham asked, aghast.

Lewrie soaked his handkerchief from the decanter and began to sponge his hat. "I told you the Navy finds it useful."

CHAPTER SEVEN

"It was pleasant and delightful,
one midsummer's morn,
when the green fields and the meadows
were buried in corn.
The blackbirds and thrushes
sang in every tree.
And the larks they sang melodious
at the dawning of the day . . ."

It was a "Make and Mend" afternoon, following the noon meal for the hands. All stores had been laded, the aired sails, hung wind-less and slack, had been furled and gasketed, and an hour's small-arms drill had been performed. Now the crew of HMS *Proteus* could "caulk or yarn" and tend to their own devices, tailor their issue clothing, shave, wash, and scrub to be presentable at Sunday Divisions, play board games, have an on-decks smoke, do carvings or mere whittling whilst they nattered of this and that, nap or sing, as suited their too-brief freedom.

"The sailor and his true love
were out walking one day.
Said the sailor to his true love,

I am bound far away.
I am bound for the Indies
where the loud cannons roar,
and I'm going to leave my Nancy,
she's the girl that I adore . . .
And I'm going to leave my Nancy,
and I'm going to leave my Nancy . . ."

Even with the duck awnings rigged over the quarterdeck and the waist, it was too warm for chanteys, horn-pipes, or reels, so the hands sang a sad forebitter, with both fiddlers, a boy on the tin whistle, and Liam Desmond droning under them, with his uilleann pipes. Desmond was a cosmopolitan sort, for an Irishman; he'd play the English tunes as readily as any from his own sad island. And "Pleasant and Delightful" was as teary a ballad of love and loss and long partings as anyone could wish for. He was equally open to Allan Ramsey's version of "Auld Lang Syne" roared along with "Hey, Johnny Cope" to sneer at an English general who'd run from Bonnie Prince Charlie back in 1745, with the few Scots aboard, turn up a weepy, lugubrious version of some Welsh dirge, or wheeze out gay horn-pipes with equal ease. He was a treasure.

Lewrie gratefully stripped out of his formal shore-going togs, completely pulled out those offending shirt-tails, and rolled up his sleeves above the elbows. With his neck-stock discarded and the front of his shirt undone, he called for a mug of cool tea from his steward, Aspinall, who brewed it by the half-gallon each dawn on the griddle in the galley; weak, admittedly, given the cost of good leaves, with lots of sugar (which in the Sugar Isles was nigh dirt-cheap) and a generous admixture of the rob of several lemons, also available for next to nothing. Let stand to cool before jugging, it made a fine thirst-quencher.

Though Lewrie did suspect that, once jugged in his large pewter pitcher, his mid-morning libations might be part of the brew from the previous afternoon's. There were some days, such as today, when that decoction could almost stand on its hind legs and toddle.

"Mister Padgett sorted yer paperwork, sir," Aspinall told him. "And there's letters, too, off that packet brig come in yesterday."

"Ah, excellent!" Lewrie enthused, rubbing his hands with false gusto at those tidings. For the last year, *no* letters from home were good news. And damme, but wasn't there a tidy pile of them, though, all thick and thumb-stained, the outer sheets whereupon the addresses were enscribed, the stamps affixed, and the wax seals poured, were now sepiaed with handling and sea transportation.

No, his official correspondence *always* took precedence. It was safer that way. The personal could abide for a piece more, after the long passage that fetched them. Whatever new disaster, insult, or calumny they contained were at least five or six weeks old, and any reply to them would take even longer, no matter how scream-inducing.

> *"Said the sailor to his true love,*
> *well I must be on my way.*
> *For the tops'ls they are hoisted,*
> *and the anchor's aweigh.*
> *Our warship stands waiting,*
> *for the next flowing tide,*
> *but if ev-ver I return, again,*
> *I would make you my bride . . .*
> *But if ever I return again,*
> *but if ever I return again. . . ."*

"In good voice, t'day, sir," Aspinall commented.

"Did they choose something cheerful," Lewrie grumbled, "I s'pose so." He had to admit, though, that the chorus of rough seamen's voices did have a more-pleasing harmony than usual, detecting the shyly, hesitantly offered basses and near falsettos from his "liberated" ex-slave sailors. The tunes and words were new to them, almost alien, and their command of the King's English marginal, yet his Black sailors had an uncanny ear for harmony. Even their unaccompanied work songs he heard when riding past cane fields ashore had been spot-on, whatever tune it was they'd sung, sometimes hauntingly so.

"Mister Motte, the Quartermaster, you can hear him there doin' the solo part, sir," Aspinall went on. "He says it come from the '60s, it did, when our Navy invaded Cuba in the Seven Years' War."

"Umhmm," Lewrie said with a nod over his paperwork, a tad irked, and peering owlishly at Aspinall's interrupting maunderings.

Aspinall took the cue, and ambled back into his day-pantry with a damp dish-clout in his hands. There to sing along under his breath, just loud enough to make Lewrie twitch his lips and furl his brows.

Damn his hobbies! Lewrie gravelled to himself; *first 'twas rope work and sennet, now . . .*

> *"Then a ring from off her finger,*
> *she instant-lye drew,*
> *saying 'take this, dearest William,*
> *and my heart will go, too' . . ."*

"Bloody hell," Lewrie muttered. "Aspinall?" he called.

"Sir?" A small, chastened voice, that.

"It's 'make and mend.' Do you wish t'join the hands up forrud and sing, 'tis your right. I'll have no need of you for a while."

"Er, thankee, sir, and I'd admire it," Aspinall cried, hastening out of his pantry, and his apron, to dash forward to the door that led to the main deck, an ever-present notebook and pencil now in hand so he could jot down the words and annotate the tunes' notes.

"Hmmpfh," Lewrie sniffed, tetchily relieved. "Peace an' quiet. Ooff!"

No sooner had Aspinall departed than Toulon, his stalwart black-and-white ram-cat, now grown to a muscular one-and-a-half stone, hopped into his lap.

"Well, damme," Lewrie softly griped. "And why ain't you caulkin' the day away . . . the way your tribe's s'posed to, hmm? Missed me, did ye? There, there, ol' puss, yes, yer a good'un. *Rroww?*"

Toulon braced himself on his hind legs to get right up against his face and rub cheeks and chin against him, play-nip at his chin and paw his collarbone for attention, grunt-mewing most-plaintive. It took a good ten minutes to cosset him, and then Toulon became a heavy, hot, and furry chest plaster which he had to stroke one-handed, and read his naval letters with the other. Toulon closed his eyes and couched his large head on forepaws high under Lewrie's jaws, all a'rumble and now a'bliss, his wee breath tickling at the hollow of his master's throat.

"You're not going to sleep, there, d'ye know," Lewrie chid him.

"*Mmrrf.*" Damn' nigh petulant, and "I will if I've a mind."

The official "bumf" done at last, Lewrie set the last enquiry aside and eyed the pile of personal letters. Padgett, his clerk, had already written up replies for him in answer to the business matters; they merely awaited his signature. Getting to the quill and inkwell, shifting Toulon, though, would be the very Devil after his two days of absence. Lewrie sidled in his chair, squirming and reaching out with his right hand to haul in a fat personal letter without waking Toulon, fingers scrabbling cross the desk . . .

"Mmarr." *You heartless bastard*, the ram-cat fussed as he was deposed. He was suffered to arch, slit his eyes, yawn, and curl about in his master's lap as Lewrie at last got both hands free with which to break the seal on a missive from his father, Sir Hugo St. George Willoughby, and unfold its several sheets. *His*, at least, were safe to read.

"Does he displease, you can eat it later," Lewrie promised his cat, who was already eying the crinkly paper with some interest.

"My dearest wastrel son," Sir Hugo's epistle began.

"I must *really* be in trouble back home," Lewrie deduced. "*Still*, rather."

"Greetings and Salutations to you, avidly gathering the flowers of the sea, far off in the Caribbean! I trust your Flowers, meaning to say, prize-moneys, blossom nicely, and that your Constitution, ever a Corinthian 'weed's' hardiness, continues to Thrive. Pardon, pray, any dis-continuity to this letter, but, the most momentous News having just arrived, I needs must convey it straightaway as the first item of interest, my previous first page be hanged.

"On the first day of August, your gallant Admiral Nelson hunted an elusive French Fleet to its lair in Aboukir Bay in Egypt, and in an action that spanned nigh eight hours, took, sank, or burned every damned one of them, their massive flagship *L'Océan*, and their plucky Admiral de Brueys (or some such-like Frog spelling!) consumed in a Twinkling when she was blown to Atoms! All London, all Britain, is agog!"

"Good Christ!" Lewrie breathed, in awe, in instant pleasure . . . and in a tiny bit of pique to be swinging at his anchors, or cruising fruitless upon a pretty but empty sea, and to have missed it! Nelson. The man had such *hellish* luck.

Though details were scanty, his father waxed most rapturous on what little he knew. The French had landed on Malta and had taken it from the decrepit and corrupt Knights of St. John, who had held it as their feudal fief since the Crusades, cutting the Mediterranean in two and giving the Frogs a base from which to oust Admiral Jervis from those seas for a second time. Ah!

"That wee Frog you spoke of, that crude Corsican upstart by name of Napoleon Buenaparte (or some such) led their army. Why the Devil a French expedition went to Egypt, God only knows. It ain't like they'd march from there to Bengal. Had I been in command, it would have been Sardinia and Sicily, my next conquest, but the tiny bastard *is* French, ever an over-vaunting and gasconading Race, are they not; hence, as Unpredictable and Inexplicable as so many young misses!"

"Yer grandfather's found himself a new dictionary, puss," Lewrie cynically confided to his cat.

"Bless me, but were you in England at this time, and did but go out in Publick in uniform, you'd not be able to buy a drink for a fortnight, Alan," his father went on. "Nor would you suffer to set foot on the ground, for being 'chaired' as lustily as a Member 'pon Hustings at a by-election. And, I dare say, even your poor wife Caroline, so hotly set against all things Nautical, might (for a brief respite, mind!) be more Forgiving and Charitable towards you."

"Hmmph," Lewrie muttered. "That'll be the day."

The second page had a great deal crossed out, as though the news had interrupted earlier thoughts; and Sir Hugo too abstemious to waste a fresh sheet of highly taxed paper on his own son.

His father had completed his London house, and was now ensconced on Panton Street, convenient to Drury Lane and the theatres, Covent Garden and the Haymarket, his haunts of old. And the comely women of the "commercial persuasion" should he get the itch. Hired an excellent man to run his acres at Anglesgreen; had taken on suitable house servants; had furnished the town house deuced well (if he did say so, himself) at a reasonable expense, thankee, with the proper style suitable to a semi-retired general officer of some means—having made the recent acquaintance of Lewrie's erstwhile admirer, Sir Malcolm Shockley, Baronet, who had put him in the way of several new investment opportunities beyond his shares in East India Company, etc. . . .

". . . though I must own that Lady Lucy, his wife, is a horrid coy Baggage, little better than a common strumpet," his father groused, at long distance. "Both times I've dined with them, both times I've dined them in in return, her slippered little toes have nigh stroked my boots Raw. What you saw in her, in your early days, I quite understand, and admire your Taste, in point of fact, for she is the most fetching Mort, but you may thank your lucky Stars you and she formed no permanent Congress, else you'd have worn her 'horns' since '84! Poor

Shockley! So unobservant to her doings—as most men are, thank God, for I in my green youth (and you in yours, no error) both profitted from 'abandoned' women.

"Hard though it may be for you to feature it, and hard as it is for me to admit, sorely tempted though I am to give her a Tumble, there *is* her Husband, a most decent Fellow, and the very idea of abusing his Trust and Hospitality quite rightly daunts me. Notwithstanding losing immense profits from our mutual Enterprises, d'ye see! Pecuniary fear of Loss is not my only motive, however. Besides, I've a new one, hired by the half-evening who bears a passing likeness to Lady Lucy, new-come from Leeds, of most fetching Aspect, and (or so I speculate) as ripely blessed, and of similar pleasingly round Dimensions, not above twenty, who avails when fantasies anent Lucy come upon me."

"Oh, good *for* you, ye old beard-splitter," Lewrie groaned.

His father had been round to see Theoni Connor and Lewrie's by-blow, Alan James Connor, too, reporting that he was now a pretty little lad of two, toddling and prattling. Theoni sent her love, o' course.

"By the by," Sir Hugo gushed onward, "that gentlemen's Lodgings I proposed, with Sir Malcolm Shockley's eager backing once I had laid out the Particulars and Advantages to him, is now open. We obtained a rather fine 1st Rate residence, only slightly gone to seed. Upon your safe return (pray God) to England, you will be in awe.

"It sits on the corner of Wigmore St. and Duke St., just off and convenient to Oxford & Baker Sts., thus easy to find, with dependable carriage service, and convenient to Govt., Finance, etc. It takes the entire corner, in point of fact, quite a *palazzo*, now set up for fifty with all the desired Amenities; common room, reading room, dining, etc. I myself, lacking my Panton St. house, would be tempted to engage a set of rooms, and, needless to say, should you and Caroline not have Reconciled by your return from foreign Service, you will be assured of a most lavish roof over your head, all at a tidy discount for kin, ho!"

"Notice he don't offer t'put me up under his own roof, catlin'?" Lewrie softly scoffed. "Nor free, either, the old miser."

He interpreted Toulon's blink and ear-flick to mean "ain't it a miserable shame."

Unfortunately, his father had had little progress to report when it came to making Caroline see sense. She was not going to pursue any Bill of Divorcement; quite rightly they had both surmised that it would be too expensive a proposition, with too much public shame attached . . . and too much enforced contact with her old, spurned beau, Harry Embleton, who, as her Member of Commons, would have to present the Bill in London. At least Caroline had sense enough to avoid *that* otter-faced fool!

There had been, by last report, no further "dear friend" notes sent her, for the simple reason, Sir Hugo concluded, that he was at sea, beyond the reach of that anonymous gossip's spiteful ken, and all his previous peccadilloes had been revealed. Supposedly.

"You are, I trust," his father had snidely penned, "if not keeping your breeches buttoned, at least possessed of enough Caution to not flaunt any of your Venereal doings in Publick, hmm?"

"As if *you* ever did," Lewrie grumbled. "Swear t'Christ, did he get to Heaven, he'd tip Saint Peter the wink, and ask where the whores kept! Ha . . . knew it, the old rogue."

For there had followed an entire paragraph touting the advantages of "balancing one's humours" with the whores, and never squiring one out in the daytime, or to any function where one's peers in Society might remark you—*hardly* the thing for an English gentleman, married or no, much less a Serving Officer, etc., and etc.

"Taught his granny t'suck eggs, too, most-like," Lewrie groaned some more. He'd heard that particular lecture at least once a month, since he'd pinched the bottom of his first pubescent scullery maid at thirteen. "Never admit paternity, were there fifty before you," Lewrie sing-songed under his breath, "never lose yer head over any coy slice o' mutton . . . think o' yer family's good name. Oh. Right. We never *had* one." He snickered, reaching for his mug of cool tea.

His father's letter *was* dis-continuous, at that, for he'd left the worst news, and three matters of the most import, 'til the last. First was the matter of young Miss Sophie de Maubeuge, his ward. She had fled Anglesgreen for London, and was now living with his father, serving as mistress (in the innocent sense, his father quickly assured him!) of his new town house!

"Caroline has gotten it into her head, and clings to the Opinion despite all Protestations to the contrary, that you and poor wee Sophie

were at one time, she cannot settle upon which, *intimate!*" Sir Hugo
informed him. "Aboard that French frigate you sailed out of Toulon,
in Lisbon before you packed her off to England, in some stolen moments during your two short shore leaves since this war began, it
don't signify to her. Either, or all, feature in her Accusations, depending upon the day of the week, and, had I not known Caroline's
sweet Nature before, I would be forced upon an initial Acquaintance
now to be convinced she was Tetched! Level-headedness and her usual
kind Demeanour quite fly her, once she gets on the Topic. Needless
to say, it all created such an impossible Situation for poor Sophie, such
glares and frowns, such harsh and quibblesome Speech, finding so
much fault with even the simplest domestic tasks, that Matters came
to a Head several weeks ago. There were shouts, Accusations made,
Refutations offered yet dismissed, to the point that Sophie packed,
summoned a coach, and turned up on my doorstoop un-announced,
reduced to Tears and Whimpers, and I could not deny her Shelter, as
I am certain you will understand. So suddenly denied any Freedom
in Anglesgreen, so isolated to the farm as she was, Sophie has at last
recovered her cheerful Equanimity, and now quite relishes going about
the City with me."

"Now that must cramp his style!" Lewrie cynically hooted.

"Daughters," his father had marvelled, "in Sophie's case, grand-
daughter, after a fashion. Somehow I feel that due to my wastrel ways
(none of which I truly regret, mind) I might have missed something
in Life by not being Engaged in Children's raisings, for young women
are quite delightful Creatures to watch blossom. I have always felt
Avuncular or Grand-Fatherly anent Sophie's development, for so she
calls me Grand-Père, but, one might almost deem my feelings Paternal,
now, when closely engaged with her Welfare, in protecting her from
the harshest Aspects of Life . . . or rake-hells such as me, in younger
guise. Rest assured that Sophie only attends the most uplifting and
chaste Amusements and Events, with me (of all people!) her guard.
Church, Theatre, Concerts, and Galleries, only the tasteful raree
shows, dines only with respectable Society, etc. And, do we attend a
Ball, Rout, or Drum, her dance partners must pass my Muster, first—
and she is home and snug in her chambers at a reasonable Hour. No
matter this places upon me a hellish restraint, I feel it is my Duty, in
your stead, to . . ."

"Knew he'd complain a tad, anyway," Lewrie chuckled, imagining how corseted the old whore-monger must be, all for appearance's sake, and for Sophie's future "respectable" marriage prospects. "And he's *not* touchin' me up for a contribution t'help dress and feed her."

The second grimmer matter concerned his boys, Sewallis and Hugh, nigh-imprisoned at their bleakly strict boarding school in Guildford. Despite how involved his father'd been with his new house, his arrangements for his country estate, and gentlemen's club, he *had* tried to keep in touch with the lads, but had gotten no responses to his letters. When down to Anglesgreen, he had called upon Caroline to enquire how they kept . . . and had not liked the answers.

The few letters that Caroline had gotten had been vague, filled with what sounded, to his suspicious ears, like rote phrases dictated by the headmaster and headmistress or their few employed instructors. This had occurred shortly before Sophie had "eloped," so Lewrie could understand, in retrospect, that the tensions had already been treacle-thick, which had not improved Caroline's acceptance of his worries; as if any questions he had concerning their welfare was a criticism of Caroline's decision to board them away at an austere public school, or a suggestion that she did not fret over them as a Proper Mother ought!

Sir Hugo had, though, received Caroline's grumpy permission to call upon them on his way back to London, so . . .

"Imagine it, dear Alan. Up pops I, in full regimental fig, in the grandest equipage going, liveried coachee, postillion 'catch-fart,' and my trusty orderly, Trilochan Singh, in the Grand Parade uniform of our old 19th Native Infantry, silks, sash, *tulwar,* and *turban,*" his father had described. We caused the most Devilish stir in the Populace as we clattered in and drew rein. Yet when I requested of the headmaster and his wife (a stout and termagant Batter-Booby) to see the lads, I was flatly Refused! Gaudy as we were, one would expect they'd have fallen on me like famished vultures, with an eye towards a lavish donation, and an annual Patronage, but no, not even that! They did *not* attempt Flattery, did *not* offer to dine me in or shew off the grounds, and, in point of fact, rather peremptorily wished me off the premises before they summoned a magistrate!

"Oh yes, says I? Indeed, say they. The school maintains a rigid *rota* from which the students are not to be taken. And what of their free time? I ask. They *pray*! I was rather brusquely told. What? your sire demanded, are they never allowed off the grounds to a sweet shop? Only under escort by instructors or proctors, says the grim wretch who rules that foul dungeon. A nastier place I never clapped eyes on, and I've *seen* Hindoo toilets, thankee very much!

"Determining that they were too Righteous to bribe, I cautioned them that I'd return before they could say 'knife,' with your, and my, solicitors, the Chief Justice to my old friend and patron the Lord-Lieutenant of Surrey, and a troop of Yeoman Cavalry, with whom to tear their Pile down round their ears, and clap them in Gaol under suspicion of Abuse of their wards, and it would be King's Bench for the both of them! I further threatened to coach back to Anglesgreen and fetch their Mother, and did they refuse *her*, I'd whistle up the troopers, and formal Justice bedamned," his father crowed in a "copper-plate" hand.

"And didn't Caroline look the place over first?" Lewrie griped as he got to his feet to fume and pace, deposing Toulon from his lap as if shedding a robe. "Damn my eyes, what *was* she thinkin'?"

"A gloomier tale never you've heard, Alan," his father went on. "They are, of course, being beaten. Were we not, all, caned in our own school days, and are now the better for it? Corporal punishment breaks intractably wild wills, and Civilises, but I fear that their treatment goes beyond the Instructive, or Necessary. Punishment is doled out for the *slightest* Infractions; for standing idle, for too much exuberance during their *rare* idle play hour, for the *tiniest* error in recitation, for chatting too loudly or happily at mealtimes! All this from adults, mind. What Sewallis and Hugh whisperingly told me passes 'twixt Elder Boys and their fags is quite another thing, quite exceeding the normal Abuse a New Boy should expect at his first school.

"My son, I strongly suspect that Torture, premeditated, brutal, and fiendish Cruelties are planned and executed nightly," his sire accused. "And where are the Instructors, the Governess or Headmaster when such occurs, I ask you? The Academy is not so large, I fear, that they might lightly send down any or all Malefactors; indeed may dread insulting the moneyed parents of such little Monsters, or lose so many of the students that their so-called School becomes unprofitable. They already accept those deemed too difficult or thick-headed, the Dregs from other schools, the Dissolute, Incorrigible or High-Flown . . ."

" 'Tis a wonder I wasn't sent there, then," Lewrie muttered, dashing a hand cross his furrowed brow.

"Even more hellish, Alan, were your sons' tremulous Intimations that such Tortures and Cruelties are dealt out to those averse to sub-mission to late-night Buggery by the older boys . . ." Sir Hugo wrote.

"Goddammit!" Lewrie yelped, hot to fly home that instant with a sword in hand, and deal out some "Jesus and the Moneychangers" justice on one and all! "My lads, oh my poor lads. What's Caroline put you into?"

"I coached back to Anglesgreen, instanter, once the lads' brief two hours of Liberty were done, and I was forced to deliver them back into that cess-pool of Corruption," his father wrote, "*not* without the severest warning to Headmaster & Headmistress that, were my sus-picions borne out, I would have the Law on them, and that Sewallis and Hugh are to be free to write whom they please, when they please, and write *what* they please. Had I the Authority, I would have snatched them out from that place at once, but, alas, in your absence that is up to Caroline. She was quite Perturbed by my sad relation of the boys' Condition. I fully expect *her* to do the Snatching. I also spoke with the Vicar at St. George's, cautioning him not to recommend that School to parents of local parish lads, and what the Devil was he thinking when he suggested it to Caroline? Are not Sewallis and Hugh mannerly and quick-witted students, in no need of such strict Chas-tisements to 'improve' their Wits or Behaviours? I left the old Goose-berry quaking in his slippers, let me tell you, in dread he was sponsoring Buggery. Passing through Guildford once more, I did call upon the Chief Justice and laid my suspicions with him, as well, so we may soon see the end of this so-called 'strict Christian' Academy, once an Enquiry has been begun.

"You must do your part, Alan, and quickly," his father stressed. "Write Caroline, urging her to remove the lads at once, and suggest *I* choose a better, this time, standing Stead for you whilst overseas on King's Business. Offer to pay fees, which I will cover, for I suspect I am more in the way of Money than you at sudden need. I did offer to stand for their Schooling, Hugh's entry into a good Regiment, and little Charlotte's Finishing, after all, do you not recall? Thence, write also to your solicitor, Mr. Matthew Mountjoy, in London, urging him to draw up a Writ on your behalf naming me as your Voice concerning the boys, strictly limited to the choice of school, and their support *in lieu* of your presence, of course, so Caroline can have no legitimate Objections to such an arrangement."

Yes, by God, he would, soon as he finished reading the rest of his father's letter.

". . . matter which has grieved you since sailing, son," Sir Hugo continued, "is your lack of news from Sewallis and Hugh. Be sure that you stipulate to Mountjoy that the boys *must* write me, as well as their Mother, concerning their Progress and their Welfare, since I will be partially *in loco parentis*. In this way, the lads will be able to write Letters to you, addressed to *me*, and you will be able to direct your Correspondence to *them*, using my Panton St. address as a Subterfuge, ho!"

That opportunity, to circumvent his wife's spite and hear from his boys once more, was almost cheering enough to mollify his earlier anger at how they had, and *might* have been, abused!

Even more wondrous, his father further suggested that Caroline was now vulnerable. His final point was that too many things bore down upon her, her fear and shame that she had unwittingly exposed her sons to pain and bestiality, that she hadn't been a Good Mother! Even more vexing had been her wrathful split with Sophie (her unallayed suspicions notwithstanding!), and . . . her elderly mother Charlotte's health was failing.

It all made, Sir Hugo slyly hinted, the perfect opportunity for him to write her, no matter that Caroline had said she'd burn anything that came with his name on it, unread.

"There is no better time for a Wife to appreciate a Husband than when crushed by Adversity," his father coyly nudged, "when the Weaker Sex, all at sixes and sevens, find need to lean upon her Stalwart Man with his innate inner Strength, and in the face of *shared* Adversities, 'form square' shoulder to shoulder in wholehearted Mutual Defence of their Children and their Welfare.

"No matter how slender a Reed that husband be (and I think we both know how Irresolute and Inconstant we Willoughby/Lewrie men turn out to be, God help our trusting Womenfolk) it is their Nature to look to Men for aid. Dispirited as Caroline is this moment, do you intend a Reconciliation someday with your good wife, then strike whilst the iron is hot, using your utmost Subtlety! Nothing too abrupt or promising at first, mind. Cajole her, with no Recriminations for her

Foolishness, with no sudden Vows or Wishes for Renewal. But then, I very much doubt that you are in need of advice when it comes to cossetting the Fairer Sex, ho!"

"Oh yes, I do!" Lewrie bewilderedly confessed to his empty great-cabins, and his nettled cat. "Ev'ry man does. And did ye ever *have* any advice, why the Devil didn't ye share it when I *needed* it?"

He plumped down in his desk chair once more, exhausted by fear and anger, by outrage. How to pen that letter to Caroline, posing stern and capable, and "reliable and trustworthy," he couldn't even begin to conjure. It would be implausible to beg her forgiveness . . . and much too soon to do so, too. He could not chide her for a brainless chit for being gulled by the vicar's advice, either.

And when you came right down to it, did he *wish* to reconcile? Hmmm . . .

He had to give that one a *long* think, turning his chair to face Caroline's portrait hanging in the dining-coach; done back when she was a newlywed in the Bahamas in '85 or '86. Dewy fresh and pretty, with her features unlined, but for the natural merry folds below her eyes; long, silken light brown hair worn long and missish under a wide-brim straw bonnet . . .

T'wasn't *all* looks, or beauty, though . . . And *damn being a sail-orman! He was gone for a year or two, sometimes an entire three years' commission, and people and things never were the same as they were when he left. Children sprouted taller, into the most amazing creatures, totally alien to who they'd been before, as strange to him as feathered savages in the Great South Seas. Wives . . .*

Had be been a landsman, even a tenant squire with even a modicum of ability to work a farm (or appear as if he even tried!) he knew things would have been different between them. There would have been no shock of *rencontre*, at the changes. They would *not* have mellowed apart, too "set in their ways" for coping with life as *independent* agents, but would have slowly, gradually adapted to each other, so that such changes never came as a security-shaking shock of recognition. They would have aged . . . together!

And, most importantly, living cheek-to-jowl with a goodly wife, standing "watch and watch" with a woman so sweet and intelligent, and compatible as Caroline, it was good chances he'd *never* have strayed.

Well, perhaps now and again, but 'twould've been *rare*. Really.

Lewrie was certain that Caroline was still more than enough for
him as a mate; hadn't he deemed her perfect marriage material once
he and she had re-met in England in '84, *long* before they'd wed?
Before that anonymous scribbler had exposed his overseas doings,
hadn't they *proved* their mutually pleasing compatibility after each separation and re-adjusted to each other, caught up? So happy and light-
hearted, so easily sociable and teasing, so much of the same mind . . .
wasn't she the same spritely but serious, level-headed but adoring girl
he'd wed?

Reconcile? Aye, he *did* wish it!

Could he shed Theoni Connor, though, and their bastard son? *Almost* completely, yes, though he did owe her an obligation. But, was
a complete break called for, then so be it. Theoni was well-off in her
own right, with no need of his financial support, or wish to bruit her
boy Alan James Connor in genteel society as a bastard.

He suspected, though, that as long as the war went on, and the
Admiralty had need of him (despite their qualms), once reconciled, he
would be right back at sea, years and thousands of miles gone, putting
into strange . . . "harbours," as all true sailors *did*, sooner or later.

Could he actually amend his roguish ways?

Sadly, he rather doubted it; or doubted such a vow surviving an
entire year, unless he spent his time completely out of sight of land.
He knew by then his own nature . . . and a lewd'un, it was, he was
man enough to confess . . . to himself, at the least.

He eyed the larger stack of letters, all from Theoni. No! His solicitor, and Caroline, now took precedence. He scooted his chair up to
the desk and stretched for paper, quill, and inkwell.

Mountjoy, then the boys, then lastly that vital epistle to Caroline.
Well, to his father, thirdly, to give thanks for his ministrations and
advice. Which thought gave him shivers! Caroline, last.

"Gawd," he said with a wondering sigh. "All this, and Choundas,
too. Well, just thankee Jesus for all this bounty."

BOOK TWO

"En labor, en odiis caput insuperabile nostris!"

"Lo! a heavy task!–this man whom
no hate of mine can overcome!"
                    –*ARGONAUTICA*, BOOK III, 510
                    VALERIUS FLACCUS

CHAPTER EIGHT

*M*ister the Honourable Grenville Pelham, with Lewrie's agreement, determined that the *Proteus* frigate, and Lewrie's tender hide, would be safer did she sail for her hunting grounds at once, with Mr. Peel to accompany her, and Lewrie, so the "game" could be put afoot immediately . . . and someone sensible kept a chary eye on her captain, to prevent further folly!

While Lewrie didn't think he had much to fear from the Beaumans and their allies, still all a'bluster with rage over Ledyard's demise, and the undying shame and dishonour attached to it (in court at least) there *had* been some disquieting rumours bandied about involving knives, clubs, and dark Kingston alleys. The principal witnesses to the affair were of too-good standing, embarrassingly alive . . . and demonstrably unbribable, yet *someone* had to pay, so . . . ! Which rumours, sworn even as the dust was pattering upon Ledyard's coffin in the churchyard, did, admittedly, force Lewrie to tug his neck-stock and gulp a time or two, and keep his head swivelling to see who was coming up on his off-side. The Beaumans always had been a crude and immoderate clan who never did anything by halves!

God sakes, look at Lucy! had been Lewrie's conclusion. Swiftly followed by *I never get in* much *trouble at sea,* then *damme, but my men are goin' stale, swinging idle at anchor so long,* and finally by *let's get after that bastard Choundas, then, at once! He's no more vicious than the*

Beaumans . . . and I can see him comin' a long way off!

So it was with A Glad Heart and filled with Righteous Duty that Lewrie ordered HMS *Proteus* to take in her kedge anchors, haul up close to her moor, unfurl tops'ls and jibs, and, on a fine and freshening slant of wind from off the distant Blue Mountains, stand out proudly past the Palisades, wreathed in the gunsmoke of her salutes to Admiral Sir Hyde Parker (perhaps with Staff Captain Sir Edward Charles eying them much as an owl might ogle an escaped tit-mouse, with shaken fist and a faint cry of "I'll have ye, yet, ye bastard!") to thread the reefs with a harbour pilot aboard, and make a joyful offing to the sparkling deeps! Where Captain Alan Lewrie, R.N., could savour the thought of . . . "Hah! Cheated Death, again!"

Despite his previous experience in the Caribbean, Lewrie hadn't known about the odd phenomenon of the sunset "green flash," that brief eye-blink of time when the sun at last declined its last hot sliver under the horizon, and the final, glorious reds, oranges, pinks, and greys were interrupted. It had been Kit Cashman who'd told him of it, over their last goodbye supper, the last night in harbour.

He had been pacing the windward bulwarks of the quarterdeck, as was a captain's sole right when not below, but crossed to leeward with his fingers crossed, hoping that Cashman hadn't been pulling his leg. Unblinking, he strained his eyes, looking directly into the sun's ball. No, not this night, for Sol blinked out, yonder over New Spain to the West, leaving only the rapidly dulling colours of the usual tropic sunset that could, at sea, turn star-strewn black as quickly as a closed window shutter.

If he had been cheated by Nature this night (or twitted by Kit's tongue-in-cheek inventions), at least the early evening was cooler than the day, and the wind rushing cross the deck was a blessing. He pushed off the bulwark, clapped his hands in the small of his back, and paced to the double-wheel and compass binnacle, now lit by a whale-oil lanthorn flickering eerily upon the faces of the quartermaster and his mate now standing their "trick" at the helm. He craned his gaze upwards to the sails and rigging in the quickly failing last light, ascertaining that everything was just so, with nothing out of order or amiss; a peek up to "weather" for threats of storm clouds; a look down into the binnacle at the compass, where the pointer wavered near to

East-Sou'east, Half East, as close to the steady Nor'east wind as *Proteus* could steer.

And damn Pelham, Lewrie thought, frowning; *sendin' us to English Harbour, Antigua, first!* Antigua lay nearly due East, demanding a hard passage "Full and By" nigh against the Trades, and days of short tacks to the Nor'west, did they get pushed too far down, alee, zig-zagging on a drunken snail's track, short "boards" almost in the opposite direction before they could come about nearer to Cuba or Hispaniola and sail a "long board" on larboard tack, right on the eye of the wind, and something *sure* to go smash aloft, with so much pressure on the rigging. He now could barely make out the forms of spare yards, booms and light upper top-masts stowed along the gangways and on the boat-tier beams, but was sure that their number would be reduced by the time they anchored.

Quartermaster Austen stood to the weather side of the helm, his Mate to the loo'rd, a larger man who braced his strength on the wheel spokes, his eyes on the sails aloft, whilst Austen kept his glued upon the compass. A big fellow, was the Quartermaster's Mate, new-come off a Yankee smuggler taken on the north shore of St. Thomas in the Danish Virgins, where *Proteus* had done a little discreet "poaching."

Toby Jugg, for that was the improbable name he'd given when he reluctantly signed ship's books as a 'pressed man, had originally been rated an Ordinary Seaman, but had quickly proven Able in the past few months, and had then "struck" for Quartermaster's Mate. Big, hulking and dark-visaged, surly and noncommunicative, Jugg had only "volunteered" to qualify for the Joining Bounty to send to his woman and child on Barbados, far to the South. Odds were, *Proteus* would never be called upon to sail there, though, and if she did, Lewrie was sure the man would jump ship, and they'd never see him again. Or he would be forced to sic the island garrison on Jugg, who would fetch him back in chains to be bound to an upright hatch grating and given four-dozen lashes for desertion.

"Not too heavy forrud, Mister Austen?" Lewrie asked the senior Quartermaster's Mate. "Not crank?"

"Erm . . . she's fair-balanced, Cap'm," Austen took a long time to adjudge. "Mebbe a tad light, forrud. But she tacks right-easy, sir."

"Watch her head close, then," Lewrie said, transferring his gaze to the inscrutable Toby Jugg. "And nothing to loo'rd, it goes without sayin', right, Jugg?"

"Y'say so, sir," Jugg growled, eyes locked on the main course.

"Ahem . . ." Aspinall interrupted, "but yer supper's ready fer servin', sir."

"Aye, thankee, Aspinall," Lewrie grunted, irked by Jugg's coolness, which was just shy of dumb insubordination. "Carry on, then, men. Mister Catterall, I leave you the deck, and the watch. Evening, all."

"Aye aye, sir," the Second Officer piped up, after hovering in summoning distance the last ten minutes. He clapped his hands behind his back and short-strutted up to windward, filled with his importance. Quartermaster's Mate Austen waited 'til he was out of earshot before he dared mutter from the lee corner of his mouth.

"Jugg, ye bloody idiot," Austen told his helm-mate. "The Cap'm ain't nowhere bad as some, an' better'n most. Keep up yer surly airs, though, an' ye'll push him t'flog ye, an' take back yer ratin'."

"Sod 'im," Jugg whispered back. "Sod all officers an' captains."

"Sod 'im, who's done right by ye?" Austen pointed out. "Ye toss yerself back t'Able Seaman, an' there's nought t'send yer ol' woman an' kid. Show willin', why don't ye? Don't cost tuppence."

"But . . ." Jugg began to disagree, his face working sorrowfully, but any explanation or relenting was stopped by Lt. Catterall.

"Minds on your duties, men . . . no talking, there," he snapped.

"Aye aye, sir," they chorused.

Mr. Peel of the Foreign Office's Secret Branch simply knew too many secrets; it was impossible for Lewrie to follow his usual custom of dining in his officers, midshipmen and "gentlemen warrants" as long as Peel was aboard. Peel, as supercargo, had to be accommodated somewhere apart from casual conversations. There was always the risk that Peel talked in his sleep, or boasted immoderately in his cups.

The only secure place where Peel could sling a bed-cot was here in Lewrie's great-cabins, and they were already cramped enough. Aspinall's little day-pantry had come down, and the chart-space had to shift aft into the day cabin, right against Lewrie's bed space; and that bed space got crowded aft and in-board into his day cabin, which had moved Lewrie's desk and chair, settee and guest chairs, portable storage chests and wine-cabinet over to larboard, nearer his quarter-gallery and his "seat of ease"—where Toulon's tin-lined sand box also was located. Toulon, usually of the most garrulous and playful nature,

had not taken all those changes kindly. Whilst he had the run of the
entire ship, his master's cabins were sacrosanct; or at least they *should*
have been. The ram-cat had not taken well to Peel, either, usually
dubiously on guard under the furniture when Peel was astir, his paws
tucked under his chest, his eyes slit in Oriental wariness.

"Evening, Mister Peel," Lewrie said as he swept back the tails of
his coat and sat himself down in the dining-coach.

"Captain Lewrie," Peel purred back, taking a place about halfway
down on Lewrie's left. "Am I given to understand that we're having
turtle soup tonight? Delightful."

"Green turtle, sir," Aspinall supplied as he poured their wineglasses
full, waving the neck briefly at the sideboard, where a tureen with the
lid off fumed. "Small'un, but tender. Turtle steaks, too."

"Our cook, Gideon, is a wonder," Lewrie boasted, discovering at
least something to lighten his grumpy mood over being turfed from
his own quarters, something with which to ease his careful formality.

"Gideon Cook . . . how apt," Peel said with a smirk as some soup
was ladled into his bowl. "Your ship's cook's name, that is."

"Cooke with an E," Lewrie corrected, as Toulon hopped up on the
table by his right hand and sat like a statue, watching Aspinall's every
move; for sure enough, once Lewrie's bowl had been filled, there was
a smaller bowl for him, mostly fine-shredded and soft-boiled meat,
with just a bit of broth. Toulon hunkered down possessively and
tucked in, now and then glaring at Mr. Peel, did he gesture too wide
or abruptly for the cat's liking.

"His old master's name, I presume?" Peel blandly commented, his
spoon poised before his mouth to blow upon, his eyes averted.

"Who knows?" Lewrie lied, tossing off a shrug of believable innocence. "Free to volunteer, at any rate."

"One may only hope, sir," Peel cautioned. "Was he a runaway . . .
the punishment for harbouring or succouring him is harsh. In point
of fact, you seem to have a great many Blacks in your crew. Howes,
Hoods? Brewsters, Sawyers, Carpenters . . . Basses and Whitbreads,
and *Nelsons?* Or Groom. Old masters, or old trades? Oh, I forgot.
'Tis Groome with an E." He gave Lewrie a questioning smirk. "But
Bass, or . . ."

"Quite a spell of yellow fever and malaria, earlier this year, Mister
Peel," Lewrie very cautiously stated, covering his lies with his napkin
to his lips. "Was *Proteus* fortunate so many locals volunteered into

her, well, I ain't picky, 'long as I can work and fight my ship."

"Odd, though," Peel drilled on, glass held pensively in hand. "That was just about the same time that a coincidental number of young male slaves fled the late Ledyard Beauman plantings near Portland Bight, was it not? One *could* wonder . . ."

Got me by the nutmegs! Lewrie frantically thought, in dire need of a panicky "Yeek!" and did he try to bluster his way out of it, he would only make things worse for himself. Panic gave way, though, to anger at Peel and Pelham, knowing they'd hold this over him to ensure his cooperation . . . when they already *had* it, the bastards!

"Most fortunate, aye," Lewrie conceded, busying himself with a spoonful of soup, taking thinking time in stroking Toulon, who had put his food away and was cajoling for more.

"Mister Pelham, now," Peel continued quite casually, "is a lad born to wealth. As we both know, respectable wealth in England means land, and property *obtaining* to the land. Tenants, and rents? He was a bit nettled, therefore, by the, uhm, coincidence. Mister Pelham, however, has the acquaintance of Sir Samuel Whitbread and the 'Great Commoner,' Charles James Fox, who are of a persuasive progressive bent. He also admires the work of the Reverend William Wilberforce and Mistress Hannah Moore, the earnest reformers. Mister Pelham is not taken quite so much by their views concerning the reform of *English* society . . . but he agrees with them about the abolition of slavery, d'ye see."

"Uhm-hmm," Lewrie commented with his mouth full, which seemed safest. *I'm ruined, I'm extorted forever . . . which?* he wondered.

"Mister Pelham now thinks the *slightest* bit better of you, sir," Peel informed him. "Did you actually have a hand in it."

"Excuse me, Mister Peel," Lewrie wondered aloud, after he got his soup down without choking in shock, or relief. "But, not two days ago, re-enslaving every last Black in Saint Domingue seemed to bother him less than a hang-nail. Damme, he's posing as a prospective slave *owner!* How can he hold both views simultaneously?"

"Ah, but they're *French* slaves, Captain Lewrie," Peel brightly replied. "Not English-owned. And anyone who tries to put the chains back on 'em will bleed money, soldiers, and grief, the whole next century. Let it be a festering boil for the Frogs, not us. L'Ouverture *is* getting the land back into limited production, so what he can do, disorganised as he is, our more enlightened British planters can do, just as well if not better. *Perhaps* with paid labour, d'ye see."

Lewrie gave that idea the scornful snort it deserved; he doubted if anyone could mention British overseas planters and "enlightened" in the same breath, and *not* be slung into Bedlam for lunacy.

"And Mister Pelham's pose is just that," Peel snickered. "For just so long as it is necessary. He'll make a great *show* of keen interest into every aspect of slave agriculture, then suffer a sudden, ah, turn of fortune that precludes the purchase of slaves, or acres."

"He'll make a pest of himself, you mean," Lewrie wryly supposed.

"Uhm!" Peel gaily agreed over the lip of his wineglass.

"Which means that I won't be saddled with you forever," Lewrie further assumed. "Your mission ends when Choundas is defeated, or when Saint Domingue explodes again? When Rigaud wins?"

"Hopefully, Captain Lewrie," Peel said with a mystifying shrug.

"Just how abolitionist *is* the Honourable Grenville Pelham then?" Lewrie queried. "Enough so to delve into slavery's horrors and write Wilberforce and Moore all about 'em? So Whitbread and Fox can screech in the Commons and expose the evils?"

"Frankly, sir, I would *not* put it past him," Peel agreed. "He *is* young, you've noticed, and, uhm, ardent in his beliefs," Peel said, with a jaded roll of his eyes at such callowness in younger men.

"Ain't he, though," Lewrie replied, chuckling; but he was more amused by the fact that Pelham was vulnerable, too. A word in the right ear, and Jamaica would shun him like the proverbial viper in the breast; an abolitionist spy out to ruin them, take their profits with emancipation and paid-for workers—steal the food from their children's mouths!

He threatens me, he goes down with me, Lewrie vowed to himself; *Pelham presses me too sore, and I'll have* him *by the nutmegs!*

"I take it that your friend, Colonel Christopher Cashman, is not enamoured of the institution either, Captain Lewrie," Peel said as his soup bowl was whisked away, to be replaced by a plate of grilled fish and simmered turtle cutlets, with small boiled new potatoes, chick peas, and fried onion slices added.

"No, he's not," Lewrie answered.

"How odd, then, that he's removed to the Carolinas," Peel said as he broke open a piping-hot roll of shore bread and slathered it with fresh butter; butter preserved as long as it lasted on the cool far-aft orlop deck, sunk in an oak pail of seawater.

"Looking at Wilmington in North Carolina, or Georgetown in South Carolina," Lewrie supplied, feeling more at ease now they were off that damning topic of his guilt. "Damme, puss, be easy! Here comes your portions. Ye ain't eatin' *mine*, damn yer eyes. Uhm, cotton, tobacco, and naval stores, mostly . . . rice and indigo from Georgetown. But he will be a factor. He told me he's placed orders for the machinery for a sawmill and rice mill. No more farming for him. I expect Kit will prosper, no matter where he lights. He's the hard-pluggin' sort."

And damme but I'll miss him, Lewrie thought once more; *Life'll be dull, 'thout Cashman t'stir things up.*

Though, after their last parting supper three nights before, it might be best if Life *did* get plodding-boresome for a while, for it had been a rowdy and "wet" night of wine, punch, brandy, and some of that infamous Yankee Doodle corn-whisky, before they'd bawled out the last *bonne chance* and *adieu*, to the great displeasure of half the sleeping residents of Kingston.

"Ah, the Americans," Peel simpered. "I'm certain that a man of Colonel Cashman's kidney will greatly improve the *ton* of their society, though he'll have to look sharp, else the Yankees skin him naked. In America, *all* is trade, everything has its price, and everything, and everyone, seems for sale. You are aware, I trust, that the Americans already trade with Saint Domingue?" Peel asked him.

"Yes, and we should put a stop to it, I take it," Lewrie said.

"Well, perhaps," Peel countered. "Before General Maitland negotiated the evacuation of our land forces, he and L'Ouverture came to what he *assumed* was a form of agreement regarding trade."

"His defeat, ye mean," Lewrie shot back, forever prejudiced to anything Maitland did. "I take it L'Ouverture reneged, and the great general was skinned by the little Black man?"

"One *could* put it that way, yes," Peel said, almost wincing at Lewrie's bluntness. "Maitland wined and dined him, held a parade for him, and fawned something shameful. Which nearly killed old Maitland's soul, since he absolutely despised him but . . . even so, Maitland is nothing if not a cunning diplomatist, so he dissembled to him deuced well."

"Piss-poor general, *and* a piss-poor negotiator," Lewrie snapped, though much intrigued by the hope of hearing more "dirt" on the man.

"Promised him the moon, did L'Ouverture agree," Peel summarised. "Our frigates to keep the Frogs at bay. British goods, arms, and munitions brought in by Yankee ships, just so long as the French didn't get the place back, if L'Ouverture would declare himself king or something and make Saint Domingue independent."

"But he didn't," Lewrie pointed out.

"Wasn't even tempted, I'm told," Peel told him, amazed by such sentiments, and what he'd have done, given the chance. "Too much in love with France and the Revolution, the mother country and the mother tongue. Though, you hear the local patter of the slaveys and even the Creoles, and it makes you wonder."

"More like, L'Ouverture knew Maitland was dealing with Rigaud, too, and saw right through him," Lewrie said with a prim sniff. "When you get down to it, do we *really* want the place? Better we blockade the coast 'til Kingdom Come . . . no *imports*, and they fall apart. No *exports*, and they go bust. More importantly, *our* planters make money with both fists, since French and Spanish colonies can't supply tuppence to the world market for sugar, molasses, and rum, and all that."

"But we must—" Peel exclaimed, as if presented with heresy.

"Have it?" Lewrie scoffed. "No, we don't. And if no one else has it, or can make ha'penny off it, it's *British* goods borne by British bottoms that rule tobacco, cotton, indigo, and cocoa . . . and Europe would shrivel up and die without 'em."

"But, surely . . . !" Peel sputtered, dabbing his lips.

"I *know*, it takes all the fun out of your plots and schemes if the Navy just closes the tap, and lets Saint Domingue rot and wither," Lewrie gleefully declaimed. "Makes your, and Pelham's, presence redundant, don't it? Why, I might actually get my cabin space back! And France, and Spain, lose *all* their overseas trade and wealth, and we whip 'em silly sooner or later . . . if their own people don't rise up to demand bread and peace, first."

"Well, I doubt we'll give up quite *that* easily, Captain Lewrie," Mr. Peel told him, once he'd gotten his breath back, so to speak. "We have *always* coveted Saint Domingue, and that very sort of exclusive possession of the Caribbean you just mentioned. If not exclusive, we would have shared it with Spain, and would have worked in concert to expel the French, the Danes, and the Dutch . . . expel the Americans, too."

"Do tell," Lewrie said, beckoning to Aspinall for more wine.

"As early as '92, there was a Lieutenant-Colonel John Chalmers, foresaw the coming war with France. He wrote the Foreign Office, and the Prime Minister, offering a plan to conquer all the Sugar Isles ... all sorts of maps and such, marked with arrows and little sketches of forts and ships ... the same sort of paper fantasies that wish-to-be generals dream up in peacetime—"

"Promising grand success ... if *they're* put in charge, hmm?" Lewrie sourly suggested. "Military, naval, *or* ... agents?"

"Well, uhm, yes," Peel was forced to admit. "Ambition grows in every breast. Anyway, Colonel Chalmers suggested that we share the island of Hispaniola, the entire Caribbean, with Spain, and urged that we form a proper alliance, with them as the weaker partner."

"Which we did, for a while," Lewrie stuck in, knife and fork in use. " 'Til Spain turned on us, and took hand with the Frogs, and God *knows* why."

"French and American ships, and trade, would have been driven out of these seas, completely," Peel continued, as casually as if he were discussing the prospects of a horse at New Market. "Spain is old, tired, and bankrupt ... what better sort of ally could one ask for? Colonel Chalmers even went so far as to propose that, with Saint Domingue in our hands, and the United States' trade eliminated, all those emigrants from Scotland, Ireland, Wales, and even England would settle down here instead of sailing for America ... depriving the Yankee Doodles of an expanding population of enterprising new-comers, and all the industries and skills they'd possess, or demand once settled. Talented Britons, who'd—"

Lewrie cocked his head to one side and grinned, setting down his wineglass so he wouldn't spill when he began to wheeze with laughter. "Mine arse ... !" he snorted, "on a band-box! Tell me you're not serious! That's the damnedest ... ! Christ shit on a biscuit!"

"Well, that's what you get when *amateurs* connive," Peel replied when Lewrie at last subsided, as if to prove that *his* hands had never touched such a scheme. "Property, property ... nothing but property, do ye know," he went on, with a worldly-wise snicker. " '*Ferrea non venerem sed praedam saecula laudent.*' 'It is not love but booty that this iron age applauds,' " Peel cited. "Tibullus."

"Bugger him, too," Lewrie retorted. "With bells on. Beg your pardon, Mister Peel, but, unfortunately, that's what you get when even the ones who should *know* better connive."

"Yes, unfortunately," Peel admitted. "You know that Maitland's gone to America? A Mister Harcourt from the Foreign Office is still in Saint Domingue, negotiating on the sly with L'Ouverture. Hope springs eternal," the elegant spy said with a faint shrug. "Maitland's brief is to negotiate covert trade arrangements, with Yankee ships to bear the goods. Unfortunately, he may be a trifle late off the mark. Their new President, John Adams, does not follow his predecessor's advice concerning foreign entanglements, as President Washington cautioned in his farewell address. Adams has already sent trade representatives to Saint Domingue, who seem to own the high cards for some reason."

"Even though twice as many Blacks are enslaved in America as there are on Hispaniola?" Lewrie said, gawping in surprise. "*They* have a bloody hope! So, do I end up chasing Yankee merchantmen?"

"It may come to that, yes," Peel intimated. "We should, uhm, *pretend* to continue in amity and cooperation with American men o' war versus the Frogs . . . for the moment."

"So all my advisories are over the side, I s'pose," Lewrie had to assume. "All that blather about equal protection for their traders and such. Sharing information with the American Navy . . . Damme, this could turn nasty if the Yankee Doodles aspire to dominate the colony's trade, without spilling a drop of blood, after we did all the—"

"Well, we won't share *all* our information, of a certainty," Mr. Peel warned. "For instance, our agents in Paris smuggled us the French private signals for the next three months, and those we shall *not* tell the Jonathons about."

"Really!" Lewrie exclaimed, a slow, devilish grin spreading on his face as he contemplated the opportunities for mayhem those signals codes might open to him.

"For now, we must be grateful the United States Navy is so tiny and weak, and most of her captains inexperienced," Mr. Peel snickered. "They barely make a show of force against the few French warships here, and those are few and far between, as we both know. Poor-cast cannon, perhaps green-timbered new-built ships . . ." he scoffed.

"You'd be surprised," Lewrie was happy to counter, recalling a visit aboard their 44-gun two-deck frigate *Hancock*. "We sell 'em modern artillery, coppering, everything they wish. A year from now, they will be a daunting challenge. We get into a new war with 'em and out come their privateers. Bad as the Frog privateers are, they're flea-bites by comparison. Do they get their hands on the exclusive Saint Domingue trade, it might be *our* merchantmen swept from these seas. If you scratch the Jonathons, you'd find they'd rather have another good bash at us than the French."

"Hmm . . . may not signify," Peel replied, grunting his skepticism at that declaration. "I doubt L'Ouverture will trust any slave-holding nation not to do him harm, in the long run. Adams's representations to him may goad the French into a real war, or force them to send an army and a fleet out here to quash any attempt to declare Saint Domingue's independence . . . or alliance with the Yankee Doodles. Which would put a better face upon our, uhm, sudden evacuation as well."

"I doubt *that's* possible," Lewrie scoffed.

"Actually, when Mister Pelham and I were about to depart, there was a lengthy article just ready for publication in all the newspapers," Mr. Peel told him with a mystifying grin. "It had been prepared by a government committee. Well, not an *official* committee, hmm? I saw. a copy of it, and fetched it along. Would you care to read it, sir?"

"Total shite, is it?" Lewrie asked.

"You must understand that it was devised to be read in Paris by the Directory," Peel related, "to create a rift, or widen the existing rift, 'twixt France and L'Ouverture, firstly. The secondary aim would be to mollify our own populace. Matter of fact, I have it here," Peel said, reaching into the breast pocket of his coat to produce a sheaf of hand-copied script.

Lewrie took it warily, sure that it would be rank drivel; and the ink would be runny, in this damp. Toulon, at least, was quickly fascinated with anything that crinkled, and pawed at the papers, and his master's hand, mouth open for an experimental nibble.

" 'No event has happened in the history of the present war of more interest to the cause of humanity or the permanent interests of Great Britain than the treaty which General Maitland has made with the Black general Toussaint upon the evacuation of San Domingo' . . . that's what they're calling it, now? Thought it was Saint Domingue."

"Less French, more Caribbean and . . . exotic," Peel explained.

" ' . . . the *independence* of that most valuable island is in fact *recognised* and will be secured against all the efforts which the French can now make to recover it. Not merely without the expense to England of fortifications or of armies but with the benefit of securing to us its exclusive commerce' ... oh, *rot!*" Lewrie spat.

L'Ouverture was lauded, though a "mere Negro and brigand," but one born "to vindicate the claims of his species and to show that the character of men is independent of exterior colour" ... "the late events will soon engage the public attention, and please all parties ..."

"Oh, please!" Lewrie gravelled, more agitated. " 'It is a great point to rescue this formidable island from the grasp of the Directory ... it is a great point gained to the cause of humanity that a Negro domination is in fact constituted'," he read, disbelief and bile in his voice, in equal measure. " ' ... that the Black Race whom the Christian world to their infamy have been accustomed to degrade ... Every Liberal Briton will feel proud that this country *brought about* the happy revolution! 'What unutterable gall! Tripe! God-rotted ... shit!"

"Ain't it," Peel rejoined, as if amused by Lewrie's naivety.

Toulon pounced upon the papers, now held in a limp right hand, with a glad little cry of victory, and many brisk "digging" motions.

"No, no, little man," Lewrie chid him, snatching them away with his left hand, and shoving them down-table to Peel. "Not these. Make you sick to your stomach. Bad as a hair-ball. Damn my eyes, Peel, who'd believe *that?*"

"Don't much signify," Peel admitted. "Once in the papers, it's official, and who's to say diff'rent? The next generation'll take this account for gospel. Think of the widows and orphans," Peel said with a dismissive sniff. "Suddenly, the kin of those hundred thousand dead, crippled, or debilitated have a crumb to cling to ... that their lads went for the good of ... humanity. 'Twas in a good *cause!*" Peel said, scornfully pontificating, as all the ministers, parish vicars, Members of Parliament (Lewrie strongly suspected) would soon tearfully declaim.

Lewrie picked up his refilled wineglass and leaned back from the table. Oh, he could have pretended to be so sickened by the whole affair that he'd been put off his victuals, but that wasn't the case; he was still hungry. Disgust had no effect on *his* digestion.

"I s'pose," he finally said, after three moody sips that nearly drained his wineglass, "the same sort of devious cant was spread in the last war ... back when I was just commissioned, or a Mid. Cant that I most-like believed."

"A glass with you, Captain Lewrie," Peel proposed, summoning

Aspinall to top them up. "To . . . an honourable world."

"Honourable world," Lewrie intoned, touching glasses with him . . . but pausing before drinking. "To the salvation of our *personal* honour, instead, Mister Peel. *Despite* the bloody world."

And the sardonic Mr. Peel surprised him by sighing, "Amen."

"Uhm . . . those private identity signals, Mister Peel," he asked after draining his glass and waving for a refill. "Ye wouldn't happen t'have those in another pocket . . . would you?"

"In point of fact, I do, Captain Lewrie, but . . ."

"Another toast, then, Mister Peel," Lewrie proposed. "To, ah . . . mischief. Mischief, and confusion to the French!"

CHAPTER NINE

Something dragged him up from the depths of an almost dreamless sleep—a commotion on deck? No, it was the faint groan of working timbers, and the motion of his sybaritic hanging bed-cot that was made almost wide enough for two, a most suspect luxury in the spartan world of the Navy. *Proteus* was still on larboard tack, her decks heeled to starboard as she rolled and ranted, and the bed-cot, hung fore-and-aft, swayed left-to-right, but with a snubbing little jerk, and a yawing, a twist every now and then. One opened eye revealed utter blackness in the closed windows of the overhead coach-top. Toulon, not liking what the cot was doing one little bit, fussed and fretted on the wood edge, ready to jump down. Lewrie flung back the single mildewed sheet that covered him and put a leg over, a foot on the deck, ready to roll to his left and leave it. There was a thud of a musket butt outside his forrud cabin door.

"Awf'cer o' th' watch . . . Mister Adair, SAH!"

"Come," Lewrie called back, groping in the darkness for a pair of canvas trousers he'd left draped over a convenient chair back.

"My pardons, Captain," Lt. Adair said, entering the cabins with a weak horn-pane lanthorn in one hand, and his hat in the other, "but the wind is come more Easterly, and the seas are getting up, somewhat."

"Felt her working," Lewrie grunted as he finished buttoning up the

front flap of the trousers, and fumbled his toes into his shoes. "What's
the time, and where stands the wind, Mister Adair?"

"Just gone Two Bells of the Middle Watch, sir," Adair replied,
"and the wind has backed a full point. We've hauled off with it, just
this minute, sir."

"But she needs easing, aye," Lewrie decided aloud, shrugging into
a thigh-length tarred sailcloth coat—now that he had Adair's light by
which to find it. "Lead on, Mister Adair."

Once on deck near the quartermasters, who were straining on the
helm, he could smell rough weather up to windward, a fresh-water
miasma that put him in mind of a water well's dank throat. A sliver
of moon gave faint light, but there were a few wisps of semi-opaque
scud near it, and just enough moonlight and starlight to reveal a solid
blankness up in the Nor'east.

"Well, damme," Lewrie muttered as the wind gusted fitful for an
ominous moment or two, and the "banshees" keened in the miles of
stays, sheets, halliards, and braces, before falling off as if dying suddenly, allowing *Proteus* to roll more upright and groan like an old
woman turning over in her arthritic sleep. "Ease her, hell, Mister
Adair, we'll rig for heavy weather. Pipe 'all hands.' We'll strike top-
masts, and take first reefs in both courses and tops'ls . . . hand the
stays'ls and outer jibs, as well. First off, hands to the braces once on
deck, and we'll ease her another point off the wind to a close reach."

"Aye aye, sir! Mister Towpenny? Pipe 'all hands'!"

"Something the matter?" Mr. Peel enquired, popping up like some
Jack-In-The-Box by Lewrie's side, wrapped in a blanket over shirt
and breeches.

"Weather's making up, Mister Peel," Lewrie snapped, wishing the
man wouldn't *do* that, coming up on his blind side and scaring him
like a graveyard ghost. "Have to prepare for it, and bear off Sou'east."

"I see. How much delay will there be, then, to our arrival at Antigua?" Peel asked, following Lewrie to the compass binnacle, where
Lewrie took a long squint at the traverse board.

"Three days?" Lewrie speculated, "A whole bloody week? No one
could tell you that, Mister Peel. Depends on how rough it's going to
get, from where the wind blows, how hard . . . if our luck's out, we'll
end up halfway to Barbados . . . or stagger down nigh to the Vice-

Royalty of New Granada. Wish t'visit the Dons and buy some *ciga-rillos*, do ye, Mister Peel?"

"Not particularly, Captain Lewrie, no," Peel said, a shakiness to his voice despite his stab at jocularity, which sound made Lewrie turn to peer at him with a faint grin. Was this "blow" Peel's first experience of heavy weather? He hadn't spent that much time on ships in the Mediterranean during their last pairing, and might have had good winds and easy seas on his way there, even in the fickle Bay of Biscay. It *had* been heard of, though 'twas damned rare.

"Ah, Mister Winwood," Lewrie said, turning his attention to the Sailing Master as he lumbered up from the gun-room and the main deck to the quarterdeck, with one of his charts under one arm, as *Proteus* awoke with a thunder of horny bare feet on oak, amid the shrills of bosun's calls. "I intend to remain on larboard tack, 'long as she'll bear it. New course, oh . . . Sou'-Sou'east, to begin with. Any dangers we should know of on that course? 'Til we run aground on Saint Vincent that is?"

"Let me consult this particular chart, Captain, sir," Mr. Winwood ponderously, soberly said, carefully unrolling it and pegging it to the traverse board, and waving a ship's boy forward with a better lanthorn so they could see it. "Ah . . . your initial estimate of landfall near Saint Vincent, should this slant of wind persist, sir, may be correct. And though the weather may plague us, I know of no shoals or reefs to the lee of the Windwards, sir."

Winwood was hopeless, Lewrie thought, following the man's ruler and course-tracing finger on the chart. He seemingly had *no* sense of humour, on-duty or off.

"A hurricane, do you think, Captain Lewrie?" Peel asked of him, clutching his wind-flagged blanket close round his chest and shoulders.

"Hurricane winds usually veer more Northerly, first, as Mister Winwood may tell you, Mister Peel," Lewrie told him.

"The counter-clockwise rotation, demonstrably proven throughout years of observation, Mister Peel, is not present here," Winwood said. "Though this is the season for them . . ." he trailed off, shrugging.

Damme, is he actually pullin' Peel's leg? Lewrie wondered, grinning at the seeming jape; *No, just bein' his own cautious self.*

"Pardons, Captain, but the hands are all on deck, and standing by braces and sheets," Mr. Adair reported.

"Very well, Mister Adair, put the helm up a point, and ease the set of the sails," Lewrie bade him, seeing Lts. Langlie and Catterall now on deck, in case something went amiss.

"Uhm . . ." Lt. Adair quailed for a second at the enormity of the task which had just fallen on his slim, barely experienced shoulders, obviously hoping that Mr. Langlie the First Lieutenant would supplant him. "Aye aye, sir."

Lewrie paced "uphill" to the windward bulwarks to observe, with the fingers of his right hand crossed in the pocket of his storm coat, his left elbow braced over the cap-rail and his left leg straddling a taut, thick breeching rope of a larboard quarterdeck carronade. After a moment, he took his hand from his pocket, crooked a finger, and bade Lt. Langlie to join him.

"Evening, sir," Langlie said, doffing his hat, which let a gust of wind dance his romantic dark curls.

"Has to learn sometime," Lewrie commented, jutting his chin at Mr. Adair, now standing by the forrud quarterdeck rail and the nettings with a brass speaking-trumpet to his mouth and bawling orders. "Do you have any qualms, Mister Langlie?"

"He's a good, seasoned lad, sir," Langlie replied, "and just as smart as paint. He'll cope with it, I expect."

"And if he don't, well here you are, Mister Langlie, ready for anything," Lewrie chuckled, leaning close to Langlie's ear so that his words didn't reach his junior-most officer. "Soon as we've eased her, strike top-masts. This *may* blow out by dawn, but . . . better safe than sorry. I'd admire, did you oversee that, sir. And, I'd expect Mister Adair will be much relieved that you *do*. Take charge until we have her reefed down snug, then let him finish the Middle Watch alone."

"Aye, sir," Langlie answered, grinning in secret with Lewrie.

"Course now Sou'east by East, sir!" Adair shouted up to them a moment later. "Broad reaching. Ready to hand stays'ls and outer jibs!"

"Carry on, Mister Adair!" Lewrie shouted back, forcing himself to slouch against the railings and direct his attention outboard, far up to weather in search of the coming storm. "Though, once we've done and he's come off-watch, Mister Langlie, you *will* inform him that my order book requires that I be summoned much earlier than he did . . . *gently*, Mister Langlie, hmmm?" Lewrie suggested to Langlie, a sly grin on his face. "A *too*-confident officer of the watch is about as dangerous as one with none."

"I half suspect he's realised his mistake, sir," Langlie said in return.

"And sometimes it isn't overconfidence that keeps the watch officer mum, but the fear of looking foolish, or incapable . . . 'til it is *indeed* much too late, sir. I'll have him supervise the lowering of the foremast top-hamper. That's a task that won't make him feel as if we distrust his abilities, sir."

"An excellent idea, Mister Langlie, thankee. Do so."

"Aye, sir."

"Take reefs, next, so no one aloft is in too much danger, Mister Langlie," Lewrie instructed, as the first few patters of raindrops hit his bare head and face. "Get her flatter on her bottom so the hands're not flung halfway to the horizon."

A brisk and efficient half-hour's labour later, and HMS *Proteus* was rigged for heavy weather, with furled and gasketed t'gallants and royals, yards, and the top-masts lowered to the decks, bound snug among the piles of spare spars on the boat-tier beams, with both fore and main courses taken in one reef, and all three tops'ls at two reefs, only the main topmast stays'l still flying 'twixt the main and the fore mast, and the two inner-most jibs on the bow still standing to balance her spanker and helm effort.

By then, it was raining buckets. Whitecaps and white horses to windward rose, heaved, and curled stark close-aboard. But they weren't breaking or flying spume off the wavetops yet. And the winds, though gusting and moaning now and again, were weaker than the gust front which had preceded the rain.

Lewrie sat and steamed in his impermeable storm coat and worst, oldest hat. He'd had his canvas sling-chair fetched up and lashed to the larboard side, near the mizen-mast shrouds, where he could keep a wary eye on things. Something else for older, more senior officers to chide him for, should they ever see it, that chair. *Real* tarry-handed tarpaulin men lived and died on their feet when on deck, never stuck a hand in a pocket, never slouched or leaned on anything . . . never had a wee nap, either! Lewrie held to *most* concepts about how a sea-captain should behave, even the one about holding the power of life and death, of being the next-best thing to God when sailing independently . . . but, did God have an idle streak, well then!

Savin' m'self for important chores, he oft told himself, as he once more did that night; *'fore called t'rise to the occasion. Didn't God Himself*

*not 'Make And Mend', the first Sunday, after six days' work at creatin'
the world? That hard a week,* I'd've *caulked away the seventh.*

The striking of Six Bells of the Middle Watch roused him from a
soggy "nod" with a grunted "Mmmph." Three in the morning, and
an hour 'til all hands were summoned again to scrub decks. It was
still black as a boot, and the seas were still lively, but the frigate was
easier in her motion, no longer yawing as she scaled the waves, no
longer in full cry of working timbers, nor jerk-snubbing twisting when
meeting a wave as her bow dipped. She sat firmly on her starboard
shoulder to the press of wind, and the faint wails aloft were the keens
of passage, not torment.

He rose and stretched, undid the buttons of his storm coat, and let
out the trapped, sweaty air, letting the coat be swept abaft of his hips
and chest. By God, but the forceful airs were almost nippy-cool, as
refreshing as a rare shore bath in a brass or copper hip-tub! Off went
his hat to allow the winds to have their way, to cool his scalp, to re-
comb his locks, and the fitful rain to rinse away a week's worth of
oils and dander.

Fitful rain, hmmm, he took note. It no longer pummeled him or
slanted in like stinging grapeshot; in point of fact, half the drops he
felt were large dollops wind-stripped from sails and rigging aloft. He
heard gurgles above the soughing roar of *Proteus*'s hull slicing a firm
way over the waves. Scuppers to loo'rd were open, and rainwater
sheeted cross the angled deck to go gargling out alee; canvas scoops
led fresh, clean water into spare casks and smaller kegs, and a work-
party under the Purser, Mr. Coote's, direction, were trundling caught
barrels on their lower rims to the edge of the companionway hatches,
to be lashed or bowsed firmly in place 'til dawn, when they would be
lowered down to the orlop, giving them a few more days of stores
with which to keep the sea just that much longer in search of their
foes.

Lewrie went forward to the nearest chute, tore off his storm coat,
and bent over it for an impromptu shower, wishing he had his bar of
soap handy, thoroughly rinsing his hair, scrubbing his face and chest,
restoring his alertness, wishing that he could shed all of his clothing,
swing the scoop over a little, and lay and wallow on deck in the steady
stream without sacrificing his dignity.

The keg was full; to hell with it!

"Lift the end, there. Direct it at me," Lewrie ordered. There! Even clad in shirt and slop-trousers, he turned under the spurts, rinsing salt crystals, mildew, and old sweat from his clothes, first, then (perhaps) cleaning his skin beneath, second.

"God, that'll wake you up," he exclaimed, for the water was as cool as the dying storm winds, while his hands stood about and gawped with broad smiles on their faces. "Everyone take the opportunity for a good scrub while it lasted, men?"

"Oh, aye, sir!" a sailor agreed.

"E'en got up enough lather t'shave with, sir," another said, for salt water would never lather with soap, and the usual issue for bodily use was a meagre cup a day, but for the happenstance of a rain shower.

"Drunk our fill, for oncet, we did, Cap'um," a third chortled.

"Who's got the cup, then?" Lewrie cried. "Give it here." And caught two full wooden piggins of sweet, fresh rainwater from the canvas scoop and downed them like a sweaty smith. "Ah, thankee. Rare treat, that. Carry on, men. And after we take Noon Sights, we'll double the water ration, for one day at least. Now we've enough to go around."

Sated, indeed with his belly sloshing, which forced a belch from his lips, Lewrie picked up his storm coat, draped it over one arm, put his hat on, and paced back to the helm, and the waiting Mr. Adair, who had less than an hour left of the Middle Watch.

"Mister Adair," he said, peering at the compass bowl.

"Captain, sir. The wind's easing, and the sea's not as boisterous. Course is still Sou'east by East, though I do believe she might abide our standing a touch closer to the wind, again, sir."

"Our run, by Dead Reckoning, Mister Adair?" Lewrie asked.

"Uhm ... half-hour casts of the log, sir," Adair said, fumbling a soggy sheet of folded paper from the breast pocket of his coat. His marks had been made with a stub of metallic lead, and done in the dark or the faint binnacle glow, so his accounting was extremely difficult to read, but Adair found a way to decypher it.

Ten knots, then eight ... nine knots, even reefed and eased ... Lewrie caught himself counting on his fingers to keep track; a spell of ten knots during gusts of the storm, three casts in a row, hmmm ...

"At least twenty miles alee of our former course, sir, and about thirty miles forrud over the ground, sorry," Adair puzzled out at last.

"Mister Winwood leave his precious chart, did he, Mister Adair?"

"Aye, sir, in the cabinet."

Lewrie fetched it out and knelt under the lit binnacle, straining his eyes to find the finely pencilled marks of their course, using a handy pair of dividers and a parallel ruler to estimate the deviation, and pace it out to leeward on Sou'east by East.

"Well, damme, Mister Adair," Lewrie said, rising. "Even if the wind shifts back to the Nor'east, we'll spend another day beating back West-Nor'west to make it up, or miss Antigua completely. Put us into the lee of Guadeloupe, even if we could return to our old course this instant."

And what was so important about putting into English Harbour on Antigua? Lewrie wondered. Was it a mere courtesy call to let the local admiral know that they were in his waters, but not under his command, on secret business? Did Peel have someone to meet there, with intelligence which might await him that was *that* vital to their mission?

He rather doubted it.

Guadeloupe, though, was South of Antigua, and not by much, just about as much as they'd lost during the storm—*if* they stayed on a course a little to leeward of their old one, even if the Trades swung back where they belonged. Guadeloupe, the last French stronghold in the Antilles—and now Guillaume Choundas's lair. Lewrie bent under the binnacle lamp to study the chart just one more time, tracing a nail to the East'rd . . .

"Aye, Mister Adair, the wind has eased," he said, rolling up the chart and stowing it away. "Try to brace her up a point to windward. A half-point, if that's all she'll tolerate, and hold it 'til the end of watch, and inform Mister Langlie when he replaces you."

He paced back up to his rightful place to windward, took hold of the bulwarks, and gripped, trying to divine what message the sea sent up his arms. They were too far out to feel the return waves from the lee shore of the distant islands, but in his mind's eye, he could see HMS *Proteus* at *tomorrow's* dawn, perhaps halfway up the coast above Basse-Terre, the main lee-side port on Guadeloupe.

Ready to raise Merry Hell with any shipping he encountered.

"Thankee, God," he whispered aloft, "for a heaven-sent slant o' wind. Now, could You give me just one more?"

CHAPTER TEN

L 1. Jules Hainaut looked about the decks of his small schooner, a captured American trader, only sixty-four feet on the range of the deck, and tried to savour his temporary "command" for as long as it lasted, tried to tamp down his disappointment that it was only for the day, and that *Le Maître*, Captain Choundas, seemed averse to ever letting him free. God forbid, but ever since Choundas had learned that his *bête noire* was in the Caribbean, the monstrous old ogre had come over all *protective*, as if he'd not risk his "pet," his "like a son to me" protégé beyond his sight until Lewrie and *Proteus* had been eliminated ... by his other, *experienced* "pets," Desplan, Griot, and MacPherson, the talented, the promising, the mature ... ! *Merde alors*, but it made Hainaut feel like a mewling infant, a kitten with its eyes barely open and vulnerable to the back-garden crows who'd carry it off like a ripe ... worm!

L'Impudente (her American name had been *Saucy*) was not even the *Captaine's* to give him, for she was basically the yard-boat Governor-General Hugues used to tour his coastal fortifications ... or sail to Marie Galante Island with his friends, wenches, and baskets of wine and food for his occasional romps ... a faded, neglected ... *yacht!*

Capitaine Choundas despised long trips in coaches, and a riding horse was pure torture on his mangled body, so, when he had decided to accompany the *Le Bouclier* frigate to Basse-Terre to complete her lading for her first aggressive cruise, he needed a comfortable way to return, and *L'Impudente* was available.

"Follow us to Basse-Terre, Jules," Choundas had ordered, "and I will take passage back to Pointe-à-Pitre with you. Try not to run her aground, *mon cher. M'sieur* Hugues would never forgive me if you wreck her, and he already despises me enough," he'd said—without humour.

Even that was galling; as if Hainaut had never been a tarpaulin man, a well-trained *matelot*, boat-handler, or *Aspirant* who had stood a watch by himself.

Well, for one day at least he was not a paper-shuffling *Lieutenant de Vaisseau*, a mere catch-fart to his master. He had challenged *L'Impudent*'s lethargic crew to sail her as she was meant to be sailed, had infused them with enthusiasm and had heated their blood with a dole-out of naval-issue *arrack*, the fierce but coarse brandy, before he even got the schooner away from the dock, with a promise of double the usual wine ration with their noon meal if they showed that magnificent frigate a clean pair of heels and danced a quadrille round her.

Even with a weeded bottom and both running and standing rigging in need of re-roving or replacement, *L'Impudente* could dance. Under all the sail she could bear, he'd stood out with the wind up her skirts to carve graceful figures beyond the harbour moles to wait for *Le Bouclier*. Then, once on course Southwest, then West, he had weaved her about from one side of the frigate's bows to the other, sometimes falling back to pace her alee, then up to windward, ducking under her stern and pretending to fire raking broadsides into her transom.

Capitaine Desplan and his officers, and the frigate's eager crew, had first good-naturedly jeered them, then later cheered them, as the aptly named schooner had taunted and flirted about her. Hainaut didn't see *Capitaine* Choundas peering over the side during his antics, which was disappointing, as he strove so hard to prove himself a trustworthy ship-handler, but surely the others were *telling* him . . . !

L'Impudente had threaded the middle of the five-mile-wide channel between the Vieux Fort and the island of Terre-de-Bas in the Saintes, with antics done for a while, and the frigate finally spreading enough sail to threaten to run her down, dead astern of her in the deeps that *L'Impudente* was sounding. She stood out a good six kilometers (Hainaut was iffy when it came to the new measurements that the Directory had invented but in the old measurements he was sure he was out far

enough to miss any reefs or shoals, and would not damage their
Governor-General's little "play-pretty."

He had turned North, with the Trades a bit ahead of abeam, and
the lithe schooner had gathered speed and heeled, dashing spray as
high as the middle of her jibs, seeming to chuckle in delight to make
such a gladsome way, as Hainaut did. Onward, rocking and romping,
ranting over the bright sea, until he was far above Basse-Terre, and
stood off-and-on to allow the frigate to sail in and anchor first, far
from any risk of falling foul of her. At last, he angled in toward the
harbour, which was no true harbour at all, just a lee-side road off the
town and its quayside street, his crew ready to short-tack once he
turned her up Eastward, planning to ghost in alongside *Le Bouclier*
once she had both anchors down.

"*Heu*, Lieutenant?" the schooner's permanent Bosun said from the
tillerhead. "There's something going on astern, I think, *m'sieur*."

"Touch more lee helm, *Timmonier*," Hainaut told the helmsman as
he stepped past the long tiller sweep to the taff-rail to raise his telescope, a particularly fine one looted from the same disgraced admiral
who had "supplied" his smallsword.

"*Mon Dieu, merde alors!*" Hainaut spat in alarm. "The 'Bloodies'!"

"Hard t'miss, thank God," Lewrie said, pointing his telescope, its tubes
collapsed, at the volcano of La Soufrière to the Southeast, and the
other peak at the North end of the island that was just about as tall.
"It appears we'll make landfall just about level with a town called . . .
Mister Winwood?"

"Deshaies, sir," the Sailing Master informed him, after a quick peek
at his chart. "About seven miles offshore, I'd make it, before we bear
away due South."

"Close enough," Lewrie said with a wolfish grin on his phyz as he
paced about near the windward ladder-head, which would soon be the
engaged side, if most French ships were inshore. "If they've watchers
ashore, we'll sail faster than a messenger can ride. And if they have
semaphore towers, it don't signify. Panic, and bags o' shit; that's what
we're here for, after all. Though I simply don't understand why we
haven't seen a single one of our warships, all the way here."

"It's possible, sir, that most of them are lurking to windward of the
island," Lt. Langlie commented, "where they can snatch prizes."

" 'It is not love but booty that this iron age applauds,' do ye know," Lewrie cited, not above borrowing from Mr. Peel's stock of erudite quotes; though the Latin had *quite* flown his head. "Tibullus, I believe. Aha! Speakin' o' booty . . ."

He lifted his glass to eye a schooner of decent size that stood abeam the wind, close inshore but heading outward. Inshore of her was a small ship, full-rigged and three-masted, that was also standing out to sea as if she hadn't a care, or an enemy, in the world.

"Time to hoist the false Tricolours, Mister Langlie," he said.

"Aye aye, sir."

"And, do I have t'fire a salute to their Governor-General, I'd not bemoan the waste o' powder, either," Lewrie chuckled. "All in the best of causes . . . ain't it, Mister Peel. All's fair in love and war."

"That remains to be seen, Captain Lewrie," Peel frostily said by his side. His nose was still out of joint that no argument he offered could dissuade the mercurial Capt. Lewrie from his enterprise . . . though Peel had to admit that Lewrie's preparations had been little short of masterful.

Proteus's masts and spars, right to the yardarm ends, had been painted in the French fashion; two large Tricolour flags flew from the main-mast truck and spanker, and even her sails had been altered with wet wood-ash from the galley fires, brushed on to mimic the different seaming system of French sailmakers. Her own Sailmaker, Mr. Rayne, and his crew had basted the jibs to appear narrower-cut, and had raised up the roach at the jibs' feet, before "painting" false seams. The bastings could quickly be freed by firm yanks on the spun-yarn small-stuff twine, returning *Proteus* to full-bellied sailpower in a twinkling.

Lastly, despite his protestations that the private signals not be used except in the most important circumstances, Mr. Peel had been forced to turn them over. With Lewrie committed to his madness, and his officers and crew so exuberantly enamoured of the plan, he could do no less, no matter that their use this day would clue the French to changing them the day after.

"She's making a hoist, sir," Lt. Adair cried, standing aft with the signals midshipman and after-guard. "An Interrogative, followed by a string of numeral flags."

"Mister Peel?" Lewrie said, turning to their resident spy.

"Ah, uhm," Peel muttered, lifting a heavy borrowed telescope to his eye, trying to keep the schooner in the ocular, and focussed, with the frigate bounding and rolling beneath him. "It is the challenge . . . to which we should reply . . ." He referred to a sheaf of papers.

"I have it, sir," Lt. Adair insisted, quickly calling numbered flags to the sailors standing by the windward halliards. French flags were numbered differently, but the stolen private signals book had the coloured illustrations in order, to sort them out. On this day in the middle ten-day of the new-fangled French month, the proper reply was a five-flag hoist . . . Nine, Two, Eleven, Thirty, Repeater; which signal quickly soared aloft as high as the mizen-mast top, each bundled flag suddenly blossoming as the light binding twine was shaken out.

"That won't put them off, will it?" Lt. Langlie fretted. "That we're miles more efficient than any Frog ship I've seen when it comes to breaking signals, sir? 'Stead of hanking them on and sending them up straight from the lockers, free to fly, and . . ."

"Hmmm," Lewrie frowned, having not taken that into consideration 'til now. Inefficiency wasn't limited to French ships, though. He'd seen signalmen start a hoist with the first flag, let it flap near to the bulwarks as the next was attached, so the message crawled up, one item at a time. "Mister Peel, what's a merchantman doing with naval private signals?" he asked, instead. "Could she be a privateer?"

"Very *possibly* a privateer, or a captured merchant ship turned to naval use, Captain Lewrie," Peel answered with an equal frown.

"*Was* she sloppy at her hoist, Mister Adair?" Lewrie demanded.

"A tad, sir, aye," Lt. Adair agreed.

"Let's call her a privateer, then," Lewrie decided, lifting his own telescope, " 'til we know better. *And* assume she'll take us for a real Frog warship, with a martinet bastard for a captain, compared to their idle ways. Just so long as it gets us within close cannon shot before her captain figures it out. 'Bout two miles, now?"

"Just about, sir," Mr. Winwood estimated aloud.

"More sails inshore, sir," Midshipman Elwes pointed out. "Wee single-masted fishermen, most-like."

"Damme, she's making another hoist!" Lt. Adair groused, waving his signalmen to haul their own quickly down. "Mister Peel, may I ask your assistance? I speak French, but translating, *and* sorting out the flags, both . . ."

"Of course, Mister Adair," Peel acquiesced, despite his opposition to the whole endeavour; as long as they were there, why not make every effort to pull it off?

"*Bienvenu* . . . 'from where bound,' she asks," Adair called out.
"Damme . . . where *are* we from, sir?"

"Rochefort," Lewrie quickly extemporised, "we've cruised along the
Carolinas with no luck, and are short of provisions. Got chased off
by American frigates, tell him. Break it up into three hoists if you can
. . . keep 'em gogglin' us. Mister Peel, what's a good name for a Frog
frigate that's been unfortunate at taking prizes?"

"Uhm . . . *L'Heureux* . . . 'Fortunate,' sir," Peel said, snapping his
fingers as if inspired, and breaking his first impish grin of the last two
days.

"Aha! Yes, make it so, Mister Adair. Quickly," Lewrie bade.

"Aye, sir. Uhm, however d'ye *spell* that, Mister Peel?"

"And now, gentlemen," Lewrie continued, turning to his assembled
officers, "let us beat to Quarters. Take your stations, and God help
the French."

Lt. Adair had to stay on the quarterdeck instead of going forward
to supervise the forrud-most guns and foremast, in close cooperation
with Mr. Peel and Midshipman Elwes to sort out the proper flags to
convey their fictitious identity and recent past to the inquisitive schooner.

She a guarda-costa? Lewrie wondered, lifting his glass one more
time. *We're close enough, now . . . I can see semaphore towers, ashore,
but they ain't wagging, yet. Waitin' for the schooner t'tell 'em who and
what we are, are they? Well, just you keep on waitin', damn you all.
You'll know us soon enough!*

"Ahem," Mr. Winwood said at his side.

"Time to turn South along the coast, I take it, sir?" Lewrie asked
with a faint grin, taking time to turn and look at him.

"Aye, Captain," Winwood solemnly agreed with a slow nod.

"Very well, sir. Haul our wind and shape the new course."

"Aye aye, sir."

"She's hauling her wind, too, sir," Lt. Adair announced. "New hoist
. . . damn, what does that mean?"

"Not for us, Mister Adair," Lewrie snapped. "Let it pass, this time.
There's a semaphore station, halfway up yonder mountain that's working its arms. Can they not read our hoists, most-like they're asking
the schooner to tell 'em what she's learned."

As *Proteus* fell off the Trades to take the wind on her larboard
quarter, the schooner angled out from the coast to close her, the gaff-

hung fore and main sails winged and bellied out as she wore across
the wind and approached at a 45° angle, aiming as if to meet *Proteus*,
bowsprit to bowsprit. The range dropped rapidly, as the frigate's crew
settled down beside their great-guns, or knelt below the bulwarks with
muskets. A keen-eyed observer *might* have noticed that *Proteus* had
her gun-ports free to swing outboard a few inches with each roll, ready
to be hauled up and out of the way the second that the order to fire
was given. The larboard 12-pounders were ready-loaded and hauled
up close to the bulwarks; a few last tugs on the tackles would jut their
snouts into firing position. The flintlock strikers were, so far, un-
cocked but primed, with the firing lanyards already in the gun-captains'
hands but held loosely.

The focs'le carronades, the quarterdeck carronades, were manned
behind closed ports, only a few designated men allowed to appear
above the bulwarks to slouch idle, prepared to wave until the trap was
to be sprung. It was a rare French man o' war that fitted carronades
so far in this war; the sight of them would have been a dead giveaway.

"Half mile?" Lewrie muttered from the side of his mouth.

"About that, aye, sir," Lt. Langlie agreed, striving to appear casual
and inoffensive as he paced about the quarterdeck.

Lewrie strode to the helm and took up a brass speaking-trumpet,
then shambled back to the bulwarks, as if he had all the time in the
world, wouldn't harm a flea, and had the most pacific intentions; just
about ready to smile, wave widely, and "speak" the Frog schooner.
He held the speaking-trumpet high, in plain sight, and, as the range
got shorter and shorter, he could see the schooner's captain standing
with his own amplifying device by her starboard, lee, rails, waiting
for the chance to "speak" him, too.

Evidently, the semaphore station had been satisfied, for after a brief
flurry of spinning telegraph arms, it had gone inert again. One quick
scan of the windward horizon showed Lewrie that the fishing boats
were still casting their nets, the three-masted ship still stood out to sea
a little beyond their bows, would pass to leeward about a mile off.
Off the harbour town of Basse-Terre, the frigate's putative destination,
Lewrie thought he could see another three-master with weary tan-
stained sails, a ship he took for another merchantman standing out to
sea. He got a glimpse of a larger three-master entering harbour, brail-
ing up as she ghosted shoreward. Close to Basse-Terre was another
schooner . . .

"Rounding off, sir!" Lt. Langlie cautioned. Sure enough, at a distance of no more than a British cable, the schooner had swung about to run alongside them.

" '*Allô, m'sieur!*" the schooner's captain called with his brass trumpet to his lips. "*Ici L'Abeille, le navire de guerre auxiliare . . .*"

"The *Bee*," Mr. Peel snickered as he came up to the windward to Lewrie's side, no matter naval custom against him being there unasked.

". . . who just got stung!" Lewrie chortled. "Run out and fire!"

Ports skreaked open to thud against the upper bulwarks; tackle sheaves squealed, and heavy carriage trucks rumbled like a stampede of cattle as the guns were run out the last few feet.

"False flags *down!*" Lewrie shouted; he'd made that mistake long ago when first as commander of the *Jester* sloop, and had caught a grim "packet" for it, no matter how successful his *ruse de guerre* had been. He had strictly cautioned the Mids and signalmen to haul the Tricolours down and get their own ensigns up as soon as the ports opened, but . . .

Halfway aloft, Lewrie thought; *close enough for king's work!*

He looked forward to Lt. Catterall, who stood in the middle of the gun-deck with his sword drawn and held high over his shoulder; who was looking most anxiously back at him.

"Fire!" Lewrie shouted as his true colours reached the tops.

"On the down-roll . . . fire!" Lt. Catterall bawled.

Three 24-pounder carronades, double-shotted with solid balls and what amounted to a small keg of plum-sized grape-shot, and thirteen 12-pounders, each loaded with *two* balls, went off almost as one, creating a sudden, murderous avalanche of metal, and a choking cloud of sulfurous, reeking smoke propelled windward, punctured by the flight of the shot, that only slowly drifted back over their own decks then alee, as the hands sprang to sponge and swab out, to charge and then reload the barrels, to prime the locks and begin to grunt and slave to run out for another broadside. . . .

But another broadside would not be necessary. The schooner was a converted trading vessel with thin civilian scantlings, framed with the parsimony of a skinflint Yankee Doodle, with light timbers put farther apart than naval practice. She was a shambles!

Both masts were sheared off just above her ravaged bulwarks, and she looked like a pheasant that had been gut-shot by a lucky, close-

in blast from a fowler's shotgun. Her starboard side bore so many
ragged shot-holes, some right on her waterline, already gurgling and
frothing with dirty spume and foetid venting air from belowdecks, that
there was no hope of saving her. They'd punched her almost to a full
stop, and she was already listing to starboard as if to hide her hurts!

"Hold fire, Mister Catterall!" Lewrie shouted forrud. "No need for
another. Drop it, lads . . . dead'un! Wait 'til we corner the *next* rat!
Mister Langlie, helm up, and hands to the braces. Lay us close-aboard
yon three-master just off our starboard bow."

"Aye, sir!" the First Officer barked, looking greedy as he began to
issue quick instructions.

"Mister Catterall, secure the larboard battery. Next victim, we will
engage to starboard!"

The runt-sized full-rigged ship quavered as if shocked, before her
topmen began to scramble aloft to free more sail, as hands sprang to
the braces to wear her a little off the wind to run due West, winds
on her starboard quarter, which obviously was her best point of sail.

"Puts me in mind of a Dutchman, sir," Mr. Winwood commented
to his captain, his face screwed up in concentration after a long study
with his telescope. "A tad shorter than your av'rage three-master, a
lot beamier, and her bows bluffer . . ."

"Shallower draughted, too, I'd expect," Lewrie added. "Bound to
be slow as treacle, even did she have a full gale up her skirts."

"Won't get far, I doubt, sir," Winwood said with a even rarer sniff
of satisfaction, nigh-even pleasure; even broke a faint smile on his
phyz! The usually stolid Sailing Master rubbed his hands together with
a sandy rasping of a practiced tarpaulin man, inured to ropes and
exposure half his entire life.

Small she might be, shabby she might be, but the merchant ship
was deeply laden with *something* sure to be valuable. If she *was* Dutch,
she was very far from home, and a very rare sight in the Caribbean
with most of the so-called Batavian Republic's colonies occupied by
British forces. Holland was occupied by the French, but it was a *cooperative* occupation, so Lewrie had heard; the "ideals" of the French
Revolution had found fertile soil in a fair number of Dutch hearts,
who had aided the earlier American Revolution so eagerly.

Allied with the Frogs, sailing from a French port, the merchant ship
was surely up to something nefarious in aid of some joint scheme. She

might be gunn'l deep with arms and munitions for Saint Domingue
... she was sailing deeper *into* the Caribbean, not for home. She'd be
what was termed "Good Prize."

No wonder Mr. Winwood was rubbing his hands together so gladly;
he was already assessing his share of her capture and sale; it was too
bad, Lewrie thought, that he was counting chickens that'd never hatch.

"Steer direct up her stern, Mister Langlie," Lewrie ordered. "I wish
to get up to pistol-shot before we bear up and rake her."

"You'll not try to, uhm ... ?" Mr. Winwood gasped, scandalised
by the loss of guineas.

"Might be a frigate I saw off Basse-Terre, Mister Winwood," he
told the Sailing Master. "No time to fetch-to, and sway out boats for
a boarding-party. Well, one boat, perhaps ... so we may set her afire
and be certain she's a total loss. Sorry. My savings could use infusions
of prize-money, too, but ..."

He swung back to look at the three-master, now pinned like some
struggling butterfly on *Proteus*'s jib-boom and bowsprit as the frigate
bore a touch alee of her, as if to intersect her course and swing about
due West to present the previously used larboard battery. A flag from
the Batavian Republic now flew above her tall, galleried stern windows.

It was too far for Lewrie to shout advice to the Dutch captain,
though he did glare at the stout figure by her taff-rail and pushed his
thoughts at him. *Strike, fool ... 'fore I'm forced t'kill you!*

CHAPTER ELEVEN

$\mathcal{N}_{ow}$ where is he going?" *Capitaine de Vaisseau* Guillaume Choundas dyspeptically said, peering out over the taff-rail of *Le Bouclier* as she drummed and thundered to the last of the "orderly" chaos of a ship come to anchor into the wind. Topmen were aloft, fisting the last sails by the brails to the yards after the tops'ls had bellied flat aback when she had steered Nor'east to brake to a stop. Men of the after-guard on the quarterdeck swarmed around him to strain against the mizen tops'l and t'gallant halliards and jears to lower the yards to the cross-tree and fighting-top. More men stood by the after capstan, with the kedge anchor's messenger line already fleeted about the capstan drum, waiting for the stern kedge to be rowed out with *Le Bouclier's* stoutest cutter and dropped. The frigate was faintly shuddering as she made a slight sternway, falling back from her best bower, paying out scope on cable run out through the larboard hawse-hole, beginning to snub to the resistance of a well-grounded anchor.

"He is having the time of his life, *m'sieur*," *Capitaine* Desplan answered with an indulgent chuckle. "Your pardons, but he has so many stern responsibilities, for such a spirited young man. And he serves a most demanding master, *n'est-ce pas?*"

Choundas painfully turned to glare at Desplan, wondering if his comments were any sort of criticism; but no, Desplan still smiled, as if he had no reason to cringe from Choundas's wrath.

"She is shabby and badly maintained, *m'sieur*, but that schooner handles as lively as a Thoroughbred stallion," Desplan went on. "Once *we* would have relished such sport . . . until stern duty, and command of ships and squadrons, forced us to growl at the world. To be that free and young, again, ah, what a brief joy. To dance with your very first little ship, *m'sieur*? Remember?"

"Umph," Choundas finally allowed. "I do, indeed. *La Colombe*, she was named, a despatch-boat . . . she, too, was an American schooner. Aptly named, she was. She *flew* like a 'dove.' Umph. Well . . ."

For a brief moment, Choundas had almost seemed human, in sweet reverie of his early days as a newly appointed Lieutenant, not even a *Lieutenant de Vaisseau* yet. But that moment swiftly passed, and he turned and clump-swish-ticked back to the taff-rail, glowering as little *L'Impudente* came about and began to gather speed to run into the port, at long last. Perhaps, Choundas thought, Jules Hainaut had suddenly remembered that the noonday meal that Captain Desplan would soon serve would be infinitely better than the cheese, sausages, and *vin ordinaire* carried aboard the schooner in a palmetto hamper. He was waving, even if the schooner was nearly a mile or more off, all of them . . . ?

"*Mon Dieu!*" Captain Desplan suddenly exclaimed, grunting as if suddenly punched in the abdomen. "*M'sieur* Choundas, the semaphore, it sends the alarm signal. What . . ."

Choundas slowly turned to watch the long arms of the semaphore tower swish, pause, then swish to a new bit of its message; an urgent signal that repeated—Enemy In Sight!

"*Capitaine* Desplan," Choundas growled of a sudden, stamping the ferrule of his cane on the deck, "get this ship underway, at once. If you have to cut your anchor cables, do it! *Vite, vite!* Before you lose her. The 'Bloodies' are paying us a visit!"

Ponderously, Choundas turned to look out to sea once more; out beyond the canted masts of Hainaut's onrushing schooner. He could see a pall of sour grey-brown smoke a few miles away, could see the tops'ls and courses of a three-masted ship headed South, see a smaller ship to the left of the smoke pall that was turning to run, one that would be a prize capture before the half-hour glass would turn.

Sudden boiling rage surged up his throat, made him wish to howl and jibber at the slackness, the inattention of the signal stations up the coast, the idle, work-a-day shamblers *pretending* to maintain watch!

And *where* was that commandeered schooner he had posted to the leeward coast of Basse-Terre to guard against such a raid? If, despite his sternest warnings and implied threats, those hapless island-born Creole time-servers had decided to tuck into the lee of Pointe Allegre and fish, or go ashore for a leisurely three-hour meal, they would learn that his threats were not empty, that even close ties to Governor Hugues would not save them.

But, no—he could not, *must* not bellow and stamp as he wished. *Le Bouclier*, caught in the middle of the evolution of anchoring and taking in all sail, was already a madhouse. Her captain, mates, and senior officers *already* made enough noise to interrupt their *matelots'* work, then rush to undo all their labours of the past quarter-hour and get way on her again.

Besides, he was Guillaume Choundas, *Le Hideux*, the ugly monster whom all feared. One thoughtless rant, and that useful aura of terror would evaporate, leaving him recalled as just another panicky officer who'd windmilled his arms and floundered; *then*, people would laugh at his haplessness *and* his disfigurements, making him a pitiable object of fun with no real authority or respect. No, he could only stand by the flag lockers and taff-rail lanthorns, leaning his bad leg against them, and drum impatient fingers on the silver handle of his cane in an outward sham of calm, as if he were quickly scheming. But *aflame* with murderous rage. The slack captain of that guardship would pay . . . and this 'Bloody' *anglais*, too! Once this marvellous frigate got sorted out and under sail, there was *still* a chance to salvage things . . . such as his successful reputation, and his continued career!

"Helm down, Mister Langlie," Lewrie ordered, as the struggling merchantman pressed on Westerly. "Course, due South for a bit. Lieutenant Catterall? Rake her as you bear."

"Aye aye, sir," Catterall shouted back, as mystified as anyone else aboard, aghast at the idea of passing up such a rich prize, of not even firing a warning shot to force her to strike.

Proteus hauled up more to windward, sailors on the sail-tending gangways freeing braces to let the yards swing to ease the press of the wind, and the increasing heel that might angle the artillery too low.

"Open ports!" Catterall cried. "Run out, and gun-captains, aim low!

As you *bear . . . fire!*" He slashed down his sword, though no gun had yet crossed the Dutch ship's stern, just a few breaths more and . . . Standing between the guns, Catterall's view was limited to the bulwarks and the open gun-ports, the cross-deck beams over his head with rowing boats stowed in chocks. To starboard, there was the gangway now full of Marines with their levelled muskets, the end of *Proteus*'s main-mast course sail, the ordered tangle of the Dutch ship's mizen-mast rigging, spanker, tops'l and t'gallant, and that Batavian Republic flag that was just starting to be lowered . . .

Catterall glanced aft at Captain Lewrie, standing four-square by the rolled-hammock re-enforced quarterdeck rails and netting that over-looked the gun-deck. *Surely*, he'd call for fire to be checked, before it was too late, before . . . now they'd struck!

The 6-pounder bow-chaser and 24-pounder carronade mounted on the forecastle went off almost as one, a sharpish barking, instantly echoed by a titanic booming, followed by the foremost 12-pounder long-barrel gun in the starboard battery as it slammed backwards in recoil, double-shotted.

Catterall turned back to the target, even more mystified, mouth open to reduce the pummeling on his eardrums as guns closer to him lit off and hurled themselves inboard, looked up as the Marines with their "confiscated" Yankee-made rifles chose targets and volleyed. Up above them and the gangway bulwark, rather significant *chunks* of timbers and gilded pieces of the Dutch merchantman's stern were soaring sky-ward in a cloud of gun-smoke and punched-free dirt and paint chips! Catterall heard the Dutch ship *scream* as her entire stern was hammered in, could hear the slamming and *rending* of the merchantman's guts as round-shot, langridge, and grape-shot eviscerated her innards as far forward as her foremast, snapping stout carline posts, knees, and hull timbers like so many frail toothpicks! The broadside swept past him, sternward, gusting hot, foul winds, gushing grey thunderheads of spent powder, and the quarterdeck carronades bellowing last, put paid to the foe. Catterall could hear human screams this time. Their flag was down, *blown* down, but the Captain was not calling the Cease Fire. *Proteus* wore about to the West as Catterall's gunners reloaded and ran out once more, to fire into the stricken ship along her larboard side this time, leaving him gaping open-mouthed, unable to feature such deliberate destruction!

"On the *down*-roll, Mister Catterall! *Sink* the bitch!" he heard.

⚓

"Not bad, not bad at all," Lewrie allowed as *Proteus* wore about Sutherly after her second crushing broadside. They had blown her stern
in, shot away both rudder and transom post, then punched great holes
on the waterline, where the ever-hungry sea now sucked and surged
into her, remorselessly. The merchantman's mizen-mast had been
sheered off belowdecks, had swivelled and fallen forward into her
main-mast's rigging to drag that shot-torn assembly into ruin as well,
to drape her larboard side like a funeral shroud.

"She's afire, too, sir," Lt. Langlie pointed out, his arm extended
toward her bows, where her galley fire, still smouldering under the
steep-tubs and grills so soon after feeding her complement, had spilled
from the brick-lined pits, catching fresh fuel alight. Hot air rippled up
from below, distorted and wavering like the air over a forge. Thin
skeins of smoke jetted from the gaps in her deck planks or side scant-
lings as if bellows-driven, with now and then a wink of tiny yellow
flamelets peek-a-booing over the bulwarks.

"Saves us the trouble of stopping to light her ourselves" was the
grimly satisfied reply he got from Captain Lewrie.

"She *began* to strike her colours, Captain Lewrie," Peel accused. "I
don't see why you had to—"

"Damn you, sir!" Lewrie barked, turning on him. "*My* word is law
aboard this ship, and I'll thankee to remember it! Her flag still flew,
her captain had *not* yielded her up, and I've no time to line my purse,
with an enemy man o' war in the offing. D'ye hear me plain . . . sir?"

"I will be forced to report that," Peel retorted, stung to the quick
by such harsh, ungentlemanly language, such a sudden challenge.

"*Damn* what you report, Mister Peel!" Lewrie sneered, his hands
clasped behind his back, leaning forward from the waist, his face close
to Peel's, forcing him to take half a step backwards. "We *came* here
to inspire *terror*, Mister Peel . . . fear of us greater than any that bo-
geyman Choundas carries with him. In their navy, their privateers,
their merchantmen, alike . . . sir!"

"But . . ." Peel was weakly forced to object, taken aback by this
new, bloodthirsty aspect to a man he'd always considered competent
but too . . . flibbertigibbet. "The consequences, our repute . . ."

"Now you just contemplate the implications of that, why don't you,
Mister Peel," Lewrie continued, in a softer voice, with slyness creeping

onto his face, "while we try our metal with yon Frog frigate. Mister
Langlie," Lewrie barked, spinning away, "shape course to stand seaward of the port with the wind a touch forrud of abeam for greater
speed. I want us at close quarters with that frigate before she gets a
goodly way on. She's still bows-on to the town, maybe had anchors
down before being alerted." He lifted his glass to peer hungrily at her,
measuring speed and distance, warily over-estimating how quickly she
could cut cables and make sail, giving the French the benefit of the
doubt as to how well-prepared they would be by the time *Proteus* was
level with her. Choundas was rumoured to have come in a frigate.
Was this his, under his direct command or not, her captain and officers
had to be a cut above the usual jumped-up radicals, with skills gone
rusty for spending too long in harbour. Lewrie hoped the enemy frigate was the one based on Guadeloupe before Choundas arrived—but
he wasn't ready to wager the lives of his crew on this being the case.

"Mister Catterall, load and then secure the starboard battery," Lewrie called to his Second Officer, "then double-shot the larboard to the
muzzles with grape, langridge, star-shot, bar-shot, and chain-shot. Hop
to it, lads! We're going to skin the Monsoors alive!"

"*Vite, vite, vite!*" Choundas muttered under his breath, as if he could
will Desplan and his crew to quicker preparation. The cables had been
cut, anchors bedamned, and the bitter ends not even buoyed for later
recovery. They could always take new ones from a fearful merchantman. Courses had been freed by energetic young topmen, who had
slashed the gaskets away. Clew lines had been freed by men on deck,
and the sails let fall on their own, not eased down. Fore course and
tops'l were now laid flat aback their masts, and the jibs were fully
hoisted, then drawn by human force to starboard to get their frigate's
head down alee. The spanker over the after quarterdeck shivered as
men of the after-guard tailed on the sheets to drag it over to starboard,
as well, to force *Le Bouclier*'s stern to walk windward and twist her
more wind-abeam to work her off the town. Blocks' sheaves cried and
squeaked as her main and mizen tops'l yards crept up off the rests one
snail-like foot at a time, to Choundas's impatient eyes. The enemy
ship was hull-up, now, dashing down upon them with a bone in her
teeth, all but her main course drawing well, and that sail showing but
a single reef, so far. Was Fate merciful, Choundas thought, they might

brail it up to reduce the threat of fire from the sparks of her own gunnery, reducing her speed, giving his own frigate a chance!

He looked over the stern, down the long transom post, past the massive pintles and gudgeons and the wide, tapered slab of the rudder. Choundas felt a cold, bleak despair settle in his stomach, as if he'd gulped down a *sorbet* too quickly. Even with the rudder hard-over, the sea round its blade only barely swirled, little stronger than a spoon in a cup of coffee. A flowing tide would spin eddies greater than that!

He stood erect, shambled about to his right to lay hold of the larboard taff-rail lanthorn-post—and found a cause for sudden hope. The steeple of a church ashore was no longer pinned over the larboard cat-heads but was now roughly amidships, right over the larboard entry-port. She was moving, falling off and making way!

"*Vite, vite, sacrebleu, vite!*" he urgently whispered.

"What should we do, *m'sieur?*" the petty officer normally in command of *L'Impudente* asked of his temporary, amateur captain.

"Get ready to fight, of course," Lt. Jules Hainaut responded.

"*Mon Dieu, merde alors,*" the petty officer almost whimpered, "but with *what, m'sieur?*" He waved a hand at *L'Impudente's* open deck and low bulwarks, where nested a pitiful set of six 4-pounder pop-guns, the shot racks beside them holding a skimpy allotment of balls. There were iron stanchions set into the railings for swivel-guns, mere 1-pounders or 2-pounders, so light that a single man could heave them up from below—empty, at the moment, as bare as a whore's arse.

"With what we have, *marinier,*" Hainaut chuckled back. "Honour demands it. *Are* the swivels below? Not rusted in a heap?"

"*Oui* . . . some," the petty officer shrugged in reply.

"Shot and cartridge bags?"

"Uhm . . . *oui, aussi.* But . . ."

"Then fetch them up, at least four of them, if we indeed *have* four," Hainaut patiently ordered, "and place them two to each beam for now. I might wish all four on one side, later, depending. Load them, then man the deck-guns."

The petty officer's jaw dropped; he almost dared to roll eyes in derision—*did* roll them, as he swung an arm at the fifteen men in the crew.

"*Officeur,* uhm . . ." Hainaut more sternly said.

"Gaston, *m'sieur*," the burly man supplied.

"You have *met* my master, *Capitaine* Choundas. What do you think he would *do* with the Frenchmen who shied away from battle? How angry do you think that he *already* is? After this, he'll be looking for any one or any thing on which to work off his wrath."

"*Eu, merde!*" the petty officer gasped, paling quickly. "*Oui*, I see your point, *m'sieur* Lieutenant. To arms *mes amis*, to arms! Fetch up the swivel-guns, *vite, vite!*"

Hainaut held his amusement in check as he watched his "crewmen" scurrying to cast off the bowsings and lashings on the deck-guns, scuttling below to fetch up swivels and powder charges, gun-tools, and more shot.

L'Impudente still stood outward on starboard tack, with the wind a bit before her beam, and with the British frigate bearing down on her like Nemesis, Hainaut thought of a sudden, recalling a scrap of classic lore that Capt. Choundas had crammed into his head whether he liked it or not. His schooner would pass out to sea a good mile before the enemy's course and his could intersect, and *L'Impudente* could be well out of her starboard battery's certain range. The frigate might try her eye on him, but it would be random and poorly directed, with low odds of a hit. He would be as safe as a babe in its mother's arms.

No, it was the *appearance* of bellicosity that was needed here, he smugly told himself. Once the frigate was off his own stern, as he held this course, he would tack *L'Impudente* and come about to tail *her*.

A few pin-prick irritations up her stern, enough to be *seen* and *remembered* by others—such hopeless bravery against such *horrid* odds!—and his master *Capitaine* Choundas could no longer deny such a plucky fellow a ship of his own, could he? Even better, Lt. Hainaut fantasised, it didn't look as if today would be a good day for the doughty *Capitaine* Desplan; his dashing frigate was going to be pummeled unless she got under way a *lot* faster, and she would barely have time to settle on a course and get her people to their battle stations before the foe was on her.

Poor, poor Navy, Hainaut more-soberly contemplated; *always the butt of the joke. Not like the tales I heard, coming up, in the* Royal *French* fleet. *Not like how equal the challenge we could make, during the last war. Now . . . the* Republic *needs dashing, plucky captains to take on the Bloodies. Captains like . . . moi!*

And if his master was slain in the battle to come (or crippled even more, to the point that he could no longer function), well, what a pity, *quel dommage*. If *Le Bouclier* lost a lieutenant or two, resulting in a shuffle from the corvettes to staff her, leaving vacancies on the other warships, his chances for advancement would be just as good.

"What *is* that British toast I heard?" he muttered to himself as he manned the tiller-bar alone. "Ah! 'Here's to a bloody war, or a sickly season!' "

CHAPTER TWELVE

"P̶ot this'un, too, sir?" Lt. Langlie asked as a saucy schooner hared off to leeward below their bows, about half a mile off.

Lewrie balefully looked at the potential prey, then forrud one more time, juggling speed and time. Three minutes more, he reckoned, and *Proteus* would just about be in close range of the French frigate. His gun crews had both batteries loaded and already run out ready for firing, ready . . . prepared in their minds, as well. To dash over to the starboard side, lever, shift, and take aim at the schooner that was opening the range rapidly, then take time to swab out, charge, reload, and run out, then dash back to larboard and *just* get their breath back before engaging a real foe . . . no, it'd only unsettle them. At that moment, they were oak-steady, whilst his view through his glass showed a French crew still at sixes and sevens; all atwitter and thinking dire, fretful thoughts, he hoped.

"Don't think so, Mister Langlie," Lewrie decided. "A waste of shot and powder. Mister Larkin?" he called to his seediest midshipman.

"Aye, sor?" the little Bog-Irish crisply replied in his "Paddy" accent, lifting his right hand to knuckle his hat.

"Keep a weather-eye on yon schooner, and sing out if she comes back on the wind," Lewrie ordered.

"Aye, Oi . . . I will, sor, Sir," Larkin amended, blushing.

"Very good, Mister Larkin. Now, gentlemen, let's be about it."

Lewrie said, rubbing his hands together in anticipation. "1 think we will take a page from their book of tactics this morning, gentlemen. Mister Catterall? Your first broadside from the larboard battery will be on the *up*-roll . . . quoins out. Take her masts and rigging down, at about two cables' range. Second broadside, you will fire on the pent of the scend, double-shotted, 'twixt wind and water, and hull her from then on."

"Aye aye, sir!"

No matter how sternly a British warship was disciplined, and no matter how cool-headed her people were to act when at Quarters, during a battle between ships, the men could not help but snicker, grin, and nudge each other, were they about to serve their foes something novel, something clever and unexpected, and this time was no exception. Alan Lewrie could almost grin in expectation, too, thinking about bar-shot, chain-shot, and bags of grape-shot waiting in the hard iron barrels of his guns. A few hands took time to look back at him as he stood over them at the break of the quarterdeck, beaming with pleasure at his sly-boots knackiness. Ship's boy-servants crouched round the companionway hatches and on the ladders that led below with leather cartridge cases ready for the second broadside; gun-captains had already selected their roundest, truest 12-pounder shot—two per barrel for a second double-shotted broadside—the best from the garlands, without filed-away rust patches, the tiny dimples and slices that would have been ignored, or hidden in the rush of battle by an extra glob of blacking, but that would send them caroming off-aim when loosed.

"Brail up the main course, Mister Langlie," Lewrie said, with an upward glance. "Wind's freshening. We still 'cut a fine feather' without it." The last cast of the log had shown nigh ten knots, and steering Sou'east with the Trades fine on the larboard quarter, their frigate would still keep a goodly speed, perhaps a whole eight knots. *Proteus* was aroar with the slick bustle of her passage, her bow waves twin, creaming "mustachioes" that hissed-sang down her flanks. "*Four* cables, now, do you judge it, Mister Winwood?"

"Under four, sir," the Sailing Master responded, after a ponder and a squint or two. "Nearing three."

"Three . . . seven hundred and twenty yards, hmmm. Ready to come to Due South, Mister Langlie, when I call. Two cables is our boy."

Lewrie lifted his glass for a final look at their foe. Topmen were sliding down from aloft, her fighting-tops were still being manned, but her scurrying crew was now mostly out of sight behind or below her bulwarks, slaving away at her starboard guns, most-likely. There! He saw the frigate's gun-ports begin to hinge upward; the muzzles of her great-guns here and there started to emerge in jerks and twitches.

They aimin' high? Lewrie asked himself. *That's their usual wont, t'cripple first. Usually do it much sooner, were they ready to fight. Take our masts down, then close. But we're already closed, ain't we?*

"Two and a half, Captain," Mr. Winwood said, tenser and edgier.

"Take aim, Mister Catterall!" Lewrie barked. "Take *careful* aim. No rushing, men. Be *sure* of your shots, with nothing wasted. By God, just 'cause you wish t'hear some more loud *bangs*, this lovely mornin'! Slack in those trigger lines, now. Easy . . . !"

"*Wait* for *it!*" Lt. Catterall was wailing, sword held high, and almost on his tip-toes in expectation.

"Two, sir," the experienced Winwood adjudged, at last.

"*By* broadside . . . on the *up-roll* . . . *fire!*" Lewrie bellowed.

Over *Proteus* rolled, with her sails straining wind-full from astern, slowly and majestically, larboard side dipping then rising up, to linger for a breath or two, pent atop the gentle scend of inshore waters.

"*Fire!*" Lt. Catterall howled, slashing down dramatically to the deck, almost bowed from the waist.

"Helm up a point, Mister Langlie," Lewrie shouted in the roar as all her guns went off together. "Due South, again!"

"Aye-aye, sir!" Langlie cried back, his voice lost in the din.

The larboard horizon disappeared in a sudden cumulus of powder smoke that the wind shoved back in their faces, keeping pace with them as *Proteus* bowled onwards, but slowly thinning to reveal . . .

"Damn my eyes, just *lovely* shootin'!" Lewrie crowed eagerly by the larboard bulwark. "Choke on *that*, you snail-eatin' bastards!" he said in a chortle that didn't carry *too* far, filled with an impatient, leg-jiggly boy's elation, as if ready to titter or giggle with the joy of a Christmas Eve's anticipation.

The French frigate's upper masts and sails had been riddled and shattered. Her main top-masts over the fighting-top had been sheered away completely, hanging to windward. Her mizen tops'l had split open and the sail-less cro'jack yard sagged in two, in a downward vee. Her spanker had been shot free of its sheets and was winged out so far that Lewrie was seeing it edge-on of its leach. Ladder-like shrouds showed gaps where star-shot or chain-shot had scissored them above and below the fighting-top platforms, which had been swept clean of sharpshooters and swivel-guns. Her fore top-masts swayed forward ten degrees out of true, her mizen top-masts were slowly whip-sawing at each long roll.

"By broadside . . . *fire!*" Lt. Catterall shrieked as the frigates fell together at an angle, gun-drunk and lost in battle lust.

The French reply broadside, rushed and disorganised, was ragged. Heavy round-shot howled past in satanic moans and keens. Amid the gun-smoke, tall white feathers of spray leaped skyward as some balls struck short and caromed upwards over the deck, missing bulwarks and attacking *Proteus* in her rigging by accident, unintentionally cracking upon masts or spars, or pillow-thumping through rigidly wind-arced sails.

Even so, there were a few parrot-squawks, the quick *rrawrks!* of shot striking home " 'twixt wind and water," along with the yelps and shrieks of alarm or sudden pain and disbelief as sailors and Marines were showered with iron shards or flying splinters, some as long as a man's forearm and half as thick!

"Well, I'm damned!" Lt. Langlie cried, wiping his face, looking outward as the gun-smoke thinned once more. "Sir! 'Less she bears up abeam the wind, we'll bow-rake her!"

The French frigate had already taken a fearful drubbing at that second broadside. Great shot-holes along her line of mid-ships ports had turned several into one long, bloody gash. Below her gunn'ls and gun-deck her glossy black hull had been punctured, leaving star-shaped holes and ragged plank ends, with one smallish one right on the waterline. And, music to Lewrie's battered ears, the Nor'east Trades bore sounds of fright, suffering, and consternation as the enemy frigate's way fell off from the loss of so much sail, and her attempt to swing abeam to them by brute helm force. She could not turn quick, though, could not protect her vitals from a bow-rake!

"As you bear . . . *fire!*"

Amid squeals of agony, many tortured *rrawrks!* of rivened wood, and the pistol-pop of stays, they bowled shot down her entire length through her flimsier bow planking. Her foremast tumbled into ruin and her mizen top-masts swayed, pivoted, then plummeted down, taking the broken cro'jack yard, fighting-top, and spanker gaff with it, burying her quarterdeck in a blizzard of trash!

"Cease fire, Mister Catterall!" Lewrie shouted, going forward. "I think the Frogs've had their fill of *us* for a good long while, hey, lads? Think we've left a calling-card they'll remember next time?"

Then, more softly to Mr. Langlie, "Take us dead off the winds, sir. Seaward, and alee of the Saintes, yonder. Stand ready to wear her onto starboard tack, the wind fine on the quarter, should it be necessary. Let fall the main course and sheet home, too. We've done a good morning's work."

"We'll not stay to *take* her, sir?" Langlie just had to wonder.

"And risk them getting even a little of their own back, Mister Langlie? I think *not*. Far as they know, we didn't lose a single man, and sank or crippled three vessels in an hour. Let 'em think on that and be daunted," Lewrie said with a smug sniff. "Damme! What in the hell . . . ?"

Light shot had moaned overhead, smacking through the mizen tops'l and t'gallant.

"That schooner, sor, he's up our stern, sor!" Mr. Larkin said, so close that Lewrie almost tripped over him.

"Hands to the braces, Mister Langlie. Mister Catterall, you will man the starboard battery, once we wear about!" Lewrie snapped. "And why didn't you alert me, Mister Larkin, when I—"

"Couldn't make ye *hear* me, sor! All but tugged at yer coat, Oi did, but niver th' . . ." Larkin spluttered in sudden fear.

"Oh," Lewrie grunted, knowing how remiss he'd been. "Thankee, Mister Larkin. My pardons, but I do that sometimes. Tug away, next time, if you must. It saves our ship and our people's lives, I'll not chide you for it."

"She'll most-like duck away, cross our stern once we've altered course, sir," Mr. Winwood sourly supposed.

"Perhaps we'll get lucky and wing her, first," Lewrie replied. "Either way, we force her to cut and run. Then we'll sail away to the Nor'west and out of reach of her puny broadsides. Like she's not worth our attention." Lewrie paced aft to stand by the taff-rail and lifted his telescope, then snorted in disgust.

"Will you *look* at this?" he scoffed. "She's firing at half a mile, perhaps a tad more . . . with four-pounders, I expect," he guessed as he gauged the keen of a ball passing to larboard, well clear of any hope of striking.

"Ready to come about, sir," Langlie reported. "Larboard guns secured, and the starboard battery manned."

Lewrie watched the schooner haring up their wake, swaying back on course after yawing to open her gun-arcs for her last "broadside." Did *Proteus* come about, she'd rapidly lose speed, whilst the schooner kept lashing along, reducing the range to a quarter-mile, hopefully too quickly for that schooner captain to appreciate his danger. One good broadside from his 12-pounders *should* put the wind up him!

"Very well, Mister Langlie. New course, Nor-Nor'west, full and by. Mister Larkin, run tell Lieutenant Catterall we'll be hard on the wind, and he's to put the quoins full-in before he fires."

"Aye, sor . . . sir!" the little imp happily cried before dashing forward, glad to have escaped his captain's wrath and to be "back in his good books."

"Oh, dear," the Sailing Master muttered as they watched the wee foeman begin to swing, as *Proteus*, too, began to heel over and change course, "but the poor fellow just chose the wrong tack to take, sir."

"Let's hope we make his life a little more exciting, the next few moments, sir," Lewrie snickered.

"Stand by!" they could hear Lt. Catterall shouting faintly, half his volume stolen by the rush of the wind. "On the down-roll . . ."

"*Eu, merde!*" petty officer Gaston muttered once again, wincing into his thin coat as the British frigate's gun-ports opened.

"Fire!" Lt. Hainaut shouted urgently. "Fire now, then get on the sheets and we'll wear about . . . quickly!"

His larboard 4-pounders fired, smouldering lin-stocks put to the touch-holes of the old-fashioned guns without even an attempt to lay or aim them. Crisp, terrier-like bangs rapped out, then a sharp double bang as the swivel-guns made their contribution. Even pointing upwards at forty-five degrees, their loads of scrap-iron and pistol balls would more likely come back down like a sudden rain squall not a third of the way to the *anglais* warship—which fired back!

Moans, keens, and shrieks of deadly, hurtling metal ran up the musical scale as they neared, some passing close enough to bludgeon men half off their feet with the wind of their passing, one smashing close-aboard, not twenty new-fangled meters from the larboard side, a monster column of water leaping skyward as high as the foremast truck, to come pelting down like the rains of a tropic hurricane, wetting everything and everyone in an instant, smothering the wind from the fore-and-aft gaff sails and jibs, knocking Hainaut's elegant cocked hat off into the filthy scuppers, and drenching his best uniform and his carefully combed coif, 'til he looked, and felt, like a half-drowned wharf rat.

"We will tack!" he cried. "Hands to the sheets. Ready to come about?" Yes, they were *more* than ready, by the look of it. "Helm is . . . *alee!*" he shouted, putting his whole weight on the tiller bar.

Away *L'Impudente* danced, force back in her sails and agile again, showing her stern to the "Bloodies'" next broadside, then swinging past the eye of the wind to run just a dab South of Due East, making herself a very small, thin target . . . incidentally.

"Now, we will haul our wind and show her our starboard sides," Hainaut screeched at his shaken crew. "We will fire one last set of shots from the starboard guns, then go back on the wind. I promise." He *had* to add that; the first part of his orders had them looking outright mutinous! "Just one more, for the honour of our glorious flag, *mes amis!* To show *les anglais* we will never be daunted!" Hainaut didn't care if shot was rammed home or not; the bangs and the powder smoke would suffice for a show of defiance. For a *show*.

"Free sheets and take a strain . . . helm's up! Ease the sheets. Wait 'til the *deck's* level, for God's sake, wait . . . Now, fire! And sheet home. Helm is alee! And we are bound for home and mother!"

"What in Hell was *that* in aid of, I wonder?" Lt. Devereux, the Marine officer, asked with a wry, gawping, one-eye-cocked expression.

"Some young and cocky Monsoor, with dung for brains," Catterall chuckled. His guns were shot out, swabbed clean, flintlocks removed, and the tompions inserted into the cooling muzzles. The gun-ports had been let drop and lashed shut, and his magnificent 12-pounder Blomefeld Pattern great-guns were now firmly bowsed to the bulwarks, their trucks chocked, and train and run-out tackle neatly overhauled. A last sponge-down to remove the powder stains, and Catterall could go aft for a well-deserved glass of claret from the gun-room stores. Looking up at their Marine officer on the gangway above him, Cat-

terall imagined that Devereux was looking a tad "dry," himself, and
might even, after such a successful morning's work, dip into his personal stores and offer to share a bottle with them. Devereux had
private funds in addition to his pay, and a much more refined palate;
his wine stock was head-and-shoulders above anything to which Mrs.
Catterall's second son could ever aspire . . . not if they kept blasting
perfectly good prize vessels off the face of the ocean instead of taking
them, that is.

"Good rub-down, Sarn't Skipwith," Devereux instructed, handing
over his Pennsylvania rifle-musket. "And do tell Private Doakes he is
not to dab gun-oil on the stock, this time, hmm?"

"Sah!"

"And did you do good practice, sir?" Catterall asked.

"Rather doubt it, Mister Catterall," Devereux dismissively said.
"Our closest approach was just under three hundred yards, and even
the rifle-musket can't guarantee accuracy that far. *Did* keep 'em worried, though, I expect, to hear balls hum round their ears that far
away."

"Lord, I'm dry as dust!" Catterall ventured, hands in the small of
his back and creaking himself in a backwards arc to resettle bones.

"We'll splice the main-brace, if I've learned anything about the
Captain," Devereux promised. "Soon as everything's 'Bristol Fashion.' "

Catterall turned away for a last look-over of his charges, making a
face at the very thought of rum, and thinking that Lt. Devereux was
a stingy bastard at times. "Oh, jolly," he falsely cheered.

"Now, Mister Winwood," Lewrie said, beckoning the Sailing Master
up to the starboard mizen shrouds, "at Nor-Nor'west, should we attempt to work our way to windward below Monserrat, or should we
stand on 'til we fetch Nevis, or Saint Kitts, before tacking for Antigua?"

"I suggest we stand on, sir," Mr. Winwood said. "The Trades're
back to normal . . . so far, that is. Not above Saint Kitts, though."

"Very well. Consult your charts and make a best guess for me, as
to when and where we may safely shave Nevis. Aye, no need to put
us on a lee shore on Saint Kitts, should the Trades back Easterly."

"Aye, sir. I shall see to it."

"Mister Peel?" Lewrie beckoned again, as Winwood went down to the binnacle cabinet. "A moment of your time, if you please."

"Captain Lewrie," Peel said, tight-lipped and still truculent.

"My apologies for any Billingsgate language in the heat of the moment, Mister Peel," Lewrie casually explained, "but if we are bound to work hand-in-glove 'til God knows when, I s'pose I *do* owe you further explanation of my . . . madness," he continued, with a disarming grin.

"I quite understand you wish to take Choundas down a peg in the eyes of his compatriots, Captain Lewrie," Peel coolly allowed, stiffly formal. "I would also imagine that tweaking his nose this morning was something personal to you."

"Quite right, Mister Peel," Lewrie cheerfully confessed. "Was he watching this morning, or will he just hear of it, he'll know the name of our ship. And you have already told me that he knows I'm in command of her. Your Mister Pelham suggested that that knowledge might lure him into folly . . . since chasing me down to kill me is personal to him, too. This little piece of work should fix his attention hellish-wondrous. Right?"

"Granted, Captain Lewrie," Peel said, gravely nodding, and seeming to relent his insulted stiffness a tad.

"But what'll it do among his smuggling captains and crews, his small and weak auxiliaries . . . his privateers?" Lewrie posed, beaming with evil glee. "I deliberately destroyed that Dutch ship to make the point that, do they cross *my* hawse, there'll *be* no mercy, 'long as they work for Choundas. That rumour will get round among 'em, count on it, soon as *Proteus*, and Lewrie, and Choundas are linked. Other warships might play by the accepted rules, but they'd best write their wills and sleep with one eye open as long as I'm at sea.

"And *any* British frigate that hauls up within their sight just *might* be *Proteus*, and Lewrie, hey?"

"Yes," Peel said after a long frown. "I *do* see your point, sir."

"So do you accept my apology, Mister Peel?" Lewrie asked.

"I do, Captain Lewrie," Peel replied with a smile, at last, and his hand out for shaking. "Do you accept mine as well. For being my own secretive self when it came to the private signals. Did we wait to use them, they would have been out of date in another two months in any event, so . . . for not going direct to Antigua, as Mister Pelham wished, too, and disputing your decision to come here."

"I will endeavour to explain myself more plainly in future," Lewrie vowed, shaking Peel's hand. "But for now, I must carry on, sir, so . . ." Lewrie said, turning away to head for the hammock nettings overlooking the gun-deck and gangways, ready to address the crew.

"Oh, Captain Lewrie," Peel called after him. "Something else I s'pose I must apologise for. Damme, but the thinking you put into your raid, it showed such unexpected, uhm . . . sagacity and . . ."

"What, Mister Peel?" Lewrie hooted. "You're sorry you thought all I could do was plod round a quarterdeck and cry 'Luff,' or 'Fetch out yer whores'?"

"Something like that, sir," Peel answered, with a faint wince to be so clearly understood. Not that he didn't think that Captain Lewrie could ever be *consistently* clever, but . . . he did have his moments!

"Accepted, sir," Lewrie chuckled with a faint bow and a grand doff of his hat. Then he was busy with the Surgeon, Mr. Hodson, whom he allowed to mount the quarterdeck to make his report, and expressing his wonder that not a single sailor had been killed, and only six men had been hurt, with the further good news that only one of the wounded hands was considered a sick-berth patient.

Sure enough, once HMS *Proteus* had made a goodly offing and had sailed the shore of Guadeloupe under the horizon, with only the twin peaks of Basse-Terre still showing, the brightly painted rum keg was fetched up from below with all due ceremony and martial music from the Marine drummers and fifers, to welcoming cheers from her thirsty, successful man o' warsmen.

CHAPTER THIRTEEN

L e Bouclier was anchored once more, to her second bower and her lesser kedge, this time with her un-harmed larboard side facing to seaward, with little *L'Impudente* tied up along her ravaged starboard side.

Saws screeched and rasped, metal hammers and wooden mauls thudded and drummed, and old wood cried as it was torn away with crow-levers for replacement with fresh planking brought up from the bosun's stores. Blocks shrilled as dis-mounted cannon were lowered back onto carriages set back on their trucks, as shattered carriages, stripped of any useful fittings, were hoisted over-side for scrapping or firewood ashore; as replacement yards and top-masts were swayed aloft, up through the lubber's holes in the savaged fighting-tops to be jiggled, then bound into place by weary topmen. The starboard gangway was heaped with the thick rolls of sails too singed or shot-torn to salvage, Fresh rolls of spare sails, huge hillocks of salvageable canvas, and bolts of new cloth smothered the forward gun-deck where *Le Voilier*, the Sailmaker and his crew, cut, snipped, basted, and sewed to patch damaged sails or start completely new replacements, installing grommets, reef-lines, and bolt-ropes inside the edging seams.

Smaller bundles, too much resembling the hopeful rolls of sailcloth, also littered the starboard gangway, and about the thick foot of the main-mast trunk in a thigh-high heap, stacked like cordwood to free deck space for the working-parties.

Those were the corpses.

The dead had been hastily shrouded, without the benefit of washing first, so their coverings were not the *écru* of new canvas, nor the darker, weather-stained parchment dun of used. They were splotched or even brightly splashed with drying gore, the bile and ordure of gutted men. Slain in mid-morning, they still awaited transport ashore to the cemetery outside the port, and it was now nearly sunset. The horrible day had been very hot and still. They already stank.

Le Bouclier's survivors avoided the stacks if they could, walking on eggs as far away as possible, but too tired, too dulled by fear and shock by then to hold their noses at the mounting reek, studiously ignoring them, most of the time. If they could.

It was only when a dead man somewhere in the sloping mass round the main-mast, swelled with rapid tropic putrefaction, vented the foul gases in eerie groans or sighs that the *matelots* would take notice and leap away in alarm, crossing themselves in dread that some poor devil under the pile still lived and was trying to worm out from under that crushing weight, calling for aid from his shipmates, with whom he had laughed and japed just a few hours before.

And sailors of any nation were superstitious. They could quite easily believe that somewhere among those bundled, shattered husks the confused, terrified spirits of the slain were beginning to stir, to walk and wail as night drew nigh to torment the living until properly buried ashore.

The stench of the dead lay over *Le Bouclier* like a harbour fog, and the Trade wind, fading with the heat of the day, could not disperse it leeward. Belowdecks, the air was even closer and hotter, even more foetid despite the rigging of wind-scoops, and the liberal use of vinegar and wash-water to scour the decks. A miasma from wounded sailors stashed below continually welled up like hot smoke from a chimney-pot, as if driven by their wails, moans, and frantic, fretful mumblings, as they weighed their odds of living, or faced the certain prospect of dying. Half-drunk on rum or cheap brandy used to dull their pains or allay the shock of amputation, their desperate prayers and weepings seemed to create the wind that wafted the stink of their wounds aloft through companionways, scuttles, and limber holes, ever renewable, no matter what brief relief a gust of the Trades might bestow.

Screams and half-shrieked pleas soared upwards, too, as the surgeon and his mates, civilian surgeons from the town of Basse-Terre, and even an exalted physician or two plied their gruesome trade. Bone-saws rasped now and then when amputations were necessary. They were necessary quite often; they were quicker than any attempt to draw out shards of wood splinters, bits of cloth, shot-scraps or shat-tered bone chips, leaving time to deal with those who needed careful attention. Supposedly, a healthy young man could recover, could live without use of a foot, a hand, an arm, or a leg.

Guillaume Choundas kept station well up to windward, as best he was able, clumsily perched atop the breech of a quarterdeck gun as doleful reports came to him. His monstrous countenance was set in a grim and stoic, brooding death-mask, broken only by a snarling decision or abrupt jerk of his head as the messengers stood near, shivering in dread of him. His cane was leaned on the gun-carriage, so he could use his remaining hand and a silk handkerchief to whisk the swarms of flies, and the stinks, briefly away.

The flies, large and pustulently bottle-green, had found them even before the frigate had begun to limp shoreward, two whole miles offshore; moments after the thrice-damned British frigate had jauntily sailed out of arcs, or reach, of their guns. The flies' numbers had only increased once they had anchored within a cable of the quays.

Though their numbers were equal to a Biblical Plague, Choundas noted that they no longer darted about quite as frantically as before. He imagined they were now sated, merely buzzing about to boast another of their . . . victories. Another of their mortal feasts!

". . . able to get one boat down before the fire got so hot that we had to abandon her, *mynheer*," grizzled Dutch captain Haljewin was explaining, a dirty, rumpled handkerchief to his own nose.

"Lost your ship, lost the munitions and rations for our General Rigaud and his Mulatto Republic," Choundas rasped, not even both-ering to glance at the man. "Better you *pretended* to strike, and fetched-to."

"The British devil gave us no chance, *mynheer*," Haljewin protested. "He crossed my stern and shattered us, crushed our side in with a second broadside, then sailed on without a second glance, as if they'd

known whose cargo it was! Had they fired a warning shot and ordered
me to strike, I would have, believe me. It would have given you half
an hour to come to my rescue, while they were fetching-to and boarding us, but . . ."

"You *knew* we were here, Citizen Haljewin," Choundas said, looking up at last, his one eye ablaze in accusation. "You saluted us as
you cleared the port, when we came in *plain* sight, rounding Le Vieux
Fort! Had you been the slightest bit clever, scared to save your . . ."

"He gave me no *time*, I tell you, *mynheer!*" Haljewin interrupted.
"Perhaps he recognised you as a frigate, and would not . . ."

"I'll take no back-talk from *you* . . . Citizen!" Choundas bawled.
"Citizen . . . not *mynheer*," he insisted, sneering over the word. "You
utter, spineless failure. You idiot! Get out of my sight!"

"I did save your sailors off *L'Abeille* . . . Citizen," Haljewin pointed
out, though gulping with sudden dread.

"But not the fool in charge of her, who should pay with his head
for her loss," Choundas barked.

"In the beginning, she did fly French flags, she *looked* so . . ." the
Dutch merchant master all but babbled in deepening dread. "I was
fooled, as were the shore watchers, I gather. She displayed the proper
identity signals. I suspect there is a British spy on Guadeloupe who
told them everything. If that is the case, Citizen *Kaptein*, I do not see
how I was so *much* at fault. I've lost my ship and half my stalwart
lads, my livelihood . . . and I saved at least a dozen of your poor
sailors. One would hope that counts for something. One would hope
that some recompense is made, in recog——"

"Go to the Devil!" Choundas roared, fumbling for his cane as an
impromptu weapon. "You knew the risks and you took them, eagerly,
for *gain*, you wheedling . . . *shop-keeper!* Get . . . off . . . this . . . ship
. . . and . . . off . . . Guadeloupe . . . Island, before I kill you myself!"
he thundered, so irate that he was almost breathless, spacing out his
words more in need than emphasis.

The Dutchman backed away, eyes saucered in stark terror, breaking
into a quick scamper for the entry-port as soon as he was past the
reach of Choundas's cane. A naval officer coughed into his fist, and
scraped his feet, having waited with his news until the dread harangue
had ended.

"What?" Choundas snapped. "You are?"

"*Pardon à moi, m'sieur Le Capitaine*," the officer, with an arm in a

148   Dewey Lambdin

sling, and his coat draped over his shoulders. "I am Lieutenant Mercier, Second Officer? Lieutenant Houdon, our First Officer, wishes to report that the shot-holes on the waterline are now plugged, with no need for entering the graving dock, m'sieur. If she is careened at the beach, permanent replacement planking can be done quickly. Pointe-à-Pitre's storehouses can supply us with new top-masts. Enough rope of sufficient thickness and quality to replace stays, and the running rigging *may* be a difficulty, unless . . ."

"We will take it from some merchantman," Choundas gravelled as he looked aloft in the fading light to assay the gaps in the maze of rigging and masts. "Why isn't Lieutenant Houdon reporting to me?"

"The First Officer, m'sieur, is aft in the great-cabins, with *Capitaine* Desplan," Mercier explained. "The *Capitaine* goes away from us," he said, using the squeamish euphemism for "dying."

Choundas had despaired. For a brief minute or two, he thought that *Le Bouclier* had won through, after all, and had gotten organised for a single-ship battle . . . 'til that first, devastating broadside in her masts and rigging that was so un-English an opening move. Draped in wreckage, gun-ports masked and artillery smothered, making it too dangerous a risk of fire to reply, he and *Capitaine* Desplan could do nothing but stand on the quarterdeck and grieve, wincing at the coming broadsides, which had killed or wounded nearly an hundred of her crew. The sad grimace on Desplan's honest, Celtic-Breton face . . . ! A moment later, and the mizen top-mast and shattered cro'jack yard crashed down on him, mashing his midsection and hips, breaking both legs in several places. Manful, without a cry, Desplan had been freed, borne aft by loyal, weeping *matelots* who truly admired him, uttering faint gasps, flinching, and going "ah-ah-ah!" at each searing jounce. He had known, even as the masts came down, that the gallant Desplan would be dead by sundown. It had been a fellow Breton's "sight."

Perhaps Desplan had felt one, himself, for he had not tried to move out of the way, but had just gazed upwards as if transfixed before being enveloped and crushed. Had *he* had a sudden foreboding that his race was run? Choundas idly drew the brass foot of his cane over the irregularities in the splintered and warped deck. Omens and portents. Signs and messages from elder Celtic gods . . . in whom Choundas still believed. For had not the ominous raven cawed and alit, on his *right*, just minutes before that *salaud* Lewrie had all but blown his arm away with an impossible single shot, three times the best musket range, the last time they had crossed swords in the Genoese hills?

Lewrie! The *Proteus* frigate! It was inconceivable that Lewrie, that swaggering, irreverent, and bawdy brute, could be that clever, that he had appeared by mere coincidence! Surely, he had been aided, *aimed* by his betters, his masters. The Dutchman, Haljewin's, feeble excuses and attempt to point the finger somewhere else just *might* have a grain of truth to them. Choundas dismissed Lt. Mercier's presence as utterly as he ignored the droning flies, in speculation of betrayal and treason done by someone close to Governor-General Hugues, or close to himself.

It would have to be someone on Guadeloupe with access to secret signal books, the new private signals that had come out from France in this very ship! Someone who could get access to fishing boats so they could be smuggled to the lurking British, or pass them to a spy already in place who could make the arrangements. Someone who had seen a copy of *Kaptein* Haljewin's cargo manifests of all they sent to bolster General Rigaud's forces, the largesse to buy his allegiance once Citizen Hédouville got ashore on Saint Domingue and contacted Rigaud with the Directory's proposal to make him the new ruler . . . in the name of France.

The British . . . such a perfidious race, thinking themselves so *very* clever and subtle, Choundas thought, sneering. Had they intended to flaunt Lewrie in his face to divert him from his plans, as if he was so brainless, so driven by a need for revenge that he'd fly after him, mewl in mad circles like a kitten chasing a streamer of wool yarn?

Well, he'd see about *that*, the fools! He shifted his good leg under him and slid off the gun breech, bracing himself erect with his cane.

"*Maître?*" he heard Lt. Hainaut say by his side. Lt. Mercier had departed, perhaps minutes before after suffering his inattention. "I thought you could use some refreshment," he added, offering a shiny pewter mug, and an arm on which to lean, but Choundas brushed him off, to make his own way to the break of the quarterdeck nettings, creaky in his joints from long stillness, and long-ago maiming.

Clump-shuffle-tick . . . clump-shuffle-tick, 'til he could lean upon the railings and discard his cane, with the ever-solicitous Hainaut at his elbow the whole way.

"Watered wine, *m'sieur*. Quite cool," Hainaut tempted.

Choundas turned his head to study him for a moment. There was a subtle difference to Hainaut's voice, to his demeanour; not quite so much smarmy deference as he usually displayed, which deference always secretly amused Choundas, to see his protégé toady so eagerly, yet be so ambitious and scheming, and imagine that he disguised it. Now he sounded . . . smug. Pleased with himself, of a certainty, but self-confident as well. Daring to be his *own* man, not Choundas's, was he?

"*Merci*, Jules," Choundas allowed, reaching out for the pewter mug, now that his hand was free, and took a long gulp or two.

"All those poor men . . . never had a chance, *m'sieur*," Hainaut mourned, removing his hat (rather the worse for wear, Choundas noted) and shaking his head sadly, as if honouring the dead and wounded.

"A waste of good material, Jules," Choundas growled. "But we will be free of them by dawn. Had we met *les anglais* far out at sea we would be cursed with them for days. After all, good Catholic widows cannot re-marry until *some* bit of their dead husbands is shipped for burial in France," Choundas said with a dismissive sing-song. "In the dirt, with the worms! Following the old customs and superstitions we would have been forced to bury them in the gravel ballast belowdecks until we came into port. *Peu!* What ancient . . . idiocy!" he scoffed.

"*Eu, merde*," Hainaut grimaced in seeming agreement.

"The 'Bloodies' shove their dead out a gun-port without even a kind word," Choundas casually informed him between appreciated sips of his wine. "Those too mangled to live, they bash on the head with gun-tools or mallets, *then* shove them over, unconcious, to drown. That is British . . . mercy, *hein?*"

"We must avenge them, *m'sieur*," Hainaut vowed with some heat to his voice. "We must strike back. We cannot let this pass unanswered."

Choundas eyed him more closely. Hainaut's zeal for vengeance sounded suspiciously like *true* conviction, not one of his usual poses. What *had* gotten into the lad? Choundas had to wonder.

"All in good time, Jules," Choundas promised with a sly smile. "But I shall not be diverted by such a silly, sentimental passion."

"Even if it was that *salaud*, Lewrie, *m'sieur?* I saw him plain, close enough to read his ship's name, close enough to recognise him at once,' Hainaut declared, half-questioning, but mostly boasting in case his master had forgotten how bravely he had shown.

Choundas uttered an evil little laugh, turning his gaze on his aide, the sort of appraisal that would shrivel the scrotums of braver men. Choundas had seen *L'Impudente*'s attack. Jules had never gotten quite as close as *that*, but . . . was there anything praiseworthy to the whole disastrous day, his terrier-nip charges had *seemed* to drive away the 'Bloodies,' in the eyes of the town's inhabitants, the uninformed.

"You did well today, Jules," Choundas decided to say.

"*Merci, m'sieur*," Hainaut responded, turning so hellishly stern and heroically "modest" that Choundas had to bite down on the lining of his cheek not to laugh in his face at such posturing.

"I must give this frigate a new captain, Jules," Choundas began.

"*M'sieur?*" Hainaut asked, as if it were grievous news to him and indeed a mortal pity, hope and greed rising despite his best efforts.

"Griot, I think," Choundas continued, between sips of his wine. "Lieutenant Houdon to take Griot's *corvette*. He could not serve under a new man, when he is senior enough for a ship of his own. He makes a good impression, *n'est-ce pas?* That fellow Mercier, I think his name is, promoted to First Officer under Griot. He kept a cool head on his shoulders during the worst of our drubbing."

And me? Hainaut furiously thought; *And what for me?*

"Griot obviously will wish to bring one of his lieutenants with him, so he has *one* familiar face in his coterie," Choundas speculated.

"Quite understandable," Hainaut allowed, though squirming with expectation.

"Leaving a Lieutenant's berth open aboard *Le Gascon*," Choundas temptingly decided. "Does anyone able spring to mind, Jules?"

"Well . . ." Hainaut began to say, averse to just blurting out to one and all his aspirations. "If he wasn't such a failure, there *is* that Récamier fellow, *m'sieur*, but . . . heh, heh."

"No, he's commanded a ship, after all. To be made Third Officer under another . . . that is not the use I eventually intend for him. After he has had enough time to ponder his 'sins,' " Choundas quibbled.

"Well, if we're *really* desperate, *m'sieur*, I could, ah . . . that is to say, might a spell of sea-duty continue my nautical education as an officer?" Hainaut finally flummoxed out. "I can already hand, reef, and steer, stand a watch, as *Capitaine* Desplan allowed me as we sailed to Guadeloupe, and . . ."

"You do merit *some* reward, Jules, *oui*," Choundas grumbled. "As junior-most officer, well . . . hmmm. I must think on that. Come. Let us board your ratty little schooner. Take me back to Pointe-à-Pitre. You can show me what a tarry young man you are, *hein?*"

"But of course, *m'sieur,*" Hainaut said with an enthusiasm that he did not feel, almost despising the sly bastard for taunting him so cruelly. But with such a cruel ogre, what could he really expect?

"And once in my own bed, after a good supper, I will sleep on it, Jules, I promise," Choundas vowed.

"You will not visit *Capitaine* Desplan, before he goes away from us, *m'sieur?*" Hainaut asked without thinking.

"I think not, Hainaut," Choundas said, more frostily, as if he had been criticised. "The good *Capitaine* fell as a true Breton sailor and warrior, without complaint or regret. To paw over him and weep a flood of loss is *womanly.* I will make a proper oration at his grave. Hurry, now, Jules. It has been a long, long day, and I'm weary."

"Aye, *m'sieur,*" Hainaut replied, walking close to Choundas for a prop, should he need it, as they went to the entry-port.

And after serving you so well, so long, Hainaut mutinously told himself; *you wouldn't even come to say goodbye to me if I fell? Your tool . . . disposable tool, and nothing more. Just give me even a tiny ship, and I'll make my own way, from here on.*

BOOK THREE

"Rebus semper pudor absit in artis!"

"Away with scruple in adversity!"
— *ARGONAUTICA*, BOOK V, 324
VALERIUS FLACCUS

CHAPTER FOURTEEN

*M*ister Peel," Capt. Lewrie said, alighting from the spavined roan "prad" which he had ridden up to, and back from, Admiralty House on its lofty, airy hilltop overlooking English Harbour. He could not quite disguise a smug expression. He had ridden, whilst Mr. Peel had been forced to take "Shank's Ponies" for his call upon the Governor-General, that is, to walk; and a long, upward walk it had been. Peel was plucking his coat and waist-coat away from his sopping shirt, and mopping his streaming face as Lewrie sprang down by the boat landing.

"Captain Lewrie," Peel finally managed to reply from a parched mouth. "Damme, you'd think there'd be a *pinch* of wind, at the least."

"Lee-side harbour, Mister Peel," Lewrie informally informed him. "Absolutely vital in the islands. The East'rd hills block most of it, and Shirley Heights polishes it off, most days."

"At least we had wind where we anchored," Peel said, fanning his hat and peering longingly to the outer roads. "Not much, but some, and some'd do for me, 'bout now."

"We'll have you under the quarterdeck awnings, soakin' yer feet in a pan of cool water, 'fore you can say 'Jack Ketch,'" Lewrie vowed. "So. How was your reception with your, uhm . . . co-conspirators in the Governor-General's office?"

"Oh, not *too* horrid, considering, sir," Peel wryly said, with a grimace, "given our use of French private signals, which, I gather, are thought too valuable to use at *all*, unless we spotted Jesus and a band of angels descending for the Second Coming. Shrieks of consternation, 'viewing with alarm' . . . all the proper forms of disapproval of which officialdom is possible. But for the fact that Mister Pelham holds superior position to them, and *might* have authorised me to employ them, at my discretion . . . a view from which I did *not* disabuse them. Might I enquire what sort of warm reception you received, sir? And that is not a pun upon today's weather." Peel grinned, regaining his breath and his equanimity after such a torrid "stroll."

"*Ginger* beer, sirs! Ginger beer!" a street vendor cried, as he wheeled a hand-cart down the stone quay near the boat landing. "Best fer tang, best fer th' bilious! *Cool* ginger beer! Who'll buy . . . ?"

"The local admiral was of much the same mind, Mister Peel. Got cobbed rather well," Lewrie confessed. "Your confederates in the Governor-General's mansion just *did* release them to him. *He* just distributed them to his captains, and now they're all for nought, so there'll be no gullible prizes brought in by guile. Hence, no admiral's *share*. Damme, I do hope he hasn't spent his expected windfall already! And we 'poached' on his private 'game park' without declaring ourselves first. *And*, damn our eyes, we didn't fetch him in even a rowboat to show for our raid. He could care less was Guillaume Choundas the Anti-Christ himself, *he's* never heard of him, so . . . you may imagine all the rest. If we do have some form of 'Admiralty Orders,' then *sail* independent, instanter! Just get out of his harbour, and his sight."

"Could we?" Peel asked. "Sail instanter? Do we need anything?"

"Firewood and water, the usual plaint," Lewrie told him with a shrug. "You?"

"Not really," Peel admitted. "There were some rather intriguin' hints that I garnered . . . 'twixt the howls, and such. Hints which we just might wish to follow up," he suggested, tapping his noggin with a conspiratorial air, and that maddening smirk of private information.

"Best we add livestock to our requests, then," Lewrie supposed. "It sounds as if we'll be cruising longer than our fresh meat holds out. Or poking our bows into waters where we couldn't buy a goat."

"Ginger beer, sir? Ginger beer fer yer cabin stores, Cap'um?" the vendor tempted. "Keeps longer'n ship's water, h'it do, an' won't go flat an' tasteless like small-beer."

"Sailor, were you, my man?" Peel enquired, taking in the ragged "ticken" striped slop-trousers the man wore, those from a much earlier issue, each leg as wide as the waistband and ending below his knees.

"Aye, sir. Th' ol' *Ariadne*, in th' last war," the man proudly said, "afore she woz hulked. Right yonder, she were, fer years an'—"

"Scrapped her, did they?" Lewrie asked, peering closely at the grizzled fellow, trying to place him, or to determine that his claims were false. Where poor old *Ariadne* had lain, stripped down to a gant-line as a receiving and stores ship, perhaps later a sheer hulk rigged to pull lower masts like bad teeth, there was now an equally sad-looking, bluff-bowed 74-gun Third Rate.

" 'Er bottom woz 'bout rotted out, Cap'um. Beached her, yonder, an' burned 'er for 'er fittings an' 'er nails," the man said. "In '89 it woz. Come out in '80, she did. I were main-mast cap'm, then. She got laid up, I went aboard th' ol' *Jamaica*, but I lost me ratin', then got ruptured an' discharged, just 'fore the war ended, in '82. Stayed out here h'ever since. Here, sir . . . I *know* ye, Cap'um?"

"Edgemon!" Lewrie exclaimed, suddenly dredging the man's name up from the distant past. "You taught me handin' and reefin'!"

"Mister . . . Ashburn, sir?" The man beamed.

"No. Lewrie," he told him, a tad abashed to be mistaken for a *much* tarrier, more promising, and *handsomer* midshipman of those times.

"Oh Lord, Mister Lewrie, aye!" Edgemon cried. " 'Twas you tried t'catch 'at poor topman wot got pushed off the main tops'l yard, wot was 'is name?"

"Gibbs," Lewrie supplied. "Mister Rolston pushed him . . ."

"Aye, sir, 'at li'l bastard!" Edgemon snarled, the memory still sour. "Beggin' yer pardon, Cap'um. 'Spect he's a Cap'um hisself, by now, an' God 'elp pore sailormen."

"No, he's dead," Lewrie happily related. "Died at the Nore, a common seaman and mutineer, under a new name."

"Hung, sir? 'Is sort's *bound* fer th' gibbet," Edgemon beamed.

"No, I killed him," Lewrie flatly said.

"Have a free piggin o' ginger beer on me then, sir!"

"I'll have a whole barricoe, sir," Lewrie declared of a sudden. "What's your charge for five gallons?"

"Lor', sir! Uhm . . . eight shillin's, sorry t'say."

"Make it ten gallons, and here's a guinea," Lewrie said, going for his purse to produce an actual gold coin, not the usual scrip that had even made its way to the Caribbean as "war replacement" for specie.

"Will that buy a piggin for me, Mister Peel, and my boat crew?"

"Cover most 'andsome, Cap'um Lewrie!" Edgemon swore. "Thankee right kindly. Alluz *knew* you'd make a right-tarry awf'cer, sir."

Oh, don't trowel it on! Lewrie thought, though smiling all the while; *the way I remember it, you despaired I'd ever master running bowlines!*

"I'll take, oh . . . one five-gallon barricoe, myself," Mr. Peel stated. "That'd be eight, did you say?"

"Ten, sir," Edgemon slyly said, tipping his former "favourite" midshipman a sly wink. Peel rolled his eyes, but paid as well.

"Mister Peel's treat, lads," Lewrie lied to his boat-crew. "He thought you looked half-strangled, sittin' out in the sun so long." As extra piggins were fetched and filled from the hand-cart, the three requisite barricoes were laid between the thwarts of Lewrie's gig.

"Do I owe *more?*" Peel whispered to Lewrie as they stood in what little shade there was, apart from the boat-crew. "And why say it was done in my name, Captain Lewrie?"

"You're not *Navy,* Mister Peel," Lewrie said in an equally soft snicker. "There's only so much jollity 'twixt a captain and his hands that is allowed, else he appears t'be playin' favourites, or goes too slack and 'Popularity Dick.' Then he erodes his own authority. Done in your name, though, and nought o' mine . . . d'ye see? What a *civilian* does, ignorant o' Navy ways, don't signify, for you ain't in the line of command, Mister Peel."

"You cannot seem to *care* for their comfort or welfare, sir?"

"Care, aye, Mister Peel. But cosset or *pamper?* Never."

"You'll recompense me my two shillings, then, Captain Lewrie?" Peel snickered. " 'Twas in a good cause, after all," he pointed out.

"Should o' bid quicker, Mister Peel," Lewrie chuckled back with sly glee. "You can't keep up with risin' prices, that's your own lookout. Ahh! That *was* refreshing! Let's get under way. Coming, sir?"

"Aye . . . coming," Peel said, snorting at his "diddlement."

"Coming . . . so is Christmas," Lewrie said with a laugh.

Peel was, indeed, sitting in the shade of the quarterdeck awning with his bare feet stuck into a wide-ish pan of cool seawater, sleeves rolled to the elbow and shirt opened to mid-chest, when Captain Lewrie came on deck, again, at the first challenging shout from the midshipman of the harbour watch, the unfortunate Mr. Burns. A rowing boat was at the starboard entry-port, and Peel sat down his mug of ginger beer.

"Boat ahoy!" Burns croaked, his pubescent voice cracking. "Who goes there?"

"Hoy, the ship!" an equally teenaged voice cried back. "Barge to the United States Armed Ship *Thomas Sumter*, with an invitation for your captain and officers!"

"Mister Burns?" Lewrie snapped from behind the gawky scarecrow, making him almost leap out of his shoes in sudden alarm.

"Boat coming alongside, sir," Burns stammered. "From the, uhm . . . that Jonathon ship lying over yonder, with an invitation, sir."

"Let 'em lay alongside and come up, Mister Burns," Lewrie decided. "Since they're almost hooked onto the main-chains *already!*"

"Uhm, aye, sir!" Burns parroted, gulping in dread before going to the entry-port to converse with the barge. "Mister Pendarves, man side-party for a Lieutenant! Turn out the duty watch."

"And we'll discuss your nodding off right after, Mister Burns," Lewrie said, glowering. "You, Mister Pendarves the Bosun, his strong right arm, and the 'gunner's daughter,' for being so remiss."

"Aye aye, sir," Burns miserably said, his lower lip quivering.

"Hmm . . . quite the uniform, sir," Peel took note with a smirk, as he came to Lewrie's side. "All the 'go,' is it? Of your own devising, I trust?"

"It was!" Lewrie snapped back, trying to ignore him.

His experiment with light cotton uniform coats instead of hard-finished wool in the tropics had been an utter failure. The dark blue coats had dyed waist-coats, shirts, breeches' tops, and anything else they brushed against, including upholstered great-cabin furniture; and the gold-lace pocket trimmings and ornate cuff detailings, even detachable gilt epaulets, had turned a suspiciously *bright* greenish tinge at the edges. Now, with most of the offending dye leached from them (and the major damage done to his wardrobe) Lewrie was left with a brace of coats of a disturbing light blue, which could still bleed faint tints if caught on deck in a driving rain. It was use them or admit to one and all his serious error, so Lewrie perversely clung to them, though their use was severely limited to clear-weather days *far* from shore or those rare days at anchor when he had no shore calls to make, and expected none in return.

"And you paid your tailor, in *full*, I s'pose, before uhm . . . ?" Peel whispered in mocking amusement.

"Yess!" Lewrie hissed back, disgruntled.

"Oh, dear," Peel commiserated.

Whatever surly rebuke Lewrie had in mind was squelched by the arrival of an officer at the lip of the entry-port, saluted by a small side-party requisite for the welcome of a Lieutenant, whichever navy claimed him . . . excluding the French, of course.

Lewrie had thought he had seen the uniforms of the new American Navy when he had been dined aboard USS *Hancock*, but this fellow looked like a relic of their defunct Continental Navy, which Lewrie could but briefly recall from one brisk encounter in his midshipman days in '82.

White stockings, dark blue breeches, dark blue coat with bright red turnback lapels and cuffs, a red waist-coat with gilt edging; and doffing a very old-fashioned tricorne hat to the saluting sailors and Marines as the bosun's calls shrilled and twittered.

"Permission t'come aboard, sirs," the strange officer called.

"Permission granted," Lewrie allowed with a "captainly" grunt.

"Allow me t'name myself t'you, sir," the man went on, sweeping his hat low in a greeting bow, though with a confused look on his phyz. "Lieutenant Ranald Seabright, of the United States Armed Ship *Thomas Sumter*. I bring an invitation from Captain Douglas Mc-Gilliveray to your captain, and such officers as he may wish t'bring, to dine aboard the *Sumter* this ev'nin', sir. Might I enquire if your captain is now aboard?"

"One of the Charleston McGilliverays, is your captain?" Lewrie asked, stepping forward with a surprised grin.

"He is, indeed, sir," Lt. Seabright declared, taken aback, perhaps, by the sky-blue apparition before him. "And you are, sir?"

"Alan Lewrie, captain of his Britannic Majesty's frigate, the *Proteus*, sir," Lewrie told him, doffing his own hat and making a bow.

"Oh! D'lighted t'make your acquaintance, Captain Lewrie, sir," Seabright said, in what Lewrie recognised as a Low Country Carolinas accent; Seabright's "sir" was more akin to "suh."

Damme, Lewrie thought, still eying the old-fashioned uniform in

some suspicion as to whether the United States Navy actually *had* one
... or did they let their officers wear whatever was handy; *Last time,
that Captain Kershaw and most of his officers were from the Carolinas.
Are there* any *Nor'east Yankees at sea?*

Lt. Seabright, though, was eying his own uniform coat with just as
much dubious suspicion, as if of half a mind that Lewrie was "having
him on," and the nape of his neck was actually turning red.

"He really is, ye know," Peel said, tongue-in-cheek.

"Once made the acquaintance of a Mister McGilliveray," Lewrie
said, "one of your merchant adventurers among the Indians to the
West. Might your captain be kin, d'ye think, Mister Seabright?"

"Certain of it, sir!" Seabright replied, more at ease suddenly. "That's
exactly what my captain's people did, before the late war."

"Then I shall accept Captain McGilliveray's kind invitation in good
expectation of resuming, as well as making, the acquaintance. Um,
how many of my officers, Mister Seabright?" Lewrie asked, still trying
to dredge up the Christian name of the McGilliveray he'd met in
Spanish Florida towards the end of the Revolution; he thought it was
something Scottish, clannish ... Highlander-ish? Unpronounceable?

"Yourself, plus three others, sir," Seabright answered. "Whomever
you choose. The captain will have *one* midshipman at-table, sir. Kin,"
he explained, with a shrug, "So ..."

"Ah! Very well, sir," Lewrie said, asking the time to be expected.
"Two Lieutenants, and one younker to keep yours company at the
foot of the table, then. 'Til then, Mister Seabright, and thankee."

"Was that wise, Captain Lewrie?" Mr. Peel said after departure
honours had been paid, and the barge was being stroked back over to
a sleek frigate-like three-master about half a mile farther up the roads.
"The Yankee Doodles ... recall what Mister Pelham told you, sir.
They are more competitors than allies. Other than our signals book,
we do not share information with them. It might be taken as, uhm ...
by our superiors, that is ..."

"Oh, rot, Mister Peel," Lewrie breezed off. "If anything, it'll prove
t'be a harmless diversion. We get a chance to see if the smaller American warships are built as stout and novel as their new forty-four
gunned frigates. I told you 'bout them, didn't I? You told *me* they've
established anchorages in Prince Rupert Bay on Dominica, and in
South Friar's Bay on Saint Kitts. Much closer to Guadeloupe, mind,

and what *they* know of these waters, and French activities, might be fresher than our information. We could learn more from them than they from us."

"If played right, 1 s'pose, sir," Peel dubiously said.

"And we, without actually *saying* that we're here on a specific mission," Lewrie slyly hinted, "discover to them who and what Choundas is. Now, do *they* feel like making the effort to stop his business as the best way to protect their own trade, we'd have more eyes and ears at sea helping us run him to ground, and all unwitting, too! They're a spankin' *new* navy, just itchin' t'beat the Be-Jesus out of the Frogs. T'gain fame and honour, t'lay the foundation for a permanent fleet not subject to the whims o' their Congress's parsimony. Damme, Mister Peel, they'd best whip *somebody* . . . soon!"

"So eager for a victory or two that they'd go after Choundas in our stead, Captain Lewrie?" Peel snickered as he saw the sense of this piddling little revelation to their supper hosts.

"Damme, they divert him from his plans, or do they *really* corner him and beat the stuffing from him, I shan't cry," Lewrie vowed. "However the deed's done, hey?"

"And there is always the possibility that, *should* they meet up with Choundas, and *lose* to his greater cleverness and skill," Mister Peel said with a quizzical brow up, "well, perhaps their Congress and voters decide having a national navy, instead of a gaggle of revenue cutters, and thirteen *state* militias at sea, is a bad idea. Hence, *no* competition in the Caribbean, and their trade protection put into *our* good hands, Captain Lewrie. Hmm . . . int'restin'.'"

"Which'd please your Mister Pelham, and his masters in London, right down to the ground," Lewrie realised, beaming at just how devious Peel could be. "Sending him home wearin' the laurel crown, gettin' him off my back . . . and you, promoted and feted, or whatever it is they do in the Foreign Office to 'good and faithful servants'?"

"They mostly came from privateersmen, smugglers, and pirates," Peel seemed to agree, ". . . our Americans."

"Set a thief t'catch a thief, you're saying?" Lewrie laughed.

"Something like that, Captain Lewrie."

"And it'll be amusing, too, Mister Peel," Lewrie brightly told him, already shuffling through his mental "muster book" for people to take with him that evening. "The McGilliveray I met was half-Scot and half-Muskogee Indian . . . whom the Jonathons call Creeks. The longer we spent up the Apalachicola River in Spanish Florida, the more native he went, 'til he got so guttural I couldn't understand half of what he said . . . and made me feel for my scalp ev'ry morning. Is his kinsman even close to the same bare-arsed, buckskin sort, you'll be able t'dine out on the tale the next five years!"

"You'll wig and powder, for safety's sake, or wear your own hair then, Captain Lewrie?" Peel proposed, chuckling.

"Oh, they hardly *ever* scalp their supper guests, Mister Peel," Lewrie cheerfully said. " 'Less they're hellish liquored up. Let's see . . . yes, Lieutenant Adair will go with me. Show 'em a real Scot for a change, not their rusticated variety. He'll most-like bowl 'em over, might even cite whole pages of 'guid auld Robbie Burns' at 'em. Don't know of him, Mister Peel? The Scot poet and songster? Oh, well. And Midshipman Grace, to pair with their 'younker.' Grace came up from the Nore fisheries not two years ago, common as anything, so he'll appeal to their egalitarian ideals."

"Whether they really practice them or not," Peel stuck in.

"Catterall? No, *he'd* scalp somebody, does he get into his cups. And there's *sure* t'be American corn-whisky. Third guest, hmm. What about you, Mister Peel? Might turn out t'be a rare treat. If not, I could take Lieutenant Langlie. He *sings* well, when liquored."

Peel and corn-whisky, though; walking on his knees and howling. *Talk about amusing, indeed,* Lewrie maliciously thought.

CHAPTER FIFTEEN

*T*he USS *Thomas Sumter* was not a true frigate, though she looked like one at first glance; long, fairly low in the bulwarks, flush-deck at the forecastle and quarterdeck, but "waisted" between her foremast and main in conventional style, with upper gangways just wide enough for sail-handling, and service of the swivel-guns that would mount on the stanchions set atop her bulwarks.

Though armed with twenty-two 12-pounders on the gun-deck, and equipped with two 6-pounder chase-guns on her forecastle and six more on her quarterdeck—making her a 30-gunner and a "jack-ass frigate" in any nation's navy—she was officially rated as an Armed Ship, in temporary service. Most of the former colonies, now states, had raised subscription funds literally by the bushel-baskets with which they meant to build men o' war, but . . . in the meantime, some of the funds were used to purchase likely merchant ships for arming and conversion until the real ones slid off the ways and got to sea.

Though *Sumter* was all trig and "Bristol Fashion," as clean and fresh-smelling as a spanking-new ship, meticulously maintained by her crew, and with her yards squared to a mathematical perfection, Lewrie wasn't particularly impressed by her, in his professional appraisal.

Sumter had very little tumble-home above her gun-deck to reduce her hull's topweight, having been designed for maximum space in cargo holds and orlop, so he suspected that she might not be as stiff as he might have liked in a blow, since, like all American-built ships he'd seen, he thought her over-sparred, and would likely carry too much canvas aloft, making her tender. Her bulwarks and hull scant-lings weren't as thick as a proper warship's, either, and from what short time they had had on an abbreviated tour before going aft, he saw that her beams, timbers, futtocks, and knees had been sawn to lighter civilian specifications, and spaced a few more vulnerable inches apart on their centres. She'd not withstand a long, drawn-out drubbing 'twixt wind and water, did she cross hawse with a French Fifth Rate frigate, perhaps not even a well-manned and gunned Sixth Rate *corvette* armed with sixteen or twenty cannon.

Those drawbacks didn't seem to faze Captain McGilliveray, though; he was immoderately proud of her, boasting of what a swift sailer she was, how capable of carrying "all plain sail" even in blustery weather . . . though with all squares'ls reduced one reef.

Lewrie had brought Lt. Adair, Midshipman Grace, and had finally chosen Peel instead of his First Officer for the third guest; the hope of seeing Peel "three sheets to the wind" on corn-whisky was just too tempting . . . and, was any intelligence to be gleaned, Peel was trained for such subtle delving and discovery, after all.

"Thought we'd begin with claret, Captain Lewrie," *Sumter*'s captain announced, opening his wine-cabinet. "Claret, not rum, appears to be the lifeblood of the gallant Royal Navy."

"And on that head, Captain McGilliveray," Lewrie responded, "I took the liberty of fetching off a half-dozen of claret from my lazarette stores as a gift to you."

"You are quite kind, sir . . . I am most grateful for your thoughtful present," McGilliveray, a well-knit fellow in his late thirties, said with a wolfishly pleased look. He was not Red Indian dark, but seamanly dark, and sported an abundantly thick thatch of ginger-blond hair, too. Nothing *like* what Lewrie had expected. "Given our present set-to with the French, you can imagine that claret is neither readily available in the States, nor anyone's first choice of potation, in public at least. Though what folk *wish* with their suppers is another matter, entirely. I fear our smugglers aren't as capable as yours, Captain Lewrie," he japed with a sly twinkle.

"Yours just have farther to go, Captain McGilliveray," Lewrie responded in kind, accepting a glass, "whereas our bold English smug-glers have but to cross 'the Narrow Sea.' I expect the Channel Isles'd *float*, for all the casks and bottles hidden in every cave and cove. As for me, though, a friend of mine . . . just recently removed to the Carolinas by the way . . . introduced me to American whisky. With such near to hand, 'tis a wonder anyone in the United States would care whether claret is available, at any price."

"Then in return for *your* kindness, sir, allow me to give a man who truly appreciates good corn 'squeezings' a barricoe of our 'portable grain'!" McGilliveray exclaimed. "After all the troubles we have had regardin' whisky, lately, I'd admire to introduce you to the best upland, Piedmont distillation."

"Highly gratified, sir, thankee," Lewrie truthfully told him.

" 'Tis mellow, amber, and actually *aged*, much like a good brandy, in oak wine casks," McGilliveray enthused. "None of your gin-clear or week-old 'pop-skull,' either. Some think it *rivals* the best brandy."

"Trouble with whisky, sir?" Lewrie asked, once glasses had been shoved into every hand, and McGilliveray had waved them into seats.

And Capt. McGilliveray took a gleeful five minutes to describe a recent "Whisky Rebellion" by back-country settlers who had objected quite vehemently to a mere penny-per-gallon tax on whisky, possibly the major trade item in the back-country, and in most instances the only medium of exchange, a replacement *money*, the coin-strapped United States had. It had taken Gen. George Washington and a call-up of the various state militias to form a field army to put it down; though once the "Riot Act, " in essence, was read, the rebellion had melted away.

"Excuse me for asking, Captain McGilliveray," Peel said, "but I was under the impression that your earlier Articles of Confederation, and your Constitution, prohibited your federal government from interfering with the sovereign states, especially with armed force."

"Aye, they do," McGilliveray, replied, frowning, "and it was indeed troublin'. Given how much Britons distrust a large standin' army, you can certainly understand *our* misgivin's . . . though it *had* to be 'scotched,' else our fragile new economy'd collapse. You ask for a payment in coin back home, taxes in coin, and God knows how folk'd be able t'pay you. Alexander Hamilton and his new national bank, well . . . mind you, Mister Hamilton's as patriotic as anyone, but it does sound so Frenchified and coin-hungry a proposition, that a great many folk hope it'll never see the light o' day."

Lewrie had taken McGilliveray's exposition on the rebellion in

mostly one ear, taking note of his surroundings, not asked for more
than the occasional "do tell" and "egad" to show interest.

Where the USS *Hancock*'s Capt. Kershaw's great-cabins had been
the opulent quarters of a wealthy man, those of a rich and titled man
back in England, McGilliveray's were spartan in the extreme. Lewrie
knew he was related to a rich mercantile family, and obviously had
been educated at considerable expense; his speech alone told him that.
The decks were covered with nailed-down and painted canvas, the
colour a drabbish solid brown, not the black-and-white parquet chequer of a British man o' war. The interior panels were off-white, and
not a single painting graced them. His desk in his day-cabin, his chairs
and such, were crudely made, dull-finished, and almost graceless. Sailcloth curtains could be drawn to cover the transom sash-windows in
the stern, but the drapes seemed an after-thought, and made from
parchment-tan *used* sail scraps. Lewrie took a peek at the waiting
dining table; dull platters and place settings of dark pewter awaited
them, with but two four-hole candelabras and a lone pitcher of bright-
polished pewter in the centre. The glasses were nondescript, befogged
by long use and many scrubbings by clumsy servants, in seawater
most-like.

Whale-oil lanthorns hung overhead—mica panels set in lead-dark
pewter or old tin, and not a single glint of brass to be seen anywhere
in the great-cabins, not a single family portrait, nothing personal to
Sumter's captain. Lewrie was put in mind of the poorest village pubs
and coaching inns he had ever seen. *Was* McGilliveray a poor relation,
or as abstemious as a prelate in a *poor* parish, eking out his dignity on
the widows' occasional charity and ten scrimpy pounds per annum?

Damme, what do they pay *Yankee captains?* he had to ask himself.

He did set a good table, though, with boiled shrimp, done in a Low
Country spice-broth, roasted chickens, *odd* yellow-orange potatoes that
he called *yams* (and were quite sweet with a slather of his fresh butter),
beef-steaks from a fresh-killed bullock, and miles fatter and tenderer
than anything he could have purchased from the British dockyard,
with lashings of cornmeal bread, island chick-peas with diced onions,
and a tangy mid-meal salad. Wine flowed, as did whisky, and Lewrie
noted that Lt. Seabright, Capt. McGilliveray, his First Officer a Lt.
Claiborne, and a fresh-faced midshipman, introduced to him as one
Desmond McGilliveray, freely imbibed the whisky like mother's milk!

Politics and religion were, of course, banned topics, and anything related to "business" was out, too, so supper conversation was limited. Americans and Britons shared little in common, the last fifteen years since the end of the Revolution, but a common language, and even that was beginning to diverge. They did not share music and song as they evolved, nor dramas, nor even London or Court gossip.

Needless to say, the aforementioned yams came in for a lot of praise and discussion, which led to longings for fresh-killed venison, comparisons of "furrin" dishes they'd come across in their voyages, or the more exotic social customs witnessed, so long as they had nothing to do with prurient or bawdy talk, accompanied by winks and nudges.

Food, it seemed, was safest, with farming practices coming in a strong second, and Caribbean cuisine third. Lewrie held forth for the Chinese or Hindoo cooking and seasonings, which led to questions about his adventures in the Far East 'tween the wars.

"A little covert work, Captain McGilliveray," Lewrie told him, with a wink, " 'bout the time your first merchant ships were putting in at Canton. Many of ours, and more than a few of yours, were disappearing. More than could be blamed on local pirates. Admiralty sent out a strong Third Rate disguised as a 'country ship,' not part of the East India Company, and sure t'be a prime target. Turned out t'be a French plot, hand-in-glove with Mindanao pirates, to build an alliance that'd capture everyone's trade but theirs, the next time war came. Well, we put paid to 'em, in the end. Couldn't blurt out that the French had a disguised squadron out there, any more than we could reveal our own . . . 'twas a hard three years, all in all, but it came right, at last."

And God, but 'twas priceless the startled, uneasy look on Mr. Peel's face as he sketched out the nub of the tale! That mission, any of its sort, was supposed to be held forever "under the rose"!

Wait for this'un, then, Lewrie mulishly thought as Peel pleaded with his eyes for silence and no *more* details, concluding with a harsh glare of warning.

"In point of fact, the Frenchman who led their activities there is now here in the Caribbean, on Guadeloupe," Lewrie told them, with a secretive hunching forward, as if sharing the unsharable. "His name is Guillaume Choundas, and I'm told he directs their privateers and minor warships. Brutally ugly fellow," Lewrie said, describing Choundas's current appearance. "You run across him, you would do your nation the greatest service by eliminating him. He's the cleverest brute ever I've come across. Most-like sent out to counter your navy's presence here."

"Don't you wish to finish him yourself, Captain Lewrie?" young Midshipman McGilliveray asked, his eyes alight at the prospects. Evidently, the U.S. Navy was not quite as tolerant of outspoken "gentlemen in training," for his captain (uncle?) glowered him to abashed silence, and the teen reddened and ducked his head.

"I'd give my right arm, young sir," Lewrie declared. "And save the world a great deal of future grief. Though I very much doubt we'll ever heave in sight of one another. Just so long as somebody does. I will spot the victor a case of champagne, do I hear the glad news. My word, what a coup that'd be for your new navy, what?"

That went down well; every American at the table got a wolfish, speculative expression at that suggestion. Promotion, glory, and honour for themselves, their new nation, and navy; a feat which would ensure a permanent U.S. Navy, never again to be laid up or sold off, once their "emergency measures" were no longer necessary.

Lewrie took a peek cross the table to Peel, who was thin-lipped and flint-eyed at how much Lewrie had revealed, at how blatantly he had tossed the bait in their direction. Their eyes met, and Peel's mouth quirked a touch, though he did incline his head in mute, and grudging, agreement. Perhaps he would have brought Choundas's name up much more subtly, but . . . it was done, and no *real* harm had resulted. Yet.

"And you, Mister Peel?" Lt. Claiborne, *Sumter*'s First Officer, enquired. "You look like a travellin' man, so weathered, an' all. Are you Royal Navy, too? I'd expect you have a favourite cuisine as well."

"Uhm, I am . . ." Peel began, flummoxing in search of a *bona fide*, of a sudden, ". . . Spain, Portugal, and the Mediterranean region, mostly. I represent Coutts' Bank in London, so I do get about somewhat."

"Old family friend of my wife's British relations, sir," Lewrie lied, covering for him. "I bank with Coutts', so when James wrote he was being sent out to search for suitable acreage for a bank's client, I offered him passage to Antigua from Kingston. Safer passage than he could expect aboard a civilian packet. My wife, by the by, originally came from the Cape Fear country in North Carolina. Upriver, near Cross Creek and Campbelltown . . . the Scots' settlements. We first met during the last war, in Wilmington."

Why, that was right up the coast! Why, that almost made her a

Scot herself, and had he ever heard the tale of Flora MacDonald, mistress of Bonnie Prince Charlie, who'd landed at Wilmington and married a local, who'd raised a Tory Highland regiment . . . unfortunately defeated at Widow Moore's Creek bridge, just outside Wilmington, but . . . !

A Chiswick, was she, why Captain McGilliveray had known of them, had met a Sewallis Chiswick before "the unpleasantness" . . . !

"My late father-in-law, sir, and the namesake of my eldest son!" Lewrie happily exclaimed. "I served with Caroline's brothers, Burgess and Governour Chiswick, quite incidentally really, at Yorktown. Rifle regiment. One of *ours*, actually, but . . ."

"Why, I do b'lieve I was introduced to them, too, must've been in '74 or '75, just before . . ." Capt. McGilliveray gleefully said. He was a Carolinian, from a distinctive region of the United States, one thinly populated compared to the northern states. And he was a Scot, a Celt, and vitally enthralled, as all "Southerners" were, by family lineages, what Caroline had once said was a parlour game more popular than Blind-Man's Buff or cards, what she'd termed "Who's Your People?"

"Just lads they were then," Capt. McGilliveray recalled with a smile, "But likely lookin'. Dash it, I even think I remember a young girl, quite the sweet miss, with 'em. Blond hair, and the merriest eyes . . . ?"

"That surely was my Caroline, sir," Lewrie agreed.

"So all the Chiswicks are in England now?" McGilliveray asked.

"No, sir. Just her immediate family. One branch remained, and still farm in the Cape Fear. Some Chiswicks, and most of her former kin, the McDaniels, who supported independence," Lewrie had to say.

"Ah, we lost so many good friends an' neighbours," McGilliveray said, sighing. "When there was no need for 'em t'cut an' run. We'd of put all the bitterness b'hind us by now."

Not if you burned each other out and murdered your own cousins, Lewrie sourly thought, careful to keep a neutral expression, as he remembered how Caroline and her family had come as refugees to Wilmington in rags and tears of betrayal.

"Now, as I recall Mister Seabright tellin' me once he returned from bearin' my invitation, Captain Lewrie," McGilliveray went on, in a playful mood, "did you not tell him that you had met a McGilliveray some time or other?"

"Forget his Christian name, sorry t'say," Lewrie replied, "but there *was* a young man name of McGilliveray with whom I served for a few weeks, in '82, just after I gained my commission. He had been London-educated . . . came out from England with an older fellow who wished to try and influence the Muskogee Indians. Your pardons, Captain, but as I recall, this particular McGilliveray or some of his kin were in the 'over-mountain' trade with the Indian tribes, and he was of . . . partial Indian blood," Lewrie stated with a hapless *moue* of chagrin, unsure of how tales of White-Indian unions went down with touchy Americans from the South, and with Capt. McGilliveray in particular. Had his kinsman been a black sheep, a "Remittance Man," or a stain on their escutcheon? Was Indian blood as shameful as a White-Negro blend seemed to be?

"We tried to get the Muskogee and Seminolee to side with us, to take on the Spanish," Lewrie further said with another apologetic shrug. "S'pose that made him a Tory, to you all. From Charleston, he said."

And let's not tell 'em the plan was t'turn the Indians loose on Rebel settlers, and drive 'em into the sea! Lewrie thought; *Devil take the hindmost, and the scalps.*

"My uncle Robert's son, my cousin Desmond," Capt. McGilliveray said primly, almost sadly, all joy of comparing heritage quite dashed. "Worst thing the fam'ly ever did, sendin' some of us to England t'make Cambridge scholars. Turned Desmond's head round, sorry t'say."

"My abject pardons for broaching the subject, sir!" Lewrie said, much abashed. "Though I'm told that even your great Benjamin Franklin and his son took opposing tacks during the Revolution. I did not—"

"Oh, 'tis long done with, Captain Lewrie," McGilliveray allowed, "and Desmond's been dead and gone, these past twelve years." He tried to placate, but only came off grumpier, more uneasy, than anything else. "Half the families in America had a Tory-Rebel altercation, if you look close. Once the war was over, though, Desmond did come home and we reconciled our diff'rences. My brothers and I inherited the city firm and the sea trade, whilst Desmond managed the hide and fur trade among the Indians. Here, sir! You actually went among the Muskogee when he did, or merely—"

"Aye, Captain McGilliveray," Lewrie replied, just about to preen a bit more and tell them another tale of derring-do, and proper modesty bedamned. "Escorted him inshore, then up the Apalachicola River in our ship's boats, then overland to a Muskogee town, the name escapes me, by a large lake. Me, him, a company of fusiliers, and a Foreign Office—"

"You knew my *father*, sir?" Midshipman McGilliveray blurted from the foot of the table, startling them all to an uneasy silence.

Lewrie turned to look at him. The lad was gape-mouthed in astonishment and sudden pleasure, the "stain" on the McGilliveray escutcheon best left unsaid or not. Lewrie suspected that the poor lad had never been told very much about his "half-breed" sire, who had served against his own kin during the Revolution, to boot, despite his uncle's declaration that they'd reconciled and put the rift behind them.

"Indeed I did, young sir," Lewrie told him. "And a formidable fellow he was, too. Brave, alert, and clever . . . skilled in the lore of the forest, *and* the nicest manners of the drawing room. At home in a *chickee* or a mansion. A bold horseman, a skilled hunter . . ."

The simple use of a long-forgotten Indian word for "hut" seemed to please the midshipman no end, for he beamed wider, expectantly, as if starved for information long denied him.

"Of the White Turtle Clan, I recall," Lewrie further reminisced. "Or was it the Wind Clan, on his mother's side? Muskogee royalty, as it were, in any event. He stood high in their councils, with their . . . uhm, *mikkos* and their . . . *talwas*! Their ministers and chiefs, as grand as peer in the House of Lords," Lewrie told him, the terms springing to the forefront of his memory after all those years. "At his urging I ended up *anhissi*, myself, toward the end . . ."

"Made 'of their fire,' " young McGilliveray exclaimed with growing excitement, "to my grandmother's *huti*. A grand honour, is it not, uncle? Captain, sorry." Young Desmond reddened.

"It was, indeed, Mister McGilliveray," his uncle gravely said.

"And . . . and were you there, then, Captain Lewrie?" Midshipman McGilliveray hesitantly pressed, his curiosity getting the better of him, and to the great astonishment of Midshipman Grace seated beside him, who had never *heard* the like back in staid old England. "Then you must have met my mother. They were married, grandfather Robbie always told me, on that trip. You must have *seen* her!"

"Ah . . . ?" Lewrie hedged, trying not to gawp. The boy's father, he sourly recalled, had been the *hugest* sort of prig, and he doubted that Cambridge had had a thing to do with it. Desmond McGilliveray,

as he knew him, had ranted like a Baptist hedge-priest against forni-
cation 'twixt the English and the Indians, forever lecturing and scold-
ing the live-long day regarding "sensible" Muskogee customs and how
stupid and "heathenish" Whites, and Lewrie in particular, were!
Frankly, Lewrie had come to quite heartily despise him! Don't even
look at an Indian woman, especially when she was in her "courses";
don't even piss in a stream above them! Lewrie couldn't recall Desmond McGilliveray even *smiling* at one of them. He'd taken no wife,
as long as Lewrie had been ashore and inland with him. Perhaps *after*
they'd sailed off, that frail little dandy-prat from the Foreign Office
dead and all their plans gone for nought, even after thinking they had
a settled agreement that the Muskogee would back England in the war.

*Only one marriage I recall, and that was mine . . . at the point of the
knife!* Lewrie thought, working his mouth in silent, resentful, reverie;
'Twas Desmond made me do it, and thought it hilarious!

"My mother was a visiting Cherokee princess," young McGilliveray
stated with a stubborn, piss-me-in-the-eye pride, as if daring anyone
to demean his antecedents; probably from long practice. "Her name
in Cherokee meant Soft Rabbit, Grandfather Robbie said my father
was dumbstruck in his tracks by her, from the very first, and . . ."

Soft Rabbit, God-DAMN! Lewrie quietly screeched, almost knocking his wineglass over; *He ain't that stiff-neck's boy . . . he's MINE!
SHIT!*

His mouth dropped open of its own volition; his eyes blared as wide
as a new-saddled colt's, as he took note of the lad's eyes. Grey-blue
eyes, just like his own. And what had his father Sir Hugo smirked
after calling upon Theoni Connor and *her* new-born bastard, right after
the Nore Mutiny? "He's got your *eyes*, Alan, me son," the old rake-
hell had cooed; followed by a gleeful cackle!

His eyes. Soft Rabbit's glossy and thick, raven-black hair; but with
a fairer Englishman's complexion that he'd *never* have gotten from a
union 'twixt Soft Rabbit and a half-blood, even were McGilliveray as
fair as a Finn! A leaner face, not rounded; a fine nose, not hawkish.

"I knew her," Lewrie confessed. "*Met* her," he quickly amended.

Damme, didn't I just! he frantically thought, recalling all the sweet,
stolen hours when they went at it like fevered stoats, like . . . newly-
weds! And the only reason he and Soft Rabbit had been made to "leap
the sword" was because she was war booty, a *slave* taken by a Muskogee war party up near the Tanasi River, far to the north. A girl

slave of the haughty Wind Clan *couldn't* birth a bastard, and holding a rantipoling "outsider" responsible was amusing to them! The poor, deluded lad, Lewrie thought.

"What was she like, sir?" young Midshipman McGilliveray begged.

"Oh, wondrous handsome!" Lewrie truthfully said. "Pretty as a picture. Not so very tall, d'ye know, but as slim and graceful as any doe deer. Sorry, but they didn't wed whilst I was at their town. And I never conversed with her. Gad, imagine lettin' an outsider, English sailor such as me, in such exalted company, what?

"Point of fact, the last time I saw your father was when he and his warriors escorted us back to our boats, then downriver to the sea. The Spanish had gotten wind of our presence, and they and the Apalachee attacked us before we started unloading the trade goods and arms we'd promised. It was neck-or-nothing there, for a bit, 'til your father rallied his warriors and ran them off. All I was left to show for it was a bayonet in the thigh, and a tale t'tell. Early spring of '83, it was."

"And he called you *imathla lubotskulgi*," Captain McGilliveray contributed of a sudden, drawing Lewrie's attention to the top of the table. "In Creek, that's 'little warrior.' Desmond told me that," he declared, seeming to gawp in wonder over such a coincidence happening in regards to his long-dead relative. "All these years, and both gone to their Maker, of the smallpox. I'd quite forgotten, but . . . well, I am dashed." The other supper guests smiled, but he didn't.

Though McGilliveray didn't *sound* "gawpish"; quite the opposite, in point of fact, as he squeamishly, uneasily looked away, eyes almost panicked and averted, "harumphing" to reclaim his proper demeanour.

He knows! Lewrie thought, cringing, fighting manfully to keep a calm exterior, himself, and *not* turn and look at Midshipman McGilliveray; *Desmond* must *have told him who really fathered the lad, he looks so English, he'd've had to. Indians annul bad marriages at the Green Corn ceremonies . . . Soft Rabbit must've said ours didn't take when I didn't come back for her, and McGilliveray took her on.* Said *he'd see to her, and didn't he just . . . the bastard.*

"Well, gentlemen," Capt. McGilliveray said, balling up his napkin and laying it aside. "Let us have the port, or the whisky, fetched out, and honour our distinguished guests with a hearty toast to the King of England. Charge your glasses, if you will?"

Lewrie again chose whisky; he was badly in need of it.

At a nod, Midshipman McGilliveray at the foot of the table rose and proposed the toast to King George III, with all the fulsome titles including "Defender of the Faith, of the Church of England"; to which Midshipman Grace responded with a shorter toast to the President of the United States—then the *serious* toasting and imbibing began.

CHAPTER SIXTEEN

"*T*hank God for a quiet day in port," Lewrie muttered to himself as he struggled out of his coat sleeves, with his long-suffering man-servant Aspinall trying to help, trying to keep up with his captain's slow, staggering circle of the day-cabin. "Wouldn't trust me with the charge of a row-boat, t'morrow."

"You circle, *I* pull yer sleeve, sir, that's th' way," Aspinall meekly suggested. "Mind yer kitty . . ."

Rrrowwr! Toulon bickered, fleeing the imminent danger from his "beloved" master's clumping feet, wisely taking his tail and paws out of reach in an offended scurry under the settee.

"Who won, Mister Peel?" Lewrie asked, rather loudly. Mr. Peel, temporarily stashed *somewhat* upright against the deal-and-canvas par-tition to his cabin, didn't answer. He was too busy contemplating his shoes, arms lankly dangling, just about ready to drool. "Them or us?"

"Uhm? Sir?" Peel finally responded, looking up blearily. "Up, the cavalry! Huzzah! Forward, the King's Own Heavy Horse!"

"Why, the damn fool's drunk as a lord!" Lewrie chortled, as he kicked a constricting shoe toward the dining-coach. He stopped cir-cling long enough for Aspinall to start undoing the buttons of his waist-coat; items which were too "scientific" for him, at the moment.

"Aye, sir . . . so 'e is," Aspinall agreed, smothering a giggle.

"Aspinall . . ." Lewrie said, peering at him as if imparting some eternal but urgent verity, "the Yankee Doodles're a *hopeless*, drunken lot. It'll do for 'em, in the end."

"I 'spect so, sir," Aspinall said, peeling the waist-coat off, setting Lewrie to circling, again. Aspinall threw a helpless look at Cox'n Andrews, who was doing for Mr. Peel and his coat and things.

"Damme, I've lost a perfectly good shoe!" Lewrie complained.

" 'Tis here someplace, sir . . . honest," Aspinall told him. "Do slip t'other off, and I'll mate 'em up. Now fer yer stock an' shirt, sir, and I'll fetch yer dressin' gown. Lean on this, sir, will ye?"

Lewrie kicked the second off; this one skittered underneath the settee, causing Toulon to yowl once more and scuttle off for someplace safer, where people didn't *shoot* things at him.

"Dry, dry, dry . . ." Lewrie carped, noting (rather squiffily in point of fact) that he'd been leant against his wine-cabinet. He felt in need of liquid refreshment, but the flimsy latch appeared too elaborate a safeguard for his fingers, too.

"Ginger beer, sah," Cox'n Andrews suggested, plumping Mr. Peel into a chair so he could remove his shoes. "Good fo' settlin' a riled stomach. I'll fetch some from yo' lazarette."

"Capital!" Lewrie crowed, swaying. "We *have* any?"

"Ten gallon, sir, fetched aboard this mornin'," Aspinall said, coming back to lumber Lewrie into a chair, as well.

"Poor Kershaw . . . the clown!" Lewrie commented, tittering over what he'd heard aboard the *Sumter*, once the dinner party had gotten so soaked that gossip had flowed as freely as the liquors.

Capt. Kershaw of the *Hancock* frigate had made a total muck of his new command, he'd been told. Lewrie had *thought* she carried too much artillery, and he was right. She'd been caught in a blow windward of Dominica, and with too much end-weight fore and aft had bucked and reared, had hobby-horsed and rolled so precipitously, that her upper masts and spars had nearly carried away, and her lower masts had been strained almost to breaking.

Capt. McGilliveray had intimated (rather slurringly in-his-cups-gleeful) that Kershaw had refused to lower top-masts 'til far too late. Then, without telling anyone at Prince Rupert Bay, he'd sailed off for Havana to make repairs, despite their Secretary of the Navy, Stoddert's, strict caution to avoid entering such a pestilential harbour! Within a week, a fifth of Kershaw's crew had gone down with Yellow Jack. Once repaired, Capt. Kershaw had taken *Hancock* back to sea, though not back to his assigned cruising ground. No, he'd taken her all the way *home*, cutting his tour in the Caribbean far too short. And, to make matters even worse, whilst on-passage up the Chesapeake to moor *Hancock* in the pratique, or quarantine, anchorage below Baltimore, had stranded her on a shoal above York River, which grounding had finally sprung her indifferently repaired foremast!

The last stroke had come when the Secretary of the Navy, Mister Benjamin Stoddert, on an inspection trip to Baltimore's dock facilities and new naval construction, had gone aboard her once she had cleared pratique and had come into Baltimore. Irked that a whole vital month of usefulness had been lost whilst quarantined (the result of ignoring his orders regarding Havana!) Stoddert had discovered Capt. Kershaw's . . . "quirks."

McGilliveray and his officers had jeeringly pointed out how sybaritic and luxurious Kershaw's cabins had been furnished, as grandiose as an Ottoman Pasha's harem, and in complete disregard of the plainer usages of "spare and simple" American virtue . . . and how Kershaw's own ideas of a fashionable naval uniform (bought from that grandee's purse for himself and his officers once they'd called at Kingston, Jamaica!) was too "Frenchified," as Lewrie had judged them when first he'd seen them.

The unfortunate Kershaw was too well connected in both Senate and House of Representatives, and too bloody rich, to sack. Stoddert could, however, "reward" him with command of a proposed two-decker 74 to be built in New York (some day when pigs could fly, perhaps) sending Kershaw to the chilly, Spartan-souled, "thou shalt not" North, and relieving him (with all due respect and ceremony) with another officer. Kershaw had been welcome to take along those of his officers who were his favourites, which "kind consideration" most-like pulled up several more cack-handed "weeds" by the roots as well.

Well, no wonder Lewrie had been confused by the plainness he'd found aboard *Sumter*. Soddenly, he supposed he'd have to strip his own great-cabins of half his furnishings, did he return the favour and dine USS *Sumter's* officers aboard . . . that, or be taken for an indolent Sybarite!

Lewrie would have put more thought into that, but he was interrupted by the harsh noise of a chair being dragged cross his blackand-white painted canvas deck covering. Mr. Peel—evidently not able to walk, but still of a mind to gab—was hauling up to him by fits and starts, hands clasped on the chair arms attempting Hindoo mystic levitation, bump by hopping bump, whilst employing his heels as oars to drag forward by main force.

"Americans're quite upset, Lewrie," Peel slurringly said, though trying to over-enunciate. He had one eye open, and was obviously having some trouble focussing that'un.

"And who wouldn't be, I ask you," Lewrie replied, without a clue as to what it was that Peel wished to maunder about.

"Kershaw . . . South Carolinian . . . one of *them*. Bad form, bein' relieved, even f'r cause," Peel tried to explain. "Massachu-mmm . . . a 'Down East' Yankee replacin' 'im *hic*. Useful . . . that." *Belch!*

"Sss-sectional bitterness-ss," Lewrie replied, so liking the sound of it that he tilted his head and hissed like a serpent for a few more moments. "Dear God, but we're foxed." Numb lips . . . hmmm!

"And who wouldn't be, I ask you," Peel heartily agreed, as their ginger beer came. "Hellish brew, corn-whisky . . . *hic!* Hellish stuff! Can't *see* how . . . Jonathons stay upright . . . past dinner. *Hic!* Worse than . . . the plague o' gin, back home. Blue Ruin."

"Tasty . . . *Belch!* . . . though," Lewrie commented.

"Oh, ahrr!" Mr. Peel vigourously said, nodding.

"So. We learn anything t'night?" Lewrie thought to enquire.

"Oh, bags, sir!" Peel enthusiastically claimed. He then paused, though, open-mouthed and cock-headed, his silence broken by a few more hiccoughs, and the odd eructation. "It'll come t'me . . ."

"Spanish Bitters, sah," Cox'n Andrews suggested, presenting them with a smallish, glass-stoppered vial, and a plate of sliced lemons, on which he liberally sprinkled the vial's contents. "Mistah Durant, sah, he say bitters an' lemons be dah grand specific fer 'hiccin's.' Settle yer bile-ish humours good as gingah beer, t'boot. Bite down, Cap'm."

"Whyever'd we come here, I wonder . . . God damn my eyes!" Lewrie grumbled as he gnawed on a quarter of lemon, then quickly blared his eyes and grimaced at the taste and smell. "*Turd* water'd be . . ." *Belch!*

Quickly followed by Mr. Peel's similar sentiment after he'd bit down on his quarter-lemon. He sucked in great gulps of air and drained his mug of ginger beer to erase the foul taste.

"Deep breath an' hold her fo' a full minute, Mistah Peel, sah," Andrews solicitously instructed, "an' yah 'hiccin's' be gone."

"Gack!" Peel replied, cheeks bulging and a hand pressed to his mouth, and the good eye floundering about for the welcome sight of any receptacle in which to "cast his accounts."

Christ, don't puke on my deck chequer, Lewrie sourly thought as he held his own breath and watched; *you've already ruined it, enough!* He ran out of wind slightly before Peel, and began to gasp, his lungs and chest gulping air like a wash-deck pump sucked spillage.

"Lord God," Peel said with a miserable groan, after a last, and stentorian and *prolonged* belch. "Think I've been purged!"

"Bettah, though, sah?" Andrews enquired.

"Yes . . . matter o' fact, I am, thankee. You were sayin'?"

"Huh? Oh. What did we learn," Lewrie reiterated. "And why'd we come to Antigua?"

"Why, we came here to introduce ourselves to the powers that be, Captain Lewrie," Peel told him, head drooping as if suddenly spent by his "dosing" with bitters. "Learn how rife are the Frog privateers . . . sightings of French men o' war . . . oh! And where Yankee merchant ships are trading. *That's* what *Sumter's* people told me! South o' here, for the most part. Where you find one, you find the other."

"Sharks an' pilot fish," Lewrie seemed to agree.

"But *some* go into Jacmel," Peel added, finally looking up; and looking as bedraggled as Death's Head On A Mop-Stick. "Didn't *mean* to reveal that, but . . . *in* whisky, *veritas,* what?"

"Ah!" Lewrie exclaimed, as if grasping an Eternal Verity or Solid Geometry. "Never mind, then. But, Mister Peel, that means that we must be two ships. Cover Jacmel, up north, or cruise far down along the Leewards, to Aruba and Spanish New Granada. Kill Choundas and his captains with one hand . . . blockade Rigaud with t'other."

To demonstrate, he held up first the left hand, then the right, and wiggled his fingers . . . of which he seemed to have twice, perhaps *thrice,* the requisite number. Rather fascinatin', really, and . . .

"No, no," Peel carped, as if dealing with a toddler's questions. "Choundas . . . on Guadeloupe. Yankee merchants . . . meet up at Dominica. *Sumter* convoyed dozens of 'em here. Hired stores ship, too, left her there . . . Prince Rupert Bay. Here, there . . . *maybe* up as far as Saint Croix. Goods for Rigaud or L'Ouverture *start* from Guadeloupe, do you see? Catch 'em . . . first leg o' their passage. *Jamaica* Squadron gets the ones headin' for Port-au-Prince or Jacmel . . . last leg, what?"

"*Stop* that," Lewrie growled. "God's sake, write it all down."

"Write it . . . *now?*" Peel gawped. "Can't even spell *ink*, in . . ."

"Now, aye," Lewrie owlishly insisted. "So *one* of us remembers it in the mornin'."

"But . . . dash it, Lewrie! I say . . . !"

"Else we'll have t'ask the Yankees all over again. Whisky an' all, Mister Peel."

"Oh. Oh!" Peel gasped. "Point . . . taken. Indeed!"

"Well, I'm for bed . . . can I find it," Lewrie announced, trying to rise of his own volition. "Lots t'do in the morrow. Re-paint all the masts and spars British-fashion . . . else the forts'll take fright an' shoot us to kindling. Stores t'lade. Naps t'take . . . oh, thankee, Andrews. Touch t'larboard, is it? Hung from the overhead, now *that's* cunning. Sways a good deal, I'd imagine. Ah! Aspinall? Do get Mister Peel ink, quill, and paper, will you?" he called out while his Cox'n took his dressing gown and "poured" him into his bed-cot. "And to all a good night."

Peel's muttered grumbles were simply music to his ears as he got comfortable. The windows in the coach-top overhead were open, with a tiny trysail set as a wind-scoop. Lewrie fanned his sheet then let it drop to his waist, savouring the rare nighttime coolness. After a bit of relative silence, marred only by Peel's faint curses and the *skrit!* of his quill nib, Toulon at last decided that peace had been restored, and slunk out of hiding in the starboard quarter-gallery storage, and leaped up to join him, slinging his bulk into the crook of Lewrie's arm and kneading for "pets" . . . beginning to purr right lustily as his master's hand stroked and wriggled upon his neck and head.

In vino, and whisky, veritas, Lewrie drunkenly thought on the verge of whirling unconsciousness; *and what'd I let slip this ev'nin'? Kindest, if the lad never knows he's my bastard. Half-Indian, Life's already hard enough for 'im. And Caroline never learns it, either! I want t'reconcile, he'd be the last straw. Damme, but I must've strewed by-blows like dust in a high wind! My "git"! A likely lookin' lad he is, though . . .*

CHAPTER SEVENTEEN

*S*hattered! Shattered in knee timbers and futtocks, from upper first futtock to fourth, amidships, along with her ribs! Her graceful stem—choke piece, knee of the head, stemson timbers and apron—including her fore rib pieces and futtocks were shattered.

Once they had stripped *Le Bouclier* down to a gant-line with only her lower masts standing, with all her ballast, stores, and guns removed, and careened her on the shingly lee-side beach near Basse-Terre, the surveyors from the dockyard had discovered just how grievous and extensive her damage was. The surveyors and the few skilled shipwrights still left on the island of Guadeloupe, after the purging and execution of the Royalists and the suspect, held little hope that the magnificent frigate could be sufficiently rebuilt. Oh, in France, *certainement*, they said with high shrugs! In the Caribbean, though, there were no stout oak trees, nor were there great, curving timbers of the proper arcs or thickness, nor the right seasoning, and just to replace her outer and inner planking, and lighter damage to carline posts, bulwarks, and rails would exhaust their scant supply of imported oak.

The shipwrights were most apologetic, but there was little they could do for *Le Bouclier*. Oh, could a ship bear a surveyor and a team of shipwrights to Cuba, or some other Spanish possession, local mahogany might serve for permanent repair materials . . . but selecting the right-shaped trees, felling them, sawing them, and transporting

them back to Basse-Terre would take months. Even then the mahogany would still require months more for proper seasoning and drying.

"Heart-breaking, *m'sieur le Capitaine*," the master shipwright, and
the *commissaire* of the dockyard, both had said. Then had fled his
presence before the expected storm broke.

Heart-breaking, indeed, Capt. Guillaume Choundas thought. What
a wondrous frigate *Le Bouclier* had been, the equal, if not the better,
of any "Bloody" warship in the Caribbean—now a useless, lifeless
hulk. And damn that *salaud* Lewrie to the deepest level of Hades.

Just as heart-breaking, though more understandable, was what he
heard from his superior, the *commissaire civil* Victor Hugues. He still
had *his* single frigate, now cruising for American prizes off the coast
of the Guyanas, far to the southwest. Did *she* come in in need of
repair, Hugues was certain that Choundas would offer bits and pieces
from *Le Bouclier*, to keep *one* powerful man o' war able to daunt the
"biftecks" . . . and that Choundas would do so in the proper cooperative spirit, in accord with the ideals of the Revolution!

"You still have two rather fine *corvettes, Capitaine* Choundas,"
Hugues had said with a vengeful smirk, "which have *yet* to put to sea
to challenge the 'Bloodies.' Let them sail singly, or as a small squadron.
Officers and men off your stricken frigate may re-enforce their crews.
Or you may transfer those now idled to *my* command, and I will put
them to good use aboard the several enemy merchant ships *I* took
before your arrival. With cannon from *Le Bouclier*, I could outfit at
least three more raiders to pursue *le guerre de course*."

"*I* am the senior *naval* officer on Guadeloupe, *m'sieur le
commissaire!*" Choundas had thundered back, "appointed by the hand
of Director Paul Barras, *premier* of the Directory of Five! They are
my cannon, *my* sailors and officers, and do they sit idle in port for
lack of cooperation from the island's *commissaire civil*, believe me,
m'sieur, he will know of it in short order, unless . . . in the cooperative
spirit, according to the ideals of *La Révolution*, prize vessels suitable
to my needs . . . which *also* now lie idle for want of cooperation! . . .
are not turned over to *me!*"

A bitter compromise had been reached. Hugues had not been sure
that Choundas's writ might prove to carry more power than his own
with the Directory, or that the ogre just might have the ear of Paul
Barras after all. Hugues got *Le Bouclier* for scrap-yard use, and four
of her great-guns, with which to form a protective shore battery at

Deshaies. Choundas received a mere two prize ships for conversion, a small brig and one schooner, to be armed with no more than ten guns apiece, crewed by as many *matelots* as he wished to employ for boarders and passage crews for any prizes taken. Wounded off *Le Bouclier* who recovered . . . they would become Hugues's. Naval Infantry, other than Choundas's personal guard detail, would be landed ashore and put under Hugues's command to re-enforce his skimpy 1,500 man garrison.

Choundas sat and sweated, stripped down to shirt and breeches and fanning himself with a "top silver" plaited palmetto hand fan. Among the princes of the Lanun Rovers or Mindanao pirate fleets, there had been tiny young girls with cool, wetted bundles of palm fronds. *Extremely* young girls, who would come whenever he had beckoned, would wind out of their colourfully printed *batik* wraps to service him, or cheerfully, submissively let themselves be pressed down, spread, and *taken*, as casually as they spat *betel* juice. Not *so* casually, the second time he took them, but their fear, then, their weak whines and pleadings, even their looks of revulsion, had been doubly sweet and invigourating. Back when he was a normal-looking man, before that *salaud* Lewrie lamed and maimed him.

He fanned a little harder, shifting his crippled leg to ease an ever-present dull ache, with perspiration popping anew to trickle down his cheeks and the small of his back—partly from the effort put into fanning for relief from the sullen afternoon's heat; partly from being frustrated to lose the tumescence in his groin that such fond reverie had engendered, and could never be relieved quite so easily as then; and partly from the intrusion of his undying hatred for the Englishman, and the harm he'd done his magnificent frigate!

His *noir* servants; *damn* Hugues for freeing them! Damn Hugues, too, for charging him *rente* on the use of them by the week! Damn *them* for drawing the line on what they would or would not do for their new master and his coterie, as if some things were below their dignity . . . as if they had any sense of dignity to upset!

They *dared* lay complaints of ill-usage with Victor Hugues's *sous commissaires civils*, they insolently dared to quit his house (when they didn't just run off!), and implored the *commissaires* for employment with *any* other house, even at lower wages, if they had to.

The *commissaires* had sent letters chiding him for harshness; he was to pay more for the services of those who remained.

There were fewer servants in his retinue doing the same amount of labour, and, illiterate or not, those remaining *noirs* seemed as if they knew those letters by heart. Cleaning, laundry, and yardwork was now done in lacklustre fashion; dishes and glassware appeared at meals spotted and stained, and had to be sent back over and over 'til he was satisfied. The cuisine, already upsetting, was now slovenly over-done or under-done, some days too spicy to be stood, and on others so bland as to be nearly tasteless, and the new male cook and his assistant had a rare knack for finding the toughest, oldest, and scrawniest victuals, whether fish, fowl, or meat. Lank, wilted, half-shriveled vegetables, half-washed salad greens almost brown or black on the leaf edges ... !

And their mute, dog-eyed, blank-faced portrayals of dumb innocence, their shambling-slow, head-scratching shows of utter ignorance! They behaved much as that Lt. Récamier had cautioned. Spoons and utensils went missing, saucers and cups inexplicably got broken or chipped, costly bed-linens brought from France got torn, permanently stained, or so poorly repaired that the caterpillar-sized seams made them useless for sleeping.

Despite constant warnings about open windows and doors, birds, lizards, and shoals of *cafards*, the huge evil-smelling cockroaches endemic to the tropics invaded, *infested* the house (and their bedding!) every night and each dawn, resulting in a stampede of *noirs* who went tittering and yelping to chase them down and expel them—resulting in something fragile and valuable being broken each time.

Merde alors, every bottle of wine that was opened tasted as if it had been *watered*, no matter that he inspected the corks and leaden seals closely, no matter that his clerk Etienne practically stood guard over his cellar, with all the crates placed in de Gougne's cramped office and bed-chamber; with a Marine Infantry sentry in the foyer right outside the doors!

And not a blessed one of them would *fan* him!

Screeching tirades made no more impression than if Choundas had howled at the tide like King Canute ordering it to go out, not in. And he could not beat them, whip them, kick them, or slap them, as one could casually do Hindoos, Chinese, or Filipinos, and it was *galling* to him. One letter had suggested spending more of his pay to purchase a better cuisine for all, including servants, of garbing them in better clothing, of supplying shoes and stockings, but he would be *damned* if he would. The cost of that notwithstanding, there was no way Choundas would stoop to "bribing" *noirs* to treat him better, or be mocked for a "soft" touch. It would be a token of total surrender, and even if he dismissed them all and started with a fresh crew of servants, word of his ineffectiveness—his de-fanging!—would be all over the island by the next sunset, making him the laughingstock of *noirs*, Creoles, and French-born alike.

He fanned himself some more, and swabbed his face and neck with a small towel that had once been coldly moist, but now reeked of sweat, mildew, and arm-pits. He painfully drew his chair up to his massive, and elegant, desk to study his manning problems.

Lt. Houdon could command the brig, the larger prize vessel now being armed and converted for a commerce raider; Lt. Mercier would be his second officer; and Capt. Griot would have to surrender one of his junior lieutenants to make the necessary third, *bien*.

Capitaine MacPherson, for all his drawbacks, was a masterful seaman, able to command *La Résolue* without his first officer; and his first lieutenant would be seasoned and made of the same mould as he by now. That officer would get the large schooner's command, *aussi bien*. Junior lieutenants would move up in seniority, *aspirants* would become acting-lieutenants aboard the *corvettes* . . .

No, the schooner needed two more officers, and the brig needed a fourth, perhaps, to serve as prize-master when she took a suitably big or valuable merchantman . . . the schooner, too? *Damn* this heat!

Choundas found it hard to think. He took a deep breath of hot, still, and musty air, squirmed about so his sweat-sodden shirt became cooler by exposure, and pored over the names in the copied musters. He ticked off a few names, chose a couple, then leaned back in frustration against the damp leather chairback, chewing absently on the end of his expensive pen's rosewood stylus. It was one of the new *steel*-nibbed pens, just coming into vogue and common use, instead of goose quills, and (he proudly thought for a moment) another example of his nation's inventiveness, like the lead-core pencil.

Récamier? No. Jules Hainaut? Hmmm. What was he to do with young Jules? he wondered.

The lad *had* shown well, the day that *Le Bouclier* had . . . died. Hainaut was tarry-handed, when he put his mind to it, and was overdue for reward for his services to him, as well as his recent pluckiness, but yet ... what that idiotic Dutch captain Haljewin had said stuck in Choundas's suspicious mind, and kept resurfacing.

Someone who had known the Dutch ship's cargo and day of her departure, *someone* who knew his plans must have betrayed her, had betrayed poor Capt. Desplan and *Le Bouclier* to the British!

How else to explain how Lewrie and his frigate had arrived just at the perfect moment? Lewrie was a swaggering dumb beast, a *weapon* to be wielded by his betters, nothing more, Choundas disparagingly sneered.

In the Far East, Lewrie had been under the thumb of a much slyer man, that murderous cut-throat, the spare and hatchet-faced *anglais* spy Zachariah Twigg. Together, they had ruined his plans a second time in the Mediterranean, in '94, despite being forewarned by Citizen Pouzin, his enigmatic civilian counterpart sent down from Paris. Posing as a mere banking clerk, a *Juif* from Coutts' Bank named Simon Silberberg of Lewrie's acquaintance, Twigg had. Hah!

Old, Twigg would be now, but Choundas did not think he could go far wrong to suspect that he still spun his webs this far from London, using a younger protégé who would find that beastly ignoramus, Lewrie, once again a useful cat's-paw. A younger spy who had *already* obtained his secret navy signals books!

And ... had not old Twigg or Silberberg, or whatever he called himself—and Lewrie!—taken one of his coasting vessels full of arms to encourage the Piedmontese and Savoyards into French service?

Another delicate mission most effectively stopped, and Jules ... Hainaut had been aboard her, had he not? Taken prisoner, and held for a mere six weeks before being exchanged for a British midshipman, then returned to his side. He'd thought, then, that it had been a suspiciously *short* imprisonment, but ...

Had Twigg "turned" Hainaut back on him as a secret informer, as Lewrie had somehow "turned" that Claudia Mastandrea slut who had been sent to milk him dry of information, then poison him, as he and Citizen Pouzin had arranged? All his schemes had turned to dust, after Hainaut had come back to him ... hadn't they?

How *did les anglais* know of his coming to Guadeloupe, learn of Haljewin's sailing day, *know* his decision to shift *Le Bouclier* over to Basse-Terre, and when? From a nest of traitors and spies already here on the island ... or from one he had unwittingly brought with him?

Choundas had always known that Jules Hainaut's eager deference was cynical play-acting. The lad was out for his pleasures, promotion, a fat purse, and his prick. He had taken him on anyway, knowing what good use he could make of a shrewd and pragmatic rogue. The Revolution badly needed men who would not flinch from ruthlessness, and Jules had proved that he could ignore false sentiments and perform what he was ordered to do. Choundas had worked round his sham, and had even found the lad amusing at times. He had groomed him, tutored him, to improve his effectiveness in the future. He didn't *wish* to think the worst of the lad. There could be a spy placed, or bought off, long ago; there could be someone whom he had yet to suspect. And it would be galling for Choundas to admit he had nurtured a viper in his breast all this time.

He would give Hainaut the benefit of the doubt . . . for now. At sea, he would no longer be privy to the plans he would improvise, now that Choundas knew that his old ones might be compromised. If Jules *was* the spy, he would have no way to communicate with the British.

Did Lewrie and the British continue to plague him with more inexplicable coincidences, Choundas would know that Hainaut was innocent.

But, did the fortunes of his small squadron and his new raiders improve beyond all hopes, and the deep investigation he would begin the very next morning fail to turn up another suspected traitor . . . !

It would be sad, but for the lack of another explanation Choundas would have no other choice but to denounce and arrest Hainaut, put him to "the question" to sear the truth from him, then turn him over to the *gendarmes* for trial, and a sure and certain execution under the blade of the merciless Victor Hugues's "Monsieur Guillotine."

And if blameless, well . . . Hainaut would get his seasoning for future duty to France as a naval officer, his fondest wish. Choundas thought to watch his reactions for carefully hidden upset, or too *much* joy. No, he'd dissemble, pretend to be glad but not *too* glad, sham sadness to be leaving Choundas's side, perhaps even pipe his eyes with "loss" at leaving the service of such a fine master . . . *pah!*

It would prove nothing, Choundas suspected; he was too "fly."

There were blank lines opposite the positions of the schooner, now renamed *La Vigilante*. Choundas dipped the steel nib of his pen in the inkwell, paused over the lines. *Dieuxième*, or *Troisième*, Second or Third officer?

"A real reward," Choundas whispered, his fiendish face even uglier as he smiled so widely, as he clumsily wrote Hainaut's name on the line for Second Officer. Written with his left hand, the name was almost illegible even to him. But Choundas was sure that his mousy and harassed little clerk Etienne de Gougne would be able to decypher it when he made the fair copies in his copper-plate hand.

And gloat with studiously hidden glee to be rid of his tormentor!

CHAPTER EIGHTEEN

*T*he two warships sailed together, clawing out their offing from Antigua to the East-Sou'east, and close-hauled to windward on the larboard tack. Though HMS *Proteus* had been quicker off the mark to seize the windward advantage, smothering the USS *Thomas Sumter* in her lee by her spread of sail, the American ship had still surged up almost abeam of her by late afternoon as the day's heat faded, as the airs borne by the Trade wind grew denser.

"Fresher from the careenage, I expect, sir," Mr. Winwood said as the reason, "with a cleaner bottom."

"Equal our waterline length, Captain," Lt. Langlie supposed as well, "so it stands to reason that both hulls perform equally. Perhaps a touch finer in her entry than ours, but . . ."

"No better handled," Lt. Catterall said with a dismissive sniff.

"Longer yards, with larger courses, surely," Lt. Adair dared to comment as they watched the *Sumter* bowl along, barely half a mile alee, "especially 'pon her t'gallants and royals. Fuller-bellied jibs . . ."

"Mmhmm," Lewrie replied to their guesses, telescope to one eye for the last ten minutes, entire, intent upon his study of her.

"Converted from a merchantman, she's fuller in her beam, too," Lt. Langlie pondered aloud, "so perhaps she sits more upright than we, just a few degrees stiffer, and sailing on a *flatter* bottom, with a pronounced shoulder . . . not as rounded as our chines, sir?"

"Mmhmm," Lewrie said again, and that only because he sensed the pregnant pause in their musings that required a response on his part.

"Merchantman or no, she's a swift sailer, I'll grant them," Mr. Winwood admitted with a hint of grumbling over any vessel that could rival a British-built, British-masted, and British-rigged ship, one set up to suit *his* experiences, and his captain's.

"Aye, swift," Lewrie mumbled. His arms tiring at last, he let the barrel of the strongest day-glass rest on the lee bulwarks of the quarterdeck for a bit. He peered about to windward, then aloft to the commissioning pendant's stiff-driven coach-whip, to the clouds on the horizon in search of dirty weather. There was none. The pendant was fully horizontal, its swallow-tail tip fluttering in concert with the lee edges of the jibs and courses. Even with the larboard battery run out and the starboard run in, *Proteus* was just a pinch slower than the Yankee man o' war, perhaps by as much as a quarter of a knot, and the cleanliness of her quickwork could not explain it. Americans simply built faster ships, Lewrie decided; just like the French did. *Proteus* had been based on a British interpretation of a captured French frigate whose lines had been taken off and copied, but . . . perhaps not copied closely enough.

"Puts me in mind of something from the Beatitudes, hey, Mister Winwood?" Lewrie asked the Sailing Master. "How does it go? That the 'first shall be last, and the last shall be first'? No matter if they out-foot us or point a degree or two more to windward, really. *Proteus* was made to dominate, not sprint . . . stay the course in all weathers, keep the seas, and *then* hammer the swifter when we finally corner 'em."

"Or simply chase 'em off, sir," Lt. Catterall said with a grunt of agreement. "Make 'em out-run us, in *fear*."

"Well said, sir," Lewrie told him with a brief grin, which drew growls of like sentiment from the rest as he turned back to leeward to raise his telescope once again, bracing the tube on the rat-lines of the mizen stays this time. He sobered quickly, though, dropping back into a brown study usually foreign to his nature, or his officers' experience with him. His statement had been his first utterance in the past hour, other than a curt directive or two to improve their ship's handling. And, intent upon *Sumter* once more, he gave all indications of ignoring anything they said.

Lewrie was not studying *Sumter* in search of a weakness that he could use to keep *Proteus* ahead, though. In fact, the idea of sailing her hull-under was the *last* thing he wished to do, no matter how competitive he would usually act to maintain the honour of the Royal Navy, his ship, or his crew. He was not, in truth, peering so intently upon *Sumter* as he was keeping an eye on one of her midshipmen . . . *his son.*

His bastard son . . . who was at that moment perched aloft high in the *Sumter*'s main weather stays, just below her futtock shrouds, with a glass in his hands, too, which he lifted every now and again to caution his captain-uncle to *Proteus*'s next race strategem. Two other boys of *Sumter*'s cockpit were perched with him, all three hooting and cheering as the American armed ship gradually gained a few more yards on *Proteus*. They'd wave their tricorne hats and whoop and halloo, teeth-bared, and mouths open in perfect O's, like a panto-mime's show against the thunder of the winds. They'd lean far out, with only a finger and a shoe heel gripping the rat-lines and stays, daring each other to greater follies of "tarry" derring-do, and each time Midshipman Desmond McGilliveray matched or bettered their feats, Lewrie sucked in his breath as if to shout and warn them to "belay all that." He could see a grizzled bosun atop the bulwarks at the base of the stays, fist shaking and mouth open to bawl caution at them, but with boys that age, what he shouted most-like went in one ear and out the other, and Lewrie still felt twinges of worry. A *father's* worry.

Desmond lifted his glass, lowered it, then waved wide, beaming, looking directly into the lens of the powerful day-glass, as if he *knew* he was being watched so closely. He raised his glass again and Lewrie lowered his, knowing *he* was being eyed, and pantomimed a solid grip on the stays with *both* hands, and was much relieved to see the lad seem to obey, and loop an arm and a shin inside the rat-lines, round a rigid stay. Lewrie made a large gesture of swabbing a coat sleeve over a "worried" brow. "Don't do that!" he silently mouthed over the water.

"Boat ahoy!" Midshipman Larkin had challenged two days following that drunken supper, and the youthful voice shouting in reply had drawn Lewrie to the deck. The turn-out for a foreign midshipman was as thin as charity, so it was Larkin who led Mr. Midshipman

McGilliveray to the quarterdeck from the entry-port with his sealed letter for *Proteus*'s captain . . . who met them personally.

"Captain McGilliveray's sincerest respects to you, sir, and I'm charged to deliver to you this message, Captain Lewrie, sir," the lad had crisply stated, doffing his hat and making a courtly "leg" worthy of an English "mid" reporting to an Admiral—though no English "mid" would ever peer so intently or so openly. And perhaps only a famous man such as Jervis or Nelson would elicit such an awe-struck expression as Midshipman McGilliveray displayed.

"Thank you, Mister McGilliveray," Lewrie had replied, properly gruff and stoical, his hand out for the letter.

"I was instructed to wait upon your written reply, sir, and . . ." McGilliveray said, stumbling for the first time. He had shown none of the usual youthful curiosity one might expect of a fellow boarding one of King George's ships for the first time, not even craning his head about to see how other navies did things, rigged things, but kept his gaze wide-eyed upon Lewrie far more intently than any courtly book of gentlemanly behaviour could advise when dealing with one's superiors, or elders.

"Oi'll see ta him, sor, whilst . . . *I* shall, rather . . . ?" Larkin offered, eyes almost crossed in concentration on "proper" speech.

"No, that won't be necessary, Mister Larkin, but thankee. I'll have Mister McGilliveray below to my quarters," Lewrie decided, which unexpected offer of hospitality confused one, but delighted the other.

"Aspinall, this is Mister McGilliveray, off the United States' Armed Ship *Thomas Sumter*," Lewrie told his cabin-steward as he seated himself behind his desk. "Mister McGilliveray, my man Aspinall, and a better 'aid and comfort' you'll rarely see. Keeps me minding my p's and q's, does Aspinall. Sit, lad, sit."

"Howdje do, sir," Aspinall had cheerfully said, knuckling his forehead.

"Draw us each a ginger beer, would you, Aspinall?" Lewrie bade as he tore open the wax seal of the letter, still faintly soft, still warm to the touch.

"Thank you kindly, sir," McGilliveray said, seated in an upholstered chair before the desk, hat in his lap, and almost squirming with some inner fretfulness, despite the half-smile he evinced. His curiosity did extend to looking about the great-cabins, finally. "Hello!"

Lewrie looked up to see Toulon, who had leaped atop the desk in curiosity of his own, perching himself on the very edge of the desk to crane his neck forward and bob, to study the newcomer.

"That's Toulon," Lewrie had told him. "Where I got him in '93, when he was a kitten. He was just about as huge as disaster, so that's how he got his name. He's *almost* out-grown his clumsiness, but he can still surprise you."

"He's a big'un, sure enough, sir," the lad said, cautiously petting the ram-cat, ruffling the fur under Toulon's intricately plaited sennet-work collar with the brass disk hung from it. "As big as a bobcat . . . nigh twenty pounds or so, sir?"

Sure enough, Toulon "surprised," stretching too far in his bliss and diving nose-first to the deck. To make it less embarrassing, Toulon leaped into the boy's lap, as if that was what he intended, all along.

Lewrie unfolded the pages of his letter and read the first lines or so, then "whuffed" in alarm. Despite any misgivings or forebodings Capt. McGilliveray might feel, the boy's uncle had determined to reveal the facts of his parentage to the lad. He had blabbed all!

"Ah, Captain Lewrie," Mr. Peel had cheerfully called out, emerging from his dog-box cabin. "A visitor, have you?"

"No one to arouse your interest, Mister Peel," Lewrie had almost snapped, regretting such a curt dismissal at once. Not for Peel's sake, but for how lightly he might esteem the lad. "Pray take a turn on deck, Mister Peel. I've a letter from Captain McGilliveray of *Sumter*."

"Very well, sir," Peel had responded, sounding intrigued as well as a tad miffed to be shooed out, as he departed.

McGilliveray had thought it odd for his kinsman to turn up with a wife and a son, especially a pale-skinned and blue-eyed infant so very unlike himself. They had stayed but briefly in Charleston after the Revolution had ended, since his "bride," Soft Rabbit, could *never* gain *entrée* into cultured society, even if she could have adapted to civilised dress—or shoes!—or could have learned to speak fluent English. It was a Muskogee marriage, after all, as informal as that of a Black city couple "jumping the broomstick" in the slave quarters.

Desmond and Soft Rabbit had resided with the boy's grandfather, Robert, at his plantation-cum-trading post on the edge of "civilisation" far up the Savannah River, and no circuit-riding parson had made it any more formal. From what Capt. McGilliveray had discovered dur-

ing their brief visit, during a later trip to "Uncle Robert's," he thought
their marriage one more of convenience than a love match, as if Desmond felt he'd had to "do the right thing" by her after her "exploi-
tation" by an English sailor-adventurer . . . for the good of his tribe
and clan name. And Soft Rabbit had acquiesced, since the babe needed
a father, and she needed support that a low-status former slave could
not get in a proud clan *huti* among the Muskogee.

Capt. McGilliveray had gently railed against his kinsman, deeming
him "a stiff-necked prig who had taken upon himself the Burden and
Duty to atone for White callousness." Desmond *did* need someone to
cook and clean, sew his clothes, and service his rare bouts of prim
desires. The boy was Desmond's "experiment." He *was* half-White
and deserved the same chance his putative "stepfather" had had, to
gain an education so he could function in the White world if he so
chose, with a solid grounding in Muskogee lore and trailcraft should
he choose that life. At best, perhaps, the lad could find a place in the
family "over-mountain" Indian trade, a symbolic bridge to Desmond's
vaunting dreams of a "partially" civilised Muskogee-Seminolee-
Cherokee-Chickasaw-Choctaw-Apalachee race co-existing at the bor-
ders of the United States, like the Iroquois League, as the semi-barbaric
German and Gallic tribes had co-existed with ancient Rome; as the various Hindoo tribes served a burgeoning British Empire in India. A project,
but never a beloved son; a comforting worker, but never a "goody"
wife, alas.

"Sadly, the Smallpox put paid to those plans," Capt. McGilliveray
had written. "Desmond and Soft Rabbit were carried off, and kindly
old Uncle Robert quite enervated, to the point that the lad was brought
to us in Charleston by Desmond's youngest brother, Iain, and an older
Muskogee nursemaid when the lad was three, and became my ward,
whereupon he did receive the best of everything we McGilliverays
could bestow on one of our own, and young Desmond's connexions
with his Indian nature were effectively severed. Curious as the lad
seemed anent his antecedents, I must confess that I can recall no true
Fondness beyond his mother. Toddler that he was when he came to
us, he held no particular air of Grief for his late Stepfather, even when
considering how Stoic our Indians comport themselves. So, when I,
at last, informed the lad of the identity of his actual Father, I—thankfully—discerned not a great Disappointment on his part, nor did Desmond evince any sudden Surprise. I suspect that the old Muskogee

nursemaid, who stayed with us 'til her Passing in '93, was present when you and Desmond took part in your Adventures, and imparted to him the Truth . . ."

Meddlin' fool! Lewrie had thought at that moment; *There's whole regiments o' lads, never knew who quickened 'em, but still prospered. Silence might've been kinder. He was settled in his mind as an orphan . . . with a silver spoon, and all. Now . . . Christ!*

"Imagine my Astonishment, two evenings past, sir, when your comments made me put two and two together!" Capt. McGilliveray had penned further. "The utter Coincidence, and the odds against such! I only knew what little Desmond had related to me, and that, long ago, anent your identity, or Character, and must confess that I knew nothing about you other than your most recent Success off Guadeloupe. Enquiries made ashore, though, sir, quickly satisfied my Curiosity as to the Illustrious Name you have gained in the Royal Navy, and the many Successes you have had against your King's foes; Fame which I was quick to pass on to young Desmond, who, enflamed by his own Eager Curiosity, made enquiries ashore whilst on his errands among Midshipmen, Warrants, and those few Officers who might deign to converse with him; such revelations assured him that he is the Scion of a most capable and honourable Gentleman . . ."

Only heard the good parts, Lewrie had silently thought, squirming in sudden dread; *Wait'll the other shoe drops. So, now what? They passin' him onto me? I'm t'be his Daddy, of a sudden? Dear God, I'm to set him an* example?

Lewrie had laid the letter aside, and looked up to see his "son" stroking Toulon, who was now all but cradled in the crook of one arm, belly exposed and paws in the air, with his head laid back in rapture to be getting such diligent attention. The lad looked him in the eyes and gulped, near to shying should Lewrie speak a single callous word.

"Well, well," Lewrie finally said, after clearing his throat. "It would appear that we're . . . kin, young sir. Now, what the bloody Hell do we make of that?"

"Don't . . . don't know, sir," Desmond meekly said, with a gulp.

"I never meant t'leave your mother . . . leave Soft Rabbit, but," Lewrie began, stammering a tad. "Your father, . . .Desmond, 'twas him, said it would be best. That he'd see to her, after I sailed away. I was wounded. Touch and go that I'd live, for a while, there, anyway, so . . . it seemed best, all round. Couldn't have taken her to London, any more than Desmond could have settled her in Charleston."

"Was she really a princess, like he said, sir?" Desmond asked, in almost a desperate pleading. "A Cherokee princess?" Lewrie sat up with a start, smothering the wince he felt.

"A *captured* Cherokee princess," he finally lied, unable to dis-abuse *all* the lad's callow assumptions, those sticking points to which his very self clung. "Man-Killer, the Great Warrior of your father's White Wind clan, raided far north and took her. Brought her back for a valuable slave. Quite a coup, they thought. She wasn't visiting . . . the Muskogee said the T'se-luki weren't the *real* People, not as good as them. Couldn't even talk right, the Cherokee, they told me."

"But they let *you* marry her, even so, sir?" Desmond pressed at him, snuggling Toulon to him as if for comfort. "Being an outsider, and all, I meant. Was it . . . ?"

"She served me supper, one night," Lewrie told him, reminiscing almost happily, despite the awkward circumstances, "and I was lost in a trice. Unmarried Muskogee girls may choose whom they wish, and we met later down at the lake . . . we talked, or tried to, and . . . she was so *very* fetching and handsome, so slim and wee, really. Very sweet and gentle a girl . . . and smart as paint, too, quick to learn things! Uhm . . ."

Randy as a stoat? Lewrie had thought; *do I dare tell him that?*

"Yet you never thought to write her, or look for her, once the war ended, sir? If you loved her as much as she . . . ?"

"I'd barely made my lieutenantcy, and the Royal Navy distrusts junior officers who marry," Lewrie extemporised, squirming in em-barassment. "We're to make Commander first, then marry some re-tired admiral's *proper* daughter. Does she come with acres attached, that's even better, d'ye see, young sir? Besides, they slung me ashore in London on half-pay, then shipped me halfway round the world to India and the Chinese coast for nigh on three years. By then, I'd met my Caroline."

"The lady on the bulkhead, sir? She's very pretty. Do you have . . . children, dare I ask, sir?" Desmond shyly probed.

"Three . . . two boys and a daughter," Lewrie said, crossing his fingers over how long that situation might continue. "And a ward, to boot. A genteel French girl, well . . . young woman, by now, whose kin were slain at Toulon. Promised a dying French officer I knew

from the Revolution that I'd see for his cousin Sophie. You'd like her,
I'll wager. Unless, of course, you have a special young miss dear to
your heart back in Charleston?" Lewrie thought to tease, to finagle
more probing, and upsetting, questions.

"Oh . . . none particular, yet, sir," the lad actually blushed, before
turning a touch gloomy. "Even as a McGilliveray, d'you see . . . we're
a long-settled and respectable family, and all, but . . ."

"But people still think you not quite . . . the *ton?* Because . . ."

The lad merely bobbed his head, as if in shame, seemingly more
intent on nuzzling Toulon to his chin; which was just heavenly to the
ram-cat.

"Well, damn their blue blood, I say!" Lewrie barked. "Uhm . . .
this sudden revelation. How widespread d'ye wish it to be, among yer
peers, and such? Would a British father make things worse for you
or better? Pardons, but I ain't had much experience at . . . this. You've
spent so much time a . . ." Lewrie flummoxed, hand waving for words.

"Bastard, sir?" the lad suddenly said, with too-candid heat.

"Well, d'ye want t'put it that way, aye," Lewrie answered, with an
embarrassed grimace. "No harm in it, really. I'm a bastard myself."

That snapped the lad's head up right quick!

"S'truth!" Lewrie vowed. "Little matter of hiring a false justice,
'stead of proper clergy, when my own father, Sir Hugo St. George
Willoughby, took my mother, Elisabeth Lewrie, to wife. A little jape
arranged by his fellow officers in the Fourth Regiment of Foot. You
know . . . the King's Own? The drunken lot o' sots. She died, soon
as I was born, and I got lost in a parish poor house nigh a year, and
was lucky to live, cruel as they care for orphan gits, 'til my father
came and got me out. Here, lad . . . does your uncle, your captain,
require you back aboard any time soon, or would you care to go
ashore with me and dine? I expect we've a lot of catching up to do."

"I expect we *do*, sir!" the lad said, almost pathetically grateful and
eager. "And I'd . . . I would be greatly honoured to accept an invitation to dine with you, sir. Because . . ."

" 'Coz I've yet t'meet a mid who wasn't half-starved?"

"That, too, sir," Desmond McGilliveray confessed, all smiles of a
sudden. "Er, should I call you 'sir,' or Captain Lewrie, or . . . ?"

"Well, once you learn what a sordid family you're kin to, make up
your own mind as to that," Lewrie allowed. "Aspinall? I'd admire did

you pass the word for Cox'n Andrews, and my boat-crew. I'll dine ashore with Mister McGilliveray," he said, springing to his feet.

"Aye aye, sir!"

"Your father's knighted, sir?" Desmond happily bubbled as they gathered hats and such. "Is he a *lord*? And, your pardons, but those medals you wore at supper t'other night . . . !"

"No, he ain't," Lewrie gleefully related. "He was knighted for bravery. A Major-General, now, though mostly retired on his estate. Nothing much, really, nothing grand. This'un's for Saint Vincent . . . we were in shoutin' distance of Captain Nelson, at that'un. And this'un's for Camperdown, when we trounced the Dutch, under Duncan the wild Scot. Oh, he's a *tall*, craggy figure, white hair stickin' up six ways from Sunday . . . !"

"And you wear a hanger, instead of a smallsword?"

"Best for boarding-party brawls, don't ye know! Cut and slash, as well as skewer, and short enough to whip about when it's shoulder-to-shoulder . . . Desmond."

To which use of his Christian name, the lad beamed so widely his face threatened to split in half, as Lewrie laid a tentative, claiming, hand atop his shoulder lightly—ostensibly to steer him ahead of him on the way out past the Marine sentry to the gun-deck.

And God help us, the both of us, Lewrie had thought.

"Signal from the *Sumter*, sir," Midshipman Grace sang out as the bunting soared aloft from the man o' war abeam of them and alee, making Lewrie shift his telescope aft towards her mizen-mast, where the powerful day-glass forced him to scan the signal flags top-to-bottom one at a time. "She sends 'Farewell and Adieu', sir . . . her second hoist is . . . 'Haul Wind' . . . for 'Am Hauling Wind,' I'd suppose?"

"Does she propose to order a Royal Navy frigate to escort her to Dominica, that's another matter," Lewrie heard Lt. Catterall gravel.

"Spell out 'Best of Fortune' to her, best you may, lad," Lewrie told Grace. "Mister Windwood?"

"Aye, sir?" the Sailing Master answered, stepping closer.

"We've enough sea-room to come about and run betwixt Guadeloupe and Montserrat, Mister Winwood?" Lewrie asked him.

"More than sufficient, Captain," Winwood soberly assured him.

"Very well, sir, and thankee," Lewrie replied. "We'll let the *Sumter* haul off well alee before we come about ourselves."

Thomas Sumter would be taking the "outside passage" to windward of Guadeloupe, that scorpions' nest, for her base in Prince Rupert Bay on Dominica, heavily laden with fresh-slaughtered and salted beef and pork, with her decks also burdened by meat on the hoof to victual any arriving American warships. Even so burdened, however, she would leap at the chance to engage any French she encountered, Capt. McGilliveray had assured in his letter's final pages.

As for HMS *Proteus*, well . . . Mr. Peel was miffed anew by what Lewrie had planned to do. When *not* at logger-heads concerning how the distant Mr. Pelham had instructed them to operate, Peel was turning out to be a rather amiable companion, and God knew that any captain needed some personal contact and conversation, besides cats, dogs, geese, and chickens . . . or himself . . . to ease the mute loneliness of command but . . . Lewrie suspected that Mr. James Peel would ever be on the *qui-vive* for his . . . inspired moments, waiting for a *heavy* shoe to drop.

Proteus would cruise past Guadeloupe to leeward, again, and do Victor Hugues, Guillaume Choundas, and their privateeers and smugglers another evil turn if they could find anything at sea to bash. Then, though, they would cruise on down to Dominica and beyond, into the seas where American merchantmen were trading, leeward of Martinique and St. Lucia, St. Vincent and the Grenadines, perhaps as far south as Tobago and Trinidad, as far west as Curaçao and Aruba along the coast of Spanish South America.

Even worse in Mr. Peel's estimation, *Proteus* would cruise along with *Sumter*, not as an *official* squadron, but two independent warships which just *happened* to be in the same waters at the same time, and did they sometimes pass within signalling distance in their rovings, well, who could fault that? Despite Mr. Pelham's strictures that the United States were rivals, not to be trusted, their merchant ships not to be aided with such diligence as long as Choundas still lived, as long as Saint Domingue was not *firmly* in Britain's grasp forever after, Amen.

"But, but . . . !" Mr. Peel had spluttered when Lewrie had revealed his and McGilliveray's scheme to him. Expostulations from both sides had taken up most of an evening, and only the downing of a consid-

erable amount of sweet, aged corn-whisky had brought him (somewhat) round to Lewrie's point of view. They wouldn't be down South
long, since trading season was ending, and all those Yankee Doodle
merchantmen would be eager to scuttle off homeward with their treasures before hurricane season. Quartering and zig-zagging the sea in
wide sweeps, always trending back North'rd, both *Proteus* and *Sumter*
would stand a much better chance of meeting up with the hosts of
French privateers bent on taking those treasures.

Lewrie had had to point out that Choundas, Hugues, and their sea-
captains weren't out here for true patriotic reasons, after all. Prize
Courts were just as respected by Republican Frogs as they had been
by the Royal Frogs, and French officials on Guadeloupe were just as
avid as Admiral Sir Hyde Parker back in Kingston for their lucrative
share, their "admiral's eighth." Starve the Prize Courts of business,
starve the privateer officers and crews of profit, and there'd be less of
it in future. Take, sink, or burn a few of them, and put the fear of
God into the rest, and that'd force them to stay home, lay up their
ships, and boast over their wine in waterfront taverns of what they'd
do, if only they could *break even* at it, if only they could find enough
hands to man their ships these days, the poltroons!

Peel *could* see the sense of it, at last (though he'd had to get pie-
eyed to do so!), that Choundas would, once stung enough, come out
personally to restore the morale of his piratical lackeys, to even the
score . . . protect his own profits, too, *and* salvage his career.

Peel had kept pointing out that L'Ouverture, the possible ally General Rigaud, and the conflict between them, was the more important
matter, that estopping martial aid to either—from the French, not their
own side, should Rigaud sign on the right line—was what Mr. Pelham
had intended when he despatched them eastward to Antigua, but Lewrie had assured him that they could accomplish that task, too . . .
indirectly, by making the short voyage seem too dangerous; by forcing
Choundas to use his men o' war in search of *Proteus* and *Sumter*, not
in convoying vulnerable merchantmen to Jacmel or Port-au-Prince;
and, by goading him so sore that he *had* to find and kill his worst
enemy before any convoy could sail.

USS *Sumter* became a bee-hive of activity as her crew scrambled aloft
and manned her braces to haul her wind and wear about due South,

and Lewrie lost sight of Midshipman McGilliveray, who became just
one more hand lined up along the yards and foot-ropes of the course
sail on her main-mast to shake out reefs, like a flock of wrens perched
on a barn roof. Lewrie finally collapsed the tubes of his telescope and
tucked it under his left arm, abandoning the lee quarterdeck bulwarks
to pace "uphill" to the windward.

"Stations to wear, Mister Langlie," Lewrie told his First Lieutenant.
"We'll come about to Sou'west-by-West, and take the Trades on the
starboard quarter. All plain sail, after that. Just 'fore sunset, we'll
shorten sail for a predawn arrival off Guadeloupe's north coast to see
what they're 'serving' us for breakfast."

"Very good, sir," Langlie replied, all dutiful and efficient a watchstander . . . but for the faintest hint of a grin at the corner of his lips.

Damn my eyes, was that a smirk? Lewrie fumed to himself. And it
wasn't the *first* he'd seen in the last day or so, either, from one and
all, even from Mr. Peel . . . once he'd gotten over his latest hangover.
It was exasperating, but Lewrie strongly suspected that his parentage
of Desmond McGilliveray was an open secret . . . which was to say it
was no secret at all. But he'd be *damned* if he didn't rip the buttocks
off the next person who found it amusing!

And how the Devil he ever thought to keep their relationship a
secret, he had no idea. After all, it wasn't every day that lofty Post-
Captains in the Royal Navy befriended lowly gentlemen-in-training
from *anyone's* navy (especially their *own*) unless they were blood kin,
cater-cousins . . . or devotees of "the windward passage" on the prowl
for pre-pubescent victims. No one who knew Lewrie would ever mis-
construe *him* for a "back-gammoner" or secret "Molly," so that left
kinship. He had hoped that *distant* kinship, some six-times-removed
cousin on his wife's side, perhaps, could explain his sudden attentive
doting, but that hope had been dashed. Too many people, from focs'le
to taff-rails, from the orlop to the mast trucks, had cocked their heads
aslant and made comparisons of their features, their very un-thought
gestures, and had come to the correct conclusion. And they'd done it
damned fast, damn 'em!

Stood up side-by-side, he and Desmond McGilliveray were as alike
as two peas in a pod.

"There she goes, sir!" Lt. Langlie pointed out as *Sumter* turned at
last, falling away Suth'rd and showing them her stern.

Little good'll come of this, Lewrie told himself for what felt like the hundredth time. He could not imagine how young Desmond could improve his situation in Life by discovering that he was *his* bastard, not the dead Desmond's, a "bastardly gullion," really—the bastard son of a bastard. *Maybe havin' more English blood than Indian makes a diff'rence,* he mused; *like bein' a Sacatra-Black, 'stead of a Griffe-Black in Port-au-Prince. Help him pass for lily-White, like the Sang-Mêlés, with one drop o' dark blood in an hundred? What'll he do, take an advertisement in the* Charleston Post and Courier, *and shout it out t'one and all? Brr!*

Such thought of adverting his kinship to the world could result in the article being picked up by London papers, which Caroline would read, and Devil take the hind-most then! Why, she'd sic assassins on him faster than the Beaumans could, for this final insult!

Hopefully, whoever his dreaded anonymous scribbler was who sent those revelatory *billets doux* to Caroline that had ruined his Domestic Joy would *never* get wind of Desmond! Safely removed (in the relative sense) from that nameless scoundrel's purview, the "log" of his scandals had dried up . . . so far. And pray God the tale stayed as dry as a Barbary desert dune!

Lewrie shook himself, rocked on the balls of his feet, and gave his neck and shoulders an easing roll to loosen the tension of intense observation and worry over young Desmond's foolish sky-larking. With an arch of his back, he turned to windward, dismissing *Sumter* and with her his secret shame.

It was actually coolish, now that it was getting on for October, and the seas were no longer simmered by the tropic sun, so soaked up a lot less warmth to be blown along on the Trades. While not nippy, the winds were refreshing, and the late afternoon sunshine was milder, and balmier, not quite so ferocious. Once the sun was down, vanishing in a finger-snap as it did in these climes, the wind would be right up the stern, flooding through his transom sash-windows, cupped by the propped open windows of the coach-top over his cabins. Despite his qualms, he would sleep well tonight, he was certain.

Sumter now sat flatter on her bottom, rapidly drawing away into the failing twilight, with yards angled and sails cupped to sail Large upon her "occasions." Though it was too far, now, to be discerned from her decks or fighting-tops, Lewrie raised a hand and waved her a pleased farewell.

Despite all . . . he *was* a likely lad.

CHAPTER NINETEEN

Soft Rabbit in a fashionable gown and picture hat was laughing with glee as he danced with her at Ranelagh Gardens, under the myriad candles, white-silk heeled shoes and stockinged ankles flirting under the froth of lace at her hems, whilst Theoni Connor stood and fanned herself near the string orchestra in livery and powdered wigs playing, inexplicably, a lively jig called "Go To The Devil And Shake Yourself." Theoni had a mug of ale in her other hand—and a Muskogee "papoosa" cross her back which bore twin boys, peering over one shoulder and beneath an armpit. Theoni *was* quite fetching in beaded buckskins, but a pair of gnarled, tanned, and sooty bare feet *quite* put him off, and . . .

"Sir! Sir!" Midshipman Grace said in a harsh whisper near his bedcot. "Mister Adair's duty, sir, and he says to tell you that the enemy is in sight, sir!"

"Woof?" Lewrie grunted, pushing himself up from his face-down frog sprawl to an elbow. "Umm . . . where away?"

"Two points off the starboard bows, sir, and almost hull-up to us, sailing about Nor'west-by-North . . . reefed down for the night, he said to tell you, sir!" Grace tumbled out with eagerness. "It is now a quarter-glass shy of Four Bells, and Mister Adair has doused all of our lights, soon as the starboard bow lookout sang out, and . . . !"

"Very well, Mister Grace," Lewrie replied, shaking his head to clear the cob-webs; the cool air streaming into his cabins had put him into a deep, muzzy, and dizzying sleep, as he had expected the afternoon before. "*Move*, Toulon, there's a good cat!" he hissed as he flung off the sheet and quilt he'd drawn up sometime after he'd caulked out cold. Toulon was curled up atop the quilt, between his spread thighs, taking his sweet time to stretch at being wakened at such an ungodly hour.

Aspinall had been summoned from his hammock a deck below in the after stores room, but was taking *his* sweet time arriving, too. Lewrie grabbed the first clothes his hands encountered off the back of a chair near his bed-cot and hurriedly dressed.

"Mister Adair is to call all hands to Quarters, Mister Grace," he snapped as he drew a shirt over his head. "No pipes, no fifes and drums, and tell him I'll be on deck, directly. Go! Scamper, lad!"

Shirt and breeches, shoes and coat, and no time to fool with a pair of stockings; a trundle cross the cabins to his arms rack for his hanger, and to hell with his hat. Within a frantic two minutes in the dark, he was out past the Marine sentry on the gun-deck and scampering up the starboard ladder to the quarterdeck scant moments ahead of the hands who'd come to strip his great-cabins of partitions, furniture, and fittings, to man the 12-pounders mounted right-aft.

"Captain, sir," Lt. Adair reported, knuckling his forehead for a salute, instead of doffing his hat. "You can see her in the night-glass, sir . . . two points off the starboard bows. Three-masted, full-rigged, but reefed down to tops'ls, jibs, and spanker for the night."

Lewrie accepted the heavy night-glass and lifted it to his eye, espying the strange ship, upside-down and backwards, as if sailing on a reciprocal course to her real one, due to requirements of the optics in the tube, as Lt. Adair prosed on to finish his report.

". . . about a half-hour before, sir, just looming behind Pointe Allegre. Her going Northerly, us fetching the point? Saw her lights, but we thought she was just a fishing smack, out night-trawling, 'til we got close enough for her sails to catch some moonlight, sir, and we divined how big she was."

"Very well, Mister Adair. My compliments to the lookouts, and to your quick judgement regarding our taff-rail and binnacle lights. I will . . . ah, Mister Langlie? That you in the night-shirt, is it?"

"Aye, sir," his First Lieutenant said, sounding sheepish about his catch-as-catch-can state of dress.

"Hands aloft, and shake out the night reefs in the main and the mizen tops'ls, let fall one reef in the main course," Lewrie directed. "Waisters to the braces, and steer for a point ahead of her bows. She shows no sign of spotting *us* yet, and bows-on to her, she might not 'til we're close-aboard! Expect to engage with the larboard battery. And where's Mister Devereux?"

"Here, sir," the Marine officer replied from near the larboard quarterdeck ladder. Lewrie could barely make him out by the sheen of his white silk shirt and white cotton breeches, quickly masked back to darkness by his batsman, who was pushing him into his red tunic, black in the faint moonlight of predawn. "Will you be requiring a boarding-party, pray God, sir?" Lt. Devereux enquired, carefully making his way over tackle, ring-bolts, and the neatly coiled jear and halliard lines by a series of shuffling, probing scuffles.

"Sorry we've proved boresome of late, Mister Devereux," Lewrie said, chuckling. "Aye. Man the larboard gangway, and be ready to go over to her, should she prove to be hostile."

There were many more comings and goings, with a deal of grunts, curses, and muffled yelps as less-careful or less-fortunate crewmen or officers stubbed their shoes or bare toes on deck obstructions in the darkness. *Proteus* thudded and slammed with the sounds of preparation for battle as sea-chests, furnishings, and partitions were slung below or out of the way, as gun-tools were fetched from the racks overhead of the raised mess tables one deck below; as shot, wadding, and powder cartridges began to come up from the rope-garlands or the magazine. A *deaf* man, Lewrie imagined, could have heard the ruckus aboard the ship off their bows, what with all the creaking and skreaking of the parrel balls binding the yards to the masts as they changed angles, the cries from the hoisting blocks, and the loud rustles of freed canvas as the night-reefs were unbound and the yards hoisted higher, the clew-lines drawing tauter, the halliards, and even the braces "sawing" cross wood belaying pins and the tops of the pin-rails.

"*Could* be a neutral, I s'pose, sir," Mr. Winwood cautioned from near the darkened binnacle cabinet.

"Then we're about to scare some poor Yankee or Dane out of his shoes, and a year's growth," Lewrie japed. "But I doubt that. Mister Adair said she was ghosting along *behind* Pointe Allegre, well within sight of Guadeloupe from her own decks, and what neutral'd risk that?"

"Mmm," Winwood pondered. Lewrie could hear his new footwear, a handsome pair of Hessian boots he'd bought at English Harbour, creak as he rocked on the balls of his feet. "Then perhaps our last raid makes them sail after sunset, hoping to be a good half-day's sail out to sea before false dawn, Captain. Beyond the ken of any block-aders?"

"I'd be gratified to hear that our last visit resulted in such a panic, aye, Mister Winwood," Lewrie snickered. "Good God, who's that?" he asked as a meaty thud, two grunts, and a faint "Dammit!" arose from the larboard ladder.

"Bosun, sir," Mr. Pendarves reported in a harsh, gravelly voice. "Ship's at Quarters, Mister Catterall begs me t'report."

"Very *good*, Mister Pendarves! And who's that with you?"

"Me, sir," Mr. Peel told him in a loud, theatrical whisper. "I beg your pardon, Mister Pendarves, for colliding with you. Seems this set of stairs isn't wide enough for two at the same time, what?"

"Ladder, sir . . . ladder!" Pendarves snarled as he made his way for-ward. "*Bloody* damned *civilian* . . . lubbers, by . . . !" They could all hear him seethe under his breath. "Clumsy, cack-handed, cunny . . ."

"Midshipman of the watch?" Lewrie softly asked, hugely amused, but holding in his guffaws. "Do you take my keys to the arms lockers forrud to the Bosun, will you? He is to arm waisters, brace-tenders, and landsmen, and be ready for a boarding action to larboard."

"Oi, sor," Mr. Larkin said, stumbling forward to take the keys, and not even bothering to disguise his sniggers as he deftly sprang to a ladder and sprinted forward.

"Now, where's our spook, goin' bump in the night?" Lewrie asked, lifting the heavy night-glass, again. She was right ahead, smothered by *Proteus*'s jibs. Quartermaster Austen and Quartermaster's Mate Toby Jugg were on the large helm, and steering as if to ram her just abaft of her starboard anchor cat-head. They could all see her without the use of telescopes, now, not two cables distant. And still as blind as a bat, it seemed! Lewrie could see people round her helm and compass binnacle, ghostily underlit by the binnacle lamps, see the amber glow of a pipe bowl as a watchstander took a deep draw on it. Her taff-rail lanthorns were merrily agleam, and another glow of light loomed below her rails and bulwarks, up near her forecastle belfry, like the lamps of a lighthouse just under the horizon.

"Dear God, but they're clueless!" Lt. Langlie chortled softly.

"Quartermasters," Lewrie bade. "We'll round up alongside her at about a *third* of a cable, thankee, our mizen even with their mizen, then let wind and sea push us down hull-to-hull. Gently, and I leave that to your best judgement t'just kiss her."

"Aye, sir," Austen and Jugg both chorused in tense whispers.

"At a *cable*, Mister Langlie, let fly all to get our way off, so we don't scud right past her," Lewrie continued. "Grappling hooks and boarding parties to be ready . . . the larboard bow-chaser to fire, when I call for it."

"Aye aye, sir," Lt. Langlie replied, leaning over the rail and nettings to pass the word forward and below to the crew. Barely had he done so when the unidentified ship's watchstanders stiffened and froze in surprise, having spotted *Proteus* bearing down on them, at last, and began to fling their arms about and tumble out a string of orders.

"*Mon Dieu, qu'est-ce que tues fous? Ça va pas, non?*" the senior watchkeeping mate howled with the aid of a brass speaking-trumpet, his voice a horrified screech. "*Détourner, détourner, maintenant!*"

" 'What the hell are you doing? Are you crazy? Turn, now,' " Mr. Peel was translating, quite enjoying the Frenchman's discomforture.

"Bow-chaser, Mister Langlie," Lewrie drawled.

"Larboard chase-gun . . . fire!" Followed by a *loud* bang!

"Open the larboard gun-ports," Lewrie instructed, "and begin to round up on her, if you please. Mister Peel, you speak good Frog. Do you inform her that we're British, and I'll blow her to kindling if she doesn't surrender, this instant. *Ici la frégate anglaise Proteus*, and all that. And we'll see which gives 'em the collywobbles . . . our artillery, or dare I hope, our fearsome name!"

Peel took Lt. Langlie's speaking-trumpet and went over to larboard—not without a new tangle with a ring-bolt and a curse or two—and shouted their identity and demands. At the same time, *Proteus* seemed to roar and snarl as the heavy gun-carriages' trucks thundered forward, as the gun-ports swung upward to bare blood-red squares above, and the sight of glossy-black muzzles below them, run out in battery.

"*Putain! Mon Dieu, merde alors! Mort de ma vie!* Aack!" could be made out among screeches, shrill screams, and distressed howls of sudden terror as the off-duty watch came boiling up from below to gape at the slaughter which lay not a ship-length from them. "*Oui!* Not to fire, we are the surrender! *Reddition*, please!"

"Ease us alongside, Quartermasters. Mister Devereux! Ready to board her and round her rabble up!" Lewrie chortled. "Ready, boarders!"

Order was being sorted out of the French crew's panicky chaos. Braces and sheets were being released from the pin-rails to allow her sails to flag and luff, powerless, as *Proteus* thundered again with the roar and snarl of defiance, from every hand's throat, this time. With throat-tearing, savage yells of triumph!

CHAPTER TWENTY

*W*hy the Devil are they lookin' at me that way?" Lewrie groused as the French captain of their latest prize and a seedy-looking Dutch "trullibubs" continued to goggle at him and shrink into themselves whenever he paced near them on the quarterdeck.

"Frankly, sir, you scare the piss out of them," Mr. Peel replied.

"Well, hmm . . ." Lewrie mused, shooting his cuffs and re-setting the line of his coat. "Good."

"And who wouldn't be, I ask you, Captain Lewrie," Peel smirked. "Considering, hmm?"

Lewrie had grabbed one of his bled-out sky-blue coats, had slung his hanger's waistbelt over his chest like a cutlass's baldric, and had a pair of his double-barreled pistols shoved into his waistband. Still without stockings or neck-stock, and still bare-headed, he had to admit that he just *might* present the slightest image of an unshaven, tousled buccaneer of the last century, of the bloodthirstiest piratical bent!

For a fillip, Lewrie screwed his face into a murderous grimace, glared at the pair of them, and uttered his best theatrical "Arrr!"

Peel had to turn his back before he laughed out loud. After he had mastered himself once more, he crossed the quarterdeck to Lewrie's side up to windward, as *Proteus* and her prize "trailed their colours" down Basse-Terre's leeward coast, just a cable or two outside the range of the French forts, but well within plain view, and with their Union Flags flying atop every mast, as well as over the biggest French Tri-colour they could find aboard the merchant ship.

"Captain Fleury, I strongly suspect, *did* piss himself after he got to his quarterdeck, sir," Peel said in a confidential murmur. "He had heard the rumours about our last raid, *and* taken the Dutch captain of that ship we sank aboard as a passenger, who'd told him all about how brutal we, and you, were. Haljewin is his name, and a fount of information, he is. Though he did manage to contain *his* bladder."

"Actually pissed himself?" Lewrie snickered. "My word!"

"Let's just say that his stockings are yellow, and his breeches buttons are rusting, sir," Peel said with a chuckle. "This Haljewin, though ... Choundas and Hugues had chartered his ship to bear munitions to Rigaud, at Jacmel or Jéremie, and we cost them sore when it went up in flames. Haljewin had a rather unpleasant *tête-à-tête* with Choundas afterward, and fled aboard Captain Fleury's ship for safety, and a way off the island, soonest. Before Choundas murdered him for letting him down, d'ye see. And before Fleury set sail, they had a week or two to hear other interesting bits, come down to the waterfront."

Dammit, but Peel was beginning to play his superior's game, that pregnant pause and brow-arched leer that would force the other person to *ask* him to continue, that would allow Peel (or Pelham) to make the un-informed party twist slowly in the wind, give them their mo-ments of smug superiority ... that, or slap 'em silly for holding out!

"Arrr?" Lewrie growled, with a black-visaged grimace at Peel.

"Won't work on me, sir," Peel assured him. But Peel did relent and inform him of how they had removed Choundas's frigate from the equation; that Choundas and Hugues were at deadly logger-heads; that there were now two *corvettes* and two additional vessels converted to privateers in Choundas's little "squadron"; and that the lack of powder and shot, of boots, tents, blankets, muskets, and such with which to bribe or bedazzle the lighter-skinned, French-educated Gen. Rigaud on St. Domingue to be Gen. Hédouville's instrument, was most effectively ruining French hopes to reclaim the island colony outright.

"Captain Fleury's ship, though, sir," Peel continued. "Just a general cargo. He'd gotten into Jacmel and back out with sugar and coffee, cocoa, molasses, and rum, and had come back to Basse-Terre in hopes of selling some of it to local merchants, getting an escort from Hugues out to the open seas, past our patrols round Hispaniola, and getting his goods back to France."

"Aye, tight as the French are blockaded, here *and* there," Lewrie surmised, "that sort of cargo would be worth its weight in gold."

"Even more relishing, sir, Fleury was chartered by Hugues," Peel added, beaming with pleasure. "He and this Captain Fleury were to split the profits. Dare I say, this loss will anger Hugues, no end. And drive another wedge 'twixt Hugues and Choundas."

"Where *was* their escort?" Lewrie asked.

"None available, since Hugues's own frigate is off far west, on the Spanish Main, searching for American prizes, sir," Peel said, "and Choundas was so stung by Hugues's criticism that he sent all his ships to sea. Six of one, half-dozen of the other. Either way, Choundas is sure to be held responsible, no matter what he did or didn't do."

"So, does this Haljewin fellow, or this Fleury, know where we'd find Choundas's privateers?" Lewrie demanded, eager to crack on sail, secure his prize with the Admiralty Court not half a day's sail South on Dominica, and start hunting them down.

"Another matter, first, sir," Peel insisted, a finger raised.

"*Arrr*, Mister Peel!" Lewrie gravelled.

"Impressive, sir, truly," Peel mocked. "No, from what Haljewin says, Choundas is turning the island inside-out, seeking a *spy*. 'Twas Choundas's conviction that *you*, sir, are simply too dim to have pulled off our raid, with such an exquisite timing as to estop a vital and secret cargo, *and* catch their most powerful frigate at the exact moment she was being moved from the harbour at Pointe-à-Pitre to Basse-Terre, without the aid of a spy in our employ. Someone close to Choundas, d'ye see, sir?"

"No, Mister Peel, I don't," Lewrie peevishly groused. "I'm just too dim . . . d'ye see. Lucky t'know how t'pee without Foreign Office assistance. Damme!"

"My pardons, sir," Peel replied. "Perhaps that *could* have been better phrased . . . firstly, that you had, uhm, directions and intelligence from British agents, in contact with a French turncoat, on which to base your actions. Rumours are, though, sir . . . dear as Guillaume Choundas'd wish to harvest your liver, he holds you to be more lucky than brilliant. He *was* heard to speak of Mister Zachariah Twigg . . . rather disparagingly . . . and was rumoured to suspect that his staff had been, uhm . . . compromised, and that Mister Twigg, or someone in Twigg's employ, was pursuing him and dogging his every move, just as he was dogged and confounded in the Far East, then the Mediterranean."

"Oh, the poor, crippled old bastard!" Lewrie chortled. "Damme, is he feelin' persecuted?"

"*And* looking over his shoulder, now, sir," Peel insisted. "You shook him by the ears, right considerable. Put him off his paces. We have partially succeeded in un-nerving him."

"Well," Lewrie queried, turning to face inward, with his elbows on the cap-rails, and not feeling quite so demeaned any longer. "Does your, uhm . . . department, bureau, or whatever actually *have* a spy close to him? Someone in your pay on Guadeloupe?"

"Now, sir," Peel demurred, sniffing. "That would be telling."

"Right, then . . . *be* insufferable," Lewrie snapped. "And may ye have much joy of it! Tell me this, then. Now that we've got the evil shit half-confounded, where do I go t'find his ships so I can plague him some more?"

"Gone South, both Fleury and Haljewin suspected," Peel told him. "Bags of Yankee trade down that way, in the Spanish South American possessions, and the Dutch islands. They're half-starved for lack of any Spanish or Dutch ships able to put in with goods. Half-starved of new trade goods, the last three or four years, and half-starved for real by way of foodstuffs on the Dutch isles. Couldn't grow half of what they needed, even before the wars began. With no takers for their formerly valuable exports, 'tis a buyer's market."

"Aye, trust the skinflint Yankees to make a killing off of 'em," Lewrie said with a sneer of distaste natural to any true Englishman of gentlemanly pretensions; money was fine and all, but one could not get caught *directly* engaged in anything so mundane as "trade" and all the "filthy lucre" that came with it. One *hired* factors too common to be further sullied; one *invested*, at arm's reach.

"And the Frogs to make their 'killing' off the Americans, sir," Peel rejoined.

"Not if we can help it," Lewrie vowed. "This suspicion of a spy lark, Mister Peel . . . think it'd be worthwhile to put a flea in one of our captives' ears, and land Fleury or this Haljewin character ashore, before we get to Dominica? Spin 'em a tale of how we knew they'd sail without escort, and when, and laid in wait for them?"

He waved an idle hand at the shoreline whipping by to windward.

"Well, I don't quite . . . hmmm," Peel commented, frowning deeply and steepling wide-spread fingers to his lips as he bowed his head in thought. "Must admit, it does entice, does it not, sir. Not exactly in my brief, though. Without approval from Mister Pelham, I'd rather not 'gild the lily,' as it were, with *too* much finesse."

"Your superior, Mister Grenville Pelham, sir, is a pie-eyed idiot," Lewrie shot back, turning so that only one arm rested on the cap-rails to face him. "One who's hundreds of miles alee, and hasn't any idea of what's transpired since we sailed from Kingston . . . just what he *wished* to happen, and that merely in a general way. Do we sit round twiddlin' our thumbs waiting for specific direction from Pelham, we might just as well sail back to English harbour and swing about our moorings 'til Epiphany. You sent him a report by fast packet, soon as we entered Antigua harbour, I take it?"

"I did," Peel agreed. "and I am mortal-certain that he would approve every step we have taken so far, and praise our industry . . ."

, "The boy might as well be in London, for all the good he is to us, Mister Peel," Lewrie pressed, "with three or four months 'twixt our correspondence. Now, do we let one or both o' these fools go ashore to tell Choundas how we took 'em, and how 'twas a traitor offered them up on a plate to us, same as his precious frigate, and Haljewin's cargo was, it'll have him tearing his hair out by the roots. You *know* how brutal Choundas is . . . recall what Twigg surely told you about him at that long meeting you had before you sailed out here? His 'charming' little . . . diversions? Like child rape, child buggery, making people *suffer* as he takes his pleasure, worse than that Marquis de Sade sonofabitch of theirs? Aye, he's most-like got fucking and torture as equal partners in his head, by now. Most-like gets a cock-stand at the smell of hot irons and melted lead.

"Most-like set himself up a dungeon and a torture chamber, soon as he lit out here. Might've been his first priority for all we know," Lewrie argued with impatient haste as the lee port of Basse-Terre loomed up, and the tiny islets of the Saintes could be made out before the bows; time, geography, and the Trade Winds were stealing any opportunity to fetch-to and send Fleury and Haljewin ashore, before they were too far Sou'west of Guadeloupe, and spend hours beating back. To drop under the horizon, then return to land captives would be too suspicious a move, but to drop them off *now* would appear natural.

"He's a vicious beast, certainly Captain Lewrie, but . . ." Peel attempted to counter.

"Choundas would *adore* searchin' for a spy in his midst, Mister Peel! They could tell him we were bound South t'hunt his privateers, too. *Us*, sir; Lewrie, and *Proteus*, out to harm him, personally! And all he can is stew and fret that we'll find one or all, and eliminate his little squadron, and there's no way he can warn them. He's *lamed*, but he ain't paralysed. He's not the sort to sit patient and trust to Fate. Damme, sir, he'll be forced t'do *something* to keep his hand in, to prove to Hugues that he's vital, capable . . . ! He's truly convinced there's a spy responsible for his troubles, Choundas will move Heaven and Earth t'find him. Does he *produce* one, he's vindicated, don't you *see*? 'Weren't my bloody fault, 'twas those damned British and a damn' traitor done it!' He'll have weeks and weeks to sit idle, 'fore those ships of his report back, and he's not the man to take his ease in an armchair and catch up on his reading."

"Hmmm . . ." Mr. Peel said, maddeningly dithering while gnawing on a ragged thumbnail, and all the while time, position, and advantage were passing by at a rate of knots! "There's truth in what you say, I grant you, Captain Lewrie, but . . ."

"But, mine arse, Mister Peel!" Lewrie spluttered. "The chances are passin' us *by*, 'long as you hem and haw. We could fetch-to right this minute . . . !"

Boom-boom . . . bo-boom, faintly from windward.

The western coast of Guadeloupe tucked in upon itself a bit as one reached its southernmost extremities. *Proteus*, standing Due South just beyond the heaviest cannon's range, had extended her distance by another mile or so as the shore trended away. Even so, the Vieux Fort on the final point below Basse-Terre had attempted to take them under fire, and by the basso notes of the bowling round-shot that went up the scale in an eerie minor key as it neared, Lewrie suspected 32-pounder or even 42-pounder guns, with which to enforce the new three-mile-limit of territoriality, their maximum range.

Sure enough, four massive waterspouts leaped for the sky, high as their frigate's fighting-tops, fat yet feathery, and aroar as tons of seawater were vertically displaced, then slowly collapsed upon themselves as torrential as a mountain river's falls. Smaller feathers of spray staggered towards *Proteus* as the massive balls caromed off First Graze to Second Graze, then Third, before losing enough forward momentum to gouge little more than leaping-dolphin splashes as they finally sank.

Proteus's sailors jeered and cat-called with derision for such a hopeless show of defiance, for their First Graze had struck the sea one whole mile or near short of her sides, with their final, weary splashes still half a mile shy.

"Better luck next time, Froggie!" Lewrie heard Landsman Desmond shrill between tunneled hands.

"Yair . . . waste yer powder, Monsewer!" his mate, Furfy, howled.

"It would appear that the French are in a bit of a pique at the moment, Captain Lewrie," Peel snickered, "and any boats despatched to port would most-like be shot to atoms long before they could be identified as truce boats. Have to make a *show* of usefulness, satisfy the honour of their bloody Tricolour rag, don't ye know. They're simply too angry to listen to reason, at the moment, so . . . it appears we can not implement your plan, for now, sir."

"Dammit, Mister Peel, they couldn't hit the ground with their bloody *hats*, we could lie off safe as houses!" Lewrie countered.

"I do not dismiss your suggestion out of hand, sir," Peel said with a pinched expression, looking as if he was wrapping resistance to the idea about himself as he tucked the lapels of his coat together. "I only say that it is a matter which will require some cogitation on my part before deciding whether it advances our enterprise, or proves to be so transparent a ploy to Choundas that we end up appearing just *too* clever, thereby, uhm . . . shooting ourselves in the foot by *forcing* him to deem the presence of a British spy in his circle groundless. I also note that we are almost past Guadeloupe. Why, it might take hours to sail back, right into the teeth of those heavy fortress guns, again. To return so quickly would be even *more* transparent to him, and—"

"*No!* Ye don't *say!*" Lewrie drawled, as if he just that instant had had a blinding glimpse of the obvious. "Really?" he sneered.

"There is hardly a call for sharp words, Captain Lewrie!"

"The hell there ain't. Our best shot at it *is* past, whilst we stood here yarnin' and . . . cogitatin'," Lewrie spat. "If not now, *do* tell me *when*, sir! Ye said yourself, 'twas a good idea, in the main. Damme, Mister Peel, I don't have 'em *often*. You keep assuring me of *that*, God knows. Young Pelham ain't here t'hold your hand and impart his . . . wisdom to you . . . !"

"Damn you, sir!" Peel barked, himself rowed beyond temperance.

"Damn you for that! I need no cosseting to do my best! For two pence I would demand satisfaction . . . sir."

Lewrie made a show of withdrawing his coin-purse from a breeches pocket, undoing the draw-strings, and delving inside for coins. Jovial blue eyes had gone cold, steely grey, and his face was a killing mask. He raised one brow in deadly query.

"Two pence, did you say, sir?"

"Gentlemen, gentlemen!" Lt. Langlie intruded, all but stepping between them in sudden worry. "Mister Peel, sir . . . Captain, sir! Do but draw a deep breath, the both of you, and consider the consequences to your good names . . . your careers, if nothing else, I conjure you."

"I'll not be insulted so publicly," Peel snapped, eyes boring into Lewrie's, not allowing Lt. Langlie a lone inch of personal space in which to part them.

"I'll not be treated like a lack-wit, too dumb t'pee on my own, either," Lewrie rejoined.

"Dear God, sirs," Anthony Langlie groused at the both of them, as softly and confidentially as he dared while still getting his point across. "Is not our King's business, and the destruction of this man Choundas, more important at the moment than either of your senses of honour and hurt feelings?"

"*Mister* Langlie!" Lewrie growled, rounding on him, as if to tear a strip off his hide for daring to gainsay a Post-Captain placed over him by that selfsame King.

"Your pardons, sir, but I cannot stand by and see you ruined," Lt. Langlie pleaded. "I know not what grievance, or difference, you gentlemen share, but surely it cannot be so dire a matter over which you must come to logger-heads. Do, pray, allow me to counsel cooler minds, some time to consider your actions before either of you does or says anything else . . . from which you cannot demur later. I know it ain't my place, Captain, and I could be broken for it, but . . ."

The desperation in Langlie's voice, the worry in his eyes, at last got through to Lewrie. He drew that demanded deep breath, then screwed his eyes shut for a long moment. With a long exhalation, he relented.

"Thankee, Mister Langlie," he said, forcing a bleak grin onto his phyz. "Thankee for your concern for me."

"And you, Mister Peel?" Langlie felt emboldened to enquire from their supercargo. "Can you not give it a good, long think before . . ."

Peel grunted as if he'd been punched in the stomach, but waved off any further "assistance" from the First Officer. "Thankee, Mister Langlie. A minor matter, as you say. But a trifling, passing snit . . . of which I shall say no more, other than to characterise it as a professional, and brief, parting of the minds. You will excuse me, sir?" Peel asked of Langlie, doffing his hat and essaying a short bow. Peel gave Lewrie a shorter jerk in his direction, too, before stomping off for the larboard quarterdeck ladder to go below.

"I'm sorry, sir, but it looked as if someone had to . . ." Langlie said with a groan of worry.

"Oh, be at ease, Mister Langlie," Lewrie assured him. "We were in disagreement over a joke I wished to play on the French. Still may, does he see his way round it. Once he 'gets down from his high-horse,' that is. 'Tis not a killing matter, 'less he wishes to make it so. I expect a decent dinner, and a bottle of *my* claret'll bring him back to his senses. Just may do the same for me, you never can tell," Lewrie concluded with a wry, self-disparaging grin.

"I am at ease, sir," Langlie replied, grinning wider, himself. "Thank God, how could I ever explain your, uhm, untimely demise to poor Sophie, or . . ."

"Now you *are* being impertinent, Mister Langlie," Lewrie chided him, putting his "stern" face back on for an instant.

"Carrying on, sir, instanter," Langlie quickly said, doffing his hat, and making a rapid escape, back to his proper duties.

Damn you Frogs! Lewrie thought, turning back to face the island as *Proteus* ran Large off the wind, now just a bit below the fort, that was still intent on wasting powder and expensive heavy shot on them; *I almost had him convinced, but for you bastards interrupting. I still think it's a good idea. Just 'cause it ain't my pigeon, not my line o' work, don't mean it's worthless. 'Lucky, but not brilliant,' am I? Just a faithful gun-dog, t'point, run, and fetch, am I? Well, we'll see about that!*

He pushed himself erect from the cap-rails, turned and stomped black-visaged past his captive captains to the binnacle cabinet, left hand flexing fretful on the hilt of his hanger. He glared at them in passing, speculating which of them, the Frenchman Fleury, or the Dutch master Haljewin (however the Hell one spelled that!), would be the better "tablet" on which to carve his mis-directing message.

Over his shoulder, he heard expostulations in wind-muffled Dutch or French, an evil snicker—followed by more unbelieving splutters.

Shoes clomped on the quarterdeck planks, coming nearer.

"Excuse me, again, Captain," Lt. Langlie said, tapping fingers to his hat in a casual salute, "but our prisoners were asking what your argument with Mister Peel was all about, and . . . I could not help having a bit of fun at their expense. I told them, sir . . ." Langlie paused, a fist to his mouth to stifle a laugh, and ruin his jape, "I told 'em that you were going to throw them to the sharks, but that Mister Peel thought only *one* should go over the side, and we'd give him the other."

"You did, did you, Mister Langlie?" Lewrie said, gazing on them past Langlie's shoulder. "Well . . . tell 'em we'll decide which later."

"Aye aye, sir!"

"*Arrr*," Lewrie called out, pointing "eeny-meeny-miney-moh" at them. Captain Fleury fainted dead away. And he really did have a very weak bladder!

CHAPTER TWENTY-ONE

*T*he Admiralty Prize Court on Dominica was ten miles or more to the south of Prince Rupert Bay and its tiny settlement of Portsmouth, at the lee-side port town named Roseau, from the times when the French had owned the island. Lewrie had been forced to trade his smart gig for a humbler but larger cutter and sail down to confer with them.

Dominica had been one of those isles infested with Carib Indians so battle-mad and death-defying that every European power that colonised the Antilles had sworn off the place in 1748, but that hadn't lasted long. Britain took it in 1763, the French got in back in 1778, then Britain again at the end of the American Revolution. The steep, fern-jungle mountains were simply stiff with Caribs, making it a real "King's Bad Bargain."

So was the Prize Court. A greater pack of ignorant "ink-sniffs," thieves, drunkards, and paper buccaneers Lewrie had never laid eyes on! And it was no wonder that they'd greeted his arrival the same way some gang of adolescent London street imps would welcome the sight of a pie-man with a tray of fresh goodies.

Half-literate, spouting "dog-Latin" legalese, their accents an echo of Cockey "Bow Bells," "half-seas-over" on cheap rum or strong "stingo" beer, and sporting mementos of their last half-dozen dinners on greasy cuffs, waist-coats, or breeches, unshaven and unwashed—

Lewrie suspected their experience of law had come from the wrong side of some magistrate's bench. He'd have rather dealt with Mr. Peel, who still sulked over their *contretemps*; it would have been safer, and he would not get gravy-spotted off the furniture, nor would he depart infested with fleas! Besides, this court would refer everything back to Antigua, and reams of paper, gallons of ink, and pounds of stamps and paste would be used up before he, his officers and warrants, or his sailors saw tuppence . . . sometime in 1810, he sourly suspected. Maybe his grandchildren might have joy of his latest capture's profit.

After that experience, which had taken up most of the morning, and a horrid dinner at a tumbledown dockside tavern, Lewrie walked out the long single quay that speared at least one hundred yards out from the beach before the waters at low tide would allow a ship's boat to come alongside, then rambled on all ramshackley for a good fifty yards more. His cutter, with its single lug-sail furled, was the only one in sight, at present, positively handsome compared to the few scabrous and half-abandoned fishing boats drawn up on the sands.

He paused to fan himself with his hat and belch biliously from his repast. The purported squab had most-like been seagull, and the "Roast Beef of Olde England" had most-like barked at the moon and run after cats before its luck had run out! The infamous two-penny ordinarys of his native London had nothing to fear for their reputations by comparison; and they had most-like not poisoned *half* as many patrons. He *might* have tried the pork roast, but the natives on the island were reputed to be cannibals, and he'd not put it past the publican to buy a side of "long pig" (as they said in the Great South Seas) and serve up the loser of some Carib feud.

"You men have eat?" Lewrie enquired of his boat crew after he finally reached them. He had let them step ashore for a meal, and the usual "wet," with instructions for everyone to be back in two hours . . . and sober, mind. A quick nose-count assured him that no one had been daft enough to take "leg bail" in such a no-hope port; no one appeared "groggy," either—well, no more so than usual.

"*Think* it was food, sah," his Coxswain, Matthew Andrews, dared to josh with him from his privileged position and long association as his sometime confidant. "It was burnt, and it come on plates."

"Law, Missah Gideon, he b'ile wood chips in slush, it would o' eat bettah, Cap'm sah," little Nelson, one of his recent Black Jamaican "volunteers" further ventured to say.

"Sorry 'bout that, lads," Lewrie commiserated, "but I do think my own dinner was pot-scrapings worse than yours. Let's shove off."

"Back to de ship, sah, aye," Andrews said, shipping the tiller-bar atop the rudder post while Lewrie was offered a hand or two on his way aboard the cutter, and aft to a seat in the stern-sheets.

Two hours later, though, as the cutter bounded close-hauled into Prince Rupert Bay, Lewrie shaded his eyes for a look round. There was HMS *Proteus*, as pretty as a painting, with her prize moored close by; there was the Yankee stores ship, attended by boats come to fetch out supplies; there was USS *Sumter* . . . but there were some new arrivals, too, including a "jack-ass," or hermaphrodite, brig that flew a small blue Harbour Jack right-forward, sprinkled with thirteen white stars, to show that she was an American man o' war; another of their bought-in and converted "Armed Ships," not a vessel built as a warship.

There were three merchant vessels flying the "Stars and Stripes" anchored in the bay, as well. Two were very large three-masted tops'l schooners, with their tall masts raked much farther aft than Lewrie had ever seen before, lying near the new-come armed brig. Farther out in deeper water, and unable to anchor closer to shore for being deep-laden, was a proper three-masted, full-rigged ship, equally as impressive a specimen of the shipbuilders' art, and "Bristol Fashion" smart.

"Damme, but those schooners look like they'd be fast as witches . . . even to windward," Lewrie commented. "Even with the full cargoes they seem to bear. Ever seen the like, Andrews?"

"Masts raked so sharp, dough, sah . . . dem Yankees mebbe crazy," was Andrews's assessment. "How dey foot 'em to de keel-steps, an' not rip right out, I'd wondah. Wadn't here dis mornin'. T'ink dem 'Mericans be makin' up a no'th-bound 'trade,' at las', Cap'm?"

"It very well could be," Lewrie agreed. "I think we'll satisfy my curiosity, before we go back aboard our ship. Steer for *Sumter*, if you will, Andrews. It appears there's a gaggle o' boats alongside of her already."

"Aye aye, sah."

"Besides, Captain McGilliveray might have something with which to settle our mis'rable dinners," Lewrie added with a chuckle.

⚓

"Captain Lewrie, sir!" Midshipman Desmond McGilliveray said at the top of the starboard entry-port, stepping forward past the Marine Lieutenant in charge of the side-party that had rendered him honours. The lad was almost tail-wagging eager to greet him, though constricted by the usages and customs of his navy to the doffing of his hat and a bow from the waist.

"Mister McGilliveray!" Lewrie cried with too much heartiness of his own, his eyes equally agleam, and his carefully stern expression creased by an involuntary smile. "Well met, young sir."

"We saw you come in with your prize, sir!" the lad exclaimed in joy, plopping his tricorne back on his head any-old-how. "Did she put up much of a fight, sir? Did she resist very long, or . . . ?"

Once his own gilt-laced cocked hat was back on his own head, he astounded the boy by extending his right hand for a warmer greeting; a hand that young McGilliveray took with a puppyish delight and shook in return, right heartily.

"Steered right up to her, yardarm to yardarm, in the dark, and only fired one bow-chaser, just t'wake 'em long enough to surrender!" Lewrie replied, proud for a chance to boast and preen. "I'll tell it all to you later, should we have the chance. But I have come to see your Captain first."

"He is aboard, sir, and aft," Midshipman McGilliveray informed him, only slightly crest-fallen. "I shall tell him that you have come aboard, Captain Lewrie. This way, please."

Lewrie's arrival alongside, though, had created enough stir to draw *Sumter*'s First Officer, Lt. Claiborne, from the great-cabins aft to the gangway, minus sword and hat.

"Ah! Captain Lewrie, good," Lt. Claiborne said, coming over to greet him, as well. "You got our captain's note, I see."

"Uhm, no Mister Claiborne, I came direct from Roseau and the Prize Court offices," Lewrie told him.

"And you escaped with your purse, Captain Lewrie? Congratulations," Claiborne replied, frowning for a second. "My captain is now in conversation with several of our merchant masters, and wished to speak with you, regarding their informations. A glad happenstance, you came to call on us. If you will follow me, Captain Lewrie?"

"Lead on, sir. Talk to you later, lad," Lewrie promised to his newly acquired "offspring."

He was led down a ladder to the gun-deck, then aft into the cabins under the quarterdeck, clutching the hilt of his hanger in one hand and his hat in the other; suddenly self-conscious to be ogled like some raree show, with many faint, fond, almost *doting* smiles to every hand. Lewrie could only conclude that *Sumter's* people had gotten a whiff of rumour concerning his relationship to Midshipman McGilliveray, who was obviously a "younker" well thought of aboard that ship to begin with.

Damme, even that hawk-faced Marine lieutenant goggled me like a new-born swaddlin' babe! Lewrie groused to himself as he was admitted to the day-cabin, where the air was close, hot and still, despite the opened windows, coach-top, and wind-scoops; where several men ceased their conversation and rose to greet him. Lewrie blinked to adapt to the dimness of the cabins, after the harsh brightness of the deck.

"Captain Lewrie, thank you for responding to my request for a conference so quickly," Capt. McGilliveray said, coming forward to take hands with him. He gave Lewrie no time to explain that he had not gotten McGilliveray's note, but began to introduce the others present.

There was another U.S. Navy officer off the hermaphrodite brig, an almost painfully tall and gaunt, dark-visaged fellow in his middle thirties, named to him as one Captain Randolph, of the Armed Brig USS *Oglethorpe*.

"Proudly commissioned in Savannah, Captain Lewrie, suh," Capt. Randolph told him with a warm smile, "an' named f'r one of your English lords, James Oglethorpe, who founded th' Georgia colony," he said in addition, and in a liquid drawl even rounder and deeper than South Carolinian McGilliveray's, were such a thing possible.

"And ya know what they say, Randolph," McGilliveray japed him, "that all the rogues went t'Georgia', ha ha!"

"*Proud* of it, suh, proud *of* it!" Randolph happily rejoined.

"And Captains Ezekiel Crowninshield and Gabriel Crowninshield," McGilliveray continued, indicating a pair of stouter and younger men who were, at first glance, as alike as a pair of book-ends; gingeryhaired and florid. "Their schooners are outta Mystic, Connecticut, magnificent and fast sailers, the *Iroquois* and the *Algonquin*."

"Twins, as well, sirs?" Lewrie asked of them after a greeting.

"Built side-by-side in the same yard, Captain Lewrie," he was gladly told in a much harsher "Down-East Yankee" nasal twang. "First swam within a week of each other, too." One brother said.

"Raced him hyuh," the other boasted. "Beat him all hollow."

"And last but not least," McGilliveray said further, "Captain Grant, off the *Sarah and Jane*. Captain Grant, Captain Lewrie, of the *Proteus* frigate."

"Your servant, sir," Lewrie politely said, though the name was nagging at him; the ship and her captain, both, as he stepped closer to take Grant's hand. "Oh! 'Tis you, sir. Well met, again."

"Why, bless my soul, if it ain't that little pop-in-jay laddy, who gave me so much grief in the Bahamas!" Grant exclaimed. "Ruint a whole cargo o' Caicos salt on me, too . . . eighty-six, was it? Just a Lieutenant, then, ye were, in yer little converted bomb-ketch . . . ?"

"*Alacrity*, Captain Grant," Lewrie supplied him. "But, then . . . you'd not have lost so dearly, had you obeyed the Navigation Acts and steered wide o' me. And the salt wouldn't have been used for bulwarks and your ship not commandeered as bait if you'd stayed in the Turks Islands and testified 'gainst Calico Jack Finney's pirates as I asked you to." Lewrie still held Grant's hand, though they were done shaking; his smile *could* have been mistaken for courteous, but there was a definite frost to his voice.

"Well, we live an' learn, do we not, Captain Lewrie," Grant at last said with a wintry smile of his own, almost pulling himself free.

"We do, indeed, sir," Lewrie replied.

"Whatever happened t'Calico Jack Finney?" Grant *had* to enquire.

"I chased him into Charleston harbour and killed the bastard," Lewrie told him in a casual, off-hand way, still grinning.

"Dear Lord, that was *you*, Captain Lewrie?" Capt. McGilliveray said with a gasp of wonder. "Why, I watched the whole thing from the Battery! My my my, will wonders never cease. That we've crossed each other's hawses, if ya will, more than once. In so *many* things, well!"

"Life is funny that way, aye, Captain McGilliveray, I grant ye," Lewrie answered, glad to turn his direction and dismiss Grant.

"Ever'body says that," Capt. Randolph of the *Oglethorpe* mused.

"but usually with long faces when they do," he japed, solemn-faced.

"If you'll have a seat and join us, Captain Lewrie. A glass of something cool? We've cold tea, or . . ." McGilliveray offered.

"Cold tea'd be capital, thankee, sir," Lewrie said as he seated himself. "I take it that you were discussing some matter concerning a mercantile nature, sirs?"

"Missing ships, sir," McGilliveray intoned as his cabin servant fetched Lewrie a tall tumbler of tea, with the unheard-of luxury of a chunk of ice in it!

"Walsham, Massachusetts," one of the Crowninshields boasted to him. "The Dons an' the Dutchies're mad for th' stuff, our New England ice. Can't pack it outta the Andes mountains 'fore it melts, I guess. Mule train's too slow."

"Too-small packets, 'Zekiel," the other Crowninshield quibbled. "Has t'be stowed in bulk, in chaff an' sawdust outta sunlight. Keeps itself frozen, ya see."

"We've lost a ship, mebbe two," the brother Lewrie now knew to name Ezekiel baldly announced, stealing McGilliveray's "thunder," as the Yankee Doodles would say in their colourfully colloquial way.

"Down South," the one dubbed Gabriel stuck in. "Sailed behind us. Had 'em in sight for a piece . . ."

"Older schooners. Slower'n ours," Ezekiel chimed in. "And we were racin' each other, like I said, so we sailed 'em under. *Mohican* was t'put in at Saint Lucia, but that'd only delay her two days or so, no more, and . . ."

"And *Chippewa* was t'come inta Roseau t'meet us," Gabriel grumbled, "but we've laid over almost a week now, and there's neither hide nor hair o' either one of 'em, Cap'm Lewrie, and we're getting worried, I'll lay ya. Coasted up hyuh t'ask of 'em, but . . ."

"Powerful worried," Ezekiel Crowninshield butted in. "Wasn't a *speck* o' foul weather on our passage, and nary even a squall astern of us did we see t'upset 'em."

"Trusted, salty masters and mates, good an' true Mystic lads in the crews, too, so . . ." Gabriel Crowninshield interrupted, shrugging in mystification.

"So, no mutiny or buccaneering," Lewrie surmised, sipping at his tea, already suspecting the worst.

"Gentlemen, I fear that those ships have been taken by French cruisers," Lewrie was forced to tell them. "When I took my prize last

night, we learned some things from our prisoners. That captain of
whom I spoke, Captain McGilliveray, that Guillaume Choundas? We
took away his best frigate a few weeks ago, but he still commands
two *corvettes* and now has converted a schooner and a brig as privateers, and our captives told us he'd sent 'em South, to prey on American ships in particular. To hurt your commerce as sorely as you've
hurt theirs. And make himself and their Governor-General, Victor
Hugues, a pile of 'tin.' If he can't challenge American warships round
Hispaniola, and further up North, he intended to put all four vessels
to sea beyond your immediate reach, and purge you from the oceans,
as you made passage home with all those rich cargoes of yours. Sorry."

*And who'd prefer lumber, ice, and barrel staves to sugar, coffee, and
cocoa?* Lewrie thought, scorning American exports and the products of
their limited industries. *Well, they do ship rum, and decent beer!*

"Onliest place they can take 'em is Guadeloupe!" Captain Grant
spluttered, breaking the stunned, sad silence following Lewrie's revelation. "Bless my soul, can't ya blockade 'em, can ya not dash back
an' . . . try to . . ."

"Intercept 'em, ayup," one of the Crowninshields supplied.

"Aye, intercept 'em," Grant gravelled. "Catch 'em before they fetch
'em into Basse-Terre or Pointe-à-Pitre. Get word t'your other warships, Cap'm Lewrie. Ya can't be th' *only* frigate in these parts!"

"Three days, into the teeth of the Trades to Antigua, and then
what, sirs?" Lewrie demanded, spreading his hands at the futility. "I
am heartily sorry for your losses, gentlemen, but do I haunt either or
both harbours in hopes of re-capturing your ships, *any* Americans
taken as prizes, I'm not fulfilling my proper duty. Better I . . ."

"Damn my eyes, Lewrie!" Grant exploded. "And here I thought ya
were a fire-eatin' scrapper!"

"Better I take *Proteus* South, sir," Lewrie reiterated with his teeth
on edge, "for do I lurk close inshore of Guadeloupe for weeks, what's
happening to a dozen, *two* dozen other American merchantmen down
South? How many ships will make it here to *form* a convoy, if the
damn' French are free to run riot? Nossirs . . . I'm away down the
Windwards, this very evening, as far as Caracas if I must."

"*Sumter*'ll clear port, as well, sir," Capt. McGilliveray vowed. "Randolph, you want to take charge here, and wait for the promised frigate
t'come in? Or would ya prefer t'sail in company with me and find a
proper fight for a change?"

"Let our consul keep an eye on things here, Cap'm McGilliveray," Capt. Randolph cried, leaping to his feet (though careful not to knock his head on the overhead beams or planking), "for sure as there's God in his Heaven, my sword, my right arm, and my ship are yours! I'd be that eager t'show those swaggerin' Monsoors what it's like to tangle with a pack o' Georgia wildcats! Bring 'em on . . . *yee-hah!*" he ended with a shout, a Red Indian warrior's feral battle-scream, that made Lewrie's hackles and nape hairs stand on end.

Aboard *Sumter*, that howl caused her crew, and Capt. Randolph's boat-crew laying alongside, to raise a screeching wolf's chorus of their own, as they suspected that they would no longer swing idle round the moorings to await the plodding drudgery of convoying, but would be going out to look for a proper stand-up fight, at long last.

"Uhm . . . given this sudden, and un-looked-for, turn of events," Lewrie carefully began to say, once he had recovered his aplomb, using caution before the unwitting civilians not privy to their government's, or his and McGilliveray's covert arrangement, "and since it is British as well as American merchantmen at peril . . . and, notwithstanding the lack of a *formal* pact 'twixt your President and the Crown, perhaps we could, ah . . . aid each other in our respective searches for the French privateers, Captain McGilliveray?"

"An *excellent* suggestion, Captain Lewrie," McGilliveray replied, shamming the utmost surprise at such a generous offer. Then, amid the enthusiastic "Huzzahs!" from Randolph and the merchant masters, he gave Lewrie an enigmatic smile, and the tiniest incline of his head as a reward. "I, and my government, stand forever in your debt for your open-handed and cooperative spirit!"

Lost in the cheering and toasting, however, was the fact that no British ships, or very few at most, were in danger; *they* didn't trade on the Spanish Main or with the Dutch isles, with both nations allies to France!

A toast was raised to Lewrie's alacrity and support, and while it was being drunk, and he posed all disparagingly "Aw, Pshaw" modest, his mind was mildly ascheme.

No matter *what* Pelham wanted, what his London masters wanted, it made eminent sense, and to the Devil with Saint Domingue and who owned it! America and Great Britain, he marvelled; sworn enemies not fifteen years past. Despite the lingering grievances and distrust created during their Revolution, their burgeoning commercial competition, and rivalry, they were going to war as temporary allies, on the same side for a blessed once! Could this lead to better things, he speculated?

And what allies they'd make, too! Even if they were so ruled by their enthusiasms, so . . . un-English in revealing their feelings, such as their screams, howls, and cheers at present.

Well, so was he, when you came right down to it. Wearing a public mask of blasé boredom definitely did not become him. In fact, he rather *liked* the freedom to howl, and wished he possessed it!

Oh, Lord, he thought, *Peel's sure t'go off like a bomb!*

CHAPTER TWENTY-TWO

*A*h, Captain Lewrie," Peel said after he had gotten back aboard *Proteus*, and had made it below to his great-cabins. Peel was sitting in the dining-coach, in the middle of writing a letter, to his master Mr. Pelham Lewrie supposed as he tore open his neck-stock, unbuckled his sword belt, and removed his coat. "You're back, at last. I have been meaning to discuss your idea with you . . . that'un you proposed on deck, yesterday, concerning the, uhm . . ." Peel enigmatically said with a vague wave of his hand in Aspinall's direction.

"Oh, yes?" Lewrie responded, feigning idle interest, and making his face a placid Englishman's mask again. "I'd relish a ginger beer, Aspinall, there's a good fellow. The Americans served cold tea when I was aboard *Sumter* just now."

"The decoction in which I indulge, sir," Mr. Peel told him, all chirpy and pleasant, as if yesterday's bitter argument hadn't happened.

Lewrie answered, "With *ice*, sir. The Yankees still had a small supply of their Massachusetts ice aboard. Worth its weight in gold with the Dons, one of their merchant masters informed me." He took a seat at the table, across from Peel.

"I am suddenly jealous, sir!" Peel said with a groan of envy at the prospect, and made a *moue* of faint distaste at his mug of tea. "I suppose we shall not see the like 'til the first American traders call at Kingston next spring, alas."

"Yer beer, sir," Aspinall said, fetching Lewrie a foaming mug.

"Thankee, Aspinall, that'll be all for a bit," Lewrie said with a brief smile. "Do you take a turn on deck and get some air. Cabins are stuffy, God knows, even with the canvas chutes rigged."

"Aye, sir, and I will," his man-servant replied, departing with a long hank of spun-yarn he quickly fetched from what was left of his tiny day-pantry, so he could continue his sennet-work.

"So, you've considered the idea, have you, Mister Peel?" Lewrie said once they were alone. He *could* not show as much keen interest in what Peel decided, for, frankly, the developments aboard *Sumter* had made the quickly spun scheme quite fly his head. He could *sham* renewed interest, though . . . and trust that fear of rejection would explain a lack of greater enthusiasm in his demeanour.

"I have, sir," Peel stated. "Once I had, uhm . . . cooled off a bit, d'ye see?" He made another *moue*, tossed off a shrug, and chuckled softly. "And I've come to the conclusion that encouraging Choundas in imagining that he's a traitor in his vicinity is actually a rather neat piece of mis-direction . . . one which I am sure that Mister Pelham would approve, were he here. One, frankly, which he might have dreamt up himself, was he privy to the intelligence we just discovered."

"Excellent!" Lewrie crowed, slapping the dining table with his open palm. "Capital! And I am certain that you've concocted a scheme for getting our prisoners back to Guadeloupe, and blabbing what you wish to Choundas. It'll be a clever bit, knowing you, Mister Peel. More subtle than any *I* could have come up with on short notice. Mean t'say," Lewrie gushed, then paused, thinking that he was laying on the praise a bit *too* thick for Peel to credit, so soon after their howling snit. He had a *very* large and heavy "shoe" which he was about to drop on the long-suffering bastard's head, after all, and it would be nice to agree on something, anything!, before dropping it.

"Well, sir," Peel continued, though he did pause a bit, himself, to give Lewrie the tiniest chary look. "Captain Haljewin was the one sprung the idea of a spy on Choundas, from what I gathered whilst interrogating the man. Haljewin had bags of unguarded time since his capture to converse with the French captain and his mates, as separate interrogations with them revealed. They are all now convinced that someone on Guadeloupe betrayed them to us last night, and I was careful to leave them with the impression that they weren't far wrong . . . without actually *confirming* the existence of a spy, or *spies*. But neither did I go out of my way to *deny* it, d'ye see, Captain Lewrie!"

Let him have joy of it, Lewrie thought; *preen gladsome, for now.*

"During my interrogations, I also discovered that Choundas has a rather small, but trusted, staff," Peel went on almost happily, in his element, privy to things Lewrie didn't know, and glad to impart them. "There's a Captain Griot, commanding a *corvette* name of *Le Gascon.* A Breton, and you know what stock Choundas puts in his ancient Celts and Veneti warriors ... men of the ancient blood, and all."

"God, yes," Lewrie agreed. "Mad for 'em."

"His other *corvette* is commanded by a Captain MacPherson, one of those *émigré* Scots who fled after the Battle of Culloden. He was born in France, but his parents were minor Scots aristocracy. Most-like landed gentry, in the 'squirearchy' with but dim and distant relation to a proper 'laird.' In France, though, 'til the Revolution, they were awarded the title of Chevalier. Or, bought it. King Louis's court at Versailles was as corrupt as the Ottoman Turks'. But, Captain MacPherson is Catholic! A breast-beater of the staunchest sort, hmm?"

"A fallen *aristo, and* a Papist, to boot?" Lewrie said with a chuckle. "That'd make him doubly suspect to the Directory in Paris ... all the anti-religion cant they spout. There's bishops back home now calling France the Anti-Christ, already. He your choice, then?"

"In a pinch, he'd serve main-well, I do confess," Peel laughed, "though he's reckoned a superb officer and ship-handler. Rather popular with his officers and men. Well thought of, in general."

"Oh well, then," Lewrie said with a shrug, and a sip of beer.

"Should a well-liked and trusted man be labeled a spy and traitor, sir, and were enough proofs manufactured to convince Choundas and Hugues of his guilt," Peel merrily plotted, "the implications of that strike much wider and deeper than Guadeloupe. Firstly, if a man like MacPherson can't be trusted, then who can? And secondly, would it not set off a frenzy of Jacobin revulsion 'gainst Catholics in France? Or create a Catholic resistance to the Directory, and the Revolution? Do you see the possibilities, sir? They're breathtaking!" Peel exulted.

"Oh!" Lewrie gasped. "It'd set off another Terror, worse than the one of Ninety-three! Half their people'd be witch-findin' among the other half, and *everyone'd* be suspect. They'd keep their guillotines workin' round the clock!"

"Decimating their officer corps, purging it all over again, of capable

people, and promoting the rabid fools most loyal to the Republic from
the rear ranks to the officers' mess," Peel chortled in glee as he contemplated the reach of his scheme.

"Turning Ordinary Seamen into Post-Captains," Lewrie added with
an evil snicker.

"Aye, he'd do right-wondrous, this MacPherson fellow. But he may
be a bit *too* straight for our purposes," Peel went on. "Choundas
maintains a very small staff, as I said. There is his aide-de-camp, his
flag-lieutenant I suppose you'd say in naval parlance. Jules Hainaut.
A *Lieutenant de Vaisseau*, now. Just a midshipman, an *Aspirant*, the
last time we dealt with Choundas in the Mediterranean. Recall him,
do you?" Peel asked, tongue-in-cheek sly.

"No, not really," Lewrie replied, frowning.

"You should. You captured him," Peel informed him, enjoying a
look of surprise on Lewrie's phyz. "Thatch-haired lout, looked like a
swineherd? Tattered uniform, all out at elbows and knees?"

"Perhaps," Lewrie had to confess his ignorance. "Can't really say.
Hmmm . . . wasn't Dutch or something, was he? My old clerk Mister
Mountjoy had to interview him? Hmmm, it'll come to me."

"The very fellow," Peel insisted. "The sort who'd sell his own
mother, did she fetch a good knock-down price, Mister Twigg determined. Parrots the right slogans, toadies with the best of 'em, and
fawns on Choundas, so he can trade on his fearsome repute, so the
Frog prisoners say. A right bastard, in their opinion, one of the *charming* rogues. For some reason, though, Choundas has sent him away
from him, after near-doting on the young sprog all these years. Appointed him aboard that new auxiliary man o' war schooner, and he's
most-like at sea now."

"Think Choundas has tumbled to him, at last?" Lewrie enquired.
"Or gotten fed up with his ways?"

"It happened *after* Captain Haljewin first brought up the topic of a
spy who'd betrayed his ship, and that frigate we smashed," Peel hinted,
tapping the side of his nose. "If this Hainaut would sell up his mother
for pocket-money, perhaps Choundas suspects he'd be open to a
shower o' British guineas, hmm?"

"But he's at sea, now, like you said," Lewrie pointed out to him.
"How could he have betrayed our prize to us?"

"Unless Hainaut was part of a whole *cabal* of agents," Mr. Peel countered, "and the very thought of that'd have Choundas, and Hugues, puttin' half the island through 'questions' worthy of the Spanish Inquisition . . . torture chambers, and all."

"Is that what you intend, then, Mister Peel?" Lewrie asked, in awe of his daring, now that Peel was hitting his full devious stride.

Dear Lord, what've I started? Lewrie had to ask himself.

"Lastly, there's Choundas's long-time clerk," Peel told him in a less enthusiastic manner, after a calming sip of tea. "He's known as 'The Mouse.' Frightened to death of working for Choundas, but too scared to leave his employ by now, I'd reckon. Knows where too many bodies are buried, all that. Meek as a catch-fart, scorned and abused by one and all. There's no love lost 'twixt him and Choundas. None lost where Hainaut's concerned, either. Who better to make a target than Choundas's sorry little long-suffering clerk, who has access to every secret and every move, and Choundas's every idle musing, hmm?"

"So," Lewrie posed, growing tired of Peel's machinations; there was a surprise to spring, a ship to get under way before dark, and the precious time in which to do both was quickly wasting. "I defer to you as to which you intend to give to Choundas, if you haven't done so already . . . let something 'oh so accidentally' slip to our prisoners? Or will you require them to stay aboard a while longer before clueing them in?"

"Impatient for them to go, Lewrie?" Peel asked him.

"The longer they're aboard, the more they might pick up of *our* doings, is all," Lewrie countered with a *minor* lie of dis-interest in them. "You can't keep secrets for very long aboard a ship, without a hint of it leakin' forrud, you know that. You've seen it. Better if we foist 'em off to the Prize Court ashore, on parole or gaoled, like we would with your run-of-the-mill enemy civilian prisoners. Else, we make 'em wonder why we treated 'em diff'rent, and start *thinkin'* about the 'why' of it, and there's your scheme taken with a grain o' salt as soon as Choundas grills 'em. Mind you, Mister Peel, he's a suspicious old shit. What's kept him alive and thrivin' all this time, hey?"

"You're absolutely right, Captain Lewrie," Peel responded, perking up with new determination and energy. "We can't risk them picking up the slightest thing that might blow the gaff, as you sailormen are wont to say. They must be put ashore at once. But with no *unseemly* haste, of course."

"Of course," Lewrie agreed, much relieved that Peel was amenable to his suggestion.

"With strict instructions that the Prize Court officials repatriate them soonest," Peel schemed on, rising to his feet to pace. "A week or so, do you think would be the customary usage?"

"Well, good luck with that," Lewrie said, sorry to disabuse him. "The Court officials are the worst pack o' drunk, slovenly lay-abouts ever I've encountered. Might take 'em weeks to recall they *have* prisoners. Might have t'bribe 'em. They're venal enough."

"Damn!" Peel spat, knocking his fists together in frustration. "The scheme must be put in play at once. Well, we'll try bribery, and see what haste the Court officials can mount then." Now that he was "aboard" the scheme, indeed its principal author, he could brook no delay in its deployment. "Choundas will be sure to believe Fleury, if not Haljewin, I'm certain of it. Or do their accounts agree with each other—"

"Thought Haljewin fled before Choundas had his arse cheeks for breakfast?" Lewrie asked. "You send him back, he's most-like dead as mutton, no matter does Choundas eat his tale up like plum duff."

"B'lieve there's a French sayin', Captain Lewrie," Peel said in a cynical drawl, " 'bout how one can't make an *omelette* without breaking an egg or two. He dined with the Devil . . . with a *short* spoon."

"Ah," Lewrie commented to that ultimate cold-bloodedness. "Oh well, then. There goes one egg . . . Who's the other? Your target."

"With MacPherson and Hainaut both at sea, we're left with just one possibility: Choundas's clerk. Name of Etienne de Gougne. He'll do . . . the covert vengeance of the meekly oppressed, the under-paid and un-appreciated," Peel sketched out, in a world-weary tone. "A hint of others already in place, who contacted de Gougne once he came ashore. The ones who run the messages out to sea . . . all that? *Vast* conspiracy. Secret Royalists and their lackeys, waging their secret war 'gainst the Revolution, and the Republic. Revenge, for those who already died under Hugues's guillotine when he retook Guadeloupe and lopped off over a thousand heads? With the ghost of Zachariah Twigg and *his* evil minions the master puppeteers behind it all with gold in plenty? Oh, perfidious Albion!" Peel mockingly cried from the French point of view. "The despicable, grasping, conniving *anglais*, we . . . *rosbifs* . . . *biftecks*, we satanic . . . *les sanglants!*"

"You could take that to Drury Lane, Mister Peel!" Lewrie congratulated, even briefly applauding him; languidly, spiritlessly, like the "better sort" of theatre-goer in London. He rose to his feet and pulled his watch from his fob pocket, opened the face . . .

Four Bells of the Day Watch chimed from the forecastle belfry—two in the afternoon, which conformed to what his watch told him. He closed the face of his watch and slipped it back into its pocket.

"Let me ask you something, Mister Peel," Lewrie requested. "I asked you once before, but . . . you and Mister Pelham got access to the French signals books, somehow. You know rather a lot about who's who on Guadeloupe, and Choundas's inner circle. *Is* there a spy, or a conspiracy of agents on the island? Do you really . . . *own* people close to the Directory in Paris, too?"

"And what did I say, when first you asked, sir?" Peel smirked, come over all superior and inscrutable again. "That I could not tell tales out of school, was that how I put it? What do *you* think?"

"That your department has the place *riddled* with spies," Lewrie declared. "Were you afraid my suggestion might expose people you had in place already? Was *that* why you rejected it out of hand? And so dismissively?" he wearily accused, their spat still rankling.

"My apologies for being brusque, sir," Peel said with a bow in his direction. "Truly. Aye, there is some *small* shred of truth in your surmise that not *all* the French on Guadeloupe are resigned to the success of the Revolution. Less effective or informative as we wish, nor as widespread as we could hope, but . . . I am *relatively* sanguine that whatever false spoor we lay for Choundas to follow, it will not lead too close to our true operatives. Do we actually lose one or two minor players, well . . . that's the cost of doing such business. Regrettable, but . . . there you are."

"Dear Lord," Lewrie gawped. He'd thought Peel cold-blooded before, but . . . that took the cake.

"Well, then," Lewrie declared, rising energetically. "Lots to do, and the hours too short, as usual. We'll up-anchor and sail down to Roseau. Deliver our prize to the Court, now they've her manifests and such . . . land our prisoners with 'em. Then," he concluded with an anticipatory wince, "we'll get under way, 'bout dusk."

"Sorry," Peel queried in surprise, "get under way, did ye say? Wherever are we bound, this time, sir? I'd thought . . ."

"Oh, didn't I tell you?" Lewrie blurted out in a rush, as if to trample

Peel's objections with his news, "The Yankees are missing some merchant vessels, and are sailing to go look for them. After I told 'em about Choundas and his four raiders bein' at sea, they swore they would run them down, too, but think they *might* need a spot o' help."

He gave Peel a rapid thumbnail sketch; Peel's mouth gaped open wider and wider, the more Lewrie explained to him.

". . . so we're t'sail with 'em," Lewrie concluded, "with three ships to make up almost a proper little squadron, and sweep the seas as far South as Caracas. Might scoop up the odd Don or Dutch trader as well, ye never can tell, Peel. More prizes'd suit, don't ye . . . ?"

"But!" Peel spluttered, turning nigh *plum*-complexioned. Both of his hands were squeezed into bone-white fists as he fought to hold in his sudden rage. "But . . . !"

"Like we *discussed*, don't ye know," Lewrie insisted. "When you got so 'both sheets aft' on whisky. We'd go south, and McGilliveray and *Sumter* would scout with us. Well, now we've *Oglethorpe* along, as well, and . . . you *agreed* to it, do you recall," he quickly pointed out.

"Lewrie, you . . . !" Peel squawked. "Damn . . . my eyes! Foreign Office . . . Maitland! Lord Balcarres, and Pelham, all their cautions! Keep the Yankees at arm's reach, half a *foe*, and . . . and you just up and decide to, on your blo—At your own *whim*! Spur of—"

"*After* gaining your *agreement*, Mister Peel!" Lewrie pouted.

"*Damn* y—Dammit, Lewrie!" Peel retorted, raising his fists as if ready to take him on, barehanded. "You just can't—"

"Our prisoners'll see all three men o' war, two American and one British, sail together, Mister Peel, and they'll dread the chance there's been an alliance made against 'em, but news of it hasn't *got* to 'em, yet. *That'll* give Hugues and Choundas something to bite on! Drive 'em bug-eatin', slung into Bedlam *mad*! Mad enough to lash out and declare real war on the United States, then we get 'em as allies, and whoever managed *that* wins himself a knighthood, and . . ."

Peel lowered his fists, exhaled long and hard, nigh to a death rattle, and dropped his head. He jerked out his chair and sagged into it, cradling his face in his hands, fingers kneading his temples.

"You need t'be *leashed*, I *swear* you do, Lewrie," he weakly said. "Leashed and muzzled, like a . . . Oh, I thought I was prepared to deal with you, thought I had your measure years ago. Twigg, he *warned* me t'keep you on a taut rein, but . . . !"

"Think of the possibilities!" Lewrie beguiled.

"Think of the disaster," Peel said with a sorrowful groan, "if it all goes bust."

"Now really, Mister Peel," Lewrie countered. "What could possibly go much wrong with chasing after French warships?"

"The mind boggles," Peel croaked. "Damn . . . my eyes, Lewrie, but you've done it to me . . . *again!* Lord, what'll Pelham say!"

"Well, I must go on deck and get us ready to sail," Lewrie told him, more than eager to get away, back on his quarterdeck where he was completely in charge. Where Peel wasn't, in point of fact.

"Don't know as I can trust you outta my sight that long," Peel almost whimpered. "Leashed and muzzled, like a dancin' bear . . ." He sounded almost wistful at that image.

"Later, Mister Peel," Lewrie said, scooping up his hat and coat and making his escape. Once on the quarterdeck, he passed the word for Lt. Langlie, to apprise him of their sailing. As he waited for him to appear, there came the sound of a mug clanking off a bulkhead. Later followed by another, and, perhaps, the sound of flung furniture.

"He's takin' that well," Lewrie could but suppose.

BOOK FOUR

*"Maturate fugam regique haec dicite vestro;
non illi imperium pelagi saevumque tridentum
sed mihi sorte datum."*

"Speed your flight and bear this word to your king;
not to him but to me were given by lot
the lordship of the sea and the dread trident."
—*AENEID*, BOOK I, 137-139
PUBLIUS VERGILIUS MARO

CHAPTER TWENTY-THREE

L *ieutenant de Vaisseau* Jules Hainaut relished pacing his small quarterdeck as the sun threatened to rise in the East. Like a proper and salted sea officer his hands were clasped in the small of his back in imitation of the *aristo* captains and lieutenants he'd served when he'd been a humble seaman. As was the custom in all navies, he could pace, or strut, alone up to windward facing the Trades and the soon-to-be-risen sun, savouring the shivery damp coolness that was so welcome before the harsh warmth of the usual tropic day.

He rocked on the balls of his feet, enjoying the creak of those bright-buffed boots on his legs, and fiddled with the hilt of his precious smallsword. The name Hainaut was sure that he had made for himself was going to be the talk of the entire colony, figuring prominently in the despatches back to Paris and the Ministry of Marine, too . . . no matter how derisive his more-experienced fellow officers aboard *La Vigilante* had been towards him. Her new *capitaine*, Lt. Pelletier from *Capitaine* MacPherson's *corvette*, had been highly dubious of his appointment into *La Vigilante* as his Second Officer, almost openly sneering at him for being a *dilettante* more suited to odious shore duties, as well as the catch-fart to such a bloody-handed ogre as Choundas. Even the midshipman, now Acting-Lieutenant Digne, the Third Officer, had seemed to mock and disdain him; jealous of not being named second-in-command to his friend Pelletier, Hainaut had thought.

Well, he had *shown* them what he was made of with an unaccustomed show of diligence and nautical skill, with saucy courage in the taking of their four prizes, and his willingness to come aboard this captured schooner, *Mohican*, as a prize-master when they had begun to scrape the bottom of the barrel for enough people to man them all, with a sham of energy and even unselfish generosity, and he had *mostly* won them over.

This schooner *Mohican*, and her near-twin that sailed not a mile alongside her, the *Chippewa*, were fine vessels— fast, handy, and sea-kindly for all their outlandish rigging and their steeply raked masts. Their valuable cargoes notwithstanding, Hainaut was sure that *Mohican* and her sister would make magnificent commerce raiders, if bought in and converted to men o' war under Choundas's control, not as privateers under Hugues. Not so large that either demanded a *senior* officer in command, too.

Lt. Hainaut had, as soon as he'd moved his sea-chest and traps aboard *Mohican*, determined that *he* would be her captain. He had at last nagged, hinted and cajoled himself away from Choundas, the damned crippled monster! and by fetching in such booty, this *Mohican* would be his permanent escape, his route to the fame, glory, and profit he wished—he *would!*—win in future. A year or two and any odium from having been Choundas's "creature" would be forgotten, and . . .

"Dawn, *m'sieur*," the older petty officer who now stood watches as a temporary quarterdeck officer announced as the sun finally burst above the eastern horizon. Lt. Hainaut crossed to the helm to take a peek at the marvellous book he'd found in *Mohican*'s great-cabins, that tabulated true sunrise and sunset to longitude. He juggled the book and the sea-chart, grunting in satisfaction as he noted that they'd made a decent distance to weather during the night, just that tiny bit farther East, and a safe haven in Basse-Terre or Pointe-à-Pitre. The casts of the knot log added up to an impressive sum of Northing, too. Hainaut set the book and the slate aside and stepped off their probable course with a pivoting brass divider and a ruler. Unless they ran into foul weather or roaming enemy warships, their entire "convoy" of prizes and raiders would make a triumphant landfall at Guadeloupe in three more days. The two *corvettes*, *Le Gascon* and *La Résolue*, with their much greater hold capacities, and the stores with which to keep the seas for months, still prowled down South nearer the Spanish Main, Trinidad and Tobago, to "show the flag" to their dubious allies the Spanish and Dutch and put iron back into their sagging spines as well as to take prizes. They would not return for weeks more, perhaps. For now, it would be this prize, these ships and their successful captors, that would arrive first to win the cheers from Guadeloupe . . . and earn the most in the Prize Court with all the valuable and tasty goods they bore.

"Very well," Hainaut said at last. "Time to send the lookouts aloft, *Timmonier*. And tell the cook he may start breakfast."

"*Oui, m'sieur Lieutenant,*" the temporary second-in-command said in reply. Hainaut was irked that he had yet to address him the way he wished, as *capitaine*. Some, it seemed, needed more convincing than others. Hainaut turned away and strode aft to the taff-rails, to stand atop the transom lockers and grip the starboard lanthorn for a better view astern, taking a moment to enjoy how straight and true was *Mohican*'s wake and how narrow the creamy-white road she cut over the sea was. Fine in her entry, slim in her moulded breadth, yet wide enough to carry cargo and be "stiff," even beating to windward. Whatever the Americans had done when forming her body below her waterline let her slice through instead of bully the waves.

She must be mine! Hainaut fervently thought again. He felt he would die, did he not keep her as his own, this rapier-quick and *épée*-slim marvel.

"Glass," he demanded over his shoulder, his right hand out to take the telescope when it was fetched to him, without looking to see if he was being obeyed. But of *course* he was, instantly.

There was *La Vigilante*, well hull-down and perhaps eight or ten *kilomètres* back, shackled to their slowest and dowdiest pair of prize trading brigs. Lt. Houdon's big brig, *La Celtique*—another of his odious master's conceits to honour his damnable "blood"—and three prizes were perhaps a mile or more astern of *La Vigilante*, but, being a much less "weatherly" pack of square-riggers, were rather far down alee. *Mohican* and *Chippewa*, even under all plain sail, had out-raced them all since sundown.

Hainaut's stomach rumbled with hunger as he lowered his glass, and hopped down from atop the transom lockers. *Mohican* was positively crammed with good things to eat on her long passage back to her miserably cold home port. Her manger held dozens of chickens, six pigs, and four sheep, and the hens laid enough eggs for a four-egg *omelette* for his breakfast. There were still loaves and loaves of fresh bread aft, with strong, piquant South American coffee beans by the gigantic sack. He'd have fresh, unwormed cheese, a whole pot of coffee, and a chicken breast with his eggs, brightened with fresh-ground Spanish pepper, with first-pressing *turbinado* sugar, with over-sweet goat's milk to whip into the eggs, to make his coffee elegantly *au lait*, with luscious jams and pearly-dewed fresh butter to smear on light-toasted bread . . . !

"*Allô!*" a lookout precariously perched on the main-mast tops'l yard shouted down. "Attention! Three . . . strange . . . sail . . . alee! Two points off the larboard quarter, and approaching quickly! *Allô?*"

"We see them!" Hainaut screeched back, even before he mounted the transom lockers once more and swung his telescope in the indicated direction.

Oui, there *were* three of them; two full-rigged ships and a brig! They were bounding along under every stitch of sail, "all to the royals" fore-and-aft stays'ls flying, and steering almost across the Trades, to the East-Sou'east . . . *thundering* up from the dark leeward horizon as if to pass ahead of *La Celtique*'s group of prizes . . . ahead of his own ship, *La Vigilante*, and her group, too!

"*Allô!*" the mainmast lookout cried once more. "I see . . . flags! They are warships! Two frigates, and a brig o' war! One is *anglais*, and two are . . . *americain!*" the lookout yelped in consternation.

"Together?" Hainaut cried, just as disconcerted as the lookout. "Americans and the British, *together*? *Mon Dieu, merde alors*, have the *Amis* declared war on France?"

There came a faint, muffled cheer from belowdecks, from their prisoners who had once owned and sailed *Mohican*, as the lookout's cry worked its way down to the fore-hold where nonplussed French sailors, just as amazed as Hainaut, guarded them, now stunned to garrulousness and loose lips.

"Someone go shut those scum up!" Hainaut shouted, for want of a better idea at the moment. "This prize can go into Basse-Terre with no survivors and no one the wiser if they keep that up, tell them!"

"What shall we do, *m'sieur* Lieutenant?" the petty officer asked from below him, standing by the transom lockers.

"Do?" Hainaut replied. He might have meant to sound angry, and properly indignant, but it came out more as a question, too. "What *can* we do?" he finally snarled, after chewing on his lower lip. "We have barely enough hands to man this prize and guard our captives ... there are only six cannon aboard, and those half-rusted. We must ... uhm, place discretion above valour. Much as it pains me, of course, *Timmonier.*"

"Of course, *m'sieur,*" the older petty officer replied, sounding just the faintest bit disgusted, despite the horrible odds. "We must run for port, *oui.*"

"Choundas and Hugues must know that the Americans and 'Bloodies' work together against us, now, *Timmonier,*" Hainaut claimed, striving to make it sound like an honourable, but reluctant, duty.

"*Oui, m'sieur.*" Stiffly and coolly, blank-faced obedient.

"Hands aloft to ... no," Hainaut flummoxed, thinking to deploy the cross-yard tops'ls for more speed, but perceiving that they were already on the eyes of the wind. "Maintain course, *Timmonier.* Signal Petty Officer Manon on *Chippewa* to stay close up with us and hold his course. At least *two* of our prizes will make port. And our terrible information. Take heart, *m'sieur.* Not *all* our profit is lost, *hein?*"

His senior petty officer did not look as if the retention of a pittance of their expected prize-money would satisfy *him*, but he did as he was bade, turning away with the sketchiest of hand salutes.

La Vigilante surely would be lost, Hainaut thought as he went forward to the helm and the compass binnacle cabinet. He waved off the ship's boy who had come to snuff the night lanthorn, long enough to produce a Spanish *cigaro* from a waist-coat pocket and lean into the cabinet to puff it alight off the flame. Lt. Pelletier would not come ashore to bolster his reputation with praise, alas. Pelletier and Digne would be exchanged, sooner or later, but that might be months in the future. In the meantime, though, whatever he, Jules, would say would be Gospel.

A modest and self-deprecating description of his own part ... with a praiseworthy display of anger that he could do no more to save them, perhaps a show of shame that there was nothing he *could* do, and play the part of the innocent man who chides himself as guilty ... hmmm. Hainaut thought *that* would redound to his continuing good credit. Well-meaning people would surely clap him on the shoulder and say that he had no reason to scathe himself. Mere bad luck, *n'est-ce pas?* And, Hainaut calculated, with even more capable officers in British or American prison hulks, there would be more ships in need of captains than there were men to command them. *Mohican* surely *must* be his, after all!

Now, had he a full crew and the weight of metal to match against the upstart Americans, if not that British frigate, then who *knew* what he could have accomplished, if only . . .

"Oh, if only," he whispered, beginning to rehearse, and script, how he would wring his hands in anguish once he stepped ashore. Jules Hainaut stood looking outboard, puffing on his *cigaro*, secretly savouring the richness of South American tobaccos, but trying on the opening "scene" and facial expressions to evince frustration and bitter sadness for his first small "audience," his own prize crew.

Yes, some good could come of this disaster, after all; good for him all round, had he the wit and *panache* with which to play it, Jules Hainaut smugly thought.

"*Allô!*" the mainmast lookout shrilled to the deck again.

"What?" Hainaut barked back in instant irritation, with a scowl on his face; he quickly amended his tone of voice and expression to one more suitable and . . . tragically heroic. "Our friends have a chance?"

"The *anglais* frigate, Lieutenant . . . I see her before. She is that *Proteus*! That 'Bloody' Devil!"

"Ah, *mon Dieu*," Hainaut gawped in true shock, a sinking feeling in his innards. "Then they are truly lost, *quel dommage. Merci*," he had wit to shout to the lookout.

"A great pity, indeed, *m'sieur* Lieutenant," the petty officer said, shaking his head in fearful awe. "How can that *salaud* be *everywhere*, as if he reads our *minds*, as if . . . ?"

"Perhaps he does, *Timmonier*," Hainaut suddenly responded, with a suspicious frown—then a wry and rueful grimace of understanding. "Perhaps this was not mere bad luck, but . . . betrayal! We *must* get word back to Guadeloupe that this devil ship and that *cochon* Lewrie have struck again, as if by a miraculous coincidence. No, this cannot be credited. He *must* have been told our every move by a traitor."

Poor Pelletier, and poor Digne, Hainaut thought, scowling over this chilling explanation for all their troubles of late. *It is all up with them. Pelletier must have had the shortest captaincy in history, and Digne in his borrowed lieutenant's coat . . . he'll still owe a tailor for the uniform he ordered, if he survives British captivity.*

Quel dommage . . . I never liked them, anyway.

⚓

"We've the angle on them, by God, sir!" Lt. Catterall exulted as they watched the sails of the French ships, the slivers of hulls on the horizon, heave up high enough to be seen with a glass. "Sharp eyes, the *Oglethorpe* had aloft, t'spot 'em so quick on the false dawn."

"Sharp eyes, indeed, sir," Captain Lewrie agreed, "we'll be up with them in another half hour. Do you concur, Mister Winwood?"

"Uhm ... the *Oglethorpe*, in a half hour, Captain. *Proteus*, not a quarter-hour later, I'd estimate," the Sailing Master answered after a *long* ponder, in his usually mournful "mooing" cautiousness.

"Then we'll take at least one prize, thanks be to God," Lewrie chuckled, "unless *Sumter* overtakes us."

"Can't share out equally, though, sir," Lt. Langlie speculated. "All three ships will be 'in sight' at the time of capture, but we've no formal alliance with the Americans which allows for sharing. And there is the strong possibility that those French prizes yonder are the missing American merchantmen they reported, so ... might not Captains McGilliveray and Randolph demand that we return the *re-taken* ships to their custody, Captain?"

"Damn my eyes, Mister Langlie," Lewrie said, turning on him, in mock anger, "but you've a quibblesome bent before your breakfast, or your coffee. Do I ask my man Aspinall to fetch us all a pot, will you let me keep just *one*?"

"Well, sir, I hardly ..." the well-knit young man began to ... quibble, but stopped, red-faced among his fellow officers' mirth.

"I know there's no profit for us this morning, Mister Langlie," Lewrie went on, awarding him a wider grin, "and indeed I shall return what American ships are possibly re-taken to our ... cousins. Is there any actual profit in our gesture, perhaps it'll come later, in a real alliance 'twixt our countries against the Frogs, d'ye see, sir. Best all round, really, if we don't even take public credit for assisting the Yankees. But their President Adams, their naval Secretary, and their Congress will learn of it, eventually. As will Admiralty, and the Crown. Secret gratitude from the Americans, and *tacit* approval by His Majesty's Government may be all we may expect."

"Yet the mightiest oaks, from little acorns grow, do they not, sir," Lt. Adair, his always-clever Scots Third Officer slyly drawled.

"They do, indeed, Mister Adair," Lewrie said with a glad nod.

⚓

Those French ships would have been so easy to miss in the grey murk of predawn, but for a very sharp-eyed lookout on USS *Oglethorpe*, in truth. *Proteus* had been half an hour into the Morning Watch, with her people's and her officers' attention engaged mostly in-board, half-past 4:00 A.M. and the summons for "All Hands" that began a ship's day.

And it had been then that a sharp-eyed lookout of their own had spotted *Oglethorpe*, at the very edge of vision ten miles aloof, up to windward at the tip of their patrol line and pencil-sketched in black against the East'rd sky. He had discerned the tiny square blocks of a signal hoist in the space 'twixt her main and mizen masts, and her new course as she foreshortened, turning more Sou'easterly to investigate something. Almost as easy to miss, had *Proteus*'s lookout blinked, was a tiny ruddy ember that winked into a brief life when she fired off a starboard, lee, bow-chaser to draw their attention.

Without being able to *read* the signal hoist, but realising that *Oglethorpe* was attempting to convey something of importance to them, Lt. Catterall, who normally stood the Morning Watch, had sent word aft to his captain, who had ordered their course altered to close the American brig o' war, hoist a signal to alert *Sumter* off to their lee down West by at least another ten miles, and fire off a starboard chase gun of their own, and the "hunt" was on.

Lewrie had Aspinall come to the quarterdeck and arranged for a pot of black coffee, then paced off alone to the windward side, with a telescope in hand. Steeling himself for the ordeal, and flexing his left arm to test its strength after his wound received at Camperdown, which had resulted in the *tiniest* bit of weakness, he clambered aloft for a look of his own—up onto a quarterdeck carronade slide mount to the bulwarks, into the mizen stays and rat-lines, up the tar-tacky and bedewed shrouds as far as the cross-bracing taut stays below the top. With a groan of rusty practice, knowing he needed a higher vantage, he cautiously threaded his body 'tween the cat-harpings, then transferred over to futtock shrouds and clambered up them until his bare head was butted against the bottom of the top platform ... *inside* the futtock shrouds, not taking the more perilous "outside passage" that required dangling from death-grips of his hands and feet like a spider hanging from its disturbed web 'til one reached the lip of the top and the maze of dead-eye blocks, to haul oneself up and over like a housebreaker breasting a brick curtain wall.

Should do this more often, he chid himself, and his well-known idleness; *I'm goin' all . . . potty, and short o' breath. Damme if I'll end up like other captains . . . all tripes an' trullibubs!*

Knowing himself, though, perhaps too well by then, such a vow he suspected would be quite forgotten by the start of the Forenoon.

Once he got his breath back to normal, and his glass unslung, he could see that Catterall was right; they did indeed have the angle on them.

The suspect horde of ships had been discovered down to the Sou'east, first of all, and USS *Oglethorpe* had made a sharp turn Easterly to stand as close to the Nor'east Trades as she could bear to place herself before the bows of the vessels she had espied flogging roughly to the North on the opposing starboard tack, and as close to the winds as they could steer, as well. *Proteus* had followed quickly and was now roughly astern of *Oglethorpe*, on the same point of sail and course. A quick look astern showed him USS *Sumter* just a bit Sutherly of their own creaming wake, to stay in undisturbed water so her hull could slice cleaner and swifter, about eight miles or so astern but gaining rapidly. It appeared that Capt. McGilliveray had not been boasting about *Sumter*'s speediness.

And *Proteus*, well . . . she was no slow-coach this morning, either, Lewrie was proud to note, thanks to her careening and hull scraping a scant three months earlier at Kingston. She would gain on Randolph's *Oglethorpe* just as *Sumter* would gain on her, 'til there might not be three miles between them when they engaged.

Now that the predawn grew lighter, Lewrie could make out that there were *three* gaggles of ships roughly three points off their starboard bows. The closest group was all square-riggers, slower and less weatherly when trying to make progress beating to windward. A little farther off and ahead of the square-riggers was a second gaggle, and they were all fore-and-aft-rigged schooners, able to point higher and out-foot their confederates. Strive as they might, though, they were just a bit too far down to the Sou'east and not fast enough to get up to windward and make it a long stern chase before the *Oglethorpe* interposed herself cross their hawses.

And there was a final brace of schooners then almost dead ahead
of the Yankee brig o' war, also close-hauled on starboard tack. Those
they'd not catch, Lewrie grumpily decided. Once a quarter-mile aloof
of *Oglethorpe*, they'd stride off like Arabian three-year-olds at the
Derby races and require a day and a night to overhaul.

The nearest group didn't have a chance in Hell, Lewrie assessed.
Stand on, tack, and come about to larboard tack to steer Easterly, or
haul their wind and scud back the way they'd come; either choice,
they'd be too slow to escape their pursuers past noon.

The trio of schooners would be the handiest and quickest. Did they
tack and run, there was a good chance that the chase could require
the whole day and some of the next. But for the fact that East of 'em
lay Grenada, St. Vincent and the Grenadines, and the maze of isles
and cays, and *coral reefs*, which lay between St. Vincent and Grenada;
all of which were either garrisoned, occupied, or patrolled by Royal
Navy vessels, not ninety miles to windward of where they stood that
instant. It would be a case of "out of the frying pan, into the fire" for
them, did they choose that course.

"Oh, you are so gloriously . . . fucked," Lewrie gleefully whispered
to himself as he closed the tubes of his telescope. "The longer you
stay blind to us, down here in the dark, the worse it'll be, too."

He re-slung his glass, squirmed about to grasp firm hand-holds and
toe-holds, and descended the inner face of the futtocks, threaded back
through the cat-harpings, turned about, and made his way back to the
bulwarks, where he could hop atop the carronade slide, then step onto
safe and sure footing on his own quarterdeck once more, scented and
smutted with fresh tar and "slush," the rancid, suety skimmings of the
steep-tubs from boiled salt-meats, that kept the rigging supple and rain-
proof.

By God, ye can't *stay clean aboard ship!* he ruefully told himself as
he swiped his tacky hands on the seat of his slop-trousers: *Go through
damn' near a quarter o' my pay with the Purser, just t'stay presentable.
Just look at Mister Coote, the greedy bastard . . . takin' my measure for
fresh-issue slops, already. Gimlet-eyed 'Nip-Cheese'!*

"Can't understand why they haven't spotted us yet," he said to his
officers. "Not that it'd do 'em much good if they did. We'll bag all
but the two dead ahead of us, one way or t'other. Ah, Aspinall!"

"Coffee f'r all, sir. No cream'r sugar, sorry t'say," his man said, passing out tin mugs dangled off a hank of twine, and holding a large black iron-lidded pot with the aid of a dish-clout.

"Your pardons, Captain Lewrie," their Purser, Mr. Coote, asked. "But I was wondering, should we serve a cold meal of cheese, biscuit, and small-beer, or do you think we might have time to boil up burgoo?"

"Cold victuals, sorry t'say, Mister Coote," Lewrie told their much put-upon older, and straight-laced Purser. "Do the French spin out a long stern chase, though, I'd admire did the people be served a hot dinner to atone for it."

"Very good, sir," Coote agreed, with a small bow. "Oh my, sir. Do you wish, I've a new bale of slop-trousers, come aboard at Antigua. I'll root out a pair or two in your size, should I, Captain?"

Mr. Coote could not fathom why Lewrie chuckled and shook his head in secret amusement before giving his assent.

"Just enough f'r one mug, sir, sorry," Aspinall said as Lewrie was served last, per his standing instructions. "Galley's stanched."

"Barely *time* enough for the one, Aspinall," Lewrie said as he accepted the searing-hot thin tin mug. "And then it'll be Frogs *à la fricasée* for breakfast. We'll relight the galley fires and grill 'em to a turn."

"Hear, hear!" his assembled officers and warrants rumbled.

For at least another quarter-hour, the *ad hoc* squadron swooped onward as the gloom of predawn gradually lightened, without the French taking any notice of them, lost in the leeward darkness. Lewrie felt sure that their straining t'gallants and royals, then the tops'ls, *must* be spotted as the bowl of sunrise spilled over and expanded, illuminating their upper canvas, almost turning them as bright as so many mirrors. Weary tan sailcloth would first appear as white as new-fallen snow, practically shouting "Here We Are!" then glow as hot as a well-stoked fireplace when the rising sun coated them shimmery gilded. But they were almost hull-up to the nearest pack, the square-riggers hull-up to them, before the French reacted.

The *Sumter* had caught up within two miles of *Proteus* by then and began to veer away, a little more off the wind on a direct course for the square-rigged ships and brigs. One mile ahead, *Oglethorpe* was within minutes of crossing the bows of the fore-and-aft-rigged group.

Lewrie, now turned out in proper uniform, including sword belt, paced the quarterdeck, waiting for the inevitable escape manoeuvres on the part of the French. They *had* to tack or wear; run Sou'east after tacking, or run South or Sou'west after wearing about.

Lewrie had also decided to allow the Yankees the principal role in the endeavour; unless they ran into trouble, he would keep *Proteus* between *Oglethorpe* and *Sumter*, like a flagship directing the activities of subordinate ships. Those two schooners, up to windward by now and safe as houses . . . He turned to look in their direction, lifting his telescope. Yes, they were at least five miles upwind, in the Nor'east, and sure to escape and carry word of this encounter to Guadeloupe, if they didn't run afoul of other British warships. And that was simply fine, to Lewrie's lights.

Except for one short fight off their own coast that had netted them a French privateer, the Yankees hadn't scored any successes, yet, and were more than due one. Reclaiming their missing merchant vessels and fighting a brace of French privateers or National ships would embolden their whole nation. That a British frigate had been a *supporting* partner might result in an even closer cooperation in future, even a formal alliance.

He *couldn't* take the lead role, though. The Americans' stubborn "younger brother" pride, and mistrust of their former enemy, would never allow him to play the old salt and senior officer on the scene. Had he tried, they'd have damned his blood and swanned off on their truculent own, Lewrie strongly suspected.

Yet . . . his standing off a bit, *appearing* in command of Yankee subordinates, would dovetail with French suspicions to a tee, he could speculate. The French espoused a lingering liking for the Jonathons. They had eagerly bankrupted themselves to support the Revolution, sent troops and fleets to aid them, and had embraced everything rustic, plain, and Yankee Doodle (including that damned song that had driven him half-daft, when he had been surrounded at Yorktown!) along with doddering old Benjamin Franklin and his ratty raccoon caps, as paragons of simple, plebeian Virtue—which had also dovetailed quite nicely with their reigning philosophers, like that Rousseau fellow with all his cant about Noble Savages, the Common Man, and Common Sense. The French had fallen in love with that wild-eyed radical Tho-

mas Paine, and his rantings on Republicanism and Democracy. So
much so that a few years later, they had staged a Revolution of their
own; one they'd mucked up, o' course . . . being French, and all.

In the beginning of the French Revolution, it had been American
grains, delivered in whole armadas of neutral ships, that kept them
from wholesale famine.

No, no matter their unofficial "war" against American traders, the
French still partways admired them. Of course, being French, the
Americans were probably seen as child-like, raw bumpkins when compared to the superiority of French society. Weak, rude and rustic in
their manners, overly prudish and Puritan in their mores, so unrealistic
as to expect honesty, fair dealing, and prim rectitude from themselves
and others . . . so hopelessly *naïve*, so un-worldly!

Hugues, Choundas, and the Directory in Paris when word of this
reached them, could never suspect the Americans of being realistic
enough to make alliance with Great Britain; too weak on land and sea
to take the lead. Too enamoured of, too *awed* by, the innate glory of
La Belle France to . . . *dare*! Those hideous English, however, were just
the sort of scheming, cynical master manipulators who could gull the
ingenuous Americans into folly, could tempt them from the eternal
gratitude the United States *owed* France!

Oh, how they'd curse, stamp their elegantly shod little feet! Lewrie
happily thought. How the Frogs would feel betrayed . . . and feel *fear*!
Fear enough to sulk for a time (as the French were wont to do) then
declare war against the United States, piqued by such betrayal?

Here in local waters, Hugues and Choundas would be piqued, for
certain, to have lost a brace of raiders, lost a flotilla of prizes; *perhaps*
gained a new foe. It would be months before packets could carry word
back and forth from Guadeloupe to France with news or instructions,
and in the meantime they would operate as if befogged. They'd keep
their main attention on British operations, but would be forced to keep
glancing over their shoulders lest the United States launch a real war,
perhaps assemble a hasty fleet to eliminate Guadeloupe as a privateering base, once and for all, by themselves, or in league with the odious
English!

And Pelham an' Peel deem me a simpleton, ha! Lewrie thought in
glee. *Well, they wanted Choundas befuddled, didn't they? And I can't
think of a thing that befuddles him better.*

"*Sumter* is firing a challenge, sir!" Lt. Langlie reported, interrupting Lewrie's musings. "And the merchantmen are wearing off the wind, to the Sou'west, it appears."

Lewrie turned his attention in the opposite direction, lifting his glass again. Indeed, he could now make out the dowdiness of the prize vessels, how deeply laden and slow they were as they wore, now they'd come completely hull-up. French Tricolours flew above Yankee "gridiron" flags at their sterns denoting them as prizes. Poorly manned prizes, he was certain. The Frogs could not allot a complete crew aboard them. Even so over-manned as French warships and privateers were when put to sea in expectation of captures, if there were now a dozen hands aboard each prize, he'd eat his hat! And half of those would have to stand guard against the original crews retaking their own ship in the wee hours of the Middle Watch. *And*, would a privateer or a warship captain willingly give up his best topmen and able seamen into a prize, weakening her own chances of survival or freedom if they met a storm or an enemy man o' war? He rather doubted it!

"The captor seems she'll play 'mother duck,' Mister Langlie," Lewrie said as he lowered his glass. "She's standing out to face the *Sumter*, to give her prizes time to get away."

"Hmmm . . . now we'll see what Yankee warships are made of, sir," Lt. Langlie said, as if sceptical of their fighting prowess. "Should we not, uhm . . . close *Sumter* and give her a hand, sir?"

"Oh, I expect Captain McGilliveray will give a good account of himself, and of his ship, Mister Langlie," Lewrie replied, chuckling almost indulgently. "*Sumter*'s indeed fast and handy. Even delayed by a short action with yonder Frog, I'm sure he'll run all the prizes to earth by mid-afternoon. They're awfully slow. And do they see their own ship . . . their 'home,' taken, the French prize crews'll be so dispirited they'll most-like have themselves a little weep, smack their foreheads, say *sacrebleu*, and strike their colours. Nowhere to go."

"Then shall we assist the *Oglethorpe*, sir?" Langlie asked, in impatience, spoiling for a good, sharp fight.

"Does she need us, aye," Lewrie replied, looking more Easterly, nearly across the bows. "Aha! See there? Yon French 'sheepdog' will challenge *Oglethorpe* as well. And her prizes seem about to tack for a run Sou'east, as I suspected. Schooners will be faster. Do you haul us up closer to weather, Mister Langlie, and hoist stays'ls. We will pursue the merchant schooners, whilst Captain Randolph matches metal with the Frenchman. Our Yankee cousins might be so pugnacious and aggressive they might forget that they sailed South to recover their missing traders. Let's get some speed on and overtake 'em for them."

"Aye aye, sir!" Lt. Langlie crisply answered, a bit mystified, perhaps, and a tad disappointed that they'd not take a larger part in the developing battle, but obedient as always.

"And Mister Langlie . . ." Lewrie added, arresting the man in midstride, "Once we've a goodly way on, you may beat to Quarters."

"Aye aye, sir!" Langlie said back, with much more enthusiasm.

"Now we'll see what this new-hatched American Navy is made of," Lewrie muttered to himself, busy with his telescope, "indeed."

CHAPTER TWENTY-FOUR

Cannon fire erupted to their starboard side, an ominous punctuation to the long-rolling drums and the urgent fifes summoning sailors from below, as *Sumter* and the French brig o' war began to trade shots. Mr. James Peel, drawn to the quarterdeck as well by their martial preparations, had learned enough by then to *ask* permission to ascend a larboard ladder before clumping up into the open air. Lewrie took scant note of his arrival, a brief smirk crossing his lips at the thought of Mr. Peel being *driven* to the deck, whether he wished to go or not. In action, there would be no sulking in his canvas-walled cabin, for partitions and bed-cot would have to come down to give gun crews room in which to serve their 12-pounder pieces aft. It was come up or get trampled.

Lewrie looked down into the ship's waist, spotting the landsmen, idlers, and waisters who were lumbering his furnishings and chests down the companionways to the orlop. There went his own sea-chest, already locked. Peel's, however, was shut but not locked, with shirt cuffs or sock ends showing under the lid; worse than a midshipman's chest . . . all on top and nothing handy, Lewrie found cause to snicker. A moment later, and here came Aspinall, clutching a sea-bag filled with his pantry things and hobby things, and Toulon cradled in one arm and none too happy about it.

"We'll not take part, Captain Lewrie?" Peel asked, after he had

himself a good look about. "Not *too* active a part, 1 trust? Ye know
what Mister Pelham'd . . ."

"I intend to allow the Yankees their due honours, Mister Peel,"
Lewrie told him. "The merchantmen are theirs to reclaim, after all."

"Thank Christ!" Peel muttered, sounding immensely relieved; for
the moment, at least. " 'Tis bad enough we're even here, d'ye . . ."

"I shan't tread on their pride, either, Mister Peel. I'll let 'em learn
to toddle on their own. 'Til they look as if they've bitten off more
than they can chew, then we'll wade in, if we must."

"I was afraid you'd say that," Peel muttered half to himself.

"For now, we're haring after yonder prize schooners, d'ye see, Mister Peel?" Lewrie pointed out, handing him the telescope. "So they
don't break free whilst the men o' war slug it out."

"Excuse me, Captain sir," Midshipman Grace said, coming up and
knuckling his forehead in salute, his waist-coat and coat sleeves wet
right through, "but the last cast of the log reads eleven and a quarter
knots, sir! She flies like a Cambridge coach, this morning, sir!"

"Damme if she doesn't!" Lewrie said, beaming with pride at his
frigate's fine turn of speed. "She's bored, and hungry today, Mister
Grace. Good ships are like fine, blooded horses. They go stale, do
you keep 'em reined back. Our *Proteus* knows when a fight's in the
offing. Like a good warhorse, she wants a part in it."

"And bless her for her spirit, sir!" Grace eagerly agreed.

"I'll never understand you sailormen," Peel grumpily confessed after
Grace had gone back to his place in the after-guard. "What mystifying
language you use, what superstitions about ships' souls . . ."

"We're a contrary lot," Lewrie allowed in all good humour as he
watched *Sumter* and the French brig o' war engaging.

"One would think Mister Jonathan Swift used your sort for cari-
catures when he wrote *Gulliver's Travels*," Peel harumphed further.

"Not *everyone* peels their boiled eggs from the *pointy* end, do you
mean to say, Mister Peel?" Lewrie pretended to find inexplicable.
"Why, I *never* heard the like, tsk tsk!"

"Oh, what's the use?" Peel groaned, half under his breath again.

"Damme, but they're good shots, our Yankees!" Lewrie exclaimed
as *Sumter* loosed her entire broadside on the French warship at a range
of about one cable. "Ev'ry ball 'twixt wind and water, by God."

The French were replying, though with a much weaker battery, it
appeared. Lewrie could detect deep bellows from some 12-pounders

mingled with the sharper barks of smaller guns among the French response. Even at such close range, the French were firing high at masts, spars, and sails, as they usually did, to cripple a foe before deciding whether to close or scamper off.

"French men o' war, Mister Peel!" Lewrie enthused, slapping his palms together with joy. "Manned by French Navy men, for certain."

"How can you deduce that, Captain Lewrie?" Peel asked.

"Privateersmen would never offer battle, unless you trapped 'em in a corner," Lewrie explained quickly. "They have too much financial stake in their own vessels, and tomorrow is another day. Run without shame today, take more prizes next time. Privateersmen can't risk damage, either. Repairs come out of their pockets, and time spent in dockyard is lost money, too."

"Whereas naval types know their government will foot the bill?" Peel sardonically supposed. "And they get paid, regardless?"

"Exactly," Lewrie said, laughing briefly. "And look you. They fire high, French Navy fashion, t'make their opponent too slow so they can get away, instead of goin' for a quick kill. There's professional Frog officers over yonder who've been schooled in their tactics maybe too long and too well. But damme, piss-poor gunners."

Sure enough, *Sumter* got off a second broadside, well-aimed and laid, long before the French could. Lewrie turned and glared at Peel, pointing at his telescope in silent, urgent demand, and Peel surrendered it, albeit in sullen bad grace, then wandered about the deck in search of a replacement, headed aft towards the binnacle racks.

The second French broadside was delayed, as the brig o' war was instantly pocked with fresh shot-holes. Chunks of gunwale and bulwark timber went flying in clouds of smoke, dust, and splinters, and the brig shuddered as if suffering the ague, sending sympathetic shivers aloft that almost spilled wind from her sails! The answering broadside, when it did come, wasn't half the strength of the first, either; ragged and stuttering, and still firing high, as if their gun-captains were too panicky to shove the wooden quoins in under the breeches to lever the barrels downward. Lewrie could gleefully think the French gunners were already near that point where the choreography of gun-drill became a teeth-chattering, snot-drooling *rota*; just do your small part, swab quick—duck; load quick—duck; run-out while squatting in dubious safety; touch-off without offering your body as a target, and *hang* aiming! Get shots off, no matter where the ball went, fast as you could, and don't *dare* look aside at the maimed and the dead, or let yourself think, imagine . . . !

It happened to the best of crews, Lewrie knew, when things got desperate. And the way that *Sumter*'s gunners were getting off three well-aimed and laid broadsides every two and a half minutes was creditable in anyone's navy.

Sumter paused in her firing as she passed down the side of the French brig, larboard side facing larboard side on opposing tacks . . . and then swung up to windward at the last moment, slewing a great foaming froth as she performed a radical turn. Her guns were run-out anew, smoke-dulled ebony muzzles levelled like the muskets of a firing squad.

"She'll stern-rake her, by God!" Lewrie exulted, full of admiration, and succumbing to "battle-fever," even if he was but a spectator and not a yardarm-to-yardarm participant for a change.

And *Sumter* did, her gun-captains igniting their powder charges as each piece bore directly up the French brig's stern, and at a distance little over a good musket shot. He did not need his glass to see the French brig o' war shiver, again, as her main-mast came tumbling down in ruin, as round shot bowled her entire length, caroming side to side in splintery ricochets that ripped the French ship's entrails out. A round-shot came bursting out from below her larboard cat-head in an immense whirlwind of broken planking, some of the inner faces painted red, perhaps . . . but it looked like a spurt of her heart's blood!

His own crew was cheering, safe themselves for a rare once, and always happy to see "Monsoor" done the dirty. A moment later, and the crew raised a louder and more enthusiastic cheer, for someone upon the French ship's quarterdeck cut the flag halliards right-aft, abaft her spanker, to let a massive Tricolour flutter down to drape her stern in sign of surrender.

"That's the way, *Sumter*, that's the way!" Lewrie hooted in joy at seeing a thing done smartly and well. He pounded a fist on the cap-rail of the quarterdeck nettings' bulwark, before remembering how glum Royal Navy captains were supposed to be—far too late, as usual.

The USS *Sumter* sailed on for a space, then hauled her wind and fell off in pursuit of the square-rigged prize vessels. Her late foe had struck her colours, and was so damaged she would not be going anywhere anytime soon, at any rate. A stern-rake would have killed and wounded so many of the French brig's crew, created so much havoc belowdecks, that it would take hours for those still on their feet to raise a jury-mast aft, plug shot-holes below the waterline, pump her out, and get any sort of way on her again. A painfully slow and crippled way, so slow that any real hopes of escape were foredoomed, if the foe decided to renege on her honour-bound pledge of surrender. A privateer might break his oath and attempt a run for it, but . . . French *Navy* officers, even jumped-up petty officers made into the gentleman-officer class, might not, Lewrie thought.

Besides, Lewrie smugly considered, the brig o' war had already been working at a disadvantage, with so many of her hands away in the prize vessels. He doubted they had enough healthy people aboard for a full rowing crew in all four of their ship's boats!

"They are, uhm . . . disturbingly good," Mr. Peel commented in the relative quiet after the guns had fallen silent. "That was a quick and brutal drubbing. Well-laid, too."

"Did you expect any less, Mister Peel?" Lewrie replied. "They may not have had much of a navy the last time round, but they're among the world's best sailors . . . as their privateers and that Captain John Paul Jones proved, time and again. Not too surprising really, when you think on it. They *are* half-British."

"Then surely not a people whose nautical aspirations should be encouraged . . . or, fostered, as it were," Peel glumly admonished.

"But of *course* they should!" Lewrie enthusiastically countered. "They're damn' good, didn't you just say so? With more ships in commission, encouraged by a few more victories like this one, they just *might* declare war on the French, and be a tremendous ally. And they wouldn't cost us a groat, not like the Austrians or Neapolitans, 'cause they're too proud to take the sort of subsidies we toss around. Millions of pounds a year, and what have we gotten for our money? Weak-kneed fools, and utter failure.

"Say we give, or sell dirt-cheap, modern artillery to 'em. It's all they need. They have Southern live oak for hulls, the tall, straight pines for masts and spars, the tar, pitch, and oils, the flax and hemp for sails and rope, and do they build a few more frigates like *Hancock* . . . I told you all about her! . . . Guns, powder, and shot are all they really lack. Say the Crown reimburses our cannon foundries so they still make the same profit as if they sold 'em direct, and that is money spent at home, not thrown away on Prussians, Hindoos, the Chinee, or . . . men in the Moon! The Crown would adore it!"

"Well, given what we've seen this morning, yes, they *seem* to be more than capable at sea," Mr. Peel tentatively acceded. "And, yes, we do waste millions in solid coin, I'll grant you. But they're *rivals* in trade, Lewrie. You give 'em an inch, they'll dominate the Caribbean, the carrying trade . . ."

"They'll never be so strong that they'd threaten our sugar colonies, though," Lewrie objected. "And, as friendly allies, with solid commercial ties to *us*, whyever should they?"

"Oh, stop!" Peel said with a groan, looking as if he wished to cram his fingers in his ears. "You make it sound too alluring. 'Get thee behind me, Satan,' don't tempt me to concede. You have led me into folly enough, thankee very much!"

"What the Crown, Admiralty, and your Mister Pelham cannot seem to see, sir, is that the Americans are a fact of life," Lewrie pointed out, sensing a victory, and becoming more diplomatic. "The French, us in some future crisis . . . *someone'd* force 'em to build a strong fleet. Now, wouldn't it make more sense to woo them while they're weak? Make the Yankees grateful for our aid? Make 'em our friends?"

"Well, it's not like training puppies, Captain Lewrie," Mr. Peel said with a snort of derision. "You can't leash-train a whole nation. Do recall that British foreign policy must be bound by what is best for us in the long run. We do not *have* friends, not permanent friends. We have *interests*, just as the Americans do. Really . . ."

"No, but you'd do best to pet, feed, and praise a litter o' pups, get 'em used to your voice," Lewrie replied with a wry chuckle. "Else you come home some dark night and find a pack o' wolves waitin' on you. Better they're glad t'get their treats and play 'fetch,' than forage on your livestock. Or confuse *you* with prey. Hmm? What d'ye say?"

"Well, it might be plausible, but . . ." Peel waffled. "Pray God this is a real insight on your part, Captain Lewrie. That it doesn't have anything to do with a certain American midshipman who might need fostering, and encouraging."

"Don't know what you're talking about!" Lewrie curtly retorted, leaning back, stiffly drawn.

"Oh, sir," Peel cynically drawled, as if preferring to talk of anything but Lewrie's madcap idea, and more than happy to change what they discussed. "Do you not! Why, it's as plain as the nose on your face. There's not a man on this ship, nor the Yankee ships, could be in doubt of him being your by-blow, once he saw you side-by-side. It might be hard enough, explaining what you just up and did on your own to Pelham ... 'gainst all his cautions and instructions, mind, if you were singly motivated to do the Crown a valuable service, based upon your appreciation of the circumstances obtaining, but ... understand, sir, that I don't wish to construe your motives ... *have* your motives construed as personal, or trivial, d'ye see ..."

"And I tell you that all I've done, I've *done* with a cold-eyed appreciation for the way things truly stand," Lewrie said, teeth gritted in response to such an insult, "*not* for a need to impress a young man. I can't *help* it if our superiors back in London are idiots, that you got sent out by lordly *sots* addled with *delirium tremens*, on their *good* days, like that Colonel of yours who thought we could starve America of emigrants if we just had Saint Domingue! What I see is a chance to rid the New World of French influence *forever*, do we do this right, and to Hell with Saint Domingue! We'd have a grand ally 'twixt our Canadian holdings and the Caribbean, with rich trade, cross a British *lake* called the Atlantic Ocean, Peel! And who's t'say Saint Domingue can't rot on the vine a few more years 'til its putrid corpse rots to the bones, then *begs* us and the Yankees for peace!"

"My God, sir, I did not ... !" Peel spluttered.

"Good God, but they're at it again," Lt. Langlie whispered to the Sailing Master near the helm, amidships of the quarterdeck.

"Aye," Mr. Windwood took sorrowful note. "And it does not help hopes of conciliation that you *blaspheme*, Mister Langlie."

"Ah, oops. Sorry."

"We never get Saint Domingue, who bloody *cares*, Peel!" Captain Lewrie was going on, with as much heat as before. "*Filthy* damn' place, in the main. American trade takes up the slack, not *just* in sugar and rum, cocoa and coffee. Prices for *those* goods go up 'cause demand is just as great, and *our* Sugar Isles fill it, at greater profit. Don't know much of trade, frankly, but ... second-hand goods through Yankee merchants, in partnership with English companies, might be arranged.

"Now, do you really think I'd go off half-cocked like a two-shilling musket, upset your precious Mister Pelham's impossible scheme for *nothing*? *Believe* me, Mister Peel, I'd not risk my command and my career on the off-chance a boy, damn' near a stranger, goes in awe o' me. And I resent having my motives being portayed that way."

Lewrie took a deep breath and calmed himself at last, frowning quizzically to see that Peel wasn't fuming like a slow-match sizzling down to ignite a bombshell.

"A lad whose existence will most-like ruin my life, anyway, if my wife ever learns of him," Lewrie concluded, his resentment spent at last, forced to grin in self-deprecating confirmation of his parentage. "And why ain't you howling, by now?" he simply had to ask.

"Because I had to know for certain," Peel mystifyingly replied. "With you, in truth, sir, who knows what goes on in your head!"

"Now, that's not strictly . . ." Lewrie flummoxed.

"See here, sir . . . no, forgive that," Peel said at last, after Lewrie let him get a word in edgewise, that is. "All you say is more plausible, and possible, than anything I heard in London, or since we arrived in the Caribbean."

"It is?" Lewrie gawped back, expecting a verbal knife-fight.

"I must own, sir," Peel most reluctantly said, "that I see the eminent sense, the rationale of your thoughts, and as far as I see it . . . God help me! . . . I can do naught but agree with your assessments."

"Mine arse on a band-box, you do?" Lewrie blurted out, with a whoosh of relief. "At long last," he could not help but add. "May I assume that your next letter to Mister Pelham will tell him of your, uhm . . . change of heart, then?"

Damme, have I actually done something clever? Lewrie asked himself, *for once in my miserable life?*

"It will, sir," Peel vowed, though looking a tad beleaguered as he pondered the personal consequences of defying the prevailing opinion of his superiors in London, not to mention the hurricane of anger that would come from the high-nosed, not-to-be-outshone Mr. Grenville Pelham. "All else is so much moonshine, wishful thinking, grossly in error or . . . hopelessly out of date."

"Well . . . excellent, Mister Peel!" Lewrie crowed.

"Well, not completely!" Peel could not help retorting, "It'll be mine arse on the chopping-block. Might as well be French . . . off with my head!" he sourly grumbled, wrapping his wide lapels over his chest as if a fell wind blew, not a tropic one. "This turns out badly, we'd best emulate your friend Colonel Cashman and flee to South Carolina. Find us a safe place to hide from the Crown's displeasure."

"Of course, does it work *out,*" Lewrie cynically pointed out in much gladder takings, almost playfully now, "your Pelham is the fellow gets

knighted for quick and clever thinkin'. I suspect our names will never
be mentioned."

"But of course," Peel answered with one of his accustomed wry
smirks, as if he was almost back to normal.

"Pity there can't be at least a wee shred o' credit for us, to improve
our standing back home, though," Lewrie alluringly hinted. "It ain't
every day I come up with a good idea. 'Tis a good day I come with
an idea, at all."

"You're fishing for compliments, you can forget it," Peel told him,
turning bleak once more, and with his hands fiddling at his coat collars
as if to armour himself against vicissitude. "*I'm* the one has to tell
Pelham. What you get won't be a jot on *my* cobbing. God, he *expected*
folly from you, but not from me!"

"Aye, I'm such a corrupting influence," Lewrie said, bowing his
head in mock contrition. "Put it down to the old Navy excuse, 'drink,
and bad companions!' Won't 'app'n, agin, yer honour, sir. Oh, well.
No thanks, no credit . . ."

Peel's answer to that was an inarticulate gargle.

"Sorry, didn't quite catch that?" Lewrie playfully enquired with a
hand cupped to one ear. It had sounded hellish-like a cranky bear-
growl. Peel turned his back and stomped rather bleakly away, towards
the taff-rails, where, Lewrie had little doubt, he would seize the cap-
rails in white-knuckled hands as if to strangle oak in *lieu* of a human
throat. Lord knew, as a junior officer Lewrie had done the same in
the face of utter frustration.

Lewrie turned his attention out-board, lifting his glass to see the
USS *Oglethorpe* brig engage the large French three-masted schooner.
The schooner had swung off the Nor'east winds to present her starboard battery, using the wind-forced heel to elevate her cannon for
the customary crippling shots at *Oglethorpe*'s rigging and sails, and
Lewrie took a deep breath and held it in dread expectation as the two
vessels' bowsprits came level with each other on opposite courses, as
the American brig blocked the schooner from view.

Their broadsides, at what he estimated as about a hundred yards,
lit off as one in the instant that both ships' hulls lay exactly opposite
each other, as if docked side-by-side, one bows-out and the other
bows-in. A massive cloud of spent powder smoke burst into existence
between them in the blink of an eye. *Oglethorpe*, up to windward, was
only partially befogged, with the smoke quickly clearing as it was

blown alee; the French schooner was the one thoroughly wreathed in it, completely blotted out from view.

Oglethorpe's masts shivered, and her forecourse yard canted and dropped, to be caught by the chain-slings rigged to prevent its total loss. Her sails were pocked and fluttered like carpets or bedding on a clothesline for dusting by *very* stout-armed maids-of-all-work. A bare royal spar on her main-mast went winging away, along with about three feet of the slim upper mast that supported it, and both standing and running rigging came snaking down as it was severed by chain-shot, star-shot, and expanding bar-shot.

"God in Heaven!" Lt. Langlie was forced to exclaim. "My word, I mean," he amended as he realised that prim Mr. Winwood was still near. *And* with his "holy" face on. "But what weight of artillery does that Yankee brig mount? How many cannon *can* a brig bear, and serve?"

The French schooner staggered out of the smoke pall. Her foremast was sheered off about ten feet above the deck, her main-mast canted so far aft that it made a rough triangle, like a mast-hoisting sheer-legs, where it rested upon her mizen. And half her starboard side was hammered so badly that one could almost make out bare ribs! Her bowsprit and jib-boom pointed down into the water like a steering oar, and her starboard anchor and cat-head were simply gone! With such a drag, she emerged bows-down, flat on her bottom and low in the water, most of her way shot clean off her, surging up a vast patch of white-foaming sea around her as if she rested atop a stony shoal where the waves first broke as they came ashore.

"Enough, and more, it seems, Mister Langlie," Lewrie said, about to dare the sea-gods and whistle on deck in admiration, or surprise.

Proteus's crew raised another gleeful cheer to salute *Oglethorpe* for her quick victory. For them, it was better than a raree show or a championship cockfight. Any day they could see the despised French getting their just desserts was simply "the nuts" to them. And the bloodier and more brutal, the better!

"Damn my . . . bless me!" Mr. Langlie further commented, a glass to his eye, as the Sailing Master pointedly coughed into his fist and issued a cautionary "Ha-Hemm!" as if clearing his throat. "Taking the lee position as she did, sir, with a fair amount of her quick-work exposed at her angle of heel, there's sure to be shot-holes below her waterline. Be a shame to lose such a fine prize, if she sinks. Why, I do believe you can already judge her down to starboard, as if taking water."

"It appears Captain Randolph is of the same mind, sir," Lewrie said in agreement with his assessment. "She *is* listing to starboard. *Oglethorpe*'s coming about and taking in sail. Save her 'fore she goes down, I s'pose. Ah, there she's struck her colours! Took them long enough. A blinding glimpse of the obvious, that. Mister Langlie?"

"Sir?"

"*Oglethorpe*'s busy," Lewrie decided, swinging his telescope to eye those French prizes, now fleeing to the Sou'east. "Wish her well, and all that, but . . . if *she* won't run down the merchant schooners, we shall. A point to loo'rd, and let's crack on. They look deeply laden to me. No matter they're Yankee-built and fast, we stand an excellent chance of overhauling 'em. By mid-afternoon, at the latest."

"Aye aye, sir. Mister O'Leary, a point o' weather helm. Haul off a mite, and shape course just to windward of the schooners, there," Lt. Langlie instructed the Quartermaster of the watch.

"They're at least six miles or better off, Mister Langlie. For now, let's stand down from Quarters and serve the crew their breakfasts. Pass the word to Mister Coote and the galley folk."

"Aye aye, sir."

"Mister Grace?" Lewrie called aft, summoning the midshipman to his side.

"Aye, sir?" the lad asked, still afire with excitement.

"Pass the word for Aspinall, and tell him I'd admire a fresh pot of coffee . . . and tell the gun-room stewards that the officers'll most-like wish a pot of their own, too."

"Aye, sir!" Grace cried, dashing off forward and below, almost breathless with second-hand battle glee that had yet to flag.

Lewrie paced aft down the windward side of the quarterdeck, as the gun crews removed flintlock igniters, gathered up gun-tools, and re-inserted the tompions in their unloaded, unfired pieces. Mr. Peel was pacing forward, nearer to the centre of the quarterdeck.

"Well, that was exciting for a minute or two," Lewrie commented.

"And we were not required to fire our guns in concert, either," Peel took fairly hopeful note, as if he had his fingers crossed behind his back—on both hands. "So far, we haven't *exactly* sinned by an act of commission, *have* we? Mean t'say . . . we didn't do anything *overt*."

"Yet," Lewrie cautioned, with a wee, sly grin that was sure to bedevil Peel's shaky qualms and recriminations.

"We were merely . . . present," Peel insisted. "Just happened by."

"Still, it's early yet," Lewrie took delight in pointing out to him. "Who *knows* what could transpire 'fore sunset," he drawled.

"God's sake, don't *do* that, Lewrie," Peel almost pleaded. "You get your sly-boots look on, and there's the Devil t'pay."

"Pelham owe you money, Mister Peel?" Lewrie badly asked.

"Of course not!" Peel spluttered, nonplussed by such a query.

"You owe *him*, then?" Lewrie went on, tongue-in-check. "Engaged to his sister or some such? He catch you with the wrong woman, knows your deepest, darkest, most shameful secret, does he?"

"No, none of that," Peel insisted, though Lewrie noted that he turned a tad red-faced, and made it too bland for complete credence. "He controls my career, reports on my fitness for future employment in our little . . . bureau."

"That surely can't be all, Peel," Lewrie said, feigning a pout of disappointment. "But in some ways, you're not the same confident fellow I knew in the Med. Mister Twigg's a horrid old fart, but I cannot recall you bein' so meek with him, nor can I recall you bein' the sort to hide his light 'neath a bushel basket and not tell him when he's wrong, or give him a better idea."

"Diff'rent era, diff'rent superior," Peel bitterly replied. "I quite enjoyed working for Mister Twigg, for I *could* be open with him. And he couldn't abide time-servers and toadies. I was his *partner*."

Peel paused, working his mouth as he realised that it was time to reveal some home truths. "I was a cashiered ex-captain of the Household Cavalry, not quite the *ton* to polite Society, d'ye see, but that never mattered with Twigg. Pelham is a different proposition entirely."

"What sort o' blottin' did you *do* in your copybook?" Lewrie queried, sure there was a tantalising tale to be heard.

"Let's say it involved the wrong earl's daughter, affianceed to a fellow officer, a Major, in the same regiment, for starters," Peel hesitantly admitted.

"Hmmm . . . do tell," Lewrie gently pressed. "Doesn't sound much like a career-ender, though. Young love . . . all that."

"Let us say that the young lady in question, and the gallant Major, *deserved* each other," Peel said with a bitter sigh. "So *easily* bored, so *needful* of amusement she was, which cost me dear. We Peels're good, landed squirearchy, Lewrie, well-enough off, but we ain't *that* rich, and the regiment was expensive enough to begin with. Cost of my 'colours' as a Cornet, then Lieutenant, then the vacancy as a Captain? String o' chargers, the proper kit and uniforms, and a sinful mess-bill each month. *Skinflint* maintenance of my dignity was half again steeper than my yearly pay, and *two* free-for-all mess-nights in a month, all the sprees about town, could put me deep in the hole. Then *she* came along, I was utterly besotted, lost my head, and then splurged my way even deeper, 'til the sight o' tailors and tradesmen'd force me to hide in stables 'til they'd gone. Toward the end I . . . our estates are entailed, so my family *could've* cleared my debts, but I was foolishly stubborn it not come to that, so I . . ."

"You robbed the paymasters?" Lewrie gently nudged.

"I . . . I cheated my fellow officers at cards!" Peel ashamedly confessed, come over all hang-dog and unable to look at anything but his shoes. "To buy her baubles, dine her out, the theatres and such, and I . . . she *swore* she'd break her engagement, that she'd marry me, but . . ."

"D'ye mean t'say, you got *caught*?" Lewrie gawped.

" 'Fraid so," Peel told him in a soft voice. "Always had a knack for cards. I usually came out ahead with *honest* play, and sure to God you know how easy it is to pluck the sort of hen-heads you find in the better regiments. Snoot-full of drink by ten, lack-wit by eleven, and ready to wager their last stitch on anything you name. Lucky to even *see* their cards by then."

"Met a few," Lewrie commented, hiding his amusement, continually amazed by how *arrogantly* dense were the second sons of peers of the realm, the sort usually found in the "elegant" regiments. And the sort drawn to cavalry were the *truly* whinnying-stupid!

"Thought I could pull it off," Peel continued. "God, after I'd skinned 'em, I even lent them some of their losses back, at scandalous interest, and they wouldn't even blink!"

"Their sort, they're lucky they could *breathe*," Lewrie chuckled.

"Anyway, one night one of 'em *wasn't* drunk as a lord, and cried 'cheater' on me, the rest took it up, and caught me with an extra card or two where they shouldn't have been, so . . ." Peel supplied, snorting humorlessly at Lewrie's observation. "I was asked for my resignation. 'Twas that, or a general court, and they'd have done anything to avoid a scandal, not on *their* hallowed reputation. They forced me to settle up with those I'd fleeced, and everyone but the foot-men had their hands out then. I was allowed to sell my commission, my string of mounts, saddlery, and all. By the time I'd cleared all my debts, though, I was barely left with the civilian togs I stood up in. *Horrid* stain on the old family escutcheon, too, don't ye know," Peel japed, trying to make light of it. "Everlasting shame . . . the black sheep?"

"Happens in the best of families," Lewrie cryptically commiserated, with the fingers of *his* right hand crossed.

"Exactly!" Peel drolly replied, looking Lewrie up and down with a tongue planted firmly in his own cheek, a cynical brow arched.

"You were sayin' . . ." Lewrie harumphed, coughing into a fist.

"I was near an American emigrant, myself, one of the Remittance Men exiled for his own good," Peel further informed him, "but for meeting Mister Twigg. Cater-cousin of my father's in the Foreign Office arranged an interview. Overseas employment, exciting doings, picking up foreign culture and new languages . . . robust, outdoorsy work . . ."

"Meet fascinatin' new people . . . betray 'em," Lewrie stuck in.

"Yes, good fun, all round," Peel said, laughing out loud for a bit. " 'Til Mister Twigg retired, it was. I suppose you *could* say I'm . . . compromised, now, in a way. See, Pelham *does* have something over me. That Major whose fiancée I diddled, well . . . *his* father's country place and *Pelham's* father's estate are nearly next door. Both fathers took their seats in Lords the same month, and both families attend the same parish church, their ancestral pew-boxes cross the aisle from each other. Knew all about me from the outset."

"Had it in for you, right off, hey? The bastard," Lewrie said. "The arrogant little pop-in-jay!"

"He is all that, and more," Mr. Peel mused. "Snobbish, impatient with his inferiors. Sure of his wits and talent, when he doesn't have a tenth of Twigg's trade-craft, nor an hundredth of his sagacity or patience, his cleverness."

"When not orderin' the murder of thousands," Lewrie sneered.

"Sublimely self-confident when he has no right to be," Mr. Peel went on, "and *not* a young fellow open to suggestions. An uncle, a former ambassador to Austria, sponsored him with the Foreign Office. Naturally, he was shoved into *our* branch. Twigg was leery, soon as he'd briefed him. Warned me to mind my p's and q's, he did. Same as he cautioned me to keep a wary eye on *you*. Sorry."

"And who wouldn't, I ask you?" Lewrie posed, too engrossed with
the hope of "useful dirt" on the pestiferous Pelham.

"Pelham put me on notice, right off," Peel told him, "that I'd best
tread wary and sing small, or I'd be an *un*-employed ex-captain of
cavalry, an *un*-employed agent, and I was no proper gentleman, to
boot! Fetch and tote, run his chores? *He'd* do the thinking, thankee
very much. Damn him, he *enjoys* having me on tenter-hooks."

"Surely he must know by now that he's been sold a complete bill
of goods on this Saint Domingue business," Lewrie scoffed. "He can't
expect to win, after better men than he broke their health and reputations trying."

"Sometimes he makes me wonder, Lewrie, he truly does," Mr. Peel
said with a slow, befuddled shake of his head. "Pelham's one of those
who think pot-holes fill before they step in them, as if the rules are
different for the rich and titled. Pelham's *smart* enough to see this
mission as a morass, but it's rare to see him suffer a single qualm.
Then he comes over all energetic, as if, does he scheme and wheedle
hard enough, he's going to win and prove his mettle, despite it being
a bloody pot-mess!"

"Let him, then," Lewrie said with a dismissive shrug. "He sent you
on a journeyman's errand to finish off Choundas, and ride 'whipper-
in' on me . . . and thank your lucky stars for't. We're a *side-show*, to
Pelham's lights, whilst he stays on Jamaica with his eyes on what he
thinks is the main prize. He won't even know he chose wrong 'til it's
much too late. Whereas the *do-able* part of his compound orders—
our part—is well in hand, and damn'-near done."

"Well . . . when you put it that way," Peel said, perking up some.

"How *did* you get saddled with this chore, and Pelham, anyway?"

"Well, other than Mister Twigg, no one else knew as much about
Choundas and his methods," Peel tossed off, as if it was of no matter.
"Then, discovering *you* were out here, so aptly placed . . . someone
else of whom I had personal knowledge . . . even Twigg said my presence was a necessity. I tried to stay in the Mediterranean, but . . ." he
said, shrugging. "Pelham came as a surprise. By then, it was simply
too late to demur without poisoning my credentials with the bureau.
And I *relish* this job!"

"Hmmm," Lewrie mused, pulling at his nose. "So all Pelham knows is what you tell him in your reports?" Lewrie broadly hinted, tapping the side of his nose sagely.

"Lewrie, that sounds suspiciously . . . mutinous," Mr. Peel gaped (or pretended to) with a hand to his chest as if aghast at what he was hearing. "You don't actually mean that I should lie to him! Or . . . are you?" Peel added, sounding almost wishful.

"Not *lie*, Peel, no," Lewrie quibbled, "just couch things in the best light. Give him chapter and verse of your best justifications as to the Yankee Doodles. Just *passing* mention of the *faint* possibility of secret cooperation leadin' to better things," Lewrie sweetly coaxed. "And make sure that Twigg and your superiors back in London are kept appraised of what a spectacular opportunity just . . . fell into your lap. *Your* lap, Peel, not Pelham's."

"Well . . . Twigg *would* like to know what we're doing, I'd wager," Peel muttered, indeed looking a trifle ill-at-ease at the ploy. "He's still got good *entrée* at the Foreign Office. And Choundas was the main target to him, all along. Twigg was never taken with the scheme about buying Saint Domingue by suborning L'Ouverture or Rigaud. In a private moment, he conjured me to not be *too* disappointed did the larger scheme fail."

"Twigg must have seen that Pelham would be in over his head, and so aspiring a twit he most-like plans t'be Prime Minister," Lewrie said with a sneer. "Yet you still go out of your way to uphold that, too."

"Do recall, Captain Lewrie," Peel said with his nose in the air, "that I, in my fashion and present line o' work, am as duty-bound as you to your Admiralty. To support my superiors in all they do and obey orders with alacrity and enthusiasm. No matter if I think them daft as bats," he sardonically commented. "Though I am no longer an Army officer, I still know how to 'soldier,' sir!"

"One hopes, when you led a troop of horse, you could adjust to changes, though, not just clatter about obedient to out-dated orders like a mechanical, clockwork toy grenadier. When out of touch with a higher authority . . . as we are at present, on a 'roving commission'?" Lewrie pressed, determined not to appear impatient with Peel's sturdy sense of honour. Surely in his line of work, such was a hindrance!

"Well, of course," Peel allowed.

"But you *think* like a soldier, not a *seafarer*, Mister Peel, and I will tell you the diff'rence," Lewrie added, smiling now, sure that he had him lured, hooked, and in play, with the gaffing and landing to come as certain as sunrise. "Can't send a galloper off to the colonel and expect an answer an hour or so later. Once out of sight of land, we're completely on our own, d'ye see, and weeks or months 'twixt new instructions, with only the vaguest idea where we'd be *found* if anyone tried. It all depends on time, distance . . . and the *winds*, Peel."

"I *have* noticed that ships *are* driven by the winds, believe it or not!" Peel retorted, getting his back up again.

"Pelham lies *downwind* of us, Peel, nearly ten days to a whole fortnight there-to-here, close-hauled to Antigua," Lewrie explained, with a smirky, confidential air. "No matter *how* angry you make him, he can only cob you long-distance. The packet brig he'd use to communicate with London starts at a disadvantage to the packets which depart from *upwind* of Jamaica, d'ye see? Do we put into Antigua, the next few days, assumin' a Jamaica packet's in port and ready to sail, your report takes a full week t'reach *him*. A day more, say, for Pelham to scream and run about in tiny circles before he damns you by post, *but* it'll be six weeks 'fore his irate scribblin' reaches London . . . and perhaps six weeks before they tell him he can lop yer prick off. And Twigg and your superiors'd have *your* reports two weeks to a month *before* that. By then, we could very well have ev'rything in our bailiwick wrapped up neat as Boxing Day gifts! Choundas . . . and a preliminary alliance with the Americans, both. *Then* who's boss-cock, and who's the goat, eh, Mister Peel?"

"Dear Lord, Lewrie!" Peel exclaimed with a shudder of dread, and looked about himself for the prim Mr. Winwood, who would chide Vice-Admirals for blasphemy. "Why is it every time you start scheming, that I suddenly feel like a prize ram being led into the shearing pen? No, worse! A *runt* ram, bound for the ball-cutter shears! These years you spent on your roving commissions, so independent . . . I fear you've been hopelessly corrupted."

"O' course I have!" Lewrie cheerfully laughed. "That, and all that 'drink and bad companions' I mentioned, too. But you *do* believe we'll get Choundas, in the end?"

"Yes, I do. I'm sure of it," Peel was forced to agree.

"Do you think we'll get the Yankees into alliance with us?"

"Well, I've my doubts on that'un," Peel demurred.

"No matter," Lewrie quickly dismissed with a wave of his hand.

" 'Tis the *effort* that matters, the *chance* that beguiles, when London hears of it . . . from *you*. Surely it's an option they already considered, but . . . to see one of their agents hard at *work* on it? One o' their *delirium tremens* dreams, most-like, right up there with . . . bright-red, man-eatin', dancin' sheep!"

"Well, there is that," Peel muttered, gnawing on a thumbnail. "By God, Lewrie, the effort would seem bold, even inspired! I do take your point. Did one wish to present the Crown with a plan more likely of fruition . . . as ambitious as seizing Saint Domingue, that's certain . . . uhm, to steal attention from Pelham, it goes without saying," Mr. Peel fretfully speculated, almost turning queasy for a moment.

"Mmm-hmm," Lewrie encouraged, with a gesture that *could* be misconstrued as miming the feeding of one's rival over-side to the sharks.

"Though some might take it as immoderate boasting," Peel fidgeted. "Tooting one's own horn, Of being *that* sort, mean t'say."

"Under-handed," Lewrie drolly supplied.

"Quite."

"Sneaking," Lewrie said on, "not the proper, gentlemanly thing."

"Well, yes . . ." Peel replied, cutty-eyed with embarrassment.

"Better than spending your whole career being thought of as an unimaginative rear-ranker," Lewrie beguiled. "A back-bencher Vicar of Bray. And disappointing old Twigg's expectations of you?"

"Well, there is that," Peel said, stung to the quick by the idea of letting his old mentor down. "One *could* express the hope. Pose the outside possibility . . . !"

"There's a good fellow!" Lewrie congratulated him.

Gaffed, landed, and in the creel! he silently chortled; *But, my God . . . what a stiff and* righteous *prick!*

CHAPTER TWENTY-FIVE

*Q*uite a stir we're causing, sir," Lt. Langlie said as *Proteus* rounded up into the wind to let go her best bower at the "top" end of English Harbour's outer roads. She had been last to enter port, after *Sumter*, *Oglethorpe*, and their five prizes, which had first been mistaken for a whole squadron of seven American warships, a sight never seen before, or even imagined, in these waters.

"And indeed we should, Mister Langlie," Lewrie smugly replied, tricked out in his best shore-going uniform and sword. He didn't envy the Antiguan merchants, once they found that the prizes would go back to their masters after a brief hearing at the Admiralty Court, and no profits would be made from their, and their cargoes', sale. What started as an eight-day wonder would become a two-day thrill, and the only ones to gain from it would be the taverns, the eateries, and the prostitutes when victorious Yankee sailors were allowed ashore.

Lewrie thought it would be interesting to see how the shoals of French prisoners were handled. Would America and Great Britain share the cost of gaoling them aboard the hulks? Which power *could* accept a French officer's promise of parole? Which would negotiate his half-pay so he could keep himself in town until exchanged? And once paid, *would* France reimburse the United States, since they were not at *full* war with each other? Lewrie snidely thought those Frogs'd most-like sulk in dockside taverns 'til The Last Trump, since France hadn't taken any U.S. Navy ships in combat, yet. And most-like wouldn't, not here in the Caribbean, at least.

Proteus had made her number to the shore forts, had fired off a gun salute to Rear-Adm. Harvey, commanding the Leeward Islands Station, and had received a proper twelve guns in reply. Just after, she'd come in "all standing," swinging up to her anchorage and furling all canvas in a closely choreographed flurry, the last scrap vanishing in concert with the anchor's splash. That impressive arrival, his news, and his testimony at the Prize Court would win his frigate, and himself, a bit of the island's adulation, perhaps enough to wake the Antigua Prize Court from its usual torpor, and bludgeon its subsidiary on Dominica into action concerning their own prize that still swung idle in Prince Rupert Bay. Frankly, he could use the extra money to spruce up the wear-and-tear on his wardrobe and his accommodations. Besides, his last good "run ashore" had been months before at Christopher Cashman's boisterous send-off at Kingston.

Lewrie rocked on the balls of his feet, eyes half-closed in fond speculation of *good* meals, fresh-water washing of all his salt-stained and itchy garments, as Lt. Langlie saw to their anchoring. Him ashore in Sunday-Divisions best, the St. Vincent and Camperdown medals algeam against his shirt ruffles. Successful frigate captains could expect a warm welcome from merchants, and from the ladies . . .

He knew Antigua of old. Why, there'd be ravishing matrons, and "grass-widows" simply bored to tears by the local society; there'd be delectably lissome young misses, with lashes and fans all aflutter as he languidly smiled, half-bowed, and doffed his hat. There'd be smiles in return from the more-promising "runners" among the ladies, the well-hooded, secretive "perhapses" if not bolder, carnal "come-hithers."

Had he at Cashman's going-away? No, and come to think on it, he had been retaining his "humours" like a Catholic monk, lately, abjuring even tame relief in the practice known in the Navy as "Boxing the Jesuit"—the one the physicians and parsons condemned for turning manly youth into feeble wheezers, with hair on their pink palms, too!

Why the Devil not? he asked himself; *a man wasn't made to* . . .

Quickly followed by thoughts of Caroline, and reconciliation . . . then of Desmond McGilliveray, and even *more* bastardly gullions turning up fifteen years hence to plague him, hmm . . . perhaps, sadly, *not*. It was a mortal pity, for the Antigua ladies were raised right in his

estimation, as round-heeled and obliging a pack of "genteel" wantons
as anyone could wish for ... the sort who'd trip you with a daintily
shod foot, then manage to be the first to hit the floor, cunningly
asprawl beneath you!

"Anchor's set, sir," Lt. Langlie reported, and Lewrie turned to take
note of Langlie's relief; at last, his onerous task of First Officer could
ease, in harbour. Well, mostly, anyway. "And the battery is secured
from the salute."

"Very well, Mister Langlie," Lewrie replied, leaving his lusty rev-
eries. "We'll row out the stern kedge to ... there," he directed, pointing five points off their larboard bows, almost abeam. "We have room
to swing by one anchor, but I'd admire did we haul her up so the
prevailing wind's off our larboard quarters, for an easy departure in a
few days. And not go 'aboard' a nearby ship, do we swing foul."

"Aye aye, sir," Langlie said, looking even more relieved.

"Your pardon, Captain, but there seems to be a boat bound for us,"
Midshipman Elwes announced. "Just there, sir."

Sure enough; once Lewrie had lifted his glass, he could see the
colours in the stern-sheets of a large rowing barge, one sporting fully
eight oarsmen, a bow-man, a coxswain, and a useless midshipman aft
by the tiller, with a Lieutenant seated forward of them, along with
another man dressed like some sort of buskined sportsman out for a
"shoot" on his private game park.

Commanding Admiral's barge, maybe the Port Captain's, Lewrie in-
tuited; *officer a flag-lieutenant, the pasty-faced shorebound sort, but why
the civilian?* Lewrie allowed himself a wry smirk, supposing that a
functionary from the island's governor-general had been sent out to
see what all the fuss was about, and had been caught sitting for a
portrait as Nimrod the Mighty Hunter, with fowling-piece, custom
rifled musket, a brace of setters at his feet with parrots in their mouths,
and all.

Damme though, he further wondered; *what's left on Antigua worth
huntin' anymore? Rats, and runaway sailors?*

"Permission to mount the quarterdeck?" Mr. Peel enquired halfway
up the larboard ladder, natty in his *other* suit of "ditto," this one in
sombre grey rather than black, with a subdued maroon waist-coat.

"Oh, shit! Oh, Hell!" Lewrie spat, lowering his telescope for a
second so he could rub his disbelieving eye.

"Well, if you feel that way about it ..." Peel griped, piqued.

"Mister the Honourable Grenville Pelham is come to call on us,"
Lewrie told him. "In that barge yonder."

"*What?* Pelham! WhatthebloodyHellis*he*doinghere?" Peel gawped,
leaping to the quarterdeck, the bulwarks, and seizing Lewrie's glass
for a gape-jawed squint of his own. "Where . . . oh. My eyes!"

"No, borrow mine, I insist," Lewrie grumbled. "God's Teeth!"

"At least he *looks* pleased," Peel took hopeful note. "He's up and
waving like his best horse just came in first. Hmmm . . . this may not
be *too* bad. '*Ne defice coeptis*' . . . 'Falter not in what thou hast begun.'
Valerius Flaccus," Peel cited, taking what heart he could.

That'un made Lewrie wince; it had been that ne'er-do-well Peter
Rushton's droll advice, just after they had set fire to the governor's
coach-house at Harrow, which had gone up in a most *spectacular* blaze,
surpassing their wildest expectations; just before he and that other
scoundrel, Clothworthy Chute, had gotten clean away, leaving Lewrie
to be nabbed with the port-fire in his hands. The caning they'd escaped
(since Lewrie was stupidly "honourable" enough not to tattle) had
been Biblical; which thrashing hadn't held a candle to the one his
father, Sir Hugo, had given him after he'd been sent down in shame
along with the long bill for damages! *Falter not*, indeed. Pah!

"My word, Mister Peel, but . . . what a load of 'balls'!" Lewrie replied. "Pass word for my servant Aspinall, there! If Pelham seems
happy, Peel, best we let him crow over whatever it is that's made him
so, *before* we, uhm . . . tell him what we've been up to. Perhaps over
a large bowl o' punch, hey? One with a *liberal* admixture o' whisky?"

"I've been to Saint Domingue!" Grenville Pelhamm boastfully announced once they were alone in Lewrie's great-cabins. "Direct action,
that's the thing, and damme gentlemen, but I do avow that we're on
the cusp of success, at long last. *Carpe diem*, what? 'Seize the day,' so
I did! Uhmm, tasty punch, this. What's in it? Diff'rent . . ."

"Oh, some celebratory champagne," Lewrie said, ticking off the
ingredients, and manfully striving not to roll his eyes at all the old
Latin adages being bandied about in Public School Boy style, with a
"pooh-poohing" wave. "properly French, o' course. Cool tea, bottle
o' dessert wine, a half-gallon o' ginger beer, sugar, and lemon. The
usual ingredients . . . mostly. Saint Domingue, though, really? Well,
well!"

"Got our Mister Harcourt to slip Toussaint L'Ouverture a letter asking to meet him on Ile Gonaves, the middle of the bay just off Port-au-Prince . . . on the strictest q.t. and he *did*," Pelham said, preening. "*Ugliest* little monkey ever you did see, but shrewd, for being a *butler* in his early days. Or so he thought, hey? *Oddest* damn' eyes, he has, too. Like a lion's. His best feature, since he's so short, squat, and bow-legged. Went . . . what's the Hindoo word? . . . in disguise, I did."

"In *mufti*," Lewrie supplied, for his father used the term after years and bloody years with a "John Company" *sepoy* regiment.

"I was wond'rin' why you were clad so, uhm . . ." Peel commented, for Pelham was still wearing a dark buff suit of "ditto" with a waist-coat in a green shade most often seen on sadly neglected houseplants, a pale tan unbleached linen shirt, tall riding boots covered by dark-brown corduroy "spatterdashes" to mid-thigh, buttoned up the outside with dark horn buttons, and had come aboard sporting a flat-crowned, wide-brimmed farmer's hat half-buried in assorted dark-brown feathers. The hat was of cheap felt, not beaver, of a colour that Lewrie could only describe as "shit-brickle" or "dyspeptic dog turd ochre." Lewrie could only assume that Pelham had struck an earth-shaking bargain with L'Ouverture, if he still felt need to sport his "costume" days or even *weeks* later, like a Muskogee warrior displaying his most-recent scalps.

"*Mufti*, that was it," Pelham crowed, holding out his tall mug for a second refill. "L'Ouverture's nigh illiterate, and cannot even speak halfway decent French, just their horrid Creole *paté . . . patois*, mean t'say. I say *paté?* Hmm."

"So, did your negotiations proceed to the point that we should offer congratulations all round, sir?" Peel asked him, sharing a look with Lewrie at Pelham's slip.

"Got a much better reception with General Rigaud," Pelham said, with a sly-boot's wink. "L'Ouverture was stand-offish, said he'd give Britain's terms a good ponder, though I think he was just stallin' for time to see what his putative master, General Hédouville, would do for him. *Slavishly* bound to France, is L'Ouverture, as we supposed, Peel. Slavish, hah! Rigaud, though . . . has fewer supporters and troops, but better organised and armed, and easily supplied through Jacmel, and a strong stone fortress to protect his rear. Whites, rich, landed Mulattoes and half-castes, the educated and civilised, as good

as any in Paris 'fore the wars, and the *ladies* . . . ! Not to boast, but
in a lone week the presence of a mannered English gentleman allowed
me more carnal pleasure than a whole six months on my Grand Tour
of the Continent, ha ha! Rigaud would take hands with Hédouville in
a heart-beat t'save his hide before L'Ouverture is sicced on him, but
Hédouville's nothing substantial to offer him, not like we could. No
British troops ashore this time, but artillery, shot, and powder, and
enough arms, munitions, boots, and accoutrements to arm more of his
followers. Enough *horses* to haul guns *and* mount a large, mobile force
that could ride circles round L'Ouverture's barefoot infantry will turn
the trick. Rigaud was all ears, let me tell you, and much more recep-
tive! Almost slavering."

"So, you will recommend Rigaud to Lord Balcarres at Jamaica, to
the Foreign Office, sir?" Peel asked with a troubled frown.

"Already have, Mister Peel!" Pelham bragged, "And lit a fire to
gather all the arms, horses, and saddlery we may, soonest. Came here
to do the same. The quicker Rigaud gets the goods the better; before
Hédouville makes *his* offer. Then, on the pretext of L'Ouverture
blocking British ships in *his* ports, even under false colours, we will
blockade *his* parts of the island, to guarantee Rigaud's success."

"I trust you were discrete, sir," Peel went on, leaning forward. "And
how did you *get* there?"

"Ain't *stupid*, Peel," Pelham griped, tossing off his third mug of
punch, and rising to get himself another refill. "Maitland will lay that
before him later. As for the how, I hired a small Bahamian boat, come
to Kingston to trade, and was headed for the Turks and Caicos for
salt. Went in my disguises, in and out of the bay at night, unseen . . .
Sailed far West before turning for Jacmel, after, so no one ashore had
a glimpse of us. Dressed as a sailor then, and Gawd what a stench it
was, all lice and fleas for days! Played as if we'd come to buy coffee
and such. But the hard part's nearly done, and as soon as we can get
a convoy to Rigaud at Jacmel, we have Saint Domingue in our grasp."

"That boat. What were Bahamians doin' . . . ?" Lewrie quibbled.

"Trading, I told you," Pelham bulled on over his objection. "A
two-masted . . . whatever you call 'em, from an island off Great Abaco,
where big merchantmen don't put in much, but *completely* English, not
to worry, Captain Lewrie. Every last one of them sounded like a West
Country peasant, or a Bristol dock-walloper. Place where they build
a fair number of boats, they said. Long settled, but sparsely peopled,

I think, and not much farmland, so it's trade where they can, or perish."

"Man O' War, Elbow, Green Turtle, Guana Cay . . . do you recall a name, sir?" Lewrie speculated aloud.

"Green . . . something edible," Pelham answered, shrugging, and sipping. "Green, boiled . . . disgusting? Anyway . . . ! Rigaud won't be cheap, Mister Peel, but I held the price down to a quarter-million per year for Rigaud, and another quarter-million for his cronies and generals, so he can pay his troops, and hire on the bootless mercenaries we abandoned when we left the island. Those who've sided with L'Ouverture for the promise of a few puny acres of plantation land? Once they get wind of Rigaud having showers of silver coin, though, we may expect at least a tenth of L'Ouverture's army changing sides and haring down to South Province, and Rigaud's so-called Mulatto Republic. Two months, four on the outside, and Rigaud will be ready to take the field against L'Ouverture. Then, perhaps a year from now, we step ashore in triumph, Mister Peel . . . Captain Lewrie, having stolen a march on the French, *and* those pesky Americans, for good and all! With not only French Saint Domingue, but the *Spanish* half of Hispaniola in our possession, as well. *Have* to invade Santo Domingo! When Toussaint L'Ouverture's slave armies are broken, that's where he will flee, and den up. When congratulations are offered, you may rest assured I will feature *your* stalwart efforts in support of my endeavours in the most appreciative terms to the Crown.

"So," Pelham barked, beginning to look a touch bleary. "While I've been up north, what have you two been up to, in the meantime, to bedevil and dethrone Guillaume Choundas?"

Pelham, thankfully, was too engrossed in dipping himself a *new* mug of punch to take note of the uneasy silence that followed *that* enquiry; and with his back turned, he could not discern the queasy looks that passed between them.

"Damme, but this is an *inspiritin'* punch," Pelham enthused with a lip-smacking grin. "Sweet, spicy, but stout. What'd you say was in it? Rum, gin, brandy? No . . ."

"Captured Guadeloupe pineapple, Jamaican cinnamon, and allspice," Lewrie said, shifting about in his chair and crossing his legs to protect his true vitals. "Sweet, dark rum, aye, and a local, er . . . spirit. Why don't *you* tell him of our doings, Mister Peel?"

Peel mouthed a silent "Damn You!" at him, then plastered a grin on his face for Pelham's benefit and gave his superior a *précis* of the raid, the latest rich prize belonging to Hugues, and her captain's loose-lipped talk of Hugues blaming Choundas for her loss, with all of Hugues's expected profits. Peel laid out the intelligence they had gleaned from their prisoners, how much they knew about Choundas's staff, his current state of health, his dealing the ruin of his frigate to Hugues for two converted raiding vessels . . .

"Choundas now only has two *corvettes* under his direct command," Peel related, merely sipping at his own punch as Pelham continued his eager quaffing, and Lewrie had a single refill. "Hugues won't give up a single *row-boat* more, sir. We learned that Choundas escorted a store ship filled mostly with munitions to Guadeloupe, with very few spare spars or canvas for his own ships, beyond what they stowed aboard."

"Short-sighted, that," Lewrie felt emboldened to add, since Mr. Pelham was soaking up the report (along with the punch) in a most amenable fashion, even going so far as to utter the odd "Oh, well played!" and "Ye don't say!" every now and then.

"There is another small three-master, a captured American ship, at Pointe-à-Pitre, awaiting convoying to Saint Domingue, that bears a cargo of armaments," Mr. Peel carefully laid out. "Both await orders from General Hédouville, whether they go to L'Ouverture, or Rigaud. I . . . that is, we . . . do not think they will ever sail, though, with our foe Choundas stripped of strong escorts. Both *corvettes* are cruising far South on the Spanish Main for prizes . . ."

"Yankee ships, mostly, this deep into hurricane season," Lewrie added. "And anyway, they can't be expected back at Guadeloupe for at least a fortnight, depending on how successful their cruise has been. We asked some Yankee merchant captains how many of their ships could still be down there, and—"

"Slim pickings, with everyone eager to get their cargoes home past the Cape Hatteras weather, sir," Peel hurriedly, dismissively explained to cover Lewrie's gaffe, and quickly changing the subject. "We've played a nasty trick on Choundas, one that will keep him busy peeking under his bed-covers. Our first raid, and destroying his frigate at her weakest moment . . . as was our second, *seemed* so timely that our recent prisoners expressed the worry that there may be a spy sneaking messages offshore to us. Choundas, as we intended, sir, *knows* that Captain Lewrie is responsible," Mr. Peel glibly said, with a confidential chuckle. "But, as we also know, Choundas holds a low opinion of the good captain's intelligence!"

"Quite right," Pelham heartily, though woozily, agreed.

"Arrr," was Lewrie's affronted comment to *that*, all but sticking his tongue out at Peel.

"And *no* one can be *that* lucky, so . . . I let slip that *another* of Choundas's ancient foes, Mister Zachariah Twigg, was out here and directing Lewrie's activities," Mr. Peel snickered. "Which accidental revelation should be reaching Choundas through our exchanged prisoners even as we speak, sir. That news, and the strong suspicion that there is someone extremely close to Choundas secretly in our pay, will drive him mad. A spy who is now collaborating with secret Royalists and enemies of his precious Republic whom Victor Hugues didn't catch in *his* initial witch-hunt, will . . ."

"Why Twigg, Mister Peel?" Pelham crossly blurted. "Why not use my name? Ain't Pelhams canny enough?"

Lewrie awarded himself a larger sip of punch from his engraved silver mug from his days as captain of HMS *Jester*, concealing a gladsome grin to see Mr. Pelham beginning to succumb to corn-whisky. He even began to hum "The Jolly Miller" under his breath, delighting in the chorus: "*the longer we sit here and drink, the merrier we shall be!*"

"Well, sir, beg your pardon, but . . . Choundas has never *heard* of you," Peel patiently explained. " 'Twas Mister Twigg, in partnership with Captain Lewrie, who bested him twice before. And the longer you are unknown to the French, the more effective you are.

"*But*, once Choundas hears that my old mentor has been sicced on him, with Lewrie for his weapon, his worst dreads will be realised. He will credit Mister *Twigg* with being able to turn a trusted subordinate against him, and that will smart considerably. Imagining that Twigg opposes him once more fits Choundas's vanity like a glove, too, sir . . . makes him feel as if our side *still* rightly fears him and his un-diminished capabilities, which made us desperate enough to bring Mister Twigg out of well-earned retirement—a retirement of which Paris surely is aware!—to estop Choundas one last time, and . . ."

"And if Choundas don't win," Lewrie felt relaxed enough to add to Mr. Peel's subtle blandishments, "he's done for, this time, and he sure t'God knows it, too. No partial coup, either. For him, it's all or nothing. He can't allow us a single trick, or he's dealt out of the game. Desp'rate enough, t'begin with. Now . . . ?"

"Until his *corvettes* return, there's nought he can accomplish," Mr. Peel continued from Pelham's other side, making that worthy swivel rather ponderously. "That's enough time to concentrate on his alleged traitor-spy, and that spy's collaborators. Why, sir, Choundas'll tear Guadeloupe down to bed-rock. He'll decimate *his* household, Victor Hugues's staff as well. *Anyone* privy to their plans will be suspect, anyone the slightest bit *connected* to people privy to plans. Mistresses, whores, body-servants . . . ?"

"No love lost 'twixt Choundas and Hugues from the very start, we . . . Mister Peel learned," Lewrie gruffly contributed.

"Hugues, we heard, suspects that Choundas was dispatched as his replacement as governor of Guadeloupe," Mr. Peel informed Pelham, with a nod and smile for Lewrie's interruption, which had slewed Mr. Pelham about again, his aristocratic head now wobbling on his neck, with one eye squinted in "concentration" or to maintain his focus. "Choundas has been slighted from the moment he set foot on the island, and hates the way he's been treated."

"Man that hideous," Pelham blearily mused, "can't have *too* many objections, when folk run screamin', or shun 'im."

"Did Victor Hugues fail to 'vet' his staff, or miss a few well-placed . . . 'reactionaries,' they call them," Peel went on, which hauled Pelham's gaze back to him, "in his brutal witch-hunt, Choundas would be more than happy to turn up a few, and make Hugues look the fool. Maybe Choundas *does* have a secret brief from the Directory to supplant him if Hugues seems to be losing his grip on things. Who knows?

"At any rate, I 'accidentally' offered up clues pointing to one man extremely close to Choundas," Peel confided to his superior, with a sly-boots' grin. "His clerk and private secretary, Etienne de Gougne. He's slurred as 'the Mouse,' a meek little scribbler too frightened of the consequences to leave his employ, we discovered."

"Him or Choundas, sooner or later," Lewrie idly stated, one leg atop his desk in sublime ease. "Choundas loses, the little bastard is done for. Knows too much, and Choundas couldn't let him live to blab, else old sins'd come back to get Choundas shortened by the guillotine."

"And we *know* Choundas's penchant for cruelty, Mister Pelham," Peel said, hiding a wider grin to see Pelham's eyes slewing beyond his head's direction, and starting to glaze over. "A shot at torturing the truth from the unfortunate fellow will suit Choundas down to his toes. Frustrate him, too, since this idiot de Gougne knows nothing and *can't* name any names . . . Choundas will go barking-mad, I expect, and turn *all* his attention on a hunt for our spies. He touches Hugues's staff, Hugues slaps him down, takes command of his remaining ships, and Choundas goes back to France in chains, disgraced and probably down for the mad-house, to boot! Driven to insanity by one too many intrigues."

"Hmmm," Pelham uttered, polishing off another mug of that perfidious punch, and dipping himself a replacement. "Don't know, Peel."

"He'll be kept so busy, so distracted . . ." Peel pressed.

"Ever think we *do* have spies on Guadeloupe, hah?" Pelham suddenly snapped. "Choundas snaps 'em up like pickin' daisies, where are we then? His clerk, well . . . dies 'thout namin' names, a wider hunt will turn up *real'uns*, shuh . . . surely!"

"Anyone *we* know?" Lewrie was forced to ask in curiosity.

"Uh er, no," Pelham had to admit.

"Anyone vital to our cause, sir?" Peel asked, too.

"I, er . . . don' know. N'body tol' *me*, damn 'em! Wouldn' trust *me* with their idet . . . ident . . . names! Their 'product' goes to Lord Balcarres, an' *he* tells me, he thinks I need it . . . *hic*. Damme, that a *cat*, Lewrie?" Pelham suddenly said, peering owl-eyed into the diningcoach, wherein Toulon crouched atop the table next to his hideous hat, head bobbing and cocking and his whiskers stiffly forward at the sight of something so alluring . . . and possibly edible.

"Why, I do b'lieve it is," Lewrie replied, feigning surprise.

"Thank God!" Pelham shuddered, sounding much relieved. "Thought it was a ship rat. Heard o' *them*, I have. *Nice* puss! *Nice* mouser!"

"So, you concur with my putting the scheme in play, sir?" Peel decided to ask, to get verbal assent before Pelham went arse-over-tit, while he could still form sentences.

"What? Oh . . . knacky ruse. Yes. S'pose," Pelham agreed, now noticeably swaying. "Clever! Amusin'. Damme, we set sail, already?"

"I'm glad you approve of my extemporaneous actions, sir," Peel most-carefully intoned, "and that Captain Lewrie may attest to such an approval." He tipped Lewrie a broad wink.

"Glad to be of service, Mister Peel," Lewrie gleefully agreed.

"Where'd those damned Colonials get all their prizes?" Pelham enquired, plopping down into his side-chair again, and tugging at his neck-stock as if strangling, or suffocating in his too-warm clothes.

" 'Bout ninety miles West-Nor'west of the Grenadines. They took four merchantmen back from Choundas's newest raiders," Lewrie casually explained, thinking that Mr. Pelham was sufficiently "liquored" to be amenable to *part* of the truth. "They also took one of his raiders into the bargain, and sank another. Picked up the survivors from that one, and fetched 'em all in. You'll have a good time interrogating 'em, I think, Mister Pelham. Once they're handed over from the Americans to our officials, that is. Should've seen 'em!" Lewrie enthused. "Ev'ry shot 'twixt wind and water, made one strike with a single broadside . . . !"

"You *there?*" Pelham gravelled of a sudden, head now well a'list and one eye screwed shut. "Yer ship'z . . . *hic!* . . . *there*, sir? Damn my eyes, you been coll— . . . collab— . . . at sea with the Yankees, 'spite my tellin' ye . . . ?"

Uh oh, Lewrie thought; *should've let him slip under the table, and kept my mouth shut!*

"God damn my eyes, you *bloody . . . WHAT?*" Pelham screeched as he shot to his feet. "*Mis'rable* idiot bastard, meddlin' . . . !"

Lewrie swung his leg off the desk as Pelham staggered forward, hands "clawed" as if wishing to strangle him, but, thankfully, he did not get that far; *couldn't* in point of fact, for Toulon, proudly bound aft toward his lair under the starboard-side settee, dragging his oversized, wide-brimmed, befeathered, and awkward "kill," overhauled Pelham's stumbling, clumping feet.

Which near-collision raised an outraged howl from the ram-cat; which howl seemed to levitate the distinguished Pelham for a startled second; which levitation made Pelham come down attempting to avoid the cat, or his costly new "sportin' hat" (it was hard to judge which), and reel and flail about for what little balance was left to him; which attempt *looked* like a marriage of an *impromptu* Irish Jig, a folk dance involving *sombreros* reported among the *mestizo* peoples of the Spanish New World, and the frantic whirlings of mystic Muslim *dervishes* in the Holy Land; which gay prancing brought forth an accompanying outburst in what *might* be mistaken for an Unknown Tongue, sounding hellish-like "*Eeh* too-ah *gaah*, shit *hic!* arr-eeh!" the last syllables a wail that ascended the musical scale as Mr. Pelham snagged a booted toe in a ring-bolt mid his descent and landed spraddle-legged on his rump with a gay thud.

"*Rrowwr!*" Toulon carped from his lair, his kill abandoned.

"Oww—hunngh!" was Pelham's response, quickly followed by a "Hhrackk!" quickly followed by the remains of his breakfast, dinner, most-like his supper of the evening before, and about half a gallon of "punch" to boot. Pelham's "casting his accounts to Neptune" didn't do his sickly green waist-coat, buff breeches, or corduroy spatterdashes a bit of good, either.

"Now I understand why they call 'em spatterdashes," Peel said, looking like to puke himself, with a pocket handkerchief pressed close to his nose and mouth. "God in Heaven, what's he been *eating?*"

Mr. Pelham caught a whiff of it, himself, and cast up another flood, just before his eyes crossed, his face went pasty, and he fell insensible to the deck on his right side.

"Pelham a Mason?" Lewrie enquired, quickly masking his own nose.

"Most-like," Peel mumbled through his handkerchief. "Most rich and titled men are. Why?"

"Just wonderin' if what he shouted was some secret language," Lewrie answered, shrugging. "Well. Shouldn't someone help him up, or . . . something?"

"Damned if it'll be me," Peel announced. " 'Twas your punch done him in. You do it."

"Aspinall?" Lewrie shouted toward the gun-deck. "Sentry? Pass word for my cabin servant . . . and Mister Durant, the Surgeon's Mate, as well. Carryin' board, and the loblolly boys," he instructed the Marine who popped his head through the forrud bulkhead door. "Mops, brooms . . . and lots and *lots* o' seawater." To himself he muttered, "May have to rig a wash-deck pump, never can tell."

" 'E looks dead," Peel observed.

"No, he'll only wish he was, when he comes round," Lewrie pooh-poohed. "God's sake, let's go on deck for some air! And when knacky little Mister Pelham can sit up, again, I want t'ask him about how he *got* to Saint Domingue. Don't care how disguised and careful he said he was, there's something about that knockabout tradin' vessel he used, bothers me. Don't know why, but . . ."

"Sounded fishy to me, too," Peel allowed as they made a rapid way aft to Lewrie's private and narrow ladder to the after quarterdeck. "Don't trust his trade-craft, the bloody . . . amateur. L'Ouverture and Rigaud, Hédouville . . . Sonthonax and Laveaux . . . those lesser generals like Dessalines and Christophe, they *all* have agents in the opposing camps. Doubt you could walk from one side of the street to the other without bumping into three or four, and a half-dozen more spies scampering off to report on your ev'ry fart and scratch."

"You think Pelham was gulled?" Lewrie asked, once they reached the brisk fresh air by the taff-rails and flag lockers, under the taut-rigged canvas awnings that now spanned the quarterdeck.

"My dear Captain Lewrie, I am almost certain of it!" Peel said with a sneer. "That damned fool, callow . . . boy! . . . let himself get used by just about everyone in power on the island, and showed 'em all just how perfidious are our dealings. After him, all our hopes for a British Saint Domingue are completely dashed. And Pelham did it, all by his little self, by being just *too* clever by half!"

"Well," Lewrie said at last. "There lies the packet brig over yonder. Four to six weeks from now, your account could arrive beside his. I'll have my portable writing desk fetched up. . . . do you decide you might need it, hmm?"

"Might fetch up Pelham's hat, too, while you're at it," Mr. Peel said with a knowing smile. "Your cat can have the feathers, for they ain't dyed. Turkey, eagle, and pelican plumes, mostly. But the hat dye might make him sick. Or as mad as a hatter."

"Good suggestion, Mister Peel," Lewrie said with a bow of gratitude. "And here, I didn't think you cared!"

CHAPTER TWENTY-SIX

Lt. Jules Hainaut had barely gotten his prize schooner tied up alongside a stone quay in the harbour of Basse-Terre when the reply to his urgent flag signals came from Pointe-à-Pitre, the other harbour to the east. The Vieux Fort semaphore tower had signalled that his hoists would be relayed to Capt. Choundas as *Mohican* and *Chippewa* had beaten a hobby-horsing way inshore. Despite the hundreds of things required of him to secure both prizes, see to the surviving crews, and turn the vessels over to the local court officials, there was no gainsaying the wax-sealed letter's pithy instruction when it came aboard stained with ammoniacal horse-sweat, and borne by an equally sweated despatch rider.

"*Come to me, quickly!*" the single sheet of paper said.

Hainaut groaned with weary misery at what strenuous effort that simple directive implied. Against the winds, a despatch boat couldn't fetch Pointe-à-Pitre 'til mid-afternoon next. The quickest way was by horseback, the only road a rain-gullied sand-and-shell track rutted by cart-wheels. Thirty-two of those newfangled *kilomètres*, at least eight hours at a trot or canter, supposing a change of horses at Capesterre or Ste. Marie was available!

Hainaut would be damned if he'd do it at a gallop all the way, Guillaume Choundas's well-feared wrath notwithstanding. Was he not a warship captain in all but name, with all the duty and responsibility that that implied? Oh, he'd make a great show of leaving with the utmost despatch . . . but he thought a brief sit-down supper somewhere on the way could be fitted in, explained by the plea of Stern Duty to his hapless *matelots*, and the safeguarding of the prizes . . . which prizes were rare and dearly earned money in *Le Hideux*'s purse, too, after all. Surely that earned Hainaut an extra, un-begrudged hour!

"*Timmonier*, I am ordered to report to *Capitaine* Choundas, quick as I may. You are in charge until I return!" Hainaut shouted with the proper seeming haste and clattered down the gangplank in the uniform he stood up in, bawling at the despatch rider for a fast mount.

"*Vous imposteur petit*," the petty officer growled to himself as soon as Lt. Hainaut was lost in the dockside throng ashore. "*Go* lick your ugly master's arse! *Et va te faire foutre*," he muttered, as he leaned over the side to hock up a hefty and derisive gob of phlegm.

"You are certain it was *Proteus*," Guillaume Choundas rasped in the ghoulishly unflattering light of four finger-thick candles mounted in a single stand on the side of his ornate desk. "You are certain it was that *diable* Lewrie?"

"There is no doubt of it, *m'sieur*," Jules Hainaut replied with the properly dramatic gravity, displaying grim assuredness, and a hint of residual anger. "Hand-in-glove with two *americain* men of war. It was *Proteus* in the centre, with one each in her van and rear. Against such overwhelming force, I regret there was nothing I could do with my two barely armed and undermanned prizes to aid Lieutenant Pelletier," Hainaut gravely explained, laying out the disastrous events as best he had observed them 'til he had sailed the action far aft and under the horizon.

Hainaut had been most careful to swath his clothing at the inn where he had dined (rather well in point of fact) so there would be no betraying food stains upon his person; but from the moment he had come to a dust-cloud halt from his last galloped leg of the journey (begun at the five-*kilomètre* post outside town to look properly winded and damp with horse-sweat) Capt. Choundas had peered so closely at him that he felt as if he were under examination with a magnifying glass, so sharp, glittery, and icily dubious was Choundas's remaining good eye on him, so high-nosed and aloof did his master regard him.

"And all three ships flew their largest battle flags," Choundas pressed. Even though Hainaut had arrived shortly after midnight, and the interrogation had been going on for more than an hour, Choundas was dressed in his best gilt-laced uniform, his neck-stock done up and all his waist-coat buttons snugly buttoned. As was his master's mind, as lucid and penetrating as ever.

"They did, *m'sieur*," Hainaut answered with an affirmative nod, even if he hadn't been close enough to the action to espy such details, and he strove to keep his face bland, but not too bland; with no owl-eyed staring, or too much rapid blinking to put the lie to his statement. Hainaut had seen Choundas conduct harsher interrogations before, and had even been instructed in the tell-tale frailties of men and women determined to bluff their way out.

"Ahum" was Choundas's response to that, taking time to swivel to face his detestable little clerk, de Gougne, who pointedly made an additional note of Hainaut's observation at his master's cue.

No wine, Hainaut thought in worry; *dry work, but no wine in the offing. How much trouble am I in? What, kill the bearer of bad news?*

In Hainaut's experience of Choundas's little "chats" with those he would expose and condemn, wine was always available to those of too much self-possession, none for the visibly nervous until they had lied their way into a corner. Wine came first for Choundas, then was given to the shaky victim with profuse apologies, as if they had survived the experience—followed by the too-casual "just a matter or two more, Citizen (or Citizenness)" to dis-arm before the verbal blow that struck below the heart. Hainaut worried (and not for the first time) exactly where he stood with Guillaume Choundas this night.

The man had aged, Hainaut noted, in the few weeks since his ship had sailed on her raiding cruise. That arc of Choundas's face he still exposed to the world was much more serely pruned than when he'd wished them all *bonne chance*; his flesh was more collapsed upon the bones and now of a sickly, pasty cast, as if he had turned hermit, not venturing outside his headquarters unless required, thinned by poor victuals, or the loss of interest in mere food in the face of all his cares and frustrations.

Hainaut almost exposed himself with a faint shudder of dread as he suddenly realised that the vaunted, clever, and capable ogre was *not* going to succeed this time. Guillaume Choundas was going to *fail*, and likely drag him down with him when he went! More so than ever, Hainaut now *had to* be free of him.

"Your prizes safely made harbour, though, Hainaut? No damage?" Choundas demanded, too solicitous of a sudden for credence, as if they didn't matter in the slightest.

"Yes, *m'sieur*," Hainaut answered, feigning gruffness, as if he were immune to the temptation of prize-money, too. "Two fine schooners belonging to the same '*Amis*' trading company. Both are about, uhm ... thirty *mètres*, and very fast, with promising cargoes of dyewood, coffee, cotton, rough wines and brandies, cocoa, kegs of limes and lemons, cocoanuts, sugar and molasses, and tons of *cigaros* or plug tobacco. In excellent condition, both of them. Lightly armed of course, but stiff and beamy enough to accept a decent battery. Six-pounders would be best, if any are available, *m'sieur*. Cannon of four-pounder measurement if not, to match their own armament. Pardon, but they would make excellent replacements for those we lost."

Choundas stared at him, disconcertingly unblinking for a *long* time, as if turned to stone by Hainaut's callow presumptions to offer "tarry-handed" nautical advice to *him*.

"Of course, in their present condition, they could make a fast passage back to France with their cargoes," Hainaut spoke up, wilting under that obsidian gaze, hating himself for making self-deprecating gestures, for altering his confident voice nigh to apologetic wheedling. "Whatever you decide, *m'sieur*."

"Indeed," Choundas intoned, with the faintest, cruelest lift at the exposed corner of his ravaged mouth. "Well, then. You have ridden hard and far, Hainaut, and must be desperately hungry and thirsty, no?"

"Ready to fight a wolf for the bones, *m'sieur*, and so dry that I could drink a river!" Hainaut exclaimed with plausible eagerness. "My poor arse ... it has been too long since I even sat a horse. Once in bed, I fear I'll sleep face-down, and need a sitting pillow for a week hence! Uhm ... what should I do in the morning, *m'sieur*? Ride back to Basse-Terre to deal with your prizes? Sail back, preferably. There is my crew to see to ... "

"One last little matter, Hainaut," Choundas interrupted, almost as an afterthought, which beguilingly coo-some tone to his voice froze Hainaut's innards, "and then I will let you refresh yourself."

"Of course, *m'sieur*," Hainaut replied, sinking back down onto his chair with his knees ready to buckle.

"Did Lewrie and the Americans," Choundas posed, leaning back in his own chair and toying with a loosely folded sheet of paper with his left hand, "seem as if they lay in wait for you? Dash straightaway for our ships? Could you see any sort of light or signal which might have *drawn* them to Lieutenants Houdon and Pelletier and their prizes?"

"All but the compass binnacle lights had been ordered doused, *m'sieur*," Hainaut answered, unable to avoid looking perplexed by such a question. "They *did* steer directly for the two larger groups, just as soon as they heaved up in view, yes, now that you mention it. But that was near dawn, and even the binnacles had been snuffed by then. It is possible that they kept mast-head lookouts aloft after dark, or sent theirs aloft earlier than ours, *m'sieur*. But I did not get the impression that they lay in wait for us. It was an unfortunate thing that we were spotted by the lead ship in their patrol line furthest to the Eastward, but . . . did they operate together to intercept any ships returning to Guadeloupe, they surely would have known to search as far to windward as possible."

"Such a *fortuitous* . . . coincidence, though, do you not believe, Jules? *Hein?* Following the first inexplicable fortunate coincidence off Basse-Terre, when we lost *Le Bouclier* and the arms shipment? You *do* recall that, I presume." Choundas sneered, all arch and Arctic cold. "Or the recent loss of a rich merchantman just off Deshaies not a week ago, when Lewrie and *Proteus* just *happened* round Pointe Allegre, just at the *instant* that a *Capitaine* Fleury's ship cleared the cape?"

"I was not aware of that loss, *m'sieur*," Hainaut said, frowning.

"No, I am now certain that you were not, for you had no way of knowing the day, or the hour, of her sailing for home," Choundas told him. "She was betrayed, *cher* Jules.

"Just as *you* were betrayed, just as *Le Bouclier* and *Capitaine* Desplan were betrayed," Choundas gravelled in a hoarse, rasping voice. "Fleury, and that fat fool Haljewin, are prisoners on Dominica, though at least Fleury had the wit to write me of his taking, of being for a brief time a prisoner aboard Lewrie's frigate. Fleury carefully wrote a veiled account of his ordeal, in a crude but workable cypher known to me. You remember that despicable old *salaud* who interrogated you when you were captured in the Mediterranean, the wicked Zachariah Twigg, or Simon Silberberg, whatever he called himself?"

"I do, *m'sieur*," Hainaut gasped for real. "Unfortunately."

"He is *here*, Hainaut!" Choundas barked, slamming his left hand on the desk-top, and making clerk de Gougne nearly jump out of his skin.

"Fleury described a civilian with Lewrie who named himself as a John Gunn, but from the description I conclude was really Twigg's old aide, a British agent named James Peel. Seeking my destruction, just one more time, they have brought Twigg out of retirement and paired him and Lewrie to destroy me and all my works. So far, they succeed, Jules."

"*Mon Dieu*," Hainaut whispered. "Surely not, you . . ."

"Not through luck, not through guile or superior numbers, *non*," Choundas snapped, "but through *treachery*. Twigg, Peel, and Lewrie are being assisted by a spy, a whole cabal of spies and traitors operating here on Guadeloupe, Jules. Under my very nose. On my own staff, among *commissaire* Hugues's most trusted people. Under my very roof, *hein?*"

"Su . . . surely you cannot suspect . . . !" Hainaut blustered, awash in sudden fear that his master thought it was he!

"I *did*, dear Jules," Choundas whispered, as malevolently cruel as a hawk honing beak and talons before tearing its quaking prey into gobbets. "Twigg had you for weeks before exchanging you for British midshipmen. The thought *had* crossed my mind, understandably so, *n'est-ce pas?*" Choundas even took a moment to roar with abusive amusement at Hainaut's gulping and blinking torment. "As false as you have played me all these years, you *did* make me wonder."

"False? *M'sieur*, really . . . !" Hainaut flummoxed.

"Don't pretend undying loyalty, Hainaut," Choundas snapped, now thin-lipped and flushed in aspersion. "I am not completely blind, nor am I deaf. You love only yourself, Hainaut. No shame in it, so long as when you *dissemble* energetic fealty to France you are useful to her . . . and to me."

"Master, I . . ."

"Do not even try to swear your undying gratitude, or loyalty." Choundas cautioned.

"While you were at sea, things on Guadeloupe have taken several turns for the worse, or the better, depending," Choundas gloomily said, grimacing with distaste. In the harsh, badly angled candlelight, his face resembled that of a satanic ghoul from folk or children's stories. "It seems that Paris is not happy with our unproductive little war on American trade. *Commissaire* Hugues has been a thoughtless glutton for money, Hainaut. He's *sold* privateering commissions throughout the Caribbean, in every Dutch, Danish, and Spanish port, not just to Frenchmen. Asks for an additional share of the proceeds from our *local* privateers, and uses his Prize Court to inflate the value of the captures for those who go along with him, and for his own gain. *Naturellement*, that makes for outright piracy preying on *our* allies, too, and threatens to upset what coalition the Directory has been able to muster against the hated British! It took me some time to discover all of this, but—"

"And now you are prepared to use it against him, *m'sieur*," Jules Hainaut said, more than happy for Choundas to turn his bile away from him, against another obstacle. Hainaut took a peek at "the Mouse" to see if Etienne de Gougne was disappointed that *his* grilling was ended, for the nonce, that the little clerk's hopes of seeing him broken were dashed, and silently relished the nonentity's tiny *moue*.

"I am, indeed, Jules," Choundas told him, smiling and nodding, "for Paris has seen fit to send us a senior official to look into the matter. One of the Directory's ridiculous creatures, all booted and spurred, in a *Tricolore* waist sash, and all those silly plumes on his hat . . . Desfourneaux is his name. I shall see him tomorrow, to lay my evidence before him. And suggest to him that Hugues has so ruined the credit of our privateering commissions that, for the moment, only good *French* corsairs remain legal, and that the best of them are conscripted into naval service whether they like it or not, to sail as warships . . . temporarily . . . to salvage the Republic's good name."

"Under *your* command, not Hugues's," Hainaut crowed, marvelling at his master's deviousness. "*Magnifique, m'sieur*. Masterfully done."

"Desfourneaux will clean up the piratical corruption Hugues has fostered, Perhaps he even has orders to place Hugues under arrest as a witless fool, who has driven the Americans into league with the 'Bloodies.' *That* piece of news you bring me will spur Desfourneaux into even quicker action to remove Hugues," Choundas slyly boasted.

"With Hugues, his staff, and his corrupt circle suspect as well," Hainaut congratulated with a sage snicker, "who, one wonders, might be left to become the new *commissaire civil* of Guadeloupe, *m'sieur?* With care, and a becoming outward disdain for greed, the vacant post could *still* prove extremely profitable . . . and pleasureable . . . for the one who proves himself capable, *n'est-ce pas?*"

"You see, dear Jules, all my efforts to educate you in the ways of the wider world have borne fruit, after all," Choundas agreed, with

an evil little laugh. "I truly never expected such an opportunity to fall
into my lap, but now that it seems possible . . . ah! And the last nail
in Hugues's coffin will be his apparent failure to apprehend the spies
who pass information to the British, because he let himself be distracted
by the lure of riches. Or perhaps the suggestion that he *deliberately*
left some untouched, were sufficiently lucrative bribes paid, hmm? Not
that he was in British pay, himself, no. That would be reaching too
far to be plausible, but . . . as soon as Desfourneaux gets his hands on
Hugues's ledgers, he is doomed, and I will be seen as instrumental to
his exposure.

"Whether I become governor or not, or become the senior naval
officer in the Caribbean, worthy of admiral's rank at long last, and
second-in-command of the island next to the *new* governor, either way
I gain, and advance," Choundas cleverly concluded. "You are *sure* you
would leave my employ, Hainaut, now that my, and your, prospects
for gaining riches, power . . . and with that power, the access to *un-
dreamed* pleasures, are so close to having? To discover the spies, I will
need the assistance of men I trust, experienced with delving into traitors' hearts and minds, experienced with my techniques of . . . interrogation. Now, could a small, insignificant ship of war, with all the
privations of seafaring, be more tempting than that?"

Jules Hainaut let his mouth fall open slightly as he cocked his head
to one side in furious contemplation. Choundas knew him down to
his boots, knew what motivated him, to what he eventually aspired,
no matter how seemingly unattainable for a half-Austrian former farm-
hand and simple sailor. Tempting as the prospects were, though . . .

"If you need me so badly you must order it, *m'sieur*, of course,"
he temporised, "but . . . I still desire command of a warship. I am not
so improved as you think. I came from before the mast, and the sea
is what I know. I do aspire to advancement, but . . ."

"So be it," Choundas growled, as if disappointed. "This schooner
you brought in, Jules, the one you *claim* would be a suitable replacement . . . you desire *her?*"

"I do, *m'sieur*, more than anything!" Hainaut vowed, though with
his fingers crossed for luck, for he'd seen his master raise the hopes
of others, only to delight in betraying them a moment later, breaking
the spirit and heart of his victims—along with the bones.

"Then she is yours, Jules," Choundas baldly told him, so firmly
that Hainaut had no fears it was a cruel ploy. "You will leave with a

new commission into her. Your orders will be to arm her with the guns off both prizes, empty them and turn the cargoes over to the Prize Court officials at Basse-Terre, and assemble the crews off both ships into her. I will send what midshipmen, petty officers, and sailors I can spare, though after our most recent disaster, experienced officers I cannot offer."

"I will make do, *m'sieur*," Hainaut confidently swore.

"Good, for I have quick need of you," Choundas said, business-like, picking up the folded letter he had toyed with earlier. "I have received a letter from General Hédouville, on Saint Domingue, at last. He intends to throw his support to that pompous Mulatto, General André Rigaud, and has urgent need for the munition ships to sail as soon as possible. With *La Résolue* and *Le Gascon* away, though, I cannot despatch the arms convoy and hope that it gets through. I can not entrust their safety to even the worthiest of our privateers as an escort, either. As soon as you are ready for sea in all respects, you must dash back down South and recall Griot and MacPherson from raiding the Americans. We must do all this before the British can act."

"I will do so, *m'sieur*!" Hainaut vowed with mounting joy.

"The vile 'Bloodies' sent an agent to Saint Domingue, to try to bribe L'Ouverture and Riguad," Choundas sneered, "a total ass. It was quite droll, was it not, Etienne?"

"Oh? Indeed, *m'sieur*," clerk de Gougne chirped back, jerked to wakefulness at the mention of his name. He had been nodding off, now that it seemed his bitterest abuser had gotten away with a whole skin, and a grand reward . . . again!

"That *salopard* Twigg does not direct every insidious scheme the British work against us, Jules," Choundas snickered. "Even he is com-partmented to deal specifically with *me*, while others woo the ignorant *noirs*. Their latest agent was so clumsily disguised he might as well have gone ashore with a regimental band! He even hired a boat to take him to Ile de la Gonave, then Jacmel, that had been at Kingston to spy for *us*, if you can believe it . . . the silly shit!"

"No! He didn't!" Hainaut hooted with open glee. "What an ass!"

"Americans, from Okracoke Island, on the Outer Banks near Cape Hatteras," Choundas cackled. "Long a pirates' and buccaneers' haven, where they make their prime living salvaging the many shipwrecks that come onshore. Perhaps *luring* some when times are lean. Who can say? A most practical and realistic lot, with a distinct English accent. They told this idiot that Okracoke was a smallish cay off the Abacos, in the Bahamas, and the ignorant *fumier* bought it! Naturally, they betrayed him for extra money, as soon as they put into both ports, being rewarded by L'Ouverture, then Rigaud, *then* by Hédouville!"

Choundas had to pause to let his harsh laughter subside.

"Before they left Jacmel, an aide to General Hédouville handed them his letter . . . *this* letter, and brought it *and* that twit straight to Antigua at the same time, then hared off here to Guadeloupe on the very next tide!" Choundas all but tittered, wiping his good eye with a handkerchief. "And he never knew a thing about it! They even taught him *sea*-chanties, and to dance a horn-pipe in his sailor's costume!"

"*Mon Dieu*, what a hopeless . . ." Hainaut wheezed, himself. "Well, I will get a few hours' sleep, then get back to *Mohican* as quickly as I can, to ready her . . ."

"No real rush, Hainaut," Choundas countered, so easily turning grim and business-like after savouring his little coup. "Your orders will take time to write, extra crew to assemble . . . The British agent promised much more than he can possibly deliver at short notice. It will be weeks before his blandishments are assembled and loaded, while ours just wait for the arrival of our ships to escort them. A midnight repast, a good night's sleep, face-down if you must, and a hearty breakfast before you depart will be allowed."

"Very good, *m'sieur*," Hainaut gratefully agreed.

"Time enough for me to discover the spy network, so this time I do not tip my hand, or the day or hour of departure to Lewrie and his spy-master," Choundas mused, looking rather weary and ill no matter if he should have been chortling over his clever master-stroke. "I have two small, additional things for you to do for me, dear Jules, if you do not mind."

"But of course, *m'sieur*," Hainaut replied, anxious to seem full of eager cooperation, now that all his dreams had been launched.

"First of all, uhm . . ." Choundas grunted, arthritically twisting in his chair, no matter how comfortably padded, and with his eyes carefully averted. "Before the arrival of Hédouville's letter and the news you brought, I was beginning to despair. *Oui*, even me, Hainaut! Time lingers heavily when plans are set in motion, and one cannot see or know how they progress, *n'est-ce pas?* Go to my bed-chamber and . . .

you will understand. A slight, amusing diversion," he said crankily. "She's very young and pretty, so you might even take joy of her, too, do you find her pleasing. If not, dispose of her. Discretely."

Hainaut chilled with foreboding as he rose and crossed to the double doors that led to his master's ground-story chambers. Hainaut gently pulled them back and stepped inside, fearing what he'd find.

A single candle burned on a night-table, a small bottle of good brandy lay on its side on the carpet, empty, along with two abandoned glasses. And a girl lay tangled in the bed-linens, her nearly White *café au lait* complexion a tawny contrast to the white of the sheets. Her hair was raven-dark and curly, now undone and bedraggled, down to the small of her back, and spilled like dried blood over the pillows.

Hainaut stepped to the side of the high bed-stead and swept her hair back from her face. She was beginning to purple with bruises his master had inflicted in his "passion," her lips split and caked with a colour darker than paste. Dried tears streaked her artful makeup, but she was indeed very pretty. Not over thirteen or fourteen, as most of Choundas's bed-mates always turned out to be, slight, slim, and petite. Child-women, with spring buds for breasts.

Hainaut put a hand under her nose and half-opened mouth to feel for breath, touched the side of her neck to see if life still throbbed in her. Yes, she was still alive. Hainaut knelt and sniffed the neck of the empty brandy bottle, and detected the aroma of laudanum, which *Le Hideux* had used to drug her into deliciously sweet helplessness, if not complaisance. Into furtive, whimpering silence, instead of wails or screams that could draw unwelcome attention from neighbours. Snuck in the back way, as always, long after full dark, muffled in anonymous cloaks or blankets. Carried *out*, before dawn, and still insensible.

Hainaut heaved a disgusted sigh before pulling the sheet up over the girl's bare shoulders and stepping out of the room, quietly closing the doors on her fate.

"Allow to me ask, *m'sieur*," Hainaut said, almost tip-toeing, and his voice a whisper, in some form of deference for that pitiful chit, "but what degree of disposal did you have in mind?"

"Scruples, dear Jules?" Choundas mocked. "This late in our association? My, my. Nothing drastic. She's a *pretty* little whore, but a whore nonetheless. Return her to her master at the *bordel* where she is employed, with a second purse beyond her rental. To compensate the *bordel* owner for his loss of earnings 'til she's presentable once

more. The whoremonger has been warned what could happen to him
if he makes a fuss. Have her out before the town wakes," Choundas
grumpily ordered, reaching for his walking-stick leaned against his
costly desk, and painfully getting to his feet at last, swaying with
weariness and wincing at the pain of an old, old man. The low candlelight limned him as an ancient, grizzled dragon.

"The last matter I mentioned may be done at the same time you
return our wee *putain. That* chore is official, public, and provides a
mask for the first."

"Very well, *m'sieur?*" Hainaut assented, perplexed again.

"Please be so good as to step out on the porch and summon the
front entrance sentries," Capt. Choundas grimly ordered.

"*M'sieur?*" Hainaut gawped in sudden, renewed dread that all he
had been offered, told, had been but a cruel charade, that all along
Choundas had been toying with him like a sly cat would torment a
fear-frozen mouse, teasing it this way and that with soft, claw-sheathed
paws.

"That spy, John Gunn or James Peel, whatever he calls himself,
boasted a little *too* much to our *Capitaine* Fleury, Jules," Guillaume
Choundas continued in a more-familiar growl, rage back in his face
and voice, "accidentally revealing to him that the 'Bloodies' have a
spy so close to me that the British might as well be sitting in this
room this very moment. Now who could it be, Jules? Who *could* it
be? Does it not make *you* wonder?" Choundas threatened, taking a
clumsy pace or two towards him, stick, boot, and brace ominously
going clump-shuffle-tick!

"He is here *now, m'sieur?*" Hainaut stuttered in surprise, and near-
terror, did Choundas still suspect him, though he'd said . . . He turned
his head to look down at Etienne de Gougne, for he *knew* it was not
him. Besides, he'd never laid eyes on this anonymous Fleury, and
could not recall snubbing or insulting anyone by that name. If this
Fleury person had laid a charge against *him* to cover the inept loss of
his precious ship, but how . . . !

"He is here," Choundas forebodingly confirmed, and slowly swept
his own gaze away and down, to peer at de Gougne as well. The little
clerk began to rise, but Choundas drove him back into the chair with
a shove of his left hand.

"The mouse? Surely . . . !" Hainaut scoffed, never so relieved in his
life.

"All these years you reported behind my back to the Directory, and their spy-master, Citizen Pouzin," Choundas gravelled. "You think I would not learn of it, Etienne, when Pouzin seemed to know too much, and so quickly, on the Genoese coast, and ever since? Don't dare deny it! Did you think he would *rescue* you, should you ever become a liability to me? Where is Citizen Pouzin now, and where are we, *hein?*"

"*M-m-m'sieur*," de Gougne blubbered in fright, barely able to find breath with which to protest his innocènce. "Master . . ."

"*That* sort of treachery I could abide, Etienne," Choundas menacingly rumbled, "such pettiness. Was it your sly, meek way to get back at me for using you like the insignificant worm that you are? But to take *British* gold to slake your wretched, pitiful, mousy *shop*-clerk's, *ink*-sniffing, *clock*-watching, *time*-server's, *slippered bourgeois*, landbound *peasant* spite on *me?* You will pay, Etienne . . . you *know* you will. I will break you into slivers. I will make blood-and-marrow *soup* with your bones, and make you drink it, before you die, with just *enough* of you left to ride the tumbril to the guillotine, so everyone can witness the reward for treason, and see justice done.

"But before that, Etienne," Choundas promised, leaning forward to whisper as sibilantly as a hideous boa constrictor, "you will name for me every traitor on this island you work with or . . . *quel dommage,*" he suddenly mused, standing upright, and instantly bemused, as if his ire had gushed away like the hot air from a Montgolfier balloon.

For clerk Etienne de Gougne had pissed himself, had even fouled his trousers, as he fainted dead away, slumped bone-white to the floor.

"*Him?*" Hainaut gaped, quite unable to believe he had it in him.

"*Oui*," Choundas confirmed, jabbing with his walking-stick. "Get *this* gaoled in Fort Fleur d'Epée. And get that trull out of my house, too, Jules. Now, *vite, vite!*"

CHAPTER TWENTY-SEVEN

*L*ewrie had given testimony before the Prize Court, and the American merchant vessels had been released to their captains to complete their homeward journeys. Crews off *Sumter*, *Oglethorpe*, and *Proteus* had been given shore liberty, with sailors of both nations reeling arm-in-arm from one public house to the next, for a whole rousing day and night.

On the *second* rousing day and night, however, the question arose to whether the Yankee Doodles had *needed* British aid in fighting a brace of French warships; whether the aforesaid French men o' war were worthy opponents, or cringingly weak and lightly armed poltroons who'd struck too quickly; whether they'd been daunted by American prowess or the mere sight of a British "bulldog" flying the Union flag.

The resulting brawls, 'twixt Yankee salts and British tars, actively aided and abetted by other bellicose drunks egging them on, *with* the eager participation in said brawls of stout British islanders and merchant seamen, by Yankee Doodle civilian sailors and gentlemen traders who'd taken manly umbrage, shortly after re-enforced by members of the watch and Admiralty dockworkers, by publicans, whores, and *their* bully-bucks and crimps, and lastly by the appearance of the heartily despised shore gangs of His Majesty's Navy's Impress Service (who came off a rather poor third) had redounded to the detriment of the publicans, their establishments, the whores, pimps, crimps, brothel keepers, and "Mother Abbesses" and *their* commercial properties, and the peaceable tradespeople and residents of English Harbour, who had forced the Governor-General to call out a company of the garrison and declare the Riot Act. Bayonets, and fall-down drunken stupors, had ended it.

Which brawl had placed HMS *Proteus*, her people, her officers, and most especially her captain in extremely bad odour, and Lewrie had had what felt like five pounds of hide taken off his backside by both the Governor-General *and* Rear-Admiral Harvey.

And to make matters even worse, Grenville Pelham was not only *not* expired, but able to sit up, take nourishment, and screech like a wet parrot!

Other than working-parties to fetch supplies, the hands off the three ships in question had been banned from further shore liberty. A day later, the Yankee merchantmen had practically been dragooned out to sea at gun-point to carry their cargoes home . . . and warned to give it a *long* think before they dared come into English Harbour again, 'less they moderated their people's behaviour.

The packet-brig, gaily flying her "Post-Boy" flag, had departed bearing Pelham's boasting reports, Peel's "yes, but" reports and codicils, and Lewrie's several hefty sea-letters to his wife Caroline and his father Sir Hugo, to his ward Sophie, separate long missives to his sons, Sewallis and Hugh, by way of his father's London lodging house, and to his mistress Theoni and his other son, solicitor, and creditors.

Lewrie could pessimistically think that keeping his breeches up and his prick to himself might just be worth it after all. He would save hundreds on ink, paper, and postage on any *more* bastards; avoiding wrist and finger cramp communicating with additional by-blows would be, he thought, a collateral blessing.

And that monstrous frigate, USS *Hancock*, had completed repairs, and had returned to the Caribbean, though it was late in the hurricane season, commanded by a spanking-new captain, one Malachi Goodell, who, or so Lewrie was informed on the sly by Capt. McGilliveray, was one of those stiff-necked and overly righteous Massachusetts Puritans and a "New-Light," a Methodist to boot; a man of rectitude who brooked as little nonsense as that famously rigid French disciplinarian General Martinet.

"And wasn't he shot by his own troops at Doesbourg, in 1762?"
Lewrie had glumly recalled.

"No matter, he's here, and senior to me and Randolph," Capt.
McGilliveray had responded with equal gloom, "and mightily miffed
our crews went on such a tear. Brought undyin' shame on our new
Navy, and our Nation, he says, and there's to be no more of it whilst
he's commanding. 'Thunderation' Goodell's a Boston 'Pumpkin,' bad
as a Cotton Mather 'Hell-fire's in your future' altar pounder. He don't
much hold with drink in gen'ral, and as for tuppin', well . . . I doubt
any of our men'll set foot ashore 'til next we dock at Charleston, and
as for lettin' the doxies an' port wives come aboard to ease 'em, that'll
be once in a Blue Moon. Put us on notice, Goodell did, come armed
with Word o' th' Lord."

"A 'Conscience Keeper' . . . God save us," Lewrie had japed. "He
cuts his hair bowl-headed like Cromwell's Puritans, does he?"

"Actually, he looks more akin to Moses," McGilliveray had sadly
countered, "so wild-haired and bearded he looks like an owl in an ivy
bush. A long, thin 'Jack O' Legs' is he. Gloom, doom, and piety . . .
and while you're up, Cap'm Lewrie, I'd admire a drop more o' yer
tasty claret, if you're still offerin', thankee kindly."

"And I am, Captain McGilliveray," Lewrie had twinkled, pouring
a topping refill with his own hospitable hand. "A good sailor, though,
I'd imagine?"

"A right scaly fish, from the cradle," McGilliveray had rejoined.
"and one o' th' first at sea when the Massachusetts Committee of Public
Safety called for ships t'face your Customs vessels. Goodell's fam'ly
were smugglin' un-taxed goods in the *large* way. Ambitious, aspirin'."

"So . . . he might be amenable to our budding cooperation, do ye
think, sir?" Lewrie had slyly queried, hoping against hope that their
new arrival would be just as eager to score a notable, newsworthy
success against the French.

"Hah!" McGilliveray had scoffed. "You'd be lucky he don't make
you walk the plank, do ya go aboard *Hancock* unbidden. He meets
you at sea, alone, and ship-to-ship, he'd like as not brace up and
challenge ya t'battle. None too fond o' th' British, is Goodell. Lost
one fine armed brig off New Bedford and had t'swim ashore in his
small clothes. Fam'ly lost a half-dozen smugglin' boats . . . burned a
sloop o' war off Rockport so your Navy didn't take her, and got

captured early in '82. Spent time in the prison hulks at New York, 'til after th' Peace got signed, long after Yorktown. Ended up a backhanded hero, for all he *tried*, but never won much success."

"But . . . he still aspires, if offered a shot at the French, and capturing Choundas . . ." Lewrie had pressed, hopes suddenly dashed.

"Oh, I'll allow he's that eager," McGilliverary had mused. "Ya show him a chance, he'll most-like go gallopin', tantwivy as hunters after th' fox. He's the fire-eatin' sort."

"A Captain Hackum, then," Lewrie had wondered, hopes rising.

"Well, aye. I *know* he's irked that our piddlin' li'l 'Subscription Ships' scored a coup, whilst he was dry-docked at Baltimore, kidnappin' crewmen. Boston 'Bow-Wows' and Northern Yankees hold low opinion o' Southerners, t'boot. Goodell met John Paul Jones, th' once and was *almost* one o' his lieutenants, and he's regretted the lost opportunity ever since. 'Thunderation' good as *said* he's anxious to tussle with th' French, t'show what the United States, and our navy, can do."

"Sounds like an enterprising fellow," Lewrie had inveigled with seeming admiration, "though perhaps a daunting one. I should meet him. Must, rather . . . duty requires. You could introduce us, Captain McGilliveray, make the way smooth and straight? Perhaps on neutral ground, not here aboard *Proteus*, given Captain Goodell's sentiments. He most-like'd suspect we'd clap him in irons again! Must I beard him in his own den aboard *Hancock*, well, then I must, I s'pose, but . . ."

"Ya *that* curious, Cap'm Lewrie?" McGilliveray had chortled, "Or are ya a glutton for punishment?"

"I'm under Admiralty orders to treat United States Navy vessels and their captains with all the respect due those deemed as 'in amity' with His Majesty's Government," Lewrie had glibly stated. "We share a foe, and would not share a signals book did not our respective governments *intend* us to work together, when our aims coincide. Your Captain Goodell, fearsome though you depict him, is the senior American naval officer in these waters, so it only makes eminent good sense to become acquainted . . . professionally.

"I doubt knowing him would be quite as pleasureable as your *own* acquaintance, Captain McGilliveray," Lewrie "chummily" had said, trying to "piss down his back" to grease the wheels, "but still, Goodell, and *Hancock*, are the most powerful force now about, and it'd be a dev'lish shame did we work at cross purposes."

"Well, there's that," McGilliveray had casually allowed, "but, Cap'm Goodell may have his own ideas about things. And he's new-come from home, so his orders're surely fresher than mine. France might've seen sense and called off its trade war, by now, and we'd know nought of it."

"I shouldn't be *telling* you this, but . . ." Lewrie had confided, leaning forward in his chair as McGilliveray had lolled on the settee. To make things even better, Toulon, having perversely taken a liking to their amiable, drawling visitor, was on the settee, too, up against the good captain's leg with his paws in the air, and twining slowly as his chest and belly were idly caressed. "We strongly suspect that the French intend to move a small convoy, but a rich'un, from Guadeloupe to Saint Domingue in the near future. Two, perhaps three, vessels, laden with supplies for the rebel slaves. L'Ouverture or Rigaud, who knows? But do either of 'em end up holdin' the high cards over t'other, they will start fightin' again. Then *all* the ports get closed, and trade be damned 'til the dust settles. Don't know who *your* country backs in that horse race . . . don't care, really," he had lied.

"Don't know as how *we've* a cock in that fight, either, Captain Lewrie," McGilliveray had lied right back. Just after, though, he had revealed a bit of his nation's preference, perhaps his own, by adding "Seems if those two do go at each other, it'll eliminate one, and make the winner so weak he'd . . . may be best do those ships get there, and let 'em fight it out and settle it, once and for all."

"Guillaume Choundas, we are *fairly* sure," Lewrie had lied some more, wondering just what it took to spur the man to further ambition, "is charged with their safe delivery. All he has left to use for that purpose are his two *corvettes* . . . what we'd call three-masted sloops of war, and moderately armed akin to our Sixth Rates. Twenty or twenty-four guns. Nine-pounders, most-like. French Navy, *National* sloops of war, not over-armed privateers. Takin' *them*, bestin' 'em in a proper sea-fight, at odds . . . ? And they'd *have* to fight, 'cause Choundas *has* t'win at something or be sacked, and to abandon the supply ships while saving themselves'd be the last straw, so they *must* stand and . . ."

"Your charmin' Mister Peel tell ya all this, did he, sir?" Capt. McGilliveray had snickered, his eyes glim-flashy in secret delight. "Or 'twas that totty-headed new-come, Pelham? Him o' th' hunt togs?"

"Don't know what ye mean, sir," Lewrie had grunted, pretending total ignorance, even going so far as to tuck in his chin and "sull up like a bullfrog."

"Yer *spies*, Cap'um Lewrie!" McGilliverary had hooted with mirth. "Yer Foreign Office, or Admiralty, or whoever pays 'em *spies*. 'Bout as secretive as house fires, th' both of 'em. Peel ain't your clergyman, God knows, he don't tutor your midshipmen, so what else *could* he be?"

"Uhm, well, actually . . . uhm," Lewrie had flummoxed, blushing, for a rare once. "Damn."

"Don't hold with spies, meself," McGilliveray had quibbled.

"Don't know why *not!*" Lewrie had quickly countered. "Your partisan rangers like Francis Marion the Swamp Fox, your ship's namesake Thomas Sumter, thrived on the aid of patriotic spies. Your esteemed General Washington, so Peel tells me, ran an intelligence network, in the face of which our Foreign Office still stands in awe. So . . ."

"I can *tell* Cap'm Goodell this?" McGilliveray had asked. "That it came from the horse's mouth, so t'speak?"

Lewrie had given that a good, *long* ponder, weighing how wroth, and *loud*, Pelham's howls would be, of how poor Jemmy Peel would whimper and beat his head against the mizen-mast trunk to have been frustrated by one of his wild-hair whims; *again!* Whisky punch wouldn't avail a second time; they were *onto* that ploy, so the screeches and expostulations'd be horrid. Weighted against all that, though, was the chance of successfully ending their "collegial" association when Choundas was at last conquered, and with a great deal of luck, he'd never have to deal with them ever again in this life.

That had taken about two ticks of his pocket watch!

"Don't see why you can't, no," Lewrie had blithely assented.

"Well, then. Well, well, well! Prizes, and battle, my, my!" the estimable Capt. McGilliveray had said, beaming and rubbing his hands with relish. "That'd take the trick, Cap'm Lewrie. Cap'm Goodell'd like nothin' better than t'beat you top-lofty Britons at your own game . . . with your own spies' intelligence."

"So, you just possibly might bring him round to continuing our cooperation?" Lewrie had posed. "Loathe us though he may?"

"There's a good chance of it, aye," McGilliveray had said. "It may be best, did we give 'Thunderation' a day'r two t'climb down from his high horse over th' riots, and let me get his ear. Then have him aboard *my* ship under some pretence or t'other, where you just happened along, with a pretence of yer own, and since both of ya are aboard, we dine t'gether, and . . ."

"I could call upon Desmond," Lewrie had quickly suggested. "In your brief fight with the French brig, by the way . . . the lad comported himself well? A credit to your ship and Navy?"

"Brave, cool-headed, and honourably, sir," McGilliveray had said with great, though more-formal, pleasure. "A credit to his blood; and, may God let me claim in all due modesty, a credit to his raisin', too."

"I should like to hear his account of it," Lewrie had replied, with a note to his voice that expressed his growing fondness. "Though I worry that so much undue attention paid a 'younker,' ahem . . . from a total stranger, really, a *foreign* Post-Captain, and from his own uncle and Captain, ehm . . . don't want his head turned, or account himself so grand or singled out that it spoils him. Others in his mess despisin' him for *seeming* cosseted, d'ye see . . . Cruelty of boys . . . all that?"

"Aye, children can be cruel," McGilliveray had glumly agreed. "Some thoughtless and repeatin' what their parents say, some spiteful and aware o' what they're doin', but had we truly cosseted him, tried t'keep him from all Shakespeare's 'slings and arrows,' we'd've done a greater harm."

"Has to stand on his own bottom someday," Lewrie had commented.

"Aye. Now, *mostly* he was in merry pin, dutiful, sweet and sly round his betters, but he *could* go cock-a-hoop wild, as all boys can, too. First to th' top of th' live oaks, a fearless horseman, a clever student . . . the sort o' lad'd make most parents pop their buttons t've raised," Capt. McGilliveray had fondly recalled. "But there was ever the slur of 'Injun,' 'half-breed,' or 'Red Nigrah,' and then he'd turn sombre and hawk-eyed . . . like a caged eagle, his gaze focussed out ten mile or better, like he was 'bout ready t'spread wings and go someplace finer. But you'd be delighted t'know, Cap'm Lewrie, your son Desmond gave as good, or better, than he got . . . though my dear Martha was put to Job's despair t'mend his clothin' whenever he came home all skinned and bloodied. But ya should've seen t'other lad he'd whipped, 'til they learned he'd take no sauce off 'em. They got older, it got more subtle, o' course. Had to, for we made certain he had th' very best trainin' with sword and pistol, as any young gentleman should, 'til he was known as a dead shot and able blade."

"The *code duello* makes for careful, *courteous* gentlemen," Lewrie had said with a knowing snicker, "and circumspect behaviour."

"Don't it just!" McGilliveray had beamed back. "It never came to such, once he and his peers entered their 'tweens. No, 'twas more a matter o' snubbin', of few invitations to social occasions, unless it was the whole fam'ly invited. Young ladies were warned he wasn't a suitable match, no matter how gentlemanly he was, how well-educated and mannerly. Not t'brag, Cap'm Lewrie, but we're a clan o' substantial means, so never doubt that the boy had the best of ev'rything, and stood second to none when it came time to 'gussy' up for church or grand occasions.

" 'Cept when he came home from play, or the hunt, lookin' as if he'd wallowed like the Prodigal Son with the pigs, that is!" Captain McGilliveray had chortled, slapping his knee in a "daddy's" reverie; a sort of reverie that Lewrie, so much at sea but for a few rare years on half-pay 'tween the wars, could but dimly understand. He hadn't been there for the outrageous, exasperating, tom-foolery of his sons Hugh or Sewallis, had no parental tales to share about his precocious girl-child Charlotte, except for distant letters, or giggly remembrances he heard from Caroline (or Theoni, now!) months or years after the deeds were done, once he crossed his own doorsill.

"Life's hard on poor orphans," Lewrie had said, squirming with embarrassment; embarrassed, too, to sound so conventionally . . . pi-. ous. "First year or so of my life I thought *I* was one, I ought to know."

"My dear sir, I'd no idea!"

"Long story," Lewrie had said, wincing and squirming some more. "Never knew my mother . . . father late to the ball, 'til he discovered me and took me in. Two wars past." Lewrie had harumphed, embarrassed, like any proper English gentleman, to speak too openly of himself.

"Pray God, though, you had *one* parent who cared enough to take you in, and raise you right," McGilliveray had rejoined; earnestly and piously, "restore to you your proper birthright . . ."

McGilliveray never did quite fathom why the estimable Captain Alan Lewrie, RN, hoicked up such a snortful bark of amusement!

"So, the lad was more than happy to come away with you and take the sailor's life?" Lewrie had quickly asked in order to cover his droll musing on what a "loving, and caring" father Sir Hugo had really been to lay public claim upon him, or the whys of his claiming.

"Somewhere on those far horizons o' his," Capt. McGilliveray had agreed, "cold-shouldered as he was, t'would've been that, or ride away cross the high mountains, among his mother's lands. Has an itchy foot, Desmond does. And though I doubt he gave it much consideration, some few years of honourable public service in the uniform of his country's Navy wouldn't go amiss, either, we reckoned. Send him to England for further schoolin' . . . where no one'd know him as half-Muskogee, right off, was another possibility. Where even did they learn of his birthright, bein' exotic might be a help, not a hindrance."

"No, I'd suspect that Desmond *did* consider it," Lewrie replied. "To take his country's colours in her time of need . . . to wear uniform and face danger, even *crave* it!" he had exclaimed, rising to fill their glasses one more time, then pace. "Even to dream of gaining his commission, of coming home one of a few, a rare breed . . . a Sea Officer with a *sword* on his hip, not a trainee's dirk, an officer and a gentleman, in an honourable, gentlemanly, and selfless, profession. I'd imagine *that* glorious return figured prominently in his fantasies, to tweak *every* tormentor's nose out of joint, put 'em all to shame, stop the wagging tongues . . . and make all those high-nosed young misses go green with regret they *ever* snubbed him. Perhaps even make one of 'em . . . *the* one he desired, forlorn and unrequited all his mis'rable 'tween years, see him in a sudden and diff'rent light."

"We never really thought . . ." Capt. McGilliveray had begun, but broke off, before bowing his head and beaming. "I, now, strongly feel that you have the right of it, sir. And are possessed of keen insight into the hearts of young lads."

"Might as well, Captain McGilliveray," Lewrie had brushed off, with a twinkle to his "top-lights" in thanks for the rare compliment. "I once *was* one . . . and may still *be*, God knows. There's more'n a few who've chid me to grow up! So!" Lewrie had chuckled, seating himself near his guest. "You do not think that my intrusive favouritism will do him lasting harm?"

"I do not, sir. You are, after all, his true father, and a man he should know, and learn from. He's *starved* for . . . repudiation, now that you state things as you have, and speak to his hopes and dreams. As his captain, I cannot dote on him, but *you*, sir, well . . . dote away!"

"And you will introduce me to your ominous Captain Goodell, as

soon as you may discover to him the, ah . . . temptation which our
mutual foe Choundas will soon put before him?"

"I shall indeed, sir," McGilliveray had solemnly promised.

"More, I cannot, in good conscience, ask, sir," Lewrie had said
back, turning solemnly grandiose, as well, "for which I am eternally
in your debt. For so much . . . in so many things!"

CHAPTER TWENTY-EIGHT

*W*hat onerous task *Lieutenant de Vaisseau* Jules Hainaut had been given, to scour the Windwards and the Spanish Main in search of those two absent *corvettes*, had barely gotten underway, when, like a pair of old shoes beneath the bed-stead, *La Résolue* and *Le Gascon* had suddenly heaved up over the Sou'west horizon not five dawns since his sailing, sullenly dragging in their wakes a lone, dowdy three-masted merchant ship, with a badly faded American "grid-iron" flag hung beneath a much brighter and larger Tricolour to signify her new ownership.

An hour later, after making their private numbers to each other, all four ships were hove-to on a gently heaving and sun-glittered sea, and Hainaut was proudly taking his first salute as the commander of a warship being welcomed aboard another man o' war. Despite the *Liberté*, *Egalité*, and *Fraternité* the Republic presented to the world, the French Navy put a bit more stock in the old customs than the Directory in Paris would have preferred. Swords swirled like mercury droplets, polished St. Etienne Arsenal muskets were slapped about to Present Arms, and well-blacked Naval Infantry boots stamped on pale sanded decks in creditable precision. Sailors stood facing the entry-port, doffing red-wool-stocking Liberty caps or tarred straw hats with wide brims as Hainaut doffed his egret-plumed, gilt-laced bicorne hat to them and stepped aboard the starboard gangway, to the surprise of a fair number of the watch officers and midshipmen of *Le Gascon.*

"You've come up in the world, Lieutenant Hainaut," Capt. Griot, the senior officer of the pair of *corvettes,* glumly commented. "With a ship of your own, so soon? How delightful for you, I am sure. And you have come South from Guadeloupe, why, exactly?" the older Breton asked, sucking on his teeth for the last bits of his interrupted meal.

"*Capitaine* Choundas sent me in search of you, *m'sieur,*" Hainaut archly replied, knowing just where he stood in the doughty Griot's estimation. "He has desperate need of you both, as quickly as you can be off Basse-Terre. I am charged to inform you that . . ."

Griot silenced him with a subtle finger upon his lips, then he pointed overside at Capt. MacPherson's gig, which was just coming near the entry-port. "We will speak of this later. Below," Griot said in a faint mutter from the side of his mouth.

"A disaster," the expatriate Scot MacPherson grunted a few minutes later in the privacy of Capt. Griot's great-cabins. "All the officers and men of both raiders gone? Poor, poor Pelletier, and Digne! There has been no word of their fates from the British, or the Americans who took them?"

"None came before I sailed, *m'sieur,*" Hainaut sadly told him as he savoured a grudgingly given glass of wine, his eyes surreptitiously evaluating Griot's taste in furnishings and estimating the depths of his purse. "*La Vigilante* sank very quickly, after a single broadside, so . . . we can only hope, *m'sieur le Capitaine.*"

"Worse, though," Capt. Griot quickly got to the larger point of things, "we very well may be in a declared war with the Americans, and they, so you report, Lieutenant Hainaut, openly sail allied with the 'Bloodies.' In spite of that, Hainaut, Le Hi— The *Capitaine* means to press on with the convoy to Saint Domingue?"

"Worse than disaster, *Capitaine* MacPherson," Hainaut said, with his nose in the air, "it was betrayal, *treason.* A ring of spies which *Capitaine* Choundas even now is rooting out. That was how the 'Bloodies' knew when *Le Bouclier* would be at her weakest, how the first munitions ship was lost the same day, and a guard schooner was lost. How one of *commissaire* Hugue's rich merchant vessels was intercepted mere hours after her sailing, and . . . so *Capitaine* Choundas believes, the 'Bloodies' and the 'Amis' certainly knew to intercept our prizes and raiders."

"Hugues, too?" Griot barked, jadedly amused. "Serves the greedy *salaud* right. Maybe teach him to stop acting like a pirate."

"Their prime source of information was Etienne de Gougne," Lt. Hainaut spat, then sat back to relish how they took *that*. "Our master has arrested him. There is a new official from France, who will likely arrest *commissaire* Hugues, too, once they get a look at his books."

"*Bon!*" Griot quite joyfully snarled. "Couldn't happen to a better person."

"With the spy ring broken, our master is certain that a convoy *can* make it to Saint Domingue . . . to Jacmel," Hainaut loftily further informed them, more than happy to be the font of all intelligence. "A letter came from General Hédouville. He's made his choice, and he now will back the Mulatto Rigaud. British agents have been on the island, courting both factions, so the convoy is urgent. Before the 'Bloodies' can put one together, with more and better bribes, *messieurs*."

"That *diable* Lewrie isn't the only British ship at sea," Griot grumbled, "no matter that our efficient superior lops off the heads of spies and traitors by the tumbril-load, there are other watchers, more warships that keep a distant blockade than that, that . . . *Proteus!*"

"And the fastest, most direct passage to Jacmel is simply stiff with British ships," MacPherson cagily muttered, stroking his six days' growth of beard. "American ships reported at the North end of Dominica on our way . . . Antigua, Nevis, and Saint Kitts, Barbuda . . . the British Virgins, and frigates from their Jamaica Squadron. This late in storm season, their ships of the line return from Halifax, freeing lesser ships from close patrolling, to range out far afield."

"And every one delighted to be so freed, and starving for prize money, and action, *aussi*," Capt. Griot chimed in, his voice "chiming" as glum as funeral bells. "Without more ships as escort . . ."

"Well, there is my *Mohican*," Hainaut gently pointed out to them, "and, now that our master is temporarily in charge of the privateers that *commissaire* Hugues directed . . ."

Hainaut's face stung as both of those tarry captains laughed in derisive glee at his expense for being so callow. Where was all their vaunted *élan*, their *esprit?* he wondered as he was forced to sit and take it. They, the hand-picked master captains, carefully chosen from

among the hundreds whom Choundas could have requested, doubted
that such a thing could be done, even if the British no longer knew
when a convoy departed. Why, they even sounded dis-loyal to *Le
Maître*, who'd *made* them, promoted them, gotten them to sea when
those hundreds he had not chosen still languished ashore without ships,
or swung idle in home ports for fear of blockading British fleets and
squadrons!

"Privateers are cowardly . . . trash," Capt. MacPherson scoffed.
"Overly cautious mercenaries at best . . . drunken pirates at worst.
Why, most of ours aren't even French! The gutter sweepings of the
Americas!"

"There is another large schooner, the equal of mine, which was
taken by *La Vigilante* and Lieutenant Pelletier, *messieurs*," Lt. Hainaut
told them, smugly proud of the success of his short raiding cruise in
comparison to theirs, "*La Chippewa* could be commissioned quickly,
given additional guns, and added to the escort. She's ready for sea."

"And manned by *whom?*" Capt. Griot snapped, not even attempting
to hide the sneer he shared with Capt. MacPherson. "Desplan's sailors
were lost with Houdon and Pelletier. We have run out of officers,
we're short of seasoned midshipmen to make *acting* officers, and those
few left are cripples, sick, or incompetent. To man your own schooner,
Lieutenant Hainaut, didn't *Capitaine* Choundas scrape the bottom of
the barrel? Do you not carry privateersmen aboard, *bribed* by extra
pay to sign Navy articles, just for a few months, not unlimited service?"

"There are a few, mostly able seamen and a gunner or two," Hainaut had to admit, reddening, and crossing his legs defensively.

"As I suspected," Griot grunted.

"To crew another escort ship means weakening ours," MacPherson
added, "using our men to brace up shirkers, incompetents, and inexperienced fools. How long would they have to work up together, two
days? It takes *months* to season a crew to competency. No, no, your
suggested armed schooner would be no help, perhaps even a hindrance.
Our strength would be diluted, making our *corvettes* less capable, and
we'd all be in the soup."

"*Messieurs* . . ." Hainaut spluttered, ready to glower and sneer at
those well-salted but faint-hearted captains, before remembering he no
longer could swagger or speak in his old master, *Le Hideux*'s, stead.

"Surely there is *something* that we may do to get the convoy through?" he wheedled.

"Pray for a gale of wind and a spell of bad weather in which a convoy may hide," Capt. MacPherson piously intoned, almost making the sign of the cross on his breast. "The British would not expect that."

"And keep *them* in port, or more concerned with their own survival," Griot contributed. "Something we can do, well . . . *oui*, our ships will crack on for Basse-Terre, quick as we can. You, Lieutenant, will take charge of guarding our slower prize ship, and make for habour as quick as *you* can. She's richly and deeply laden, *gosse*. You lose her or cost us a *sou* of her value, and God help you, *hein?*"

"I understand, *m'sieur*," Hainaut crisply responded, as a junior should; though seething to be called *"gosse"*—a youngster! Hainaut promised himself to remember that slight, and somehow, someday, find a way to make that shit-arsed Breton oaf pay for it.

Clump-swish-tick—clump-swish-tick. Guillaume Choundas took a deep breath of clean air on the ramparts of Fort Fleur d'Epée, after the long, exhausting climb from its cells, far below ground next to its magazines and powder rooms. Even with Victor Hugues suspended from his office, Choundas could not order things to suit him. Hugues was gaoled in relative comfort in his own quarters, under honourable arrest. His loyal staff, smug in their graft and greed, continued much as they had before, expecting Hugues to be exonerated and freed after the new man, Desfourneaux, had received the proper "emolument," so an office for Choundas was still impossible; and prisoners were *never* put in chambers with easy access, which amounted to easy egress or contact with co-conspirators, so there would be no chance to whip up matching stories, or let those already caught escape. Besides, the *noises* that those under rigourous interrogation made disturbed the *digestion*, and a Frenchman could *never* risk such harm to *Le digestif!*

Choundas had barely gotten his wind back, and ached like sin in his over-worked good leg and bad, braced, one, when his weary leaning on the parapet was interrupted by the brisk arrival of that officious, pompous prig Desfourneaux, who came clattering up the stone stairs in his colourful waist sash, costly sword, and belt, and that ridiculous hat of his, bound with another heavily tasseled *Tricolore* sash for a

band, and red-white-blue plumes jutting upward to mark him as one
of the Directory's own.

"Your work goes slowly, *Capitaine?*" Desfourneaux asked him with
a faint whinny.

"Slowly, yes, Citizen. And yours?" Choundas asked in return.

"Oh, we'll have him in the end," Desfourneaux idly vowed, waving
a hand as if shooing the ever-present island flies. "Paris has enough
reason to recall Citizen Hugues already. But to *profit* so massively
from the execution of one's proper duties . . . ! The Directory is *most*
upset that the infernal man took our *reasonable* edicts regarding the
control and identity of neutral merchant shippers who might aid those
invidious British so literally. His overzealous prosecution at regulation
of that trade, he turned into a vicious *guerre du course*, and an unfortunate, uhm . . . diplomatic incident. Now it looks as if the Americans
have rewarded our gracious aid to their Revolution with typical Anglo-
Saxon churlishness and become British allies in open war . . . *if* your
young officer's report may be credited. One would *expect* formal declaration of war sent here by a truce ship, first, but those rustics may
not understand how nations are supposed to deal with each other. I
fear Hugues's greed, and zeal, caused *another* war. One which our
hard-pressed Republic cannot afford."

"Then he should lose his head," Choundas decided aloud, feeling
uncharitable to both Hugues *and* Desfourneaux, and averse to pleasantly idle palaver. "And my suggestions, Citizen? What of them?"

"Withdrawing Letters of Marque and Reprisal from all but French
owners and masters, yes, at once," Desfourneaux said, nodding, as if
a committee decision was instantly enforceable law in every port in
the Caribbean, no matter how far-flung; as if those just shy of piratical
endeavours would cease their depredations when they heard the news!
A snarl at Desfourneaux's idiocy escaped Choundas's lips.

"Conscripting the rest into the Navy, though, arming and training
a whole squadron of small ships under your command," good Citizen
Desfourneaux maundered on, making a *moue*, "might be too expensive,
for now . . . marvelously effective though they might prove, under
your well-famed and experienced leadership, *m'sieur Capitaine*, ha ha!"

"Not all, then, merely the best dozen or so," Choundas pressed,
though he'd be damned if he would plead or bargain.

"Well, perhaps two or three more, for now," Desfourneaux said as
he shrugged. "Paris sent me to *curtail* Hugues's war on commerce,

fearing his excesses would *lead* to war with the Americans."

"The privateers will then be idle, in need of employment! If I can offer the best, the largest and best-armed naval commissions . . ." Choundas insisted, "it will keep them from *real* piracy . . ."

"Which requires naval *pay*, which France cannot afford, *m'sieur!*" Desfourneaux quickly told him. "I will, of course, write Paris to ask for a proper squadron be sent to these waters, a real fleet, capable of facing the British . . . possibly the Americans, too, to guard Guadeloupe and Saint Domingue against invasion. *Then*, there will be a place for a man such as yourself as . . . Commodore of the small ship flotilla. Such a position *could* make you an Admiral, *hein?*

"As long as nothing, ah . . . unfortunate occured in the meantime," Desfourneaux slyly added. "As long as you executed your present duties so well until their arrival that I could recommend you?"

Choundas bristled with resentment. Was the bastard hinting at a bribe, or was he about to propose another onerous, thankless chore for him to perform, just like the *aristos* had trotted him about the world like the donkey forever chasing the dangled carrot? Though Desfourneaux wore his neck-stock and shirt collars loose and open like a good Republican, or the revolutionaries of the Bastille's storming, what was he but a canting *shop-keeper*, a jumped-up . . . *attorney* mimicking a real zealot, sent to salvage the mess made by governmental idiocy!

"What did you have in mind, Citizen?" Choundas gravelled.

"To fulfill General Hédouville's demand for the convoy to Saint Domingue, *Capitaine*," Desfourneaux smoothly replied. "Quickly."

"The munition ships are ready to sail, and my *corvettes* will be here, perhaps within days," Choundas promised. "Storm season is nearly over, and the cooler winds of winter will speed them along, once they depart. I am *more* than ready to fulfill the general's demand, so . . ."

"Your spy . . . who flourished undetected for so long, almost in your very pocket, *Capitaine*," Desfourneaux interrupted, with a snarky little shark's grin, shedding his airy unconcern and amiability. "He has confessed? He has named others? Your probes yield results?"

"Not yet," Choundas said with a frustrated grunt through gritted teeth. "The little traitor's resistance is surprising, coming from a meek worm such as he. I am unable to employ my usual techniques, you see," Choundas said, raising his remaining good hand, "and people in Hugues's employ are so oafish that de Gougne would perish under their clumsy brutality before he could *begin* to break. I have arrested all the servants, as many suspicious coastal dwellers and fishermen as we could, but, with so little help, it may be weeks before I get round to 'putting the question' to them all, you see . . ."

"What do the 'Bloodies' say," Desfourneaux smirked, "that 'it's a poor workman who blames his tools'? Your clerk had but a few hours, at best, between your opening General Hédouville's letter and his arrest, no? You've thrown in gaol half the poor fishermen and regular, visiting tradesmen to your mansion, all your house servants. Patrols prowl the shores and the docks. Odds are, you caught those who'd pass messages. Odds are, your de Gougne never had a *chance* to pass on his discovery . . . assuming he's a spy in the first place, hmm?" Desfourneaux slyly suggested. "De Gougne, well . . . a rather large black mark to be expunged from your records, *Capitaine*. If he truly *is* employed by the British. You agree with my assessment, then?"

"*Most* of what you say is true, Citizen," Choundas was forced to admit, "though the letter from Fleury, the British agent's slip . . ."

"You are sanguine, then, that the convoy may sail without risk of betrayal?" Desfourneaux pressed. "Come, come, give me odds that the munitions will reach Saint Domingue," he prissily requested.

"Uhm . . . nine or ten to one, against interception," Choundas grudgingly had to say, after a long, irate fuming. "With three ships to escort two . . ."

"And since you yourself admit that the back of the spy ring is at least severely hampered, if not broken," Desfourneaux said with an expansive grin, "there is no reason why *you* could not take command of the enterprise and *personally* see it through . . . before completing any investigations here on Guadeloupe. After your triumphant return."

"But, of course, Citizen, I . . . !" Choundas blustered, insulted and angered, and mightily taken aback, both.

"Such a coup would go a long way to excuse your harbouring of a possible spy . . . *and* in expunging what so far has been a long, and sad, string of failures that your seeming lack of attention concerning your own staff allowed, *hein?*" Desfourneaux said with a leer. "Such an act of personal responsibility, and daring, might even allay the niggling suspicion that your clerk was not the *only* person on your staff covertly corresponding with the British or their local informers."

"*Moi?*" Choundas thundered. "You suspect *me* after all I've done . . . all I've suffered from the God-damned British? Is *this* the way I am to be repaid for my loyalty to the Revolution, to the Republic, and to *France?* How *dare* you, you tawdry, tarted-up little slug! You wish me to command the convoy? Good, I will, and bedamned to you!"

"Run the same risk as your followers, my dear Choundas. Prove by your being there that it will get through," Desfourneaux answered, lazing at sublime ease against the parapet stones, as if Choundas was no threat to him; his howling rage just a passing gust of wind. "That is all I ask. Though we *will* have a little talk about your insulting manners . . . when you return, *hein?* Too many years of operating on a roving commission, with too free a hand in the disordered early years of our Revolution, has made you incapable of proper subordination, *n'est-ce pas?* Perhaps a few weeks at sea will give you time for much-needed introspection."

"Bah!" Choundas snarled, raising his walking-stick. "You . . . !"

Hard as it was for him to do, he swallowed his ire and lowered his hand, knowing that Desfourneaux was more dangerous than he seemed, that Hugues could have company on his way home in irons!

"You see, dear *Capitaine*, you begin to learn circumspection and manners already!" Desfourneaux gleefully pointed out, departing.

CHAPTER TWENTY-NINE

*W*elcome aboard, Captain Lewrie, sir," Lieutenant Seabright said after Lewrie had doffed his hat to the assembled crew on *Sumter*'s deck and plopped it back on his head. "Captain MacGilliveray has been expecting you, and is waitin' aft," he added, offering his hand, with a grin struggling to split open his face, making Lewrie wonder what he thought of getting introduced to Capt. Malachi "Thunderation" Goodell.

Lewrie cocked a brow at him in query as they stood close.

"*Okracoke*, sir," Lt. Seabright whispered, sniggering and about to bust.

"Heard o' that, have ye?" Lewrie whispered back with a careful grin of his own. Evidently, the Yankees had gotten wind of Mr. Peel's questions ashore—*he* hadn't been in the riot!—and the discovery of how completely the foppish Mr. Pelham had been gulled. Despite misgivings that fellow Americans were in the pay of the French, it was proof positive that lofty British aristocracy, the oppressive "Mother Country" in general, was *both* heels short of a whole loaf.

"Sorry, sir, does it cause you any harm, but ya must admit it's droll," Lt. Seabright snickered. "Ah . . . Mister McGilliveray. Do you escort Captain Lewrie aft to the captain's cabins."

"Aye aye, sir!" Desmond McGilliveray piped up, stepping forward from his deferential place beside the clutch of U.S. Marines, aquiver with expectation. "Welcome aboard, sir," he stated, face abeam.

"Thankee kindly, uhm . . . Mister McGilliveray," Lewrie answered, tipping the lad a sly wink and smiling back. "I've, ah . . . taken the liberty of fetching off a few items which might prove instructive for your nautical education," Lewrie said, swinging a British Marine's issue haversack forward from off his right hip and shoulder. "Some books of mine you may find useful . . . my first copy of Falconer's *Marine Dictionary*, the 1780 edition, sorry, but it can't have changed that much . . . When ashore I did discover an edition of the *Atlantic Mercury*, which depicts every pertinent feature of the North American coasts and harbours . . . so you don't run aground more than *once* in your career, d'ye see, uhm . . ."

He had also thrown in his second-best set of nautical instruments; parallel rules, dividers, and such, a shore-bought pencil case, folding nib-knife, and a full dozen virgin wooden pencils, to boot; and a small block of Brazilian gum eraser.

Desmond's face glowed as he opened the stained and bedraggled Falconer's and read the inscription in the inside cover: "Alan Lewrie, *HIS* book, Jan. '80. Like Hell, it's yours!"

"Thank you . . . !" Desmond gushed, ready to tear up, quickly adding "father," in the faintest of whispers, in such a manner that Lewrie was like to cough, choke, and "spring a leak" as well. He put the book back in the haversack and slung it over his shoulder. "I found something I thought *you* might like when we boarded our foe, too . . . sir!" Desmond announced. "A small relict of taking a French man o' war. Well, not such a big foe, but . . ."

"But 'tis early days," Lewrie assured him. "Who knows what a week might bring? Next year? Uhm . . . we mustn't keep your uncle, and captain, waiting, though. Or Captain Goodell. As forbidding as they say, is he?" Lewrie asked, with an expectant grimace.

"That, and more, sir!" Desmond answered, rolling his eyes, and looking as if, did naval custom and usage allow, he might fan himself.

"Well, let's get on with it, then. Lead on, young sir."

"I'll fetch your present, soon as you're aft and below, sir."

"That'd be excellent, thankee. And for your thoughtfulness," he told his bastard son, hoping that pilfering valuables out of a prize-ship didn't run in the family blood; recalling a hidden chest of gold aboard a French ship, from which he had "borrowed" a considerable sum whilst in temporary command of her in the last war.

Though I could *use money, if he's offerin'*, Lewrie thought.

Captain Malachi Goodell was indeed forbidding, and *did* resemble an "owl in an ivy bush," as Capt. McGilliveray had said. Great, fierce glowing eyes flew open as soon as Lewrie was admitted to the great-cabins, then slitted in panther-y study, as he had himself a good look-see. A long, curving, beak-like raptor's nose jutted from the thatch of a sleek, plump beard. Lewrie assumed that Capt. Goodell had teeth and lips under there somewhere, though they were hard to espy. Goodell was as tall and straight as a musket stood on end, and just about that lean. *Big* hands flexed, as hairy-backed as his chin; *big* feet clumped on the deck in awkward pique at the sight of their *British* interloper; legs encased in unadorned, well-blacked boots as tall as a dragoon's—though with the usual knee-flaps cut off.

"So *thou* art the British Captain Alan Lewrie," Goodell rasped, "of whom, of late, so much has been related to me, *sir*."

"I am, sir, and honoured t'make your acquaintance," Lewrie pleasantly purred back, even if he did feel the "nutmegs" in his groin pucker and "tuck up" at the sight and sound of that ominous worthy.

"Captain McGilliveray told me thee might come aboard, whilst I was here, Captain Lewrie," Goodell grumbled, "though, surely, he hath told *thee* of my lack of fondness for the British."

"Captain McGilliveray discovered to me your experiences in the last war, Captain, aye," Lewrie replied, "for which I can but offer a poor and unofficial apology. Times change, however. Circumstances are different, and, one may hope, old grudges are set aside in the face of the new situation which obtains, so we may . . ."

"President Adams and our Navy Secretary, Mister Stoddert, whom I hold to be otherwise sensible men, order me to share signals with thee, and fodder off thy dockyards and chandleries, to . . . cooperate," Capt. Goodell rumbled, owl-eyes asquint and teeth bared, turning "cooperate" into an epithet, "but *not* to take hands with thy Royal Navy openly. Captains Randolph and McGilliveray have already hove up a cable shy of open alliance, sir . . . for which inconsiderate actions I have chastised them. Now, here thee cometh, with yet another beguiling fruit from off the Tree of Wickedness. To tempt me as the

Serpent tempted Eve, as Eve corrupted Adam, sir?" he growled in righteous indignation.

"To present you with a chance to use your *Hancock* in the way she was intended, sir," Lewrie calmly rejoined, feet apart and hands behind his back. He tried on a grin, and a casual tone. "One would assume by now you've shifted *Hancock*'s battery, since last I was aboard her, and lightened her of end-weight? Captain Kershaw *had* burdened her with too many guns. So freed, she must represent the very best your nation may field, in terms of speed *and* weight of metal, so . . ."

"Shalt never tell thee what armament a ship of the *United States* Navy bears, sir!" Goodell barked, tilting his head back and looking down his nose.

So much for tarry yarnin' 'twixt professionals! Lewrie thought, wincing; *the brute loves me like Satan loves holy water!*

"Twenty-four pounders on her lower deck, twelves above," Lewrie surmised aloud, "perhaps even long twelves as chase guns, none of which signify, Captain Goodell. You may black 'em with paint, cruise about and show the flag, even daunt the odd French privateer, then plod home with a trade convoy when your biscuit and beer give out. Or . . . you could black 'em with powder smoke and eliminate any present, or future, threat to American-flagged vessels in the Caribbean, *and* ham-string the rebellious slave armies of Saint Domingue, for lack of arms. Whatever designs the United States has on that half of Hispaniola would be furthered, as well, sir," he baldly stated.

"And unwittingly playing cat's-paw to further *British* designs on that benighted isle, sir? No, never!" Goodell spat back.

"For *all* of Hispaniola, I don't give a tinker's . . . fig!" Lewrie honestly told him, though doubting that the prim Goodell would care for him saying "damn."

"So thou *sayest*, sir, though thy *spies* yet scheme to seize it," Goodell accused.

"Aye, they *do*, sir," Lewrie admitted without a qualm, "and much joy may they have in the doing. It keeps them occupied, and gives the Crown the impression they're earnin' their pay. But we both know that the task's a bootless endeavour. Much the same could be said for *your* agents, too. L'Ouverture, Rigaud, some ambitious Black general no one suspects . . . none of 'em'll ever trust Whites t'deal fair. Your ships and ours may someday trade there, but that'll be all we'll do, 'cause the Black rebels will fight tooth and claw, to the last drop of

White blood, to stay independent and un-enslaved. We took *our* shot and lost an hundred thousand men. Britain won't try again, and I doubt that America'd spend her soldiers' lives that prodigal, either. Speak to your consuls, *your* spies, on Saint Domingue, they'll say the same."

"My country does not spy, I tell thee!" Goodell snapped.

"Moses and *his* generals did," Lewrie said tongue-in-cheek, "as they entered the Promised Land, sir. Washington did. Every—"

"Thun-der-*ation!*" Capt. Goodell roared, clapping his hands aft of his back and stomping about to give Lewrie his insulted back. "Infuriating . . . base . . . cynicism. Pah! Idolatrous mockery!"

"I am all that, and more, sir," Lewrie cheerfully confessed to him. "Ask Mister Grenville Pelham or Mister James Peel, they'll give you chapter and verse. *Our* spies, sir . . . the ones I know of. I care not, does Saint Domingue go 'poof' like Sodom and Gomorrah. And no matter what sealed orders you have from your esteemed Mister Stoddert, sooner or later you'll come to the same conclusion. What counts in the end is keepin' all this double-dealin' muck off our escutcheons . . . and doing the honourable thing in our nations' names."

Goodell whirled about to face him, eyes blared deep in his overhanging hair and cheek-high thatch, this time flatly astonished, as if someone had tweaked Noah on his buttocks.

"Thou just up and *names* thy schemers, Captain Lewrie?" Goodell hissed, goggling. "Surely, thou art like no British officer it's been my sorrow to experience. Why dost thou do so, sir?" he demanded.

"B'lieve me, sir, you ain't the first ever accused me o' bein' diff'rent," Lewrie said with a self-deprecating chuckle. "As to why, it's 'cause the prize they seek is Fiddlestick's End, when the biggest threat is Guillaume Choundas, his warships, *and* his convoy, and do *you* stop his business, 'stead o' me, I care not a whit. Captain Mc-Gilliveray's told you of him, sir? Of his utter, depraved vileness, his penchant for torture, his pref'rence for childr—?"

"Hisst!" Capt. Goodell snapped, raising a hand as if to ward off the Devil himself. "Do not, I conjure thee, sully great Jehovah's own sweet air with talk of such un-natural abominations, sir."

"Sorry, but that's what he is, sir," Lewrie said, admonished.

"Foetid spawn of Satan," Goodell ominously growled, "is what he is! Oh, that noble France could fall under the sway of such evil men! Deluded first by wicked Popery, and despoiled second by those spiteful of even *mistaken* creeds! Now we see the rotten fruits of a tyrannical Catholicism for what it truly is, where its vaunting pomp and mindless rituals lead . . . to the very rim of Hell's bottomless pit! Now, they besmirch the sweetest words of all, I say! Liberty, Freedom, and Democracy, wrested from the cruel grasp of an oppressive despot, from the maw of Mammon, the very bed-rock of our new nation, the best hope for Mankind in all the world, is sullied and become accursed, is become a stink in the nostrils of those who'd yearn to emulate us!

"All due to the grievous excesses and bloody-handed terrors of a revolution betrayed, its finest sentiments satanically twisted into a lust for conquest and despotism in the name of 'The People,' for *Man* not God . . . its pure authors slain on the altar of . . . Reason, but not Faith!" Capt. Goodell ranted, his voice rising, as did his bile, arms flogging the air as he angrily paced McGilliveray's great-cabins like a "Leaping Methodist" preacher at a Welsh revival meeting.

Lewrie was, when pressed to it, officially a congregant of the Church of England, hence, leery of too *much* enthusiasm. McGilliveray was from its off-shoot, what the Yankees had professed since their new Book of Common Prayer of 1789 as "Episcopalian"; in essence the Church of England minus King or Archbishop of Canterbury as defender or final arbiter of the faith. Both looked glumly at each other, fearing that, once launched, the estimable Capt. Goodell might flail and blather on 'til the Second Dog Watch.

"Amen, sir!" Lewrie declared, hoping it might cut him short. A sudden rapping on the great-cabin doors facing the gun-deck provided a better reason for pause, though.

"A Lootenant Adair, f'om th' *Proteus* frigate, sir!" the Yankee Marine sentry called in, properly stiff-backed, but with a taint of a sly dubiousness to his voice, too.

"My pardons, gentlemen," Lewrie said with a frustrated frown on his phyz. Just when Goodell had *sounded* like he was haranguing himself into *some* sort of decision, and now *this!* "Aye, Mister Adair?" he snapped, tromping forrud as if to say "this had better be good!"

"Beg pardon, Captain, but we've received an urgent query, sir," the immaculate Mr. Adair said in a soft, shy voice, little louder than a confidential whisper, "from the Prize Court ashore, Captain, sir . . . rather embarassin', really. The prize we left at Dominica, d'ye see? It, uhm . . . seems to have gone missing, Captain. It isn't there any longer."

"*What?*" Lewrie all but shrieked. "Mine . . . ! That's . . . ! *Hey?*" he flummoxed, mindful of a righteous glare astern of where he stood. He crooked a finger to draw Lt. Adair even closer, a few more guarded steps nearer Capt. McGilliveray's chart-space. The revelation was too shameful for even the cockroaches to hear. "Whatthebloody-helld'ye*mean* it's gone?" he hissed almost in Adair's shell-like ear.

"The Antigua Court sent word to the Dominica office at Roseau to fetch her off to English Harbour to be valuated, sir," Adair said, all but wringing his hands, no matter that it wasn't his fault. "But she'd *already* sailed, sir. The Roseau office thought she'd been sent-for two days ago. Their letter stated that Quartermaster's Mate Jugg came ashore, said that Midshipman Burns and the Bosun's Mate, Mister Towpenny, had got orders to sail here, so they let 'em clear harbour, sir, and . . ."

"Jugg!" Lewrie muttered, as if gut-punched. "That motherless damned ingrate! Why'd I *ever* trust him with a rope-end, I . . . Damn! Back aboard *Proteus*, Mister Adair, and tell Mister Langlie he's t'get her hove in to short stays. We're off, soon as I can return, myself. A wife and child on, where was it? Barbados! Sure as Fate, that'll be where he's bound. After that, who knows, now he's a'ship, with a rich cargo t'sell. Go, Mister Adair. Be off with you!"

"Aye aye, sir!"

Who else had been in the harbour watch he'd left behind to see to the prize, Lewrie asked himself, purpling with fury at the embarrass-ment, and dread of monetary loss, in equal measure. What loss to his reputation, well . . . that didn't bear thinking about without a bottle of brandy near to hand!

Willie Toffett, another hand he'd pressed off a Yankee smuggler in the Danish Virgins; he'd *seemed* innocent, harmless, and easy-going. Had Jugg led him by the nose into folly? Jugg, damn him! He'd trusted and promoted him, had let him have the guinea Joining Bounty so he could send it as a note-of-hand to his alleged wife and child on Barbados! With the ship, he'd lost Midshipman Burns, too, who was even duller and stupider than he *looked*, but . . . to lose an anchored ship in a friendly harbour? And Mister Towpenny, the wily and ex-perienced Bosun's Mate. Surely *he'd* have stayed loyal, and awake, if Burns had not!

"Something the matter, Captain Lewrie?" McGilliveray enquired, sounding solicitous. "Bad news, is it, sir?"

"Hah?" Lewrie barked, startled from his sudden funk. "Why no, naught at all, Captain McGilliveray. News, of a certainy. For good or ill, well . . . hate to seem ungracious, but I must be off. Can't dine, as I wished. Captain Goodell, happy to have made your acquaintance. Sorry we could not have spoken further," he said, coming aft to fetch his hat. "Do consider all I said, though, pray. Perhaps when I come back, we may discuss our mutual interests, and discover a way to . . ." he hedged, wishing to flee before word of shameful foolishness came offshore to the Americans.

"Return, good sir?" McGilliveray pressed, surprised. "You are to *sea*, Cap'm Lewrie?"

"Fear I am, sir," Lewrie told him, reddening. "Small chore . . . that sort o' thing. Salutations, and *adieu*, gentlemen, 'til next we meet." Lewrie sketched out an abbreviated bow in *congé*, with a hasty sweep of his hat, then turned his back on them and almost sprinted to *Sumter*'s starboard gangways, and entry-port, thanking God that Andrews his Cox'n had already been alerted, and was standing by, the oarsmen of his gig already drawn from their yarning with the American sailors and waiting for him over-side.

"Captain . . . Captain Lewrie, sir?" a tremulous voice froze him in his frenzied tracks, though. Desmond had been aft on the quarterdeck, and had scampered forward at the first sign of scurry. "You're going, before dinner, sir?" His new-found son sounded forlorn and abandoned, and for the life of him, Lewrie *couldn't* depart and disabuse him, was there a king's ransom in the offing.

"I fear duty calls, young sir," Lewrie sorrowfully said, hoping the lad wouldn't be too hurt by his haste, though Desmond's face was clouding up with the quick grief of a broken promise, a dashed hope. "My Mister Adair brought me urgent news, which I must act upon, quick as you can say Jack Ketch. I *did* hope we could dine together, but . . ."

"I understand, sir, really," Desmond swore, though his protestation sounded thin. "Time and tide . . ." he added with a brave smile, and a wise shrug.

"Old Navy sayin' . . . 'growl ye may, but go ye must,' " Lewrie told him, stepping closer. "Once I'm back, I promise I'll make up for it. A whole *day* ashore, the two of us, does your uncle, Captain McGilliveray allow. Swear. Cross my heart an' hope t'die."

And how many promises of that sort had he made to Sewallis and

Hugh, to little Charlotte and Caroline, in his time? And how many
had he broken when Admiralty called! How many vows had Desmond
heard in his short time on Earth, too, from those he wished to trust.

"Can't leave without your present," Desmond muttered, playing up
manful and game. He pushed forward a hat-box that had seen better
days. "I hope you like it, fath— . . . sir. You will take it·with you?"

"But of course!" Lewrie exclaimed, taking the battered hat-box from
him, and feeling something inside shift its balance. "Now, what in the
world do we have here, I wonder?" he teasingly cajoled, forced to
kneel so he could remove the lid, with Desmond squatting down aside
·him and taking the lid for a moment. "My . . . word! Now ain't *he* the
handsome one!" Lewrie congratulated, feeling anything *but* thankful.

Christ, what'll I do with this'un? Lewrie asked himself, aghast.

For inside the hat-box was a stripling kitten, white-furred in the
main, with a grey tail and nose, two large dark grey smudges above
his eyes and 'twixt his ears. Two huge, impish pale-green eyes peered
up at him, goggling in wonder as its head bobbed and cocked, half
from curiosity and half from catling-clumsy imbalance. The kitten
uttered a wee, shrill but *loud* "meek!" and a shut-mouthed little trill.

Gawd, Toulon'll kill him! Lewrie sadly thought; *he won't last a dog
watch! All that white fur, too . . . there go my uniforms. Play up gladsome, fool. The poor lad* meant *well.*

"Damned if he isn't almost Toulon's exact opposite, white where
that little scamp's black, and all! What a thoughtful gift, Desmond,
my boy. Most thoughtful, indeed!" he gushed, most insincerely, as he
reached into the hat-box and lifted the kitten out.

"After we boarded the French brig o' war, I saw him, cowering
and mewing on her boat-tier beams," Desmond happily babbled, "under a smashed-up cutter, and how he survived our broadsides, I can't
rightly say, fa— . . . sir. I took one step in his direction, and he just
dashed to me, and almost clawed his way up my boot and breeches,
then started in to purring like he'd bust, soon as I took hold of him.
Oh, he's just as smart and clever as a lady's bonnet, he is, father! He
took to bed in Midshipman Alston's hat-box, so I had to buy it off
him . . ."

"I'll recompense you for . . ."

"No, 'twas his old'un, and part of the gift, since he's so fond of it,"
Desmond objected, "and the little fellow's already figured out the right
place to make, isn't that clever?"

"Well, you give any of 'em a nice box o' sand or dirt, a little privacy, and that's pretty-much bred in the bone," Lewrie chuckled as the kitten dug his claws into the gilt-laced lapel of his dress coat and made loud sniffing noises. *And* purring fit to bust. "Don't know how Toulon'd like a playmate. He's set in his ways, but . . . I'm sure they'll take to each other."

Sooner or later, he silently hoped; *please, Jesus!*

"You like him, sir?" Desmond said as Lewrie pried the kitten off his coat and gently set him back in the hat-box. He put the cover on, and he and Lewrie stood back up.

"Absolutely delighted!" Lewrie lied most earnestly. "You could not have *bought* a better, were you rich as King Midas. You're a grand young lad, Desmond. I'm proud of you, for being so quick aboard your foe. Your uncle tells me you're shaping main-well as a gentleman-in-training . . . though more attention to your studies'd not go amiss!" he said, playfully making as if to tweak the boy's nose. He hadn't a clue about Desmond as a scholar, but such flummerous words always *seemed* to hit near the mark where midshipmen, and boys, were concerned. "Proud of your thoughtfulness, too, and your generosity."

"I call him Snowflake," Desmond proudly imparted.

"Well, early days . . . he might grow up t'be big as Toulon, and who ever heard of a champion, two-stone ram-cat named Snowflake, hey?" Lewrie chortled, then softened, in dread of hurting the lad's feelings. "Mean t'say . . . ye can't insult a proud, willful creature with a wrong name. Have to observe for a time, before the apt name comes. Might end up a Smudge, a Scamp, or a Rascal, you never can tell. Well . . . I *must* go, son. Thankee, again, and soon as I'm back, you'll come aboard and dine with me, and see how little No-Name fares, right?"

"I shall look forward to it . . . father!" the lad replied, with a covert wink before they did their appropriate goodbyes, dictated by Society and naval etiquette.

Another bloody cat, Lewrie told himself, settling in the stern-sheets of his gig with the hat-box in his lap; *first of a curmudgeon's round dozen, like poor old Captain Lilycrop back in '82? Christ, just spare me! Still . . . the boy meant well by it. I'm sure he did.*

CHAPTER THIRTY

*H*MS *Proteus* was driven like Jehu had driven his chariot, sails set "all to the royals," stays'ls bellied out between her masts everywhere even the tiniest zephyr of wind could be caught, cupped by heavy flax or cotton and used to impart power. Stuns'ls were boomed out on her course and tops'l yards, and the rarely employed sprits'l beneath her plunging jib-boom and bowsprit had been spread, now stiff with the furious boil and bluster of salt spray flung up from the cutwater and the frigate's fine entry.

Driven though *he* was, Lewrie did take time to thank *Proteus*'s builders, the Nicholson yards at Frindsbury on the Medway, for "Frenchifying" her and improving on the numerous *Thames* class frigates. What he knew about ship design could fill a thimble, admittedly, and the new science of hydraulics, as the learned half-English half-Swede director of the Royal Dockyards at Karlskrona, Fredrick af Chapman, wrote of it, was quite beyond him. All he knew was that *Proteus* was swift.

His Surgeon's Mate, the scholarly French *emigre* Mr. Durant, once a university-trained Physician before fleeing the Terror in France, had taken time to read up on his new surroundings in all its contrary, esoteric mysteries, and was the only one who could explain it.

"T'ink of ze seawater as treacle, ze molasses, *Capitaine*," Durant said over supper in Lewrie's great-cabins, to enlighten his commanding officer's "darkness," exasperated at last, perhaps, by Capt. Lewrie's befuddled look. "Ze faster you go, ze more ze water is compressed by ze bows, but water, any liquid, you *cannot* compress, *comprends?* It bash back at you, it makes ze stone wall. You must *cut* ze water, never try to batter t'rough it. Ze ladle floats on treacle, you cannot submerge it easily. Ah, but ze knife blade, *hawn-hawn!*" he had triumphantly concluded, replete with that snorting nasal laugh to which Frogs seemed so damnably partial.

Proteus's fore-end frames stood narrower to her keel, sacrificing beaminess and storage capacity, surrendering just a bit of forward buoyancy, rising straighter and more vertically near her stem pieces to narrow her lowest forefoot and entry. Her planking had required more costly steaming and bending to create a rounder and more grace-ful arc, more of a hemispherical bow moulding than the usual nearly square-cut form. Nowhere near as fine as the bows of a cutter, gig, or fishing boat, for Nicholson's naval architects could but create a compromise . . . but a highly pleasing, and swift, compromise she was.

So, HMS *Proteus* stood Sou-Sou'west from Antigua, determined to give French-held Guadeloupe a wide berth this time, and with the wind fine on her larboard quarter she was making nearly eleven and a half knots, still "battering" her way against those "treacly," glittering seas, not as fast as the Trades blew, but close, so that hands on deck could get a bit of cooling respite from the afternoon heat and savour the impatient keen and hum of the Trades in the rigging, the drum-ming and booming of her stout-planked hull as she met the long-set four- or five-foot seas, and the waterfall's, dragon's hiss, of her wake.

"Sail ho!" a lookout in the main-mast cross-trees cried. "Two point off th' larb'd quarter! One . . . two . . . *three* sail, astern!"

"Astern of us?" Lt. Langlie said with a puzzled grunt. Lifting his brass speaking-trumpet to his lips, he shouted aloft, "Can you make them out?"

"Tops'ls, t'gallants an' royals t'th' first'un! T'gallants an' royals t'th' second . . ." the lookout shouted back. "Last'un, I kin see royals, only, sir! Two ships, an' a brig! First'un *might* be *Sumter!*"

"Mister Grace, my duty to the Captain, and inform him that the Americans might be out, astern of us, and following," Lt. Langlie said.

⚓

"Now now, lads . . . behave," Lewrie cajoled his cats. "No Name" was inside his hat box, forepaws, eyes, and muzzle peeking playfully at its rim, and madly scrambling to get out for the *fifth* time, trilling and mouse-squeaking. Toulon stood a foot or so aloof of the box, with his tail bottled up, ears laid flat, his back arched, and his fur stood on end. *His* comment to such mediations was a long, wrathful moaning, followed by a fang-baring hiss of equal duration, punctuated by a spit, and a testy chop-licking. "No Name," far from being daunted by such a welcome, seemed to regard Toulon's action as a delightful raree-show, and an invitation to play. "Christ Almighty, now . . ." Lewrie sighed. "Damme, I *know* he meant well, but . . . Aye, Mister Grace?"

"Mister Langlie's duty, sir, and I'm to tell you that the American squadron *seems* to be astern of us, sailing on our same course."

"Oh hell, this could get embarrassing," Lewrie muttered, contemplating what a horse-laugh the Yankee Doodles would have when they got wind of *why* he'd dashed out of English Harbour so frantically. "Aspinall, er . . . I'm going on deck. Do you *try* to keep the littl'un alive 'til I return."

"Aye, sir," Aspinall replied, though regarding such a Herculean task with a dubious, much put-upon expression. "Here, Toulon! Here's yer 'toe-y'! Play 'chase' with yer fav'rite 'toe-y'?"

He dangled a much-clawed and gnawed red wool ball on a length of spun yarn, a toy that usually sent Toulon into transports of joy, and could be counted on for a half-hour of energetic distraction. Today it elicited an edgy hiss-spit, and several crocodile swishes from his bristled-up tail before he returned to his "death watch."

"Sure it's the Yankees, Mister Langlie?" Lewrie asked, once on the quarterdeck.

"The lookout's familiar with their appearance, sir. We believe so, aye," Lt. Langlie replied as they both raised telescopes to study the tiny slivers of sail that barely peeked above the horizon. "They are ten miles or so astern of us, their royals or t'gallants in view, perhaps a sliver of the lead ship's upper tops'ls now and then, when the sea lifts both of us together."

"Making up to us?" Lewrie asked, mentally crossing his fingers.

"But slowly, sir. *Sumter*, for so the lookout supposes her to be, leads them. They must have cleared harbour not two hours after we did."

"Well, damn," Lewrie grumbled. "Swift as they've proved in past, they'll most-like be *abeam* of us by sunset. I'll have to dine 'em in, and *never* be able t'live it down. We sailed so quickly, they must imagine I'm after Choundas and his convoy and want a piece of the action. Damn-*nation!*"

Lewrie gloomily speculated that he could *just* sail the brig o' war USS *Oglethorpe* under, and might elude the three-masted *Sumter*, as well, but *Hancock* and her humourless master Goodell . . . ! He hadn't a hope in Hell of out-footing *her*, with her taller masts and over-long spars, her larger spread of canvas, and her impressive length of keel. Once she got "the bone in her teeth," USS *Hancock* could outrun terns!

"Do we not light the taff-rail lanthorns, nor show any binnacle lights, we mask all the stern windows, and your gun-room and I dine in the dark," Lewrie hopefully said, "then add a radical change of course . . . say due West just after full nightfall, they might stay on their present heading."

"Which would place them ahead of us, to the Suth'rd, sir," Lt. Langlie glumly commented, "and *sure* we'd stumble over them within the week. And *then* what'd we say . . . sorry?"

"Own up that we're a pack o' fools," Lewrie spat, lowering his telescope, "who can't keep proper guard on an anchored ship."

"I simply can't imagine that Mister Jugg turned pirate on us, sir," Langlie said, sighing as he took off his hat and trailed fingers through his dark and curly locks. "A surly, glum bastard he was, but he'd settled in main-well, and was ever in a fair way of performing his duties. Mister Burns, well . . . *there's* hen-headed for you, but Mister Towpenny and four reliable hands, even Toffett, to overcome on his own, sir? Idle hands the Devil's workshop or no, Captain, they'd only been becalmed aboard the prize a little more than a week. No, I can't see an uprising. More like, I suspect one of Choundas's small privateers sneaked in and cut her out in the dead of night, when only two or three were awake."

"*Supposed* t'be awake," Lewrie snidely retorted. "Was it Mister Burns who had the deck, t'other hands could've set *fire* to her without a harsh word from *him*, the quakin' dullard. So timid he wouldn't say 'Boh' to a goose!"

"She could be alongside the Basse-Terre quays on Guadeloupe by now, sir," Lt. Langlie went on. "That devil Victor Hugues's valuable cargo back in his hands . . . that ogre Choundas laughing like a loon at re-taking her from *you* the best of all to him, sir," Langlie remorselessly fantasised, "getting *some* of his own back at our expense in more ways than one, d'ye see, buffing up . . ."

"Yes!" Lewrie finally barked. "I *do* see, Mister Langlie, clear as a bloody damn' bell!"

"My pardons, sir, I . . ." Langlie said with a wince.

"Arrr!" Lewrie gave vent to a piratical growl, an expression he was becoming rather fond of; it was brusquely eloquent, in its own inarticulate way.

"At least, sir, the rapidity of our departure spared us Mister Peel's, or Mister Pelham's, presence," Langlie pointed out, trying to salvage something worthwhile from the ongoing fiasco.

"Proving that God is, when it suits Him, just, Mister Langlie."

"We stand on as we are then, sir?" Langlie enquired, happy for a change of topic. "Until dark?"

"Aye," Lewrie grunted. "Little more we can do. We could hang the crew's clothing in the rigging for a quarter-knot more speed. *If* there was a spare inch o' rigging left. I'll be below."

"Uhm . . . how is Toulon taking to his new, uhm . . . ?" Lt. Langlie just *had* to ask.

"Oh, simply bloody *fine*, Mister Langlie! Like chalk an' cheese they are," Lewrie gravelled, slamming the tubes of his telescope shut. "Oil and vinegar . . . ham and bloody eggs, thankee for askin'."

Lewrie stomped forrud to the larboard, windward, ladder to the gun-deck, tromped the steps downward and turned at its base, forcing a Marine sentry in full kit by his doors to stiffen, ready to salute.

"Sail ho!" the main-mast lookout cried, again.

"Now, bloody what?" Lewrie grumbled to himself.

"*Two* sail . . . four points off th' starb'd bows! *Three* sail . . . sailin' athwart, an' bound West-Nor'west!" the lookout further howled, which tweaked Lewrie from his funk and made him scamper to the quarterdeck, again.

"Just about due West of us," he said half to himself, deploying his much-abused telescope once more by the barricade of hammock nets.

"*Four* sail, now!" the lookout shrilled. "Four points off th' starb'd bows!"

"Mister Langlie, hands to stations to wear ship," Lewrie snapped. "Make our new course Nor'west by West. They could be another

American convoy, late departin' for home, *but* . . . we'd better investigate."

"Ahoy, th' deck!" a lookout called down from USS *Sumter*'s mainmast cross-trees. "Th' frigate's wearin' about t'starb'd tack!"

"Now where's he goin'?" Capt. McGilliveray wondered aloud. "I could o' sworn he was bound for Guadeloupe, but here he goes a'harin' off to th' Nor'west. Most p'culiar."

"Maybe she's spotted something, sir," Lt. Claiborne, his First Officer, supposed. "Or . . . what intelligence he received that caused him to tear outta port came a day late."

"Aye, and th' onliest thing that'd whip Cap'm Lewrie t'sea that I know of'd be news that th' French convoy's sailed," McGilliveray replied, "like we finally decided. Maybe that's why *Proteus* wasn't bound direct for Guadeloupe in th' first place, that a British spy got word of their *departure*. Time a boat could get to Antigua, they'd be about this far out, on course for Jacmel on Saint Domingue. Damn my eyes, sir, but I do b'lieve Cap'm Lewrie's got lucky, and espied 'em, after all! Desmond? Mister *McGilliveray*, mean t'say? Make a hoist to the *Hancock*, lad, an' make it . . . 'Alter,' 'Nor'west,' and 'In Pursuit.' In pursuit o' what, we don't rightly know yet, but there's somethin' he's caught scent of that's put his tail up. Mister Claiborne! We'll wear ship to Nor'west, if ya please."

"Aye, sir."

"And no wonder Lewrie was so secretive," Captain McGilliveray said, half to himself, slamming a fist on the nearest bulwark. "Dour as ol' 'Thunderation' treated him, he doesn't want t'share 'em. Well, we'll see about that, won't we, ha ha!"

"*Sumter* signals that *Proteus* has worn about to the Nor'west and seems to be in pursuit of something over the horizon, sir," Goodell's First Lieutenant related to him with the sombre *gravitas* their stern captain demanded from men he intended to groom and mould as gentlemen officers . . . if it killed them.

"Ah, hmm," Capt. Goodell replied, clearing his throat. "Do thee summon the hands to wear about as well, sir. So much undue haste is indicative of something worth chasing, aye, even in one so idle and

indolent as Captain Lewrie struck me. Like all the *British*," he glowered, "Thun-der-*ation*, what hypocrites are they! Beguile me for cooperation in his quest after *one* despicable Frenchman, appeal to honour
. . . then dash off to have it all for himself, didst his intelligence smack
of too *much* potential plunder, pah! Hypocrites, liars, and tyrants, every
last one of those enervated . . . Babylonians!"

"*Une voile!*" the lookout atop *Le Gascon*'s main-mast cried. "A sail,
to windward! One point aft of the starboard beam! Royals, and top-
gallants . . . studding sails on topsail yards, I see!"

"*Mon Dieu, merde alors*," Capt. Griot said with a grimace. "The
enemy has found us, after all." Griot raised his telescope and swept
the tubes to their full extension, though there was little chance that he
could espy anything from the quarterdeck, yet.

"What course does she steer?" Capt. Guillaume Choundas shouted
upward, clump-shuffle-ticking to the starboard side.

"Bows on . . . no! She shows her larboard bows! Steering North-
West!" the lookout responded.

"How *many* masts?" Choundas cried, his throat rasping harshly in
unwonted effort, and with his eye shut in furious contemplation, with
an imagined chart of the Caribbean in his mind.

"*Two!* So much canvas, *messieurs*, I can only make *out* two!" the
lookout cried, after a long, frustrating pause of half a minute.

"Out of Antigua, for certain, *Capitaine*," Griot fretted, as he paced,
"which lies almost due East of our present position. Shaping course
to the North-West . . ." Griot was hushed by the raising of his master's
left hand, for Choundas was still thinking, and would not be distracted.

"Two-masted, flying studding sail booms, hmm . . . bound out of
Antigua to the North-West," Choundas muttered to himself, transferring his left hand to massage his throat, for it had been years since
he'd actually commanded at sea where shouting orders had been required. "I think we see a British packet brig, Griot. North-West,
perhaps a half-point more Westerly, would be the shortest course to
Jamaica. She might be carrying despatches or orders. At speed."

His good eye flew open and transfixed the scowling Griot like a
collector would pin a butterfly to a board.

"Their *Contre-Amiral* Harvey to their *Vice-Amiral* Sir Hyde Parker
at Kingston, perhaps?" Choundas said with a wicked smile. "If she

stands on, she falls into our laps. What the accursed Huguenots, the so-called Acadians call a *lagniappe*, Griot. 'A little something extra' to make our success complete. Stand on, as innocent as you please. I think a false-flag ruse may serve. American would be best. We could appear as a late-season convoy on our way to America. The few trifling excuses for warships the Americans have in these seas are much the size and strength of ours."

Choundas took hold of a mizen shroud and swivelled about slowly to clap eyes on his convoy. *Le Gascon* and *La Résolue* lay to windward of the merchant ship and trading brig by at least two miles, out near where the greatest threat could make the most likely approach. One of them, *La Résolue*, lay aft and to windward, about four miles astern of *La Gascon*, on the convoy's rear flank. Hainaut's much faster and much handier armed schooner scouted ahead by at least another four or five miles, quartering back and forth like a bloodhound casting for spoor.

Choundas shut his eye, again, recalling how *La Résolue* looked; could she pass for a merchantman? Perhaps, he decided. Jules out so far in advance of them, though . . . that would never do. If any ship could resemble a typical American trader, his *La Mohican* was it.

"Signal to Hainaut," Choundas briskly ordered, his eye and his mouth snapping open, "to take close station at the head of the convoy. Spell that out, if you must. Then make signals to *Capitaine* MacPherson in *La Résolue*. He is to close up as the last ship in column, astern of the three-master. No national flags aloft, 'til ordered, and then the first to be displayed will be the American. *We* will remain in position, to appear as the only escort to a convoy of four, and will hoist the American flag when queried."

"She might not wish to come that close, *Capitaine*," Griot said.

"Let her fear be only slightly allayed, Griot, let her maintain her present, quick, and direct course for Jamaica, and our bows will at some point come within a few scant miles of intersecting. I think she will bear off a *little*, to pass ahead of us without forcing us to back and fill, or alter course. And that will be close enough for a quick dash out to snap her up."

CHAPTER THIRTY-ONE

*O*ne *brig*, sor!" Midshipman Larkin, precariously perched aloft on the main royal yard where it crossed the slim upper mast, reported. "There's one *schooner* . . . and *three* . . . full-rigged *ships*, sor!"

"Very well, Mister Larkin!" Lewrie cried back, hands cupped at his mouth. "Now, lay below and make me a fuller report!"

Midshipman Larkin, as agile and sure-handed as the best of the frigate's elite topmen, slung his borrowed telescope like a musketoon and descended to the cross-trees, down the narrow upper shrouds, and then found a back-stay round which he wrapped his limbs and slid like a street-pedlar's monkey to the starboard gangway, where he landed with a solid thump, to a round of cheers and a clap or two from his mess-mates in the cockpit, and the hands. Larkin took a brief second to doff his hat, perform a bow from the waist, then trotted aft to the quarterdeck.

"Show me," Lewrie bade, handing the incorrigible young fellow a wood-framed slate and stub of chalk, and Larkin quickly bent to sketch out several sharp-pointed long ovals, with dashes for masts. Halfway through, Larkin had to snort and snuffle, then wipe his runny nose on his coat sleeve; still panting like a pony from his exertions.

"That's why they put buttons on the cuffs in the first place," Lt. Langlie commented, "so well-dressed nobles wouldn't use fine clothing as snot-rags and chin-wipes, Mister Larkin."

"Sorry, sor . . . touch o' sniffles. Here, Cap'm, sor. Schooner's ahead, three-masted. Full-rigged ship aftermost, another ship, then a brig, and closer to us, another full-rigged ship, sor. Sir, I mean."

"Standing out like an escort?" Lewrie puzzled, aloud.

"Aye, sir, seemed t'be," Larkin answered, his shaggy head cocked to one side over his sketchy results. "Th' schooner 'twas showin' 'er tops'ls, but begun t'take 'em in whilst I was watchin'."

"Sight of a frigate in the offing, sir, I'd reduce sail and get snug to my fellows, too," Lt. Catterall deduced in his gruff and blunt way. " 'Misery loves company,' so they say, hey?"

"Any flags showing, Mister Larkin?" Lewrie asked.

"None, sor . . . sir. Though . . . this ship here," Larkin said, as he tapped his stub of chalk on the slate by the ship closest to them, "she was runnin' up sets o' signal flags, an' then t'others . . . this'n far aft, and th' schooner, seemed t'answer her, sir."

"Like other escorting vessels, Mister Larkin?" Lewrie pressed.

"Uhm, well . . . sorta like, sir, aye," Larkin ventured, nodding.

Lewrie clapped his hands in the small of his back and rocked on the balls of his feet, beginning to beam a sly grin. "What, gentlemen, did the learned Doctor Samuel Johnson call it, what was the word in his *Dictionary* for when you go in search of one thing, but find a better, all unexpected? Mister Adair, you're our resident scholar . . . ."

"It is 'serendipity,' Captain," Lt. Adair supplied, grinning in mounting expectation. "We've discovered the French *convoy*, sir?"

"I do b'lieve we have, sir," Lewrie replied. "Mister Langlie, a point more Westerly, do you please. Put us bows-on to them, so they see *a* ship, for now. And I'll have the stuns'ls, sprits'l, and royals taken in, to boot. We may need to manoeuvre hard on the wind. Chain-slings to be rigged on the other yards, and boarding nets fetched out ready for hoisting. Mister Grace?"

"Aye, sir?"

"Bend on and be ready to hoist our number and the challenge in this month's private signals book . . . the one we share with the American Navy," Lewrie slyly said, "and dig into your flag lockers and get that Yankee courtesy flag ready to hoist as well. With our own near to hand, of course. Hop to it, gentlemen, make it happen, instanter!"

Was the convoy British, he'd eat his hat. It could *only* be the Americans, or the French—Choundas's convoy! The Jonathons would form much larger convoys, with dozens, or scores, of home-bound ships;

and he either knew the names of every United States Navy warship sent to the Leewards to escort them, or he already knew them by sight!

Now, just let 'em hoist Yankee colours, and I'll know for sure, Lewrie gloated; *let 'em try to answer with the right signals. Even if they got their hands on 'em, somehow, they can't bluff their way out with false identities!*

"Aloft, there!" Lewrie cried to the lookouts. "How stand those American ships, astern of us?"

"Lead ship's nigh hull-up, sir!" one of them responded. "Rest are close astern o' her, showin' tops'ls *and* courses!"

"Uhm . . . I'll have to hoist the American flag from the foremast, sir," Midshipman Grace piped up near his elbow. "With the wind on the starboard quarter, and our bows direct at them, they'd not be able to see it plain, else. But Mister Elwes has the private signals ready on the larboard mizen halliards, sir."

"Very well, Mister Grace, scamper forrud and bend it on, then hoist it soon as you may," Lewrie bade him impatiently, and Mr. Grace scuttled off with the "gridiron" flag lightly bound in twine under his arm. Moments later, it was soaring aloft, still a colourful ball 'til it reached the halliard peak block, where a twitch and the power from the wind let it burst open like a bright flower to stream alee. One long minute passed before they got a reply.

"Deck, there! Near ship's hoisted colours . . . American!"

"Excellent!" Lewrie chortled. "Now, Mister Elwes, hoist away! And make what ye will o' *that*, Monsoor Frog."

The signals soared aloft and broke out in a string of nine code flags. The "convoy" was drawing closer, the nearest almost hull-up to *Proteus*, so there was no way they could *not* reply to them. But Lewrie had to pace about and stew for what felt like five minutes before that lone "escort" whipped off an answer.

"Well?" Lewrie demanded of Mr. Elwes, who was frantically flipping through his signals book.

"Can't make it out, sir," Elwes fretted. " 'Tis nothing current, not in the past six months' codes, at least. She shows a private number for the USS *Pickering*, but *Pickering* is a Revenue Service *cutter*, and she hoisted her private number and the reply to our challenge out of proper sequence, sir."

"Then she's lyin' through her teeth," Lewrie gladly concluded, clapping his hands in glee. "Make to her the usual jibber-jaw, 'where bound' and such. Hah! Ask her if she's seen USS *Sumter*! That'll be int'resting. And on the *starb'rd* halliards, Mister Elwes, where *she* can't read 'em . . . hoist *Hancock*'s number, followed by 'With All Despatch' and 'Enemy In Sight.' "

"American," Choundas muttered, sullenly fuming at this sudden and disturbing revelation. "*American*, of all things. Signal the rest of the ships to hoist American flags, Griot. We will bluff her."

"*Oui, m'sieur*, but . . . she hoists another set of signals. How do we answer them?" Griot asked him, striving to maintain the required *sang-froid*, but revealing his worry anyway. "She names herself in new codes that we do not possess. We were fortunate I had an out-of-date copy in my desk, but . . . is she a merchantman, or a man-of-war, we do not know until she closes us."

"Two corvettes and a well-armed schooner against a single brig of war, Griot?" Choundas scathingly sneered. "Merchant or warship, in another hour it will not matter, for she'll be our prize. We *do* know the code flag for 'Repeat.' Angled as she is on the Trades, her flags are difficult to read. She must come closer, fall a bit astern of us, or press a bit ahead, to make them readable. Close enough for you to sortie out and take her under fire, quickly re-enforced by *La Résolue* and Hainaut's schooner. Tell them we lost the latest signals book in a hard blow, and must fall back on the old one. Surely, they have it, still, and will accommodate a . . . fellow countryman." He chuckled.

"*Ohé!*" the main-mast lookout shouted. "Ships ahoy! Two . . . no, *three* ships to the starboard beam, astern of the nearest one! Three sets of topsails, top-gallants, and royals . . . headed North-West!"

"*Merde*, that close?" Griot griped, dashing back to the bulwarks with his telescope extended once more. "This near one must have masked them, if we see topsails, already. They could be up to us in another hour or so. *Mort de ma vie, m'sieur*. What if they are war-ships?"

"And what if they are a whole convoy?" Choundas barked back, in sudden loathing for the usually stoic Griot's uncharacteristic "windiness." And he'd thought him a Breton paragon, all this time, a worthy scion of the ancient Veneti, courageous as himself!

⚓

"They're almost hull-up to us, from the deck, sir," Lt. Langlie announced. "Six miles, perhaps? And our Yankee 'cousins' are closing us rapidly," he said, swivelling about for a peek aft.

"We'll be close-aboard the French in half an hour on this wind," the Sailing Master, Mr. Winwood, soberly opined. "And the Americans, so I do adjudge, will be up to broadsides a half hour after that, sir."

"Mmhmm," Lewrie absently acknowledged them, all ascheme, and a bit too impatient to create a little inventive mischief and mayhem to wait that long. The strung-out convoy arrayed in-line-ahead was split in equal halves by *Proteus*'s bisecting bowsprit. They could haul up harder on the wind and cut them off, they could wear once more and duck astern of them, go dashing for the lee-side and the vulnerably slow escorted ships . . . which?

Didn't plan on it, but I've led the Yankees to a fight, Lewrie pondered; *I commit to battle, and Goodell'd never forgive me for wadin' in before he could get up, and there goes his grudgin' gratitude, and any chance o' future cooperation. Two* corvettes, *mayhap the schooner is an armed auxiliary, too, hmm . . . discretion the better part o' valour, for once? Use my bloody* head, *for a rare once?*

"Mister Langlie," Lewrie finally said, turning to face his execcutive officer. "We will bear up hard on the wind. New course . . . Nor-Norwest. Mister Grace, you still with us? Once we're settled on our new heading, you will lower the Yankee flag and break out our true colours. Smartly. And make a hoist to the convoy to heave to and prepare to be boarded, that same instant." To Langlie, he gleefully explained, "we'll sit out here off their starboard bows and let 'em sulk on things for a bit. Pull their hair and kick furniture, if they've a mind. They wish to come out and fight, we'll be more than happy to oblige 'em. Give the Americans the chance to participate, if they dally long enough, too."

"*Ohé!*" the lookout screamed, a minute after the "brig of war," or the "merchant brig," had worn about, revealing herself as a three-masted ship. "She is *anglais!*" Choundas ground his teeth, despising the shouts, and the man who made them. "*Mille diables*, she is a frigate!" he wailed, spreading consternation by reporting so emotionally.

"Damn it!" Choundas rasped, stamping his cane on the deck.

"*Ohé!* She is that devil ship *Proteus!*" the lookout howled.

"Shoot that dog!" Choundas barked. "Do you not train your men to report correctly, Griot?"

"*M'sieur,* I ..." Griot stammered, as flustered as his sailors at the sight of their nemesis. "How? How *did* he find us? Who could have betrayed our sailing, after all you did to stamp out traitors?"

"You are French, Griot! You are *Breton!*" Choundas bellowed in rage, his face gone the colour of red plums. "Behave accordingly, as a warship captain, or ... !"

"*Ohé,* the deck!" the lookout shrilled once more, "the ships to the East are warships! Flags at every mast-head! A *corvette,* a brig of war, and ... perhaps a small frigate, astern!"

"*Damn* that man!" Choundas spat, glaring upward as if his look could kill. "Lewrie is *not* a devil, Griot, he's but a man. A stupid, idle, arrogant British ... amateur! He sits out there from fear, waiting for the Americans to come up before he acts. Americans! Revenue cutters armed with pop-guns, thin-sided merchant ships turned into poor substitutes for men of war! We sortie now against him, and we'll have nearly an hour to swarm over him. Three ships to one, and with him taken or crippled ... Lewrie *dead,* at last, yes! ... they'll stand off in fear of us! Oh, Lewrie dead at long last ..."

"*Proteus* is a Fifth Rate frigate of thirty-two guns, *Capitaine,*" Griot recited, suddenly so calm that Choundas got a crick in his neck from turning his head to glare at him. "Her main artillery consists of twelve-pounders. Her weight of metal is greater than ours, together."

"Get those damnable rags down, Griot," Choundas coldly ordered. "Hoist our glorious *Tricolore,* and signal *La Résolue* and *La Mohican* to form line-of-battle on us. We will fight, and ... we ... will ... conquer, do you hear me, *hein?* Do it! *Vite, vite!*"

"And our charges, *m'sieur?*" Capt. Griot asked. "What should we do with them?"

"Order the convoy to wear about and make the best of their way back to Guadeloupe, Griot," Choundas quickly decided. "If they cannot drive that close to the Trades, they must run East-Sou'east, at least, until we come to fetch them, say. For now, they are no longer our main concern," he disparagingly said, hope, and rage, and a long unused acuity for tactics awakened in his breast, "We have a battle to fight!"

⚓

"Three-to-one, sir," Lt. Langlie said, slyly grinning. "Almost even odds, that. After all, they *are* French!" he japed.

"Takin' 'em long enough," Lewrie grunted back, brooding on the larboard bulwarks facing their foes. "They beat up to us, they'll hope to bracket us. I would, in their position. The lead *corvette* to lie off our bows, the second abeam, and the schooner t'play the 'bull-dog' and stern-rake us often as she can. Our Yankees?"

"*Oglethorpe* has worn about, and is after those merchant ships," Langlie said, craning about for a good look. "They're mostly out of it, bound due South, or thereabout, sir. *Sumter* and *Hancock* are still bound directly for us, 'bout five miles up to windward."

Lewrie took himself a long look-see, too, feeling oddly calm, and satisfied. *Proteus* still lay Nor'east of the French, only slowly angling closer to them as the escorting warships swanned about to get ready to fight. They were separated by little more than two miles of water, now, tantalisingly beyond even extreme gun-range. The leading French *corvette* was bound Nor'west, as close-hauled to the Trades as she could bear. The second *corvette* was still about a mile astern of the first one, perhaps a quarter-mile alee of her consort, and unable to pinch or claw up closer. The armed schooner showed much more dash, though; her fore-and-aft sails allowed her another point higher on the eyes of the wind, steering North-by-East, almost bows-on to *Proteus*'s larboard quarter. Lewrie turned to slouch with his right arm on the bulwarks, most un-captainly-like, and squinted at her. He imagined a "dashing" schooner captain might haul up close, then tack and try to rake him, getting in his licks before the others, perhaps to fire up into his frigate's rigging and carry away something vital that would allow the *corvettes* to get into knife-fighting distance. Well . . . two could play that game, Lewrie thought. His ship had not yet reefed or clewed up her main course, which would be drawn up out of the way for fear of fire once the guns began to sing; she still had all the power of the wind to utilise. *Proteus*'s yards, though she steered a point "free" of close-hauled, he'd had drawn in loose-braced, not *quite* gathering as much wind as they could if braced in sharp. Not that obvious to the approaching French yet, letting them gain, but . . .

Yes, there she went, starting to tack . . . the ambitious young shit!

Get a bit to windward, then tack and fall down on his vulnerable stern
. . . or so he thought!

"Mister Langlie, brace in hard and get a proper way back on her.
Then we will wear," Lewrie decided of a sudden.

"And close them, sir?"

"For a while, Mister Langlie," Lewrie cheerfully replied. "In the
process, we'll force them to tack, if they want at us that badly, upset
whatever they're planning, and . . . bear down on yon schooner so
frightful we'll make her commander squirt his breeches," Lewrie
quickly sketched out. "Once about, we will go close-hauled on larboard tack and chase the little bastard, splitting their forces and iso-
lating him. And give the 'cousins' the time to get up and have a proper
whack at 'em.

"I'm feelin' devilish generous today, Mister Langlie," Lewrie said
with a chuckle. "New course, East-Sou'east."

"Aye aye, sir," Langlie said with a sly grin.

"She wears!" Griot exclaimed.

"Then get us about, too, at once!" Choundas snapped. "Signal to
La Résolue to conform to our manoeuvres."

"At once, m'sieur," Capt. Griot said, turning to pass the order to
his First Officer, then turning back to Choundas. "Such a tack will
bring us much closer to the American warships. Once we engage
Proteus they will have time to sail up and take us on our dis-engaged
side."

"If I cannot have that salaud Lewrie this time, I will at least damage
him in passing, Griot," Choundas growled. "A quick action at three-
to-one odds to cripple and kill, then we will break away and go to
the rescue of our merchant ships . . . hacking that puny American brig
of war apart in the process. Perhaps even taking her and teaching a
lesson to those rustic ingrates. Oh, to be just a mile closer . . . what
Hell we could play upon Lewrie as he wears!"

For HMS Proteus was coming about, first swinging to present her
stern to the Trades, then only slowly, handsomely, swinging her yards,
jibs, and stays'ls as she wore across the eyes of the wind, offering up
her profile to the French corvettes, which were swinging their bows at
her as they tacked. The slowness of the British frigate's manoeuvres,

and their tacks, brought all three square-riggers closer to each other —
yet still frustratingly out of even a most hopeful gunner's attempt to
hit her, one mile beyond Range-To-Random-Shot.

Guillaume Choundas hobbled to the head of the larboard gun-deck
ladder, wrapping his left arm about the stanchion for a swivel-gun, his
walking-stick tucked under his arm, and thumping his fist on the rails
as if to flog *Lé Gascon* into a break-neck gallop. Griot, canny sailor
that he was, had the larboard guns run out and the starboard artillery
run in near to amidships, to loading positions, to get her flatter on her
bottom. *Le Gascon*'s, and *La Résolue*'s, bottoms were mostly clean,
their entries were finer than most, and their length of keel was just a
bit shorter than the frigate's. Given enough time, and both *corvettes*
should stride up to *Proteus* and bracket her between their guns. Lewrie
could squirm about, but that would only quicken his death.

He looked Sutherly, noting that *La Résolue* was positioned for an
engagement on Lewrie's starboard side, while *Le Gascon* was high
enough to take him under fire on his larboard side, even allowing for
leeward slippage, which was unavoidable going hard to windward.

"Your *protégé*, Hainaut, has courage, *m'sieur*," Griot commented.
"His schooner might get to her before we do."

"Yes, he does," Choundas replied, irked that his vital calculations
of wind, leeway, and speed were interrupted, yet with a sound of
grudging pride in his voice, even so. "Cleverness, too."

"Let us hope more cleverness than brute bravery, *m'sieur*," Capt.
Griot gloomily intoned. "Once we savage *Proteus*, and get past her,
we must bear away Southeast, else we approach the Americans, line-
abreast . . . unable to aid each other, *m'sieur*," he pointed out.

"I do not fear their rough-cast, home-made, and light *pop*-guns,
Griot!" Choundas declared with a sneer. "American foundries and
powder mills are . . . *merde*. And their gun crews a pack of clumsy
children in comparison to how well you and MacPherson have trained
ours."

"Very well, *m'sieur*," Griot said, keeping his voice neutral, in dread
of what Choundas might order in the heat of rising expectations for
battle. He feared pointing out how quickly the Americans stalked down
on them, were starting to haul their wind a point or so, as if to aim
between *Proteus*'s stern quarters and his own ship's bows, and cut them
off from pursuit. Capt. Griot was fearful, too, to express what qualms
he felt after taking a long look at the trailing "small frigate" that his

lookouts had reported, as she loomed taller and taller in his ocular, beginning to appear as massive as a cut-down Third Rate still bearing two decks of guns. . . . *Madness*, the doughty Griot thought, his heart heavy; *we are sacrificed to this* ogre's *revenge. Madness!*

"The Frog schooner's now about one mile off our starboard quarters, sir," Lt. Langlie adjudged, his telescope to his eye, "and those *corvettes* are a mile and a half astern, but coming fast. One about dead astern, t'other on our larboard quarter."

"And our Yankees only four miles up to windward," Lewrie added, with a satisfied sniff. "Time for some fun, Mister Langlie. Haul our wind and steer due South. Mister Catterall?" he shouted forward, over the hammock nettings. "Stand by, the starboard battery, and take that schooner under fire once we've fallen off! Your best gun-captains, to fire as they bear, mind! Let 'em take their time at it!"

"Aye *aye*, sir!" Catterall bellowed back, pleased as punch to be loosed on their foes, at last. "Right, you bawdy whore-sons . . . !"

Proteus heeled, groaning, almost putting her starboard outboard shroud chain platforms into the sea as her helm was put up, as braces and sheets were eased. Once settled on her new course due South, the port lids swung up to make a regular blood-red chequer against the pale paint of her gunwales, and the heavy truck-carriages rumbled and squealed as her 12-pounder guns were run out in-battery. A long minute passed as gun-captains fussed and fiddled with the elevating quoin blocks, directing their crews to shift aim left or right with the long crow-levers to "sweat" tons of oak and iron a few inches. Rope tackles and blocks were overhauled for clear recoil paths, before the experienced gun-captains took up the lanyards to their flintlock strikers, then shot their free fists skyward to show readiness, reducing the slack in the lanyards to the last, remaining inch . . .

"As you bear . . . fire!" Lt. Catterall roared.

Bow to stern, her thirteen starboard 12-pounders stuttered out a bellicose thunder, some gunners waiting for the scend of the sea to raise the decks nearer to dead-level before jerking their lanyards; in ones, twos, and threes the guns erupted and lurched inboard, with both guns right-aft in Lewrie's great-cabins adding the final kettle-drun *coda* of a quick *Boo-Boom!* To Lewrie's ears it was almost excruciatingly . . . musical!

The French schooner had been almost bows-on to *Proteus*, following her turn off the wind, and her stunned master had kept her bows-on . . . most-likely to present the slimmest target he could to that sudden broadside. Great, lovely columns and feathers of spray leaped skyward about her . . . to either beam, or short before her bows, but terrifyingly *close*, and bounding upward as darting black specks from First Graze, barely slowed to howl, keen, or shriek over her decks or down both of her sides, as if she had been assailed by a flying coven of witches!

Thinking quickly, the schooner's captain ordered her helm hard over to leeward to tack her Northward towards the nearest *corvette* to escape a second pummeling, hoping to flit beyond *Proteus*'s limited gun-arcs. As she bared her starboard side to them, rolling, heeling, and every sail panic-flogging, *Proteus*'s gunners raised a jeering howl at the sight of holes that their shot had punched in her canvas!

"Now, back on the wind, Mister Langlie!" Lewrie ordered. "All for now, Mister Catterall, sorry! Close your ports, but reload, then stand by to serve 'em another!"

"We've lost a quarter-mile to the *corvettes*, sir," Lt. Langlie pointed out.

"Aye. Temptin'," Lewrie snickered, beaming fit to bust, with a playful double-lift of his brows, "ain't we. Those poor bastards back yonder, Mister Langlie . . . they *should* be running, but they're not. I doubt they could scuttle back to Choundas, 'thout dirtyin' their guns a time or two. He'd scrag 'em for cowardice, else. Counting on it!"

The schooner ploughed on Northerly for a minute longer, before tacking again to lay herself half a mile in advance of the nearer *corvette*, now up on their larboard quarter. Some quick flag hoists were made, then both vessels hauled their wind a point free, to fall off on a bow-and-quarter line, "lasking," 'til they lay off *Proteus*'s starboard quarters once more, then came back to in-line-ahead, hard on the wind. The far *corvette* had fallen off, too, to match the distance to leeward that *Proteus* had lost with her Sutherly swing, all of them yet intent on bracketing, then pummeling, her.

But, by then, they had left it too late, and the Americans were upon them. *Sumter* swept in, abeam of *Proteus* and thrashing between on a furiously boiling bow and quarter wave, her gun-ports already opened and her curious bright red figurehead of a fighting cock with its neck outstretched and its wings spread in anger catching the reflections of sea-glint and appearing as if alive.

The French schooner hauled her wind, again, ducking to leeward to upset the aim of *Sumter*'s larboard gunners, showing the Yankee her stern. As she turned, she fired a ragged salvo from her larboard pop-guns, moments before *Sumter* returned the favour, and the sea about her frothed, leaped, and feathered anew with near-misses. And the schooner visibly trembled as heavy round-shot hammered into her. The French *corvette* astern of her hauled her wind, too, beginning to swing Sutherly. To stand on close-hauled to windward would open her vulnerable bows to a punishing rake, and to haul her wind too late would make the bow-rake even closer and more damaging! She would match her larboard guns to *Sumter*'s starboard cannon while running for home, and hope for the best!

While *Hancock*, massive as a rocky island fortress, bore down on the farther *corvette*, remaining upwind of her to oppose larboard guns to larboard guns . . . and just *slavering* for the Frenchman to haul off and expose her fragile stern timbers.

"Mister Catterall, stand by to engage the schooner, again! Do you haul off South, Mister Langlie," Lewrie bade.

Sumter arrowed in at an angle before swinging abeam of her foe, and both broadsides went off almost as one, instantly wreathing both ships in an angry grey thunderhead of spent powder smoke; upon which the schooner stood out in stark profile after *Proteus* had altered her course. The range was only half a mile, this time, but . . .

"Hold fire, Mister Catterall, 'til she sails below *Sumter*! We don't want t'hit our friends with 'overs'!" Lewrie cautioned. But all four vessels were running off the wind to the Suth'rd, denying *Proteus* a clean shot for long minutes whilst topmen aboard the schooner raked her tops'l gaskets free and let her extra canvas fall. With more sail aloft, she slowly began to inch ahead—then had the sauce to let loose her starboard guns at *Sumter*'s dis-engaged side, and, once settled down on course, raised her larboard ports and let fly at *Proteus*, to boot! The sharp, yipping bangs didn't amount to guns much larger than 4-pounders, and her small-diametre shot grazed twice or thrice, before sinking close-aboard with no effect, but Lewrie found it galling. And, as she finally sailed alee of *Sumter* and the battling *corvette*, out in clear air where they could fire on her, *Proteus* had to swing two points to windward so her guns could bear, even as the range began to open . . .

"Fire!" Lt. Catterall at last could howl, slashing his sword at the deck after long stomp-about-cursing moments of utter frustration. Low-aimed roundshot pillared and columned the waters round the French schooner, bounding from First Graze to dash low over her decks, gnaw a vicious bite from her bulwarks here and there, but . . . she sailed on, still firing—as if it were an equal contest!

"Point more to windward, Mister Langlie! Hit her, again, lads! *Gut that poxy, slug-eatin' whore!*" Lewrie raged, *knowing* that the schooner was out-footing his frigate, that if they didn't cripple her soon, he'd be forced to fall in astern of her and spin out a day-long stern-chase, in hopes of a few lucky hits from his forward chase-guns to whittle off her speed advantage. Had he been able to fire on her when she'd been closer, and dead abeam . . . !

Far down to leeward, USS *Oglethorpe* had merged with those fleeing merchantmen, a quick peek with a glass showed him. It looked like they had already struck their colours and fetched-to.

There goes all hope o' profit, Lewrie miserably surmised; *damme . . . I said I was feelin' generous, but not that generous, by God!*

"*Hancock* is engaging, Captain!" Lt. Langlie screeched, the only way he could be heard over the general din.

"This ought t'be int'resting," Lewrie muttered, turning aft.

The American frigate had clewed up her main course, and had let her way fall off a bit. Better than a mile and a half astern, she now appeared close enough to the French *corvette* to crash her yardarm tips against the French ship's yard ends, though there probably remained at least two cables' separation between them.

There was a concerted crash as *Hancock*'s weather-deck guns, the 12-pounders mounted on her stout and wide gangway, went off together, stabbing hot amber and red daggers at the *corvette*, creating a pall of gun-smoke that drifted down on the French warship. And the *corvette*'s sails and yards were savaged, spindly top-masts and shattered yardarms sent flying in ragged chunks, her dun-coloured sails clawed and bitten into great rents, whipping and collapsing in on themselves.

Hancock altered course in the last seconds as the two warships' images overlapped, laying her beam parallel to the French ship's side, and then . . .

"God help the Frogs," Lewrie muttered; rather insincerely, that.

Hancock's heavy lower-deck 24-pounders raged, and even at that distance it looked as if the *corvette* rocked and tipped, bobbing like a folded-paper boat on a pond, assailed by a heaping handful of pebbles flung by a spiteful child. Then, almost mercifully, all sight of her was blotted out by a titanic pall of powder smoke that blew down upon her, hiding her hurts from view. Even hidden, *Hancock*'s massive guns, firing as they bore and not in broadside, still thundered.

"Gawd!" was all that Lt. Langlie could say after seeing that.

"Exeunt, one French *corvette*, stage left," Lewrie said, awed by such a powerful display. "Damme if she ain't completely dis-masted . . . right down to the level of her bulwarks," he pointed out, as the smoke drifted alee and clear of the *corvette*, which now wallowed with all her motive power, and most of her way, stolen.

For their own part, Lt. Catterall was getting off another broadside at the French schooner, gnawing her just a bit more, peppering the sea about her, but inflicting no lasting harm. *Proteus* had to turn up to windward two more points to keep her guns aimed at her, but at the same time the schooner was hardening up to the Trades, too, and was in the lead, curving out a course ahead of their frigate's starboard bow.

Lewrie grimaced in frustration. The schooner would prove to be handier and more weatherly. *Proteus* could press up another point, and then she'd be close-hauled, sailing on the ragged edge of the wind and could go no higher. The schooner with its fore-and-aft sails could go at least a point higher, and end up directly ahead of them, where only the pair of chase-guns could worry at her, and not very effectively at that, as the bows plunged and soared, bludgeoning their way windward.

Within an hour, Lewrie knew, the schooner would be far enough up to windward on the larboard bows that only *one* chase-gun could fire; a swing to leeward to use all his larboard battery would put *Proteus* even farther behind and alee. One hour more, and the schooner would be out of gun-range.

He looked about for aid, but there was none. *Oglethorpe* was now back under sail after securing her two prizes, but was too far down in the South, alee of *Proteus*, to be of any avail. Oh, he could continue to chase the schooner, but he doubted he could catch her *this* side of Guadeloupe, unless something in her rigging carried away.

Lewrie drew a deep breath, held it, then let it out in a bitter sigh. He had the Americans to flatter and congratulate, in hopes that their sudden and complete victory might make them so giddy they might leap at continued cooperation, even alliance; and that was worth much more in the long run than a puny armed schooner taken as prize.

A *lack* of gunfire turned his attention Westerly. Far off, now almost hull-down, *Sumter* and the other French *corvette* had ceased firing, and were now cocked up to windward, fetched-to. No flag flew on the Frenchman's masts.

"Well, damme," Lewrie groaned aloud. "Might as well secure the guns, Mister Langlie. We'll not overhaul our Chase before beaching us on Guadeloupe. Do you concur, sir? Or do you prefer a shore supper?"

"Sadly, I do, sir," Langlie said, pouting with distaste and disappointment. "Game's not worth the candle. That is one fortunate Frog captain, out yonder. Skillful, too, sir."

"Aye, damn him ... whoever he is," Lewrie spat. "I fear we will hear more from him, in future. Very well, sir. Secure the guns, then get us about and lay us alongside *Hancock*. Where I must come over all 'Merry Andrew' and back-slap 'em. Makes me wish Mister Pelham had got aboard before we sailed ... he'd know how to 'piss down their backs' in the proper manner. *He's* the smarmy skill to appear sincere."

" 'Til they serve him boiled *okra*, sir," his First Lieutenant chirped, tongue-in-cheek. "Green, boiled, disgusting ... did he not say, Captain? With a dash of ground coal stirred in, too, sir."

"Hey?"

"Okra, and ashes from a coke furnace, Captain ... okra-*coke*, do ye see?" Langlie further japed.

"Now you're *really* reaching, Mister Langlie. Lame, lame, lame!"

"Very good, sir."

CHAPTER THIRTY-TWO

*I*t was a rather crowded little assembly as Lewrie's gig stroked over to the USS *Hancock*. *Oglethorpe* had fetched up her two prizes, as had *Sumter*, now looking a little worse for wear after fighting the longest engagement of the day with *her* French *corvette*. Eight vessels, now cocked up to windward within the compass of a quarter-mile, with boats bearing victorious officers back and forth, other boats transferring a host of prisoners into custody aboard the Yankee ships, or transferring U.S. Marines aboard the prizes to guard captured ships' companies.

Hancock's wide weather decks were crowded, too, as Lewrie stood atop the entry-port lip to receive the side-party's salute, smiling as pleasant as anyone could wish as he doffed his hat and looked about to see what damage the two-decker frigate had taken.

None, was his assessment! What little harm the *corvette*'s lone broadside had done aloft had already been most efficiently re-roved and only a few hands were still in her rigging, tidying up with paint, tar, or galley slush.

"Ah, Captain Lewrie!" the stern Capt. Malachi Goodell bellowed with uncharacteristic good cheer. "The author of our triumph over the idolators, I am bound, the very fellow who drew us on, like the pillar of smoke by day drew Moses through the Wilderness. Welcome aboard to thee, sir. Wilt thou partake in a celebratory cup of cider, Captain?"

"I would, Captain Goodell, and gladly offer you and your fellow captains my congratulations," Lewrie replied as a steward offered him a mug of something wet from a handsome coin-silver tray. Goodell's cider potation was cool, sweet, yet sprightly on the tongue . . . and vaguely alcoholic? Lewrie noted.

"Normally, I eschew befuddling spirits, sir," Goodell explained, to answer Lewrie's mildly puzzled look, "and encourage others to shun the demonic lure. A home-made and slightly aged apple cider, though . . . in strict moderation . . . may, on certain rare occasions, prove harmless. Though I still lament how prodigally our honest Americans imbibe the harder ciders, ladies, men, yea, even suckling babes in their cradles."

"Quite tasty and refreshing, Captain Goodell," Lewrie complimented him, despite the sermonising. "And with a full measure, may I propose a toast, gentlemen?" he said, perking up the assembled officers—McGilliveray, Randolph, and their first officers, along with commission officers in *Hancock*. "To the gallant Navy of the United States of America . . . may today's victory be but the first of many!"

"Hear, hear! Aye! Huzza! *Yyee-hahh!*" The last from the plump-phyzzed Georgian, Captain Randolph and his First Lieutenant; evidently Goodell's *mildly* aged cider was more inspiriting than Captain Goodell imagined, if taken aboard in sufficient quantities. And since cheers made for dry throats, the servants were hard-pressed to refill all the empty mugs.

And aye, McGilliveray had had a hard fight of it, for his opponent, *La Résolue*, had resisted bravely 'til her unfortunate Capt. MacPherson had perished, and all his deck officers had fallen, leaving it to a wounded Master Gunner to strike her colours, and *her* slaughter had been simply frightful, McGilliveray relished to inform him, but "Have no fear, Cap'm Lewrie, Desmond came through without a scratch, and he showed as cool and brave as ever ya could ask for. First across, when we come up close-aboard and stormed her. And how's that new kitty he gave ya, he begged me ask?"

"Missed *all* th' fun," Capt. Randolph imparted, between mugs of "sore-needed refreshment." "Mount fourteen spankin' fine twelve-pounders, and only fired six o' th' starboard batt'ry, at two ships, and they struck quick'z a wink, they did. Aye, fourteen of 'em, an' long-

nines on focs'le and quarterdeck, too, twenty-two guns. Don't that
beat all for a li'l ol' converted brig o' war? Oh, too bad that schooner
out-footed ya. A clean sweep'd been sweeter by far, but . . . somebody
has t'run back t'Guadeloupe with his tail 'twixt his legs an' bear th'
bad news to that devil Choundas, don't ya know."

"Perhaps next time, so well-armed, sir, your gallant *Oglethorpe* will
be the one to surprise greedy and unwary Frenchmen," Lewrie said,
feeling unctuous . . . and irked, though striving to please. "Assuming
they'll feel pugnacious, after such a drubbing as you gave 'em today.
'Twas smartly, quickly, and efficiently done, sir. My congratulations
to you, and your accurate gunners."

"A moment, Captain Lewrie?" Goodell intruded, now more formal
in mien. "Wouldst thou care to meet one of our unfortunate French?
Allow me to name to thee *Capitaine de Vaisseau* Humbert Griot of *Le
Gascon*. Captain Griot, may I present to thee Captain Alan Lewrie, of
His Britannic Majesty's ship *Proteus*?"

"Captain Griot," Lewrie said, shifting his cider mug to his left hand
and doffing his hat with his right, making a formal "leg" to that
grizzled, unshaven worthy. "My regrets for your loss this day, sir."

"*Capitaine* Loo— . . . Lew-ray," Griot grumbled back, with a quick
doff of his own hat, but no bow; he was an anti-*aristo* Republican to
the soles of his shabby boots. "So . . . *you* are ze devil I meet at las'
. . . ze one 'oo obsess *Capitaine* Choundas to ze frantic. But for a spy
e *vous, nevair* you find us, I am thinking, *non*?"

"Tosh, sir," Lewrie scoffed, though tapping sagaciously at the side
of his nose. "I was lucky, was all. Spies! What rot! Your old master
Choundas was born with spies on the brain, sir. And how is the poor
old fellow, might I enquire?" Lewrie said with a lofty smirk.

"Why, thou mayst ask him thyself, Captain Lewrie," Capt. Goodell
said, his eyes merry with delight, and his teeth bared 'neath his hedge-
like beard and mustachios. "For here that fiend doth arrive, even as
we speak." Goodell chuckled, waving a hand towards the sound of
blocks squealing above the starboard side.

Jerking foot by jerking foot, a bosun's chair slung from a main yard
rose up over the *Hancock*'s bulwarks, bearing a bedraggled figure who
sat slumped defeatedly, one palsied and liver-spotted hand clinging to
the canvas chair-sling. Pasty-pale, that long-despised face as it weakly
swung its gaze in-board in the dullest curiosity, or an attempt at proud
disdain, to regard its conquerors with that one good eye.

Uniform tar-stained and smutted with powder smoke and sailcloth dust, rumpled and suddenly too big for his frame, his hat gone and his thinning reddish hair wildly disarrayed, Capt. Guillaume Choundas would have seemed a pathetic apparition. He had also suffered a wound in his bad leg, the red-spotted bandages visible through the rent that a surgeon had made in the thigh of his trousers; with a second gash high on his forehead, right on his receding hair line.

"And *that*, in the end, is thy wily, implacable Nemesis, Captain Lewrie?" Captain Goodell sourly wondered aloud. "Tsk, tsk."

"*Fou!*" Lewrie heard the sullen Griot whisper under his breath. "*Qu'il aille au diable! Nom d'un chien . . . engoulevent!*" Which slurs made Goodell stiffen in pious indignation. And Lewrie smile wickedly; for Griot had called Choundas "fool," had damned him, had accused him of being a "God-damned goat-sucker," to boot!

"*Vous!*" Choundas snarled, soon as he clapped eyes on Lewrie, in a vitriolic snarl that conveyed nearly fifteen years of brooding anger and pain, his undying lust for revenge, since that bright tropic morn when he'd fallen to Lewrie's sword on the pristine beach at Balabac in the Spanish Philippines.

"Why *hallo*, 'Willy'!" Lewrie gaily rejoined in a mocking drawl, and tipping his hat with glee once he'd gotten over his utter surprise. "Havin' a bad day, are we . . . ye foetid old bugger?"

"Captain Lewrie, really!" Goodell primly chid him. "Such abuse for an honourably surrendered and now-helpless foe . . . thy long-standing personal *animus* notwithstanding . . . I'll not have it, not aboard an American man o' war, sir! The gentlemanly and honourable courtesies will be observed 'twixt foes, who are, in defeat, foes no longer."

Choundas was swung in-board and lowered to the deck, landing on his good leg but instantly collapsing like a sack of clothes when his hamstrung leg tried to share the load. With a hiss, Choundas summoned the reluctant Griot to his side to help him stand, to shake his uniform into better order, and take a few steps.

"*M'sieur*," Choundas said, blatantly ignoring Lewrie to concentrate on Goodell, "you 'ave ze best of me, *Capitaine*, an' 'ave honourably defeated me. To you is ze *victoire*, an' I 'umbly offer to you my sword," he concluded, knackily shamming nobility, to play off Lewrie's churlishness. With Griot's help, Choundas freed his scabbard from his belt-frog and extended the costly and ornate blade hilt first.

Oh no, don't . . . ! Lewrie thought, in a panic, dreading what was coming. Sure enough, *Le Hideux*'s good eye darted at Lewrie, with his lips curled in a tiny smirk of triumph.

"Ahem . . . !" Lewrie began, like a first attempt to call a waiter.

"Thy reputation precedes thee, Captain Choundas," Goodell said, looking down his raptor's beak at the man, and the temptation of that priceless smallsword that could grace Goodell's mantel for generations, "and I tell thee plain, *monsoor*, wert thou capable of offering an *iota* of resistance or deviltry, what I know of thee tempts me to clap thee in irons, regardless of thy rank and dignities . . ."

That's the way, man! Lewrie silently exulted; take *that sword, and guard him close!* Deep *on your orlop, among the rats!*

"Nonetheless, I feel it my duty as a Christian gentleman, and a fellow professional officer of my country's Navy, on which I will allow no slur concerning the proper treatment of prisoners that might sully its glorious name, to take thee as thou stands, an officer and a gentleman of *thy* navy, who may freely and honourably offer his parole, on thy personal bond of honour . . ."

"*Bluck!*" Lewrie objected, stupefied past real words!

". . . strictly admitting that the betrayal of such personal word will redound to the greatest discredit upon thyself, thy navy, and thy Republic," Goodell concluded, casting a dubious look at Lewrie. "Wilt thou offer thy parole, or wilt thou surrender, sir?" he posed.

"To such generosity of ze spirit, ze Christian spirit, *m'sieur*, *naturellement*, I am mos' 'appy to accept your offer of parole, *merci beaucoup bien!*" Choundas rasped back, his cruel, scarred lips forming a creditable facsimile of a lamb-innocent, and grateful, smile.

"Mine arse on a band-box!" Lewrie said in a fretful whisper: "I fear I *must* protest, Captain Goodell! Christian charity aside, sir . . . most creditable to you . . . Choundas simply *can't* be trusted. He should be *my* prisoner. His Majesty's Government has the older, and greater, claim on him, and . . . !"

"Did *thy* ship vanquish his, Captain Lewrie?" Goodell cooed back, suddenly come over Arctic ice, his owl-eyes asquint as if focussed on prey. "Did he strike his colours to *thee*? He did *not!* Were he thine, he would languish in chains and filth aboard a prison-hulk at English Harbour for years, as *I* languished in British captivity, sir . . . just to satisfy thy *animus*, which is unbecoming in an officer and gentleman of thy repute, sir! Though his soul be sold to the Devil long ago, and his sins the vilest scarlet, yea, even so, I could never subject even *him* to such cruelty. Captain Choundas is now *mine*, taken in honourable battle. Unless and until he does anything to violate his sacred honour, I am honour-bound to take his parole at face value, or defame my country's trustworthiness. Captain Choundas is an *American* prisoner, sir, the fruit of an *American* victory, and I will brook no further dispute of the matter."

"But France isn't at *war* with the United States, he'll be let go, he'll . . . !" Lewrie spluttered, appalled.

"Thun-der-*ation*!" Goodell bellowed. "Did I not say the matter is closed, sir? Thou wouldst gainsay me on my own quarterdeck, sir?"

Lewrie withered under Goodell's fury, blushing furiously to be dressed-down before the American officers and sailors like an idiotic midshipman . . . before Choundas's sly scorn! "He's dangerous, he . . ."

"No longer, Captain Lewrie," Goodell said, seeming to relent. "At limited liberty ashore in the United States, Choundas will work no more deviltry. And since no formal declaration of war exists, there will *be* no prisoner exchanges possible, Captain Lewrie. Neither do the French yet hold a single U.S. Navy officer of comparable rank to *offer* in exchange . . . dost thou *see*, sir?" Goodell concluded in much calmer voice, his beard-shrouded lips curling in the faintest of grins and his owl-eyes, for a brief moment, twinkling with glee.

Damme, did the old stickleback just wink *at me?* Lewrie gawped.

"Captain Choundas will be sent to an American seaport, with my report of his capture . . . and his *nature* . . . made public knowledge to one and all, Captain Lewrie. He will work no further havoc. Nor, return to France before the turn of the century, in my estimation. That is the *most* I may promise thee, sir, and thou must be satisfied with that."

Lewrie realised that the game was blocked at both ends; he had lost, and must put the best face he could on his defeat. He heaved a bitter sigh, then said, with passable good grace, "I s'pose I must, at that, sir. Please forgive my zeal to see such a dangerous foe placed where I'd *know* he could do no more mischief. *Had* I captured Choundas, I could do no less, *did* he offer his parole . . . no matter how *galling*! My congratulations to you, sir, and I wish you all the notice and fame that pertains to such a triumph. To yourself, your officers and tars . . . and to the glory of your Navy, and the United States of America."

I nabbed him, though, Lewrie grimly told himself; *I'd not have given him the* chance *to hand over his sword. Board his ship and shoot him down, run him through . . . not give Choundas time to strike colours! Could I have . . . in the heat of the moment? Or lose my command and my honour, get court-martialed for murderin' a prisoner? God,* please, *he looks so old and sick, You could pluck him with a fever, or something! A bad batch of oysters . . . any cause! He has to die, else I'll never be able to rest easy! Hmmm . . . there must be a way . . .*

"Zealousness in the pursuit of one's duty is ever forgivable, sir," Capt. Goodell was saying, stroking his whiskers in glee to have a Briton apologise to him for *anything*, "even though thy zeal might be adulterated by personal motives. Thank thy Maker, Captain Lewrie, that, in thy pursuit of just revenge upon such a monster, personal zeal did not overcome the *professional*, and that thine own hands, and immortal soul, remain unsullied. Great Jehovah's justice will grind Choundas, be sure of that, yea, even unto chaff and powdered, blighted seed, so black and withered that his evil will be spurned even by the hungriest birds of the air or beasts of the field . . . and shalt never take root in the fertilest soil."

"Amen, sir," Lewrie replied with a fervor he could not really feel; what he felt was oily and unctuous to sham piety, but . . . needs must. "Well, then sir. I will take my leave. You will sail back to English Harbour, Captain Goodell? Good. Please allow me to request that you bear my despatches about today's action to my superiors."

"Thou will not enter harbour, sir?" Goodell asked.

"Fear I'm bound away on another matter, sir," Lewrie answered, tipping him a conspiratorial wink, as if a duty of even greater import awaited him, one of a secret nature. "I shall say my goodbyes to Captains McGilliveray and Randolph. My congratulations, again, and . . . do we have future occasion to work together, to the confusion of the French . . . or *another* mutual enemy, please recall that I owe you a duty, and a service, and would move Heaven and Earth to fulfill it."

"Loath though I am to admit it, Captain Lewrie," Goodell said as he tentatively offered his hand, looking down at it for a moment as if he could not credit that he was doing so, or that his hand moved of its *own* volition, "I find myself almost looking forward to such cooperation. Should my country and thine find common cause, mind."

They shook on that informal bargain; even though Goodell's paw felt much like a limp, dead flounder, they at least shook on it.

"Off again, are ya, Cap'm Lewrie?" McGilliveray said, frowning. "I was hoping you could dine aboard just one more time. The lad—"

"Fear I must, sir," Lewrie said, shrugging sadly. "Promise me that, if *Sumter* bears Choundas to America, you watch him close, parole be damned, will you?" he urged. "And keep Desmond away from him, every minute! If Choundas learns who he is to me, and he will, I'm certain of it . . . he has his ways! . . . he'll find a way to take revenge on me and kill him, if he can. Cripple him as bad as he's crippled, at the least! For God's sake, I beg you, Captain McGilliveray, don't trust Choundas with a rusty fork."

"I will, though I don't quite—" McGilliveray quickly vowed.

"Before I depart, I'll send a letter aboard for the . . . for my son, telling him the same, and that . . . that he's . . . that Desmond is shapin' main-well to become a fine young man, and I wouldn't want any harm to come to him. Which I hope you'll say, as well, sir, from me?"

Lewrie dug out his wash-leather coin-purse and clawed down for a few shillings. " 'Til we meet again, he might find need for some things at the chandleries and shops, so—"

"No need o' that, Cap'm Lewrie," McGilliveray protested. "He's his Navy pay, such as it is, and a modicum o' private means as my adopted nephew. Desmond needs time with his real father, more than money. Once you're back from your pursuit, sir, we'll make time for that to happen. For the nonce, count on me t'keep him safe, and well t'windward of that devil."

"I could ask no better than that, Captain McGilliveray, thankee kindly," Lewrie responded, somewhat eased in his mind, but knowing his foe of old, worries for the lad's safety would not quite disperse that easily. He put his purse away, chiding himself for a callous bastard, for feeling relief that "fatherhood" wouldn't *cost* too much; that his new-found son Desmond came with his own sustenance!

"A lucky lad, sir," McGilliveray commented, "with two families, two fathers, really . . . so concerned for his wellbeing."

"One who left it much too late, sir, but . . ." Lewrie confessed.

"But makin' up for it in splendid fashion," McGilliveray told him warmly. "God speed your fine ship, Cap'm Lewrie, and your return."

EPILOGUE

"You lead a charmed life, Lieutenant Hainaut," Representative-on-Mission Desfourneaux told Jules over a convivial glass of wine, at the end of his verbal report. "So . . ." Desfourneaux said, prissily setting his wineglass down on his "appropriated" marble-topped desk with a precise little *click*. "The redoubtable *Capitaine* Choundas was taken, both *corvettes* and the arms convoy were taken, by the Americans, you say, not the British. Yet Choundas's *bête noire*, Lewrie, discovered it, and led them to it . . . yet took little part, hmmm. A failure. A regrettable failure, and a great loss to France."

"Yes, Citizen, assuredly," Hainaut replied, not sure of what he could say, in safety. Would he be blamed for surviving, or did their representative from the Directory imagine that he was the one who had alerted the British and the Americans?

"In the long run, though, your former master had outlived his usefulness," Desfourneaux went on with a wee *moue* of regret. "He was ill, one could see that, and as a result his faculties were diminished. Had this Lewrie person not been present as a lure, Choundas might have put about and saved the convoy for another try, later on. Might the British have planned to use Lewrie as bait, because your former master had become too . . . predictable in his lust for revenge?"

"It is possible, Citizen Desfourneaux," Hainaut allowed with an enigmatic shrug. "He *was* obsessed by Lewrie, for a certainty."

"To the detriment of all else he was trusted to do, alas," the voice of central authority grumbled, leaning back in his comfortably padded chair, and sighing theatrically. "Both Hugues, and Choundas, lost to the Revolution's further service. A clean . . . sweep, hah!" Desfourneaux chirped as if secretly pleased. "Both too brutal and direct. Useful, in the early days and the Terror, but . . . France is now in need of subtler, cleverer men. Men of action, naturally, but those who understand when to employ wits, *or* the sword. Men such as you, I do believe, Lieutenant Hainaut."

"Indeed, Citizen?" Hainaut perked up warily.

"Indeed," Desfourneaux reiterated, turning more business-like. "With the loss of *Capitaines* Choundas, Griot, and MacPherson, and the earlier loss of *Capitaine* Desplan and *Le Bouclier*, our naval power in the Caribbean is gone. You, and that Lieutenant Récamier, whom Choundas needlessly relieved of sea-duties, just to make him a scapegoat and object lesson, some few others, must make do until my reports to Paris produce a re-enforcing squadron. Choundas . . . *Le Hideux*," Desfourneaux said with a simper, as if emboldened by Capt. Choundas's enforced absence to damn him with his behind-the-back slur, "recommended you highly. His papers, which I seized after his departure, also absolved you of any suspicions of treachery, or any hint of collusion with British agents."

"I see, Citizen," Hainaut replied, allowing himself the tiniest smirk of derision for his former employer, as if sharing Desfourneaux's disdain. "Although I feel insulted that I was *ever* suspected, after serving him so well." Though Jules Hainaut could not help worrying about what else the ogre had written about him.

"Récamier I appoint a *Capitaine de Vaisseau*," Desfourneaux intoned formally, "and will assign him the best remaining ship suitable for conversion and arming. From what others here on Guadeloupe say of him, he is much too good to idle ashore, and was treated most shabbily by that vicious old cripple. He will command all our ships, now."

"An admirable choice, Citizen, pardon me for saying."

"Related by marriage to a dead naval hero," Desfourneaux chuckled, waving a hand in the air dismissively, "Admiral de Brueys. Fool that he was to lose his whole fleet to that Nelson at Aboukir Bay. As harmful as it was to the *esprit* of the revolutionary masses, it wasn't *all* his fault. That ambitious climber, General Bonaparte, might just as well have staked him out for slaughter. Rest assured, *mon cher*, in our good time the Directory will make *that* upstart pay, too. For you . . . you, Hainaut, ahem. By the plenipotentiary power granted me by the Directory as their *Représantant-En-Mission*, you I make a *Capitaine de Frégate* . . . to serve as Récamier's strong right arm and second-in command."

"I . . . I don't know what to say!" Hainaut exclaimed in wonder.

"A small *merci beaucoup* will suffice," Desfourneaux simpered at him. "I confirm you in command of your schooner *La Mohican*, and will assign another into the, uhm . . . *Chippewa?* . . . to pair with your vessel. Of course, France expects great things from you, *Capitaine* Hainaut," he said, turning serious. "When strong enough, eventually, this 'Bloody' *Capitaine* Alan Lewrie you must eliminate. Do not take it as your sole task, as your old master did, but . . . he must be cornered and defeated. He must be seen by our *people* to pay for the loss of such a hero as . . . Guillaume Choundas," Desfourneaux sardonically sneered.

"I will do it . . . someday, Citizen," Hainaut eagerly vowed.

"*Bon!* For now, though, concentrate on British shipping. The Directory has disavowed our war on American trade as Victor Hugues's doing." Desfourneaux paused to shrug. "Perhaps in a few months, they will again be 'good prize,' who knows? The last packet that slipped through the blockade bore no news about an Anglo-American alliance, or an American declaration of war, so, for now, we will not take actions that *goad* the 'rustics' into taking hands with the 'Bloodies,' nor declaring open war. But some victories over the many small cutters and sloops of the British blockade would not go amiss, *n'est-ce pas?*"

"I am looking forward to them, Citizen Desfourneaux, and thank you, again, for your trust in me," Hainaut declared, knocking back his glass of wine in celebration, now that he knew (for the *moment*) where he stood in the Directory's estimation, and firmly vowing to himself that he would do nothing to lower that estimation; would indeed wreak such havoc on the British that the Directory raised their opinions of him, paving the way for even higher rank, and fame.

An intricate ormulu clock chimed on the marble-topped sideboard in Desfourneaux's pleasant office in the upper levels of the grim Fort Fleur d'Epée, and the man slapped his leather-bound workbooks shut in a fussily pleased fashion. Desfourneaux rose and poured both of

their wineglasses full, again, gave Hainaut a playful little smile, and
then crooked a finger to command him out onto the stone balcony
overlooking the courtyard of the fort.

"Now that our business is at an end, *Capitaine* Hainaut, we will
witness the end of another, less fortunate, bit of business. Do bring
the bottle . . . this may take some time," Desfourneaux directed.

The fort's massive gates had been flung open to allow the towns-
people and islanders inside. A battalion of the garrison stood rigid,
under arms, as the tumbrils rolled into the large courtyard, drawn by
artillery horses. The tall wooden wheels of the tumbrils groaned and
clattered on the cobblestones, wobbling on their hubs; the un-greased
axles keened dirge-like, and the fairly open-woven wicker frames atop
the tumbrils' beds shook and trembled, in tune with the men and
women who rode them, wide-eyed and refusing to believe, as the short
line of big carts slowly rolled to the foot of the steps that led to the
high wood platform, and the waiting guillotine.

The crowd began to titter and jeer, to cat-call and curse those people
in the carts. The soldiers were allowed to raise their muskets and shake
them in anger, too, as the taunts of the crowd built in rage and volume,
as the first of the condemned were led or dragged aloft to the executioners, to answer for their crimes of treason, treachery, the betrayal
of so many gallant officers, warrants, and beloved sailors lost with the
convoy, and that hero of the Republic who had succumbed, not to
superior force, but had been sold out to the despised British, for
"Bloodies'" gold.

The heavy, slanted blade rose slowly, foot by agonising foot as if
to draw things out for the mob's screaming pleasure, before the pincer-
like release mechanism locked in place. The names, the crimes, the
sentences were screeched out over the crowd roar, the lanyard was
tautened, and then the blade flashed down to slam its great weight and
its razor-sharp edge into the bottom of the blocks. And the heads of
the criminals and traitors flew off, to land in the bushel-baskets, teeth
in those harvested heads still chattering, lips still writhing with a final
prayer or protest, eyes rolling like a slaughtered heifer's, and a gout,
a fountain, an eruption of blood gushing outward as the hearts in those
"shortened" bodies continued to beat in thudding terror for a moment
or two, and members of the crowd howled and shrieked with glee,
rushing to catch droplets on scraps of cloth for souvenirs.

Last came the arch-traitor, the one who had betrayed a paragon of the Revolution, his own master. Etienne de Gougne was hauled down from his tumbril, its last occupant, with his shirt open, and his neck bared. His long, Republican locks had been shorn at the nape so nothing would impede the blade. Hands bound behind his back, bound from chest to waist in old, cast-off naval ropes, too, de Gougne tried to struggle even so, thinly screaming his innocence, damning Choundas as a bitter, overly suspicious fool, which protests made the mob shout even louder, booing and laughing at his ridiculous desperation.

There was a drum-roll that went on and on for what seemed like a whole minute after Etienne's head was locked in place. The mob *liked* suspense, those executioners knew. Finally . . .

Shisshh—thud!—"Hurrah!" and the entertainment was done.

"Thus perish all who would spurn the superiority of our glorious Republic," Desfourneaux intoned, one hand lifted over the balcony balustrade like a church noble bestowing his general blessings. "Well, so much for that, Hainaut," he continued, turning amicable. "This puts an end to most of our spies and traitors, for now. Some few may have eluded us, but there is nothing like wholesale executions to run the rest into hiding, or ineffectiveness. We will get the rest eventually. I am nothing if not a patient man," he said with a supremely satisfied sniff, tossing off the rest of his glass of wine.

"I still can't believe that de Gougne, that timid little mouse, could have—" Hainaut dared to say.

"Guillaume Choundas was noted for his nose where spies and reactionaries were concerned," Desfourneaux interrupted. "If in little else of late. I am utterly convinced his instincts were correct. Choundas gone . . . de Gougne and his suspected collaborators gone? The end of a problem . . . *chop!* Ha ha!" Desfourneaux tittered.

Hainaut resisted the urge to rub the back of his neck to assure himself that his head was still attached, and would most likely remain where God intended it, for the nonce.

"You and *Capitaine* Récamier must dine with me tonight, Hainaut," Desfourneaux happily suggested. "Shall we say at eight, when the heat of the day is dissipated? I have appropriated Choundas's town mansion, so you know the way. I also sleep in your old bed-chamber. What tales it could tell, *hein?*" he said with a sly leer.

"Well . . ." Hainaut smirked, shrugging like a man of the world.

"Executions, ah . . ." Desfourneaux frowned, lowering his voice to cordial intimacy. "For some reason they excite me, much as they did the amatory humours of the masses in Paris in the early days. Going at each other in the court balconies, the doorways of Place de Bastille. An affirmation of life in the face of death, perhaps? You are known as one familiar with this island's, ah . . . pleasures, Hainaut. Maybe you could recommend to me a lady, or ladies, amenable to an evening of dalliance. Clean, mind . . . no English Pox!" he blushingly quibbled. "Handsome, it goes without saying. Young and pretty, not too tawdry? *Not* as tender as those your old master preferred, *Mon Dieu, non!* You understand."

"Completely, Citizen," Hainaut replied, his smirk turning to a knowing leer. "Just the one as a mistress, or a new one each *evening?* Two, three at a time? French-born, Creole . . . part-White, or a swart tigress for a change of pace? On Guadeloupe, everything is for sale, anything is possible. And so willing to please, ah! But of course I can aid your search, Citizen!"

Hainaut had whore-mongered for Choundas when succulent prisoners or their tender daughters were unavailable; pimping for a Voice of the Directory could prove equally favourable to his cause. M. Desfourneaux at least had *conventional* tastes, he suspected, so the courtesans he'd already sampled would suit admirably.

And as long as he pimped, he might as well profit from it. A pact with madames and *bordel* owners, the girls themselves, could fill his own purse. He contemplated strumming them first, *then* escorting them to Desfourneaux "prepared for battle" so to speak—with what the British termed "battered buns"?—serving to Desfourneaux his "fresh-served" seconds might prove to be the drollest kind of *geste.* Overcharge him for island-made sheep-gut cundums . . . ?

"Would this afternoon prove soon enough, Citizen?" *Capitaine de Frégate* Jules Hainaut lazily enquired. "I have in mind a delectably sweet Octoroon, just barely seventeen, but already possessed of skills one could not find in Paris, itself. Petite, playful . . ."

"As a matter of fact, Hainaut, I think I *will* go home at once. Take my mid-day meal, so many preparations for our supper, tonight . . ." Desfourneaux announced, all but fingering his crotch in anticipation. "Uhm . . . by three this afternoon, you might . . . ah?"

"By half past *one,* Citizen," Hainaut promised, him. "And may I wish you . . . *bon appétit?*"

⚓

Late that evening and far out to sea to windward of Guadeloupe, USS *Hancock* prowled a moon-drenched sea hungry for prey, like a wraith on All-Hallow's Eve. While Citizen Desfourneaux improved his *digestif* with a *second* courtesan fetched as a house-warming present by his old aide-de-camp, *Capitaine* Guillaume Choundas sat on the edge of the hard bunk in his tiny deal-partitioned cabin forward of the officers' gun-room, beset by American cuisine. Salt-pork, soup beans, yams, ship's biscuit, and greasy gravy griped his innards like smelting lumps of ore, and bile surged up now and then to sear his throat. As for that corn-whisky they had offered . . . pah!

Griot, in the insubstantial next-door cabin, snored away, insensible to swinish victuals, defeat, and captivity alike, making Choundas despise his peasant's dullness. His own ears and face burned with the utter shame of loss, of being out-witted, of failing so completely . . . of being so *wrong*! His repute and career were utterly *lost*, his place sure to be awarded to one of the *handsome*, swaggering charmers, and all *he* had done would be forgotten, dismissed as ancient history if remembered at all. The Americans might hold him, gallingly inactive; months and months, *years*! of penny-pinching, miserly parole.

And that swaggering pig Lewrie still lived! As if his life was charmed! As if the very Heavens, the fickle ancient gods, conspired to preserve and reward him!

Choundas fantasised that he'd find a way to kill him, slip into England as a crippled *émigré* beggar and murder his wife and children, if nothing else, but *how?* All his fortune would be gone, he would be penniless! And Choundas could feel that *time* for revenge was growing shorter. His marvelous body, his iron constitution, was betraying him. If Lewrie were to die by his hand, it *might* be with his last breath, as he had always vowed, never suspecting . . . !

Nonetheless, Guillaume Choundas vowed that he *would* murder his Nemesis; find a way to delude the simple-minded Americans and escape; destroy Griot for letting him down, for being a dull shop-keeper fraud in bear-skin slippers, not a Venetic conqueror! He *would* take revenge on faithless Jules Hainaut for abandoning the battle like the cynical coward he really was, he *would* win back his position and honours . . . !

But he had to press a grimy towel to his lips to stem a flood of bile and vomit; had to squeeze his buttocks together to prevent an even greater shame before he could stagger aft to the quarter-gallery with

the aid of a crude loaned crutch. His bowels screamed in stony rend-
ings, and shuddery looseness, both, while fiery stabbings in his stomach
popped cold, woozy sick-sweat that flooded his body like an Arctic
dunking. Weak and faint, his sphinctre failed him, and for the first
time in his life, Guillaume Choundas succumbed to despair, giving out
a faint, bleak whimper as he crammed the end of the towel into his
mouth to deny the world the pleasure of hearing his helplessness. Hot,
galling tears trickled from his eyes, searing his cheeks, to make his
humiliation complete.

"I must not die before he does, please!" Choundas whispered to the
groaning oaken darkness, almost in prayer. But to which gods?

The hilltop overlooking the vast encampment was bathed in moonlight
as General Toussaint L'Ouverture stood under the fly of a grand
pavillion that once had sheltered a French General of Brigade in splen-
dour, looking down at his sleeping army and its guttering cook-fires,
and felt his own despair for his long-suffering but hopeful people . . .
for the future of St. Domingue, which some had begun to call Haiti
in Creole *patois*. Its reluctant leader, short, bandy-legged, and unre-
markable, plied a cane fan, seeing not a rag-tag army, but an island
beset on all sides by a brutal, opportunistic outside world, just as the
encampment was girded by forbidding forests and jungle.

The Americans threatened; those bland-faced, smiling *slaveowners*
must be shown that they could never buy or steal part, or all, of Haiti.
He must *use* them, but keep them at arm's-length. Else their merchants
would buy, or raid for, slaves close to home, much cheaper than
human chattel shipped from West Africa. Sadly, there were "Haitians"
who'd be *more* than happy to profit in such an evil trade, preying on
their darkest and poorest, just like the kings of far-off Dahomey or
Guinea.

The aggressive and wily British, who'd sent that perfect *fool* to
barter with him, still lusted for St. Domingue, though they ruled all
the other Sugar Isles already. Their "gifts" and pledges would bring
fresh chains for his people, too. And so, must be beguiled and strung
along, yet ultimately spurned.

And—heart-breakingly—Mother France plotted to restore the plantation system, to fill her war coffers with gold, and if that new-come
General Hédouville's schemes bore fruit, hordes of the *grands blancs*

would flood back in, with a huge army of occupation, to enforce their will. Vast profitable plantations would re-arise, their workers only *half*-starved this time, paid *next*-to-nothing, if not re-enslaved outright . . . after the requisite bloodbaths and "taming" massacres.

Hédouville craftily hoped to divide, conquer, and weaken, play rivals off in another "War of the Skin," then crush the feeble winner. To stave him off, to counter that brute, there was only one course of action open, though Toussaint L'Ouverture dreaded the price his people would have to pay. But St. Domingue—Haiti—must be one, or it was doomed, so the island's reluctant, unschooled master of war *could not* shrink from it if he wished his people's fragile freedom passed to their future generations.

So . . . in the morning, before first light, his sleeping soldiers must march on South Province, make a pre-emptive "War of the Skin" on those who would rule a breakaway *part* of the whole, for the profit of a *few*, armed, succoured, and beholden to the re-enslaving outsiders, and make *all* the blood, fire, and horror suffered so far—enough for the entire world, enough for a millennium!—to have been in vain.

Before first light, Toussaint L'Ouverture would march against the Mulatto Republic, and faithless General André Rigaud.

Under that same moonlight, HMS *Proteus* snored her way Sutherly under all plain sail, to the West of Guadeloupe, her eerie ghost-grey sails spiralling metronome-fashion against the star-strewn sky. Five Bells of the Evening Watch were struck up forward, slowly tolling half past Ten—*dong-dong . . . dong-dong . . . dong*—that the ship's boy at the belfry let echo brassily on as he turned the half-hour glass, and went back to nodding.

Captain Alan Lewrie, RN, lay nude under a sheet in his swaying wide-enough-for-two bed-cot, flat on his back with his hands enlaced under the musty down pillows, striving for sleep. He'd dined on fresh red snapper that Gideon, the frigate's talented cook, had caught in a slack-wind hour that morning; he'd washed it down with a whole bottle of tangy, fruit-sweet Beaujolais from a mixed case that the Georgian, Capt. Randolph of USS *Oglethorpe*, had presented to him off one of those rich prizes they'd taken. He *should* have been snoring, but he wasn't.

He should have been pleased—yet he wasn't.

Lewrie could congratulate himself that he had his great-cabins to himself, that he'd rid himself of that callow idiot the Honourable Grenville Pelham, even Mr. James Peel, as if he'd made them "walk the plank" or marooned them on infamous and desolate Sombrero Cay like the pirates of old. He could happily savour, too, the fact that *his* part in their schemes, the do-able part of all-but-impossible orders from the Crown, was over and done with, and he could not *imagine* a reason why they'd call on his services, ever again. Sometimes surliness and truculence had their uses, he could gleefully contemplate!

Yet he still heaved frustrated sighs, stretching and wriggling to wring wakefulness from his body, his mind still stewing on his one failure. For Guillaume Choundas, though captured and defanged, still *lived*, damn his eyes! The look on the bastard's face, when he at last tumbled to how confining a gaol his parole had committed him to, was simply priceless. Yet . . .

Choundas was still so *very* clever! Lewrie was mortal-certain he'd find a way to delude his Yankee captors, then do *something* that'd prove to his masters in France that he was still useful and effective. Play-act meek, crippled, and inoffensive, spy on them, then sneak his observations to the Directory somehow?

Or would Choundas think that revenge against him mattered more? Did he discover that Desmond was his, so young and trusting, he *still* could find a way, even in ball-and-chain, and . . . !

"And what am I doing with a half-grown son?" Lewrie groaned in the darkness. "Haven't known him a Dog-Watch, so why's he so dear?"

Lewrie hoped that his hastily penned letters might bear fruit. One to James Peel, boasting his victory, yet suggesting that, had he ever done HM Government good service, could he shepherd the lad when he stepped ashore on Antigua, if Choundas was landed there as well . . . that James Peel should do what should be done with Choundas's life if there was a way, *before* that monster could get to his new-found son.

Several letters, copies of the same one really, to Christopher Cashman; to every seaport town he'd mentioned before sailing away to a new life in America—Savannah, Charleston, Georgetown, or Port Royal in South Carolina, Wilmington or New Bern in North Carolina; Beaufort, however differently pronounced, in both states. Letters which pleaded with him, that, should he *ever* have loved him as a friend, Kit might take time from establishing himself to ascertain in which naval port that ogre Choundas would spend his parole. Hire a crew of bully-bucks, for which Lewrie would gladly reimburse him, and ". . . I implore you my dearest friend, for my peace, and the peace of the world, *slay him!*"

A letter to warn Desmond, though how *fearfully* on-guard a bold, callow 'tween would bear himself did not bear thinking about. One to his adoptive uncle and captain, too, though no matter how careful that Capt. McGilliveray had vowed to be, he simply *couldn't* grasp just how dangerous Choundas was, and . . .

Something heavy up forrud slid, then went thump! Thence came a Crash-Thud that roused Lewrie to his elbows. "*What* the bloody Hell?" he groused, rolling out of bed and wrapping himself in the sheet, then padding towards the sounds to see what was the matter.

Even by moonlight streaming in through the overhead coach-top, Lewrie could see that his chart-space was a mess. Rolled charts were scattered, several books from the fiddle-rack shelves were now on the slanted desk-top, and brass dividers and rulers were underfoot, along with several pencils, and Capt. McGilliveray's parting gift of a brace of rare and costly steel-nib pens he *thought* he'd carefully stowed.

"Good God A'mighty," he muttered, padding aft again. And *there* were his house-breakers! Two sets of eyes peeked over the rim of the hat-box, reflecting moonlight like four green glimmers of fox-fire . . . wide and innocent "t'weren't us yer honour, sir, honest!" eyes.

"Boys, boys," he said, sighing as he knelt before their hat-box lair; Toulon taking up most of it. "I expect such from Chalky, he's a new-come, but I thought *you* knew better, Toulon. Settle down to *sleep* like cats're *supposed* to, can't you?"

Some eagerly received pets and strokes, and they *did* curl up in a furry heap, Chalky the kitten swarming over Toulon to cuddle and lick his elder's head, which prompted grooming licks in return from his partner in crime . . . and how they'd come to such a close, mischievous companionship so quickly, Lewrie couldn't fathom; though it beat the first few days' slanging matches and hostilities all hollow, he could gladly admit to himself as he clambered back into bed and settled his sheet.

Thumps and grunts, slaps and high-toned trills, and deep meows.

Then the hat-box was overset and a new romp was on, paws thundering on the canvas deck-cover, from the transom settee to the gundeck door.

"Gawd," Lewrie implored the night and the overhead deck beams as he pummeled his pillows. "Give me patience . . ."

CPSIA information can be obtained at www.ICGtesting.com
Printed in the USA
LVOW11s0305270214

375172LV00002B/2/P